THE PERFECT PLAN

CAITLIN WEAVER

Storm
PUBLISHING

Ebook ISBN: 978-1-80508-926-1
Paperback ISBN: 978-1-80508-928-5

Cover design: Rose Cooper
Cover images: Shutterstock

Published by Storm Publishing.
For further information, visit:
www.stormpublishing.co

ALSO BY CAITLIN WEAVER

Such a Good Family
Things We Never Say
Who We Used to Be
The Good Mothers

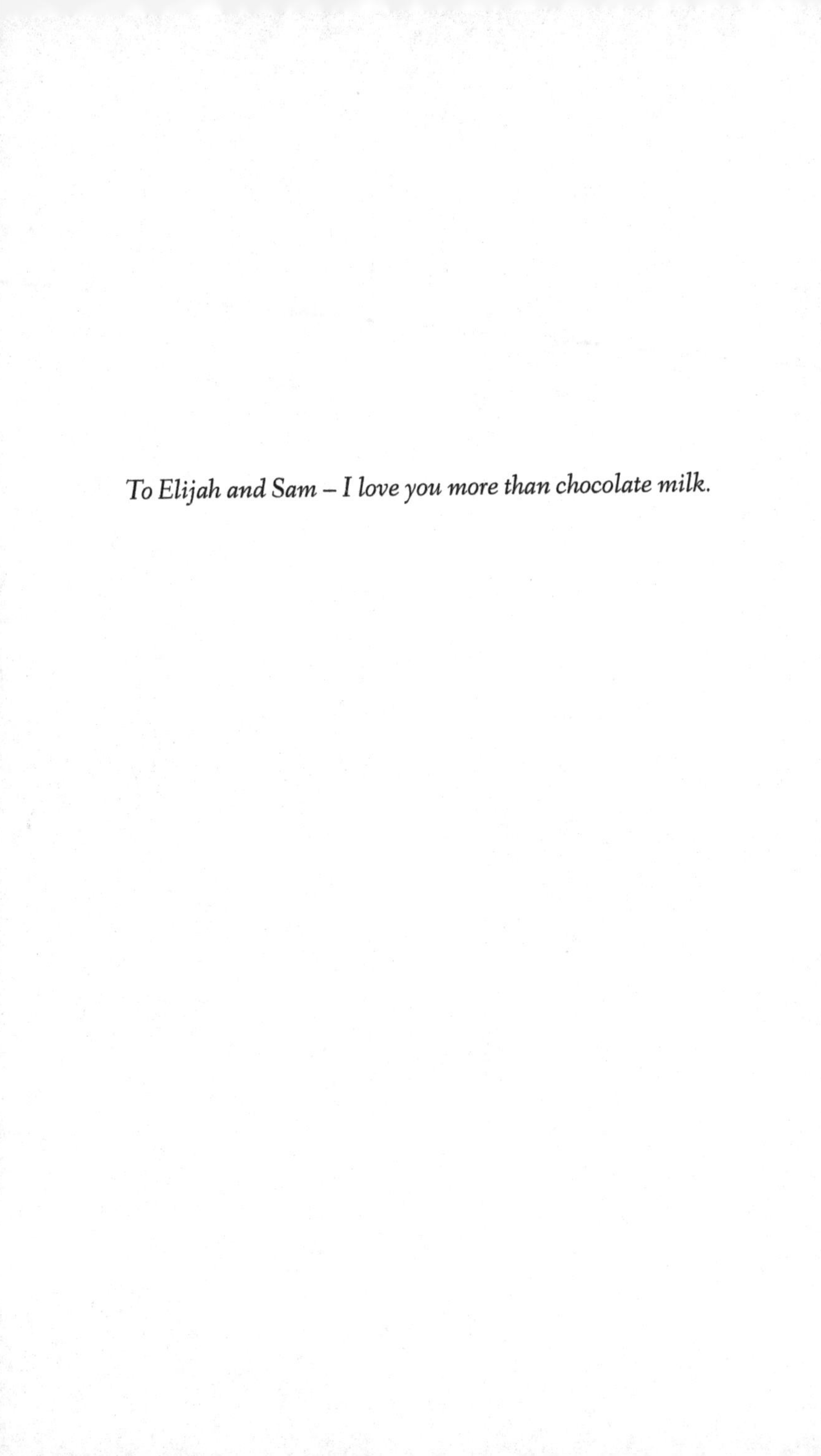

To Elijah and Sam – I love you more than chocolate milk.

PART ONE

ONE

To the casual observer, the three friends looked to be enjoying a leisurely Sunday brunch. Except instead of French toast and omelets spread before them, the restaurant table was covered by stacks of printouts neatly clipped together. And instead of a mimosa, each woman held one of the packets of paper, eyes tracking the words like a typewriter, pausing only for a sip of coffee. When one of them finished reading she set the papers back on the table where another of the women would pick them up. The three of them continued this rhythm for several silent minutes. Read, sip. Read, sip, switch.

"What about her?" Fabiola pushed a printout across the table. "I liked the letter she included to prospective parents. She talks about how much she loves her own kids and how she really wants to give that gift to another family." She pulled her long, cinnamon-colored hair back and tied it in a loose knot on top of her head—her "thinking hair" as her husband called it.

"I read that one." Alice raised her eyebrows. "Hopefully she loves her kids enough to let someone else teach them how to spell."

Fabiola groaned. "That's so not the point." She pushed up

the sleeves of her chunky, marigold sweater and fanned herself. The calendar, which said September, had fooled her into thinking it was fall.

Across from her Liz stifled a laugh. "I mean, she's not wrong about the spelling..."

Fabiola rolled her eyes and fiddled with the bracelet she'd bought at a vintage shop. It was inlaid with tourmaline, which the shop owner said was supposed to bring prosperity. Fabiola hoped that was true. It wasn't like she wanted to win the lottery or anything; she just wanted to stop worrying about how to pay for the kids' summer camps and the repairs to their aging Subaru.

"I like her." Alice pushed her clear-rimmed glasses back up her nose and lowered the papers she was holding to the table, tapping the top sheet with a long, pale finger. Her unpolished nails were filed short and round, and the plain gold band on her left ring finger was the only jewelry she wore.

"Why?" Liz asked. She twisted a strand of shoulder-length, honey-colored hair between her index finger and thumb, the same way she'd done since college.

"Well, for starters, she has two kids of her own and she works full-time as an ultrasound tech. So she's clearly good at multitasking. Plus, she says she's open to following a specific diet if you want her to, which demonstrates that she's flexible and responsive to feedback."

"Alice, we're choosing someone to have Liz's baby, not do office work," Fabiola chided.

"But all the skills that make someone a good employee translate directly to motherhood," Alice insisted. "Listening, following through, attention to detail." She ticked things off on her fingers as she spoke.

"Except I'm going to be the mom. She's just carrying the baby," Liz reminded her. The three women went quiet. "I'm going to be a mom," Liz repeated in a softer voice, a note of disbelief creeping in.

"Yes, sweetie, you are." Fabiola reached across the scuffed table and squeezed her friend's hand, noting the contrast between her olive skin tone and Liz's paler fingers. "You absolutely are."

"It's just, how do I choose?" Liz gestured to the papers spread before them. She wore a crisp white button-down shirt over dark jeans and calf-high suede boots. The outfit, combined with the pretty flush on her makeup-free cheeks, made her look like she'd just returned from a horseback jaunt in the countryside or finished filming an organic yogurt commercial. "I mean, they all sound good on paper," Liz continued. "Good medical histories, they passed a psych eval, they're financially stable. But I'm going to be trusting this person with the health of my child —not to mention spending a lot of time with them."

"If only there was a screening question about whether or not they touch the magazines in doctors' waiting rooms," said Alice, suppressing a smile. "Or consider kale to be overrated."

Fabiola snorted. Liz was both a notorious germaphobe and a food snob, though she preferred to call herself "discerning."

"Hey, Swiss chard has way more nutrients than kale, and it actually tastes good," Liz protested. "By the way, have either of you been to the new restaurant from the Top Chef guy? It's supposed to be, like, back-to-basics, authentic Korean food. The kimchi is literally made by someone's Korean grandmother." She flicked her hair over her shoulder. "I could probably get Michael to call in a favor and get a reservation for some time next week if you want to go." Michael was Liz's boss and the founder of the private equity firm where she was a partner.

Alice made a face. "Meh, I'm not a huge fan of Korean food. And I hate kimchi."

"Alice, you're Korean," Fabiola said with a shake of her head.

"I *am?*" Alice pretended to look shocked. "Maybe that explains why people look confused when they ask where I'm from and I tell them the Upper East Side."

Fabiola had grown up thinking of Alice's adoptive parents, the Borowitzs, as her second family. She'd spent almost as much time at their light-filled classic six on East 91st Street as she had at the small, two-bedroom in East Harlem that she'd shared with her father after her mother vanished from their lives.

"I'd love to go," Fabiola said, "but with the back-to-school frenzy for the twins and Vivi..." She trailed off, knowing she didn't need to say more. The rest was assumed. The kids were always her excuse.

"Oh, come on, guys," Liz wheedled. "We haven't all had a night out together in forever."

"OK, fine," Alice said. "I'll go as long as I don't have to eat kimchi. Anything to get out of doing bedtime."

"Fabi?" Liz turned to her. "Can't Aron help next week?"

Fabiola looked down at the dregs of her Americano. "Aron's hours are really long at his new company. And September is always one of my busiest months at work." She wrapped her hands around her empty mug, trying not to let her resentment show. It was so easy for Liz, and Alice with just the one child—which was practically like having no kids at all—to be spontaneous. While she was always boring Fabiola, stuck at home with her three kids. Except, and this was the part she never said out loud, she kind of liked it that way.

Unlike Alice, Fabiola hated missing bedtime. At nine years old the twins were in constant motion, always throwing a ball back and forth or knocking something over for her to clean up. Bedtime was the only time they sat still enough for her to cuddle with them, one on each side of her on the bottom bunk as she read aloud chapters of *Harry Potter*. And even Vivi, suddenly surly at fourteen, would sometimes still let Fabiola sit on her bed and brush her hair before she turned out the light.

"No worries, Fabi." Liz smiled at her. "You'll come next time."

"OK, let's get back to the task at hand." Alice glanced at her watch and refocused on the papers in front of them. "I have to leave soon to pick Abigail up from Hebrew school."

Liz eyed the printouts and chewed on her bottom lip. "I don't know, this feels so... subjective. I brought my laptop, so maybe we could come up with ranking criteria and I can build a decision model."

Fabiola's eye caught on the large diamond on Liz's left hand as her friend drew a silver laptop out of her bag. *Peter picked that ring out for her*, she thought. She tried to imagine her old friend standing in Tiffany's looking over a selection of rings nestled on a blue velvet tray. No, Peter wouldn't go to Tiffany's. He'd have a connection, someone trying to settle a karmic debt after Peter had cut a tumor out of their brain and who was also conveniently in the diamond business. That's how Peter's life worked.

Fabiola cocked her head and examined Liz's determined face as her fingers began to fly across the keyboard. "Liz," she said, leaning forward. "Sweetie, I don't think this is something a spreadsheet can help you figure out. These are people we're talking about."

"People who will be getting paid to carry our baby," Liz pointed out. "This is a very expensive, um, transaction. I want to get it right."

Fabiola tightened the hair knot on the top of her head. "Look, the agency already screened them all for the medical stuff," she said. "So, in that sense, all the profiles are the same. All that matters in the end is that you trust them. But you can meet them, right? Before you decide? So do that. Talk to them. Let them tell you about themselves, about why they want to do this—"

"They're doing this because they're being paid a lot," Liz interjected.

"It can't be just that," Fabiola insisted. "It's a special kind of person who wants to do this. Someone who needs to fulfill a bigger purpose. To bring new life into the world. It's... transcendent." She smiled, remembering her own pregnancies.

"Funny, I don't remember pregnancy as transcendent," Alice said, with a raised eyebrow. "Mostly I remember how I threw up every day until my third trimester. And my stretch marks. Those are unforgettable." She smoothed a hand over her stomach, flat under a plain black T-shirt tucked into black jeans. Everything Alice owned was black, white, or gray. She was a firm believer in the capsule wardrobe.

Liz toyed with her napkin. "Is it bad that I'm relieved I don't have to be pregnant? It sounds, like, very inconvenient."

"I loved it." Fabiola's gaze softened as she remembered how beautiful she'd felt with the curve of her belly and the new roundness in her chest and hips. The hormones had left her feeling mildly euphoric all the time, like being on a constant, low dose of nitrous oxide—and doubly so with the twins. And the sex. Oh God, the sex. She'd wanted it all the time, and Aron had been thrilled. They'd never before had such fiery, urgent sex—or since.

"Can I get you anything else?" An apron-clad waiter appeared at their table holding their check and glanced pointedly toward the entrance of the restaurant where several parties waited for open tables. The three women had been lingering at their table for almost two hours, a lifetime in New York minutes.

"No." Liz shot him a look so stern Fabiola felt him wither inside. Liz had that effect on people.

"Pushy, pushy!" Alice said, nodding toward the waiter after he set their check down on the table and backed away. "When did this place get so trendy, anyway? It was a total dump back in the day. Remember how the tables were always sticky?"

Their weekend brunch tradition had started when they'd all moved to the city after Vassar, where Liz had been assigned as the third to Alice and Fabiola's dorm suite. They'd chosen to meet at the restaurant near the Flatiron Building purely based on location—it was equally inconvenient from all of their neighborhoods, Liz in Tribeca, Alice on the Upper East Side, and Fabiola in Park Slope, Brooklyn. Over the years sometimes they'd met once a week, sometimes once a month. And though the restaurant name and décor had changed several times, they remained loyal to the location.

Now, as Fabiola gazed around the table, she wondered how she'd been lucky enough to have both Liz and Alice by her side for so many years. With them, every cliché about best friends was true. They were her ride-or-dies, her kindred spirits, her one phone call. She would do anything for either of them. In fact, sometimes she wished she could do more, but both Alice and Liz were so... self-sufficient. Fabiola was always the one who seemed to need career advice, an emergency babysitter, or a fashion intervention.

As she thought about this, an idea formed in the depths of her mind. Maybe there *was* something she could do. Something big. The idea blossomed quickly, as though it sprung up in a shaft of focused sunlight. In the space of seconds, it transformed from a passing notion to a conviction she felt deep in her belly.

"I'll do it," she said, her gaze refocusing on Liz.

"Don't be silly." Liz waved her hand and reached for the bill. "You know it's my turn to pay."

"No, I mean I'll do it. I'll be your surrogate." As soon as the words left her mouth she felt a flicker of unease as she thought of Aron—but surely he'd support her in this, wouldn't he? He knew how much Liz meant to her.

Liz's hand froze in midair over the table and her eyes

widened. Alice let out a small croak and placed her palms on her chest.

"It makes sense, if you think about it." Fabiola rushed to fill the void of silence that had settled over the table. "I love being pregnant. I'm *good* at being pregnant. Aron and I aren't planning on having any more kids, and, like, it's *me*, Liz. Your best friend. What could be more perfect, really?" She paused to take a breath. She could do this. She could finally be there for her best friend in a way that truly mattered.

Across from her Liz gripped the table with both hands, processing. "Fabi, it's too much, I couldn't let you—" Her voice quavered.

"Please, Liz." Fabiola clutched her mug. "Let me do this for you. I'd love to." Tears sprang to her eyes, and she felt a sudden, wild desperation to be the one to do this for Liz. Liz and Alice had seen Fabiola through so many ups and downs. She'd take a bullet for either of them. Except, in this case she didn't have to. She could grow a baby instead.

Liz lowered her eyes for a beat. When she looked back up, Fabiola could see her friend's mind whirring as she analyzed the idea.

"Fabi, are you sure? I mean, this is a big decision. Don't you want to talk to Aron?"

"Of course, I'll talk to him, but I'm sure he be on board."

"And Peter... well, Peter loves you, of course. This will just be... a lot to digest."

Fabiola closed her eyes, trying to imagine Peter's response to Liz telling him she was going to have their baby. Would he feel happiness? Trepidation? The same swirling mix of emotion soup she was feeling right now? She shook away the thoughts and refocused on the tentative smile spreading across Liz's face.

"Yes." Fabiola nodded. "Of course. But he'll see it makes sense." Of that she was certain.

Liz inhaled a deep, raspy breath, then let out a shaky laugh.

Her eyes were shiny, and a tear leaked onto her cheek. "OK, then."

Liz was not a hugger, but Fabiola rose from her chair and wrapped her arms around her friend, who squeezed her hard in return. Soon Alice had sandwiched her from the other side. With her arms around Liz, Fabiola's mind again strayed to Peter, and she felt the briefest tingle of guilt. She shoved the thoughts aside and instead buried her face in Liz's hair and squeezed Alice's hand around her waist. She was going to give her best friend the world's greatest gift. For now, that was all that mattered.

TWO

The pizza was burning. Fabiola could smell it from upstairs in the boys' bedroom where she was putting away their clean laundry. She sniffed the air again as she balanced a stack of underwear in her hands—red for Liam and blue for Ben, to ensure there was no tussling over having to wear underwear the other brother had certainly farted into at some point.

She cocked an ear towards the stairs to see if she could hear Aron in the kitchen. He'd offered to make dinner and had spent the afternoon dusting the counters with flour as he made homemade pizza dough, while Fabiola did the laundry that had piled up during the week. Despite the fact that she'd tried many times to teach the kids to wash their own clothes, neither the twins nor fourteen-year-old Vivi seemed to notice when their hampers were full.

"Honey?" Fabiola called downstairs. "Honey, I think the pizza's ready." Silence. Apparently, "making dinner" included only the combining of ingredients for said dinner and not ensuring that food actually made it to anyone's plate.

Hurrying downstairs she opened the oven to reveal a pizza with heavily browned cheese and a blackened crust on one half.

She grabbed a dish towel and yanked it out of the oven, nearly dropping the heavy pizza stone Aron insisted on using in the process.

"Hey." She turned to see Aron in the doorway. "I was just coming in to grab that."

"I would have checked on it earlier. I didn't know you weren't watching it." Her tone was neutral, but the accusation was clear.

"I was watching it. I was just out on the stoop talking to Jer." He flicked his head to move his brown hair away from his eyes. It was shaggy, hanging down over his ears. Fabiola would offer to get the clippers out tonight to cut it for him.

Fabiola suppressed an eye roll. Jeremy was Aron's closest friend and lived down the block with his wife and two daughters. He was usually the source of Aron's interest in new hobbies, which tended to involve lots of expensive equipment and time away from Fabiola and the kids. Training for a triathlon was his latest obsession.

"It smells delicious," Fabiola said, trying for a lighter tone. "Why don't I make the salad?"

"That'd be great, hon." Aron shot her a grateful look. They both knew he hadn't been planning to make one to begin with.

She busied herself with chopping cucumbers and late season tomatoes from the farmer's market. She could hear the boys in the living room muttering to each other as they played video games and a quick glance at the clock told her Vivi would be home shortly from her best friend Harper's house. She wasn't going to get a better moment.

"So, I had brunch with the girls this morning," she said.

"Oh yeah, right. I meant to ask you how it was." Aron fished his phone out of his pocket.

"You know how Liz and Peter had decided to go the surrogate route."

"Mm-hm." He began to scroll. "Good for them."

"I agreed to be their surrogate."

Aron's thumb froze over his screen and he jerked his head up. "You did what?"

Fabiola took a deep breath to steady herself. "I said I'd do it." Saying it out loud, it seemed obvious now that she should have talked to Aron about it first.

The worry lines on Aron's forehead eased and he laughed. "Good one, hon." He looked back down at his phone.

Fabiola tilted her head. "I'm not joking. I think it's the right thing to do. This is important to me."

Aron's shoulders tensed as he lowered his phone to the counter and stared at her. "You can't be serious."

"Why not?" Fabiola crossed her arms. "After all this time, my best friend is finally trying to become a mother; how could I not want to help her with that?"

Aron snorted. "Well, for one thing, you're too old."

"Excuse me? Plenty of people have babies at thirty-six." Annoyance ripped through Fabiola. She set her jaw, indignant. While she had expected Aron might be caught off guard by her announcement, she hadn't expected to be laughed at.

"Fabi, we have enough going on already." Aron waved his hand like a teacher dismissing his students.

"I want to do this." She swallowed hard. Of course Aron wouldn't understand. He didn't have the kind of friendships she had with Liz and Alice. Sure, he had a group of college friends who went to Vegas together every two or three years, and work friends with whom he went to happy hour, but there was no comparison. For a split second she felt almost sad to think that he'd never had what she had with Liz and Alice. Then she saw his eyes narrow and anger gathering on his face like an approaching thundercloud.

"Jesus, you're actually considering this, aren't you?" he said.

Fabiola wavered in the face of his dissent, then straightened to her full height. "I told you, I'm more than considering it. I told Liz I'd do it." She was not one to back down from a promise, especially something as important as this.

"Without talking to me first?" Aron's hands shot out to his sides and his voice ratcheted up in volume. "Um, you didn't think to run such a major decision by me? That maybe you should ask how I felt about it?"

"You didn't ask how I felt about you quitting your job to found a start-up." A surge of resentment propelled the words out of her mouth like a bottle uncorking after years of being under pressure.

Aron stiffened. "That's different," he shot back. "You knew that was always my plan."

Yes, down the road when we actually had some money saved, thought Fabiola. Pivot, Aron's fledgling company, was based out of a Red Hook warehouse-turned-office-space. It was an online publication that covered sports through a lens of racial and gender equity and, Aron assured her, was only months away from being acquired by a big media company that would definitely, probably, maybe, make them a lot of money.

"And this is a crucial time for me at work," Aron continued. "What with both Vice and Buzzfeed feeling us out. I can't be distracted."

Fabiola pressed her lips together. Why was she insisting on this, anyway? Aron was right, it was a big decision. A huge one. They *should* have talked about it. That's what healthy couples did. And that's what they were, right? Healthy-ish, anyway. She closed her eyes for an instant, thinking of how to communicate the visceral need she felt to do this, to support Liz in such a tangible, substantial way. And Peter, of course.

She opened her mouth to reply just as the front door creaked open. "Vivi?" she called. "Is that you?" The door shut with a loud bang. Definitely Vivi.

"Hey." Vivi breezed into the kitchen and opened the fridge, oblivious to the sparks of tension in the room. She wore black spandex shorts and a lavender sports bra she claimed was a crop top and thus perfectly fine to wear in public. Her long, dark hair was coiled up and tied in a knot on top of her head.

"Hi, sweetie," Fabiola said, grateful for the distraction "How was your afternoon?" Out of the corner of her eye she saw Aron stalk out of the room. "How is Harper?" she continued, refocusing on her daughter. "Was Izzy there, too? What did you girls do?" Vivi, Harper, and Isabelle had been a trio since they'd met in nursery school.

Vivi stuck her head further into the fridge. "Izzy wasn't there and me and Harper just, like, hung out."

"Harper and I," Fabiola corrected. Growing up with a Spanish speaking Peruvian mother and a Jamaican father, she'd often had her own grammar corrected in school. Especially once she'd started at Dalton, the exclusive Upper East Side prep school.

"We're out of yogurt, *again*." Vivi closed the fridge door with a hard thud.

Fabiola winced at the sound of jars rattling inside and pursed her lips. "Add it to the grocery app, OK? Anyway, we're eating in five minutes. Go tell your brothers; they're playing video games."

Vivi rolled her eyes and yelled in the direction of the living room. "Mario! Luigi! Dinner in five!" Then she disappeared up the stairs and banged the door to her room closed behind her.

Fabiola winced again. She hoped at least the twins would be in a good mood at dinner, and that she and Aron could fake it.

"Mo-om, I'm hungry." Ben appeared in the doorway, his T-shirt on inside out and backwards. His summer buzz cut, Fabiola's specialty, was growing out and his dark, springy curls were re-emerging.

"Sooo hungry," Liam agreed, slouching in behind him. A head taller than Ben, he had Fabiola's thick, red-tinted hair which stood on end when he ran his fingers through it, making him look even taller.

"Well, you're in luck." Fabiola brandished the pizza cutter. "Grab a plate."

Dinner went better than Fabiola had expected, with only a handful of fart jokes and just one food throwing incident. Aron offered her his we'll-talk-about-this-later smile in a kind of truce, and even Vivi's normally truculent temperament seemed brighter after spending most of the day with Harper.

After dinner, once the boys had been forced into the shower and then rewarded with an hour of screen time, and Vivi had sequestered herself in her room with her phone, Fabiola paused in the doorway to their bedroom. Aron was sprawled on the bed scrolling through his phone. His relaxed posture reminded her of how he had looked back when they met. She'd been fresh out of Vassar. Six years older, he'd been well into his career as a sports and technology editor for *Esquire* magazine. He'd worn his hair longer then, down over the collar of his button-up shirts, and she'd thought it was sexy. Now, though, his shaggy hair had the look of someone who'd been slacking on their personal hygiene.

"I could get out the clippers for you," she said, extending a peace offering. She'd started cutting Aron and the boys' hair during the pandemic, teaching herself with YouTube videos. Now it seemed silly to pay for someone else to do it, especially when she'd finally gotten good.

He looked up at her and hesitated, running his hand through his hair, then nodded. "Sure. OK."

In the bathroom he sat on the closed toilet lid and pulled off his faded gray Notorious RBG T-shirt. "Not too short," he warned.

Fabiola draped a towel around his bare shoulders. "It grows fast, remember?" she said.

"Still."

She nodded and went to work. As she cleaned up the hair around his neck and started working her way up his head, the hostility from earlier began to evaporate and a buffer of comfortable silence settled over them. This was what marriage was, after all. Waiting things out.

She switched to scissors, measuring the hair between her fingers before cutting. "I want to do it," she said in a low voice.

The tendons in Aron's neck tensed. "Why?"

She hesitated, trying to wrangle the burning need inside her into a reasonable explanation. "Because she's my friend," she said. "Because I'm good at being pregnant. Because given her history Liz doesn't exactly trust the medical community, but she trusts me. Because it's the right thing to do." She met his eyes in the mirror.

Liz had been diagnosed with cervical cancer during their sophomore year of college. Fabiola and Alice had seen her through the sprint of freezing her eggs "just in case" and her emergency hysterectomy—only to find out two weeks after surgery that the pathologist had misread the biopsy report, which was benign. There had been a lawsuit and a good deal of money after that. Fabiola didn't know exactly how much, but it had been enough to pay for Liz's Tribeca apartment straight out of Vassar, and then her MBA at Columbia.

"So not because of... Peter." Aron's mouth twitched.

Fabiola sighed. She'd hoped this wouldn't come up. While Aron and Peter had a cordial relationship, they'd never completely warmed to each other. Before they'd gotten married, Aron had asked her if there had ever been anything between her and Peter. "You two just seem really... close," he'd said.

"I've known Peter forever," she'd told him, avoiding the question. "He was my first friend when I started at Dalton in junior high. I was the new kid plus I was on scholarship and everyone knew it. Peter made all that OK."

Now, she kept her tone measured as she snipped the hair

around Aron's ears. "Of course I want to help Peter, too. He's my oldest friend, and he's married to my best friend." She shrugged, as if it was a no-brainer.

"I don't like it." Aron shook his head, and she steadied it between her hands. "It feels... complicated."

Fabiola set down the scissors and picked up the blow dryer. Turning it on, she blew it over Aron's neck and ears, watching the short, dark hairs scatter into the air. "All done," she said, switching it off.

Aron regarded himself in the mirror. He always looked older after a haircut, his cheekbones sharper, the veil of hair across his forehead disappearing to reveal the light lines etched there. He turned to face her. "OK," he said. "I'll think about it."

Fabiola felt a twist of hope, and something else she couldn't name, coil inside her.

THREE

Monday morning was choreographed chaos. Aron's alarm went off early and he performed the charade of trying to be quiet while he rummaged in the closet for his triathlon cycling clothes, rattling hangers and opening and closing drawers with dull thuds. When he exited their bedroom, the door creaked like it was auditioning for a radio show sound effect. He'd been meaning to put WD-40 on the hinges for weeks now. Turning over in bed Fabiola mentally transferred that task from his to-do list to hers.

Fabiola worshipped lists. Lists were a way of lighting the way forward and creating order from disarray. She loved the sense of hope they gave her so much she'd built a career around it.

She hadn't meant to organize people's closets for a living—she had a degree in Anthropology from Vassar, for God's sake. And she'd certainly never meant to be both the primary caretaker and the primary breadwinner. But, thanks to the rise of America's obsession with Marie Kondo and The Home Edit, what had started as a fun hobby now earned her enough—

barely—to support their family while they waited for Aron's company to become profitable.

She rubbed her eyes and sat up, knowing she wouldn't be able to fall back to sleep. She needed to wake the twins up soon, anyway, to make sure they were dressed, fed, and out the door in time for her to walk them the three blocks to their elementary school. She'd packed their backpacks last night and placed them in the woven storage baskets that stood next to the front door, one for the detritus of each kid. She hoped Aron would remember to wake Vivi when he got back. That and make coffee.

When Fabiola returned, however, Vivi was still sleeping, and the coffee maker was empty. She cast an accusing glance at Aron, who'd draped his sweaty cycling jersey over a kitchen chair and was standing shirtless, sipping a brownish smoothie concoction. He'd always been thin and lanky, but recently he'd developed the slightest of bellies, a puffy rise of white skin that looked like it would deflate if pricked. *Too much home-brewed beer*, Fabiola thought, wrinkling her nose at the thought of the yeasty concoction. She couldn't wait to quietly dispose of the brewing equipment that cluttered their basement, once Aron was distracted by a new hobby.

"Vivi has to leave in thirty minutes, and you know how long it takes her to get ready," Fabiola complained. Since starting high school the week before, Vivi spent at least a half hour each morning trying on outfits, the mound of discarded clothes on her bed growing larger by the day.

He raised his hands in defense. "I made her a smoothie." He pointed to the counter, where a second glass of brown sludge sat.

That was the problem, thought Fabiola as she ignored the smoothie and headed upstairs to her daughter's room. Unlike some of her Brooklyn mom friends' husbands, Aron could never be faulted for doing nothing. He was helpful, just usually not with what she needed.

Vivi was unhappy to be roused. She appeared downstairs twenty-five minutes later wearing the same black spandex shorts as the day before and a baggy T-shirt with *Mediocre Vibes Only* printed on the front.

"Let's go," Fabiola said. "Dad made you a smoothie."

Vivi glanced at the glass on the counter and made a face. "Eww."

"Fine." Fabiola held up her hands in surrender. "Eat this. You need something in your stomach." She handed Vivi one of Aron's protein bars and pushed her toward the door. "Get going. And you better text Harper to tell her you're running late." Each morning Vivi walked the five blocks to Harper's house before the girls continued on together to the high school.

"Harper started early morning swim practices this week," Vivi said, her face sullen. Harper and Izzy had both made the varsity swimming team, composed mostly of juniors and seniors. Vivi, who had been relegated to the junior varsity team, had promptly quit swimming in protest, earning her a lecture from Aron on commitment and perseverance while she rolled her eyes.

Fabiola was determined to stay positive in the face of Vivi's dark cloud. "Have a good day, sweetie," she chirped, and steered her daughter toward the door. "I love you!" Her phone chimed with an incoming call as she waved goodbye to Vivi's back. Looking down, something in her chest fluttered.

"Hey," she answered, trying not to sound breathless.

"Fabi, hi." Peter's voice was warm and husky, like a wool blanket draped over your shoulders at a campfire.

"Hi. Sorry, I already said that."

Peter laughed. "How are you?"

"Good. Great. You know, the usual back to school madness." She leaned against the kitchen counter to steady herself. While she and Peter exchanged the occasional text, he never called her out of the blue like this.

"I'm sure. I don't know how you do it all."

Fabiola sighed. "Yeah, me neither."

Peter cleared his throat. "So, um, Liz told me about your... offer. To be the surrogate."

Fabiola nodded vigorously, then remembered he couldn't see her. "Yes. I did. Offer, that is. If you want me to, of course. And no pressure, obviously, I just thought..." She trailed off. What had she been thinking, exactly? That she wanted to help was the main reason. And the main reason was the most important one, right?

"No, it's an amazing offer, really. I can't believe—" He paused and for a moment she thought he almost sounded choked up. "I can't believe you would do that for us."

"I'd do anything for you," she said, adding quickly, "You and Liz mean the world to me."

"Well, you know how much we love you," he said. The "we" hit Fabiola like a bullet discharging from a gun she didn't know was loaded. Peter paused. "Look, I was thinking, if this is really going to happen, maybe the four of us should get together to, you know, um, approach things as a team."

Fabiola's chest tightened. "Yes, great idea," she managed.

"OK then." Peter sounded relieved. "I'll run some dates by Liz."

Fabiola heard Aron's feet on the stairs. "Sounds good. Sorry, Peter, I have to run—work stuff. Talk to you soon." She hung up as Aron entered the room. His hair was damp, and he was dressed in his typical work outfit of jeans and a vintage concert T-shirt. Today's listed R.E.M.'s Out of Time tour dates.

"Who was that?" he asked.

Fabiola waved her hand. "Just one of those recorded info calls from the school."

"Oh." Aron's brow creased as he glanced at his phone. "I didn't get one."

"I think they do them in waves. You'll probably get one later." She fiddled with a lock of her hair. "Hey, so, about our conversation last night..."

Aron pursed his lips and rubbed the back of his neck. "Hon, I have a really busy day and I'm late. I just, I still need time to think."

"OK, sure." She bit back her annoyance. Why did he think this was his decision to make?

He leaned forward to kiss her goodbye. "Love you."

"Love you, too."

FOUR

After loading the dishwasher and wiping down the counters, Fabiola raced to get herself ready for work, throwing on a forgiving olive-green maxi dress. She'd long given up striving for Liz's toned, athletic body or Alice's naturally rail thin frame. Her curves were her curves, even if she sometimes wished for more of them in some areas and less in others.

She pulled the front door behind her and quickened her step, hoping to make the fifteen-minute walk over to 6th Avenue in ten. The morning was already warm even though the calendar read September. As she started down the street her phone rang and a picture of her father's face grinned up at her from the screen. It was an older picture; these days his neatly trimmed beard was more salt than pepper, but his eyes still crinkled the same way when he smiled.

They talked almost every day, and normally seeing his name on her screen made her smile. Today, though, a bubble of unease formed in her stomach. If she became Liz and Peter's surrogate, she'd have to figure out how to tell him. Though he'd lived in New York since he was eighteen, he was often befuddled by what he called her "American life."

"Hi Papa," she said. "How are you?"

"Happy to have my feet on the ground and not in the clouds," he said, his typical response. His voice still carried the island lilt of his childhood. "How are you, sweets?"

"I'm good, but rushing to work so I can't talk. You're still coming for dinner tonight, right?"

"I wouldn't miss it."

"OK, see you then. Love you."

"Love you, too."

As Fabiola rounded the corner onto 6th Avenue she spotted her assistant, Hayley, standing in front of an unassuming brownstone. The hot pink tips of her white-blonde ponytail bounced as she typed on her phone at light speed with one hand and balanced an iced coffee with the other. Hayley did everything at light speed.

"Hi." Fabiola waved as she got closer.

"Hey!" Hayley said. Her greeting always contained a note of exuberant surprise, as if seeing Fabiola was a delightful coincidence despite their pre-arranged meeting. "I'm so excited for today! My first client!" She clapped her hands together and bounced on the toes of her Adidas sneakers which she wore under rust-colored wide-legged pants and a plain white T-shirt.

"Yeah, well, you've earned it." Fabiola smiled. Hayley had been working part-time for her for three months, helping with her calendar, creating a client database, and designing a newsletter for her. Already Fabiola had no idea how she'd operated without the young woman's help for so long.

Hayley squinted up at the building. "OK, so Karl Noss. Age eighty-two, wife died a year ago. His kids are pressuring him to finally get rid of their mom's things. They've offered to do it for him but—"

"—he doesn't want their help," Fabiola said. This was good. Karl had already recognized what many people didn't; that having his children involved in the process would only make it harder.

"Right." Hayley nodded.

"The apartment is five thousand square feet, give or take." Hayley gave a low whistle. "God, this thing must be worth a fortune."

Fabiola shrugged and twisted her thick hair up off her neck, securing it with a scrunchie. "I'm sure it wasn't when he bought it." She knew this type of client. Karl Noss and his wife had likely lived modestly in that same brownstone for decades and raised their children there. Along the way they'd accumulated layers of theater programs and photo albums, pants that might fit again one day and bottles of perfume with a few drops left; all of which Fabiola would sort through like an archeologist, painstakingly sifting and sorting away the unnecessary while taking care to leave the memories intact.

Mr. Noss greeted them at the door and was exactly as Fabiola had pictured him, tall with a full head of white hair and small, wire rim glasses perched on his nose.

"Please," he said as he walked them through the space. "I leave it in your hands. I've kept trying to go through her things myself but—well, I never get very far." His mouth curved down and Fabiola resisted the urge to reach out and squeeze his hand.

"I appreciate your trust," she said, giving him a warm smile. "Please, feel free to go run some errands or get a cup of coffee. We'll be here for a while."

Fabiola and Hayley were in the bedroom sorting through Mrs. Noss's clothing when her phone rang. Her heart sped up as she glanced down at the name on the screen. *NYC Public Schools*.

"Hello?" she answered.

"Hello, Mrs. Butler, this is Vice Principal Gonzalez from Marie Curie High School. I'm calling regarding Vivian—"

Fabiola's fingers tightened around her phone as scenes from

news clips of any number of recent school shootings flashed through her mind. "Is she OK?" she interrupted, her pulse thudding in her ears.

"Yes, she's physically fine," the woman said, her tone brusque. The relief that flooded Fabiola's body left her knees weak and she sank down onto the bed, pushing aside a pile of neatly folded cashmere cardigans. "Unfortunately, there's been an incident involving the school dress code," the vice principal continued. "Someone will need to come pick Vivian up."

"The dress code?" Fabiola pictured Vivi's baggy T-shirt from that morning. In the closet Hayley had stopped pulling clothes from their hangers and was staring at her, not even pretending not to listen. "She needs to be picked up? Are you sure that's necessary?" Annoyance crept into Fabiola's voice. At the other end of the line the vice principal's sigh was so loud she held the phone away from her ear.

"Yes," said the woman. "I'm afraid it is."

Fabiola's annoyance turned to resentment. Why didn't they ever call Aron? She was actually working, while he was probably at his office playing foosball and "brainstorming," which as far as Fabi could tell meant talking a lot without actually doing anything.

"I can totally stay and finish up if you need to go," Hayley said when Fabiola hung up, the eagerness in her voice apparent. Fabiola gave a tight smile and held up a finger while she rose to her feet and dialed Aron's number.

"Dress code violation? What kind of bullshit is that?" he demanded after Fabiola filled him in.

"I'm not totally sure," Fabiola replied. "But she needs to be picked up. Can you do it? I'm at a client."

"I really can't, I'm sorry, hon." He didn't pause long enough to even pretend to consider it. Unless it was a true emergency, their unspoken agreement was that she was the default parent for situations like this. This flexibility was the whole reason she worked for herself, though she wondered if it was time to revisit this agreement now that she had a wait list for clients.

Aware that Hayley was watching her, Fabiola bit back the sharp remark on her tongue. "I get it," she said, her tone clipped. "See you later for dinner." Turning back to Hayley she rearranged her face into a smile. "Can you handle this?" She gestured to the room.

Hayley nodded vigorously. "Oh yeah, definitely."

"Send me a picture of anything you're unsure of," Fabiola instructed, pointing to the piles. "The hard part comes after the sorting, when you bring him into the room to select items for the memory box. Two articles of clothing, max, preferably accessories. Don't rush him. It's important to honor the process." She nodded toward the wooden box the size of a large shoe box sitting on the dresser. In situations like these she'd learned it was best to curate the surviving spouse or children's mementos gently but firmly. "I'll call you to check in as soon as I can."

With gritted teeth she located her purse and turned to go. Vivi had better have a *very* good explanation.

FIVE

Vivi sat glowering in the Uber Fabiola had called to take them home from the high school. As soon as they'd stepped outside the school building, she'd ripped off the baggy T-shirt with the school's logo that she'd been forced to put on. Under it she wore a tight, off the shoulder, black shirt that barely grazed the top of her shorts. Fabiola had never seen it before.

"We do not allow exposed shoulders or midriffs," the vice principal had explained. "But again, Vivian is welcome to stay and wear a different shirt."

"I was in the middle of a meeting with a client," Fabiola told Vivi now, exhaling her frustration. "Why couldn't you just have worn the other shirt?"

"What? No way!" Vivi looked as though Fabiola had suggested she shave her head.

"So you'd rather miss school and have me miss work?" Fabiola's voice grew louder.

Vivi crossed her arms again and turned away to stare out the window. "I'd rather not be objectified by a sexist dress code."

Fabiola tried to stay calm. She didn't recognize the angry teen girl next to her. Where was her sunny, smiling daughter who'd been content in sweatpants and her Dolphins swim team T-shirt until just a few months ago? "Where did you get the shirt, anyway?" she asked.

Vivi picked an imaginary piece of lint off her lap. "It's Layla's."

"Layla? Have I met Layla?" Fabiola clicked through her mental yearbook of the kids from Vivi's junior high.

"She's new," Vivi said. "She just moved here from California to live with her dad. She said the shirt would look really good on me and she liked the one I was wearing so we traded this morning."

"So you agreed to wear a shirt you knew would get you into trouble."

Vivi made a disgusted noise in her throat. "The dress code is stupid and sexist. Most of it just applies to girls—we're being oppressed."

"Oppressed?" Fabiola held back a laugh. "Because you couldn't wear a shirt I wouldn't have let you wear anyway? Please." Vivi scowled and Fabiola sent up a silent prayer for patience. "Look, I agree that it's a stupid rule. But sometimes it's easier to follow a stupid rule instead of wasting your time getting into trouble."

Vivi rolled her eyes so hard Fabiola worried she might pull a muscle. "You *would* say that, Mom."

"What is that supposed to mean?" Fabiola frowned, examining Vivi's face for clues to the riddle her daughter had recently become. She felt a stab of sorrow thinking about how, when Vivi was younger, her face would light up whenever Fabiola entered a room, as if her happiness was suddenly complete. The distance of that memory made Fabiola heartsick.

"Oh, please. You've never broken a rule in your life," Vivi said.

Fabiola closed her eyes and inhaled deeply, summoning her equilibrium. Her daughter had no idea the rules she'd broken.

The car slowed to a stop in front of their brownstone and Vivi wrenched open the door. "Stop," Fabiola said, holding out her hand. "Give me your phone."

Vivi clutched her backpack to her chest. "What? Why?"

"Because I said so," Fabiola snapped. Her equilibrium had vanished, replaced by a flash of anger at Vivi's pure selfishness. "You can have it back when you've shown me you know how to make good decisions."

Vivi's lips curled in rage and her glare was so hostile that for a split second Fabiola wondered if she'd lost control of the situation. But then Vivi heaved her backpack at Fabiola's chest. "Take it all," she said, then climbed out and stomped up their front steps.

"Don't think you get to lie around here all day," Fabiola called after her as she got out of the car. "If you insist on being sent home then I have plans for you."

After a morning of folding laundry and cleaning her room, Fabiola gave Vivi her phone back. "Thirty minutes only, while you eat lunch," she said. "Then I need you to pick a developing country and write a two-page report contrasting the role of women there to the role of women in the United States. After that we'll discuss the true meaning of oppression." Fabiola folded her arms across her chest, pleased with herself. She hadn't gone to Vassar for nothing.

Aron arrived home as Fabiola was pulling a roast chicken and baked potatoes from the oven. "Hey," he said, kissing her, his beard tickling her cheek. He'd grown one over the summer, and to her surprise she liked it. It disguised the sharp point of his chin. "How was your day?"

"Not what I'd hoped for," she said dryly, tenting foil over the bird to let it rest.

"Oh, right. Vivi," he said, thumping his laptop bag down onto the counter. "I mean, it's ludicrous. The more I thought about it, the madder I got. I mean, what right do they have to police her body?"

Fabiola raised an eyebrow. "You didn't see the shirt."

"But it shouldn't matter. They have no right. This is about body autonomy," Aron countered, stabbing a finger in the air.

"She's obviously not grown up enough to make smart choices for herself."

"Oh, come on, she deserves more credit than that." He crossed the room, heading for the refrigerator.

"So do I, Aron." She cocked her head at him, aware of the land mines she was picking around.

He stopped mid-stride, then turned toward her and pinched the bridge of his nose. "The surrogacy thing again." He shook his head. "Look, you know I do my best to support your decisions. It's just—"

"Then support me in supporting Liz," she said. She stepped toward him and laid a hand on his arm. "That's what we do for each other, right? Support each other's dreams? I supported you with Pivot," she pointed out.

"That's different—" He moved away a little and her hand slipped from his arm.

"It's not. Dreams are dreams. My best friend has a dream of having a baby. I can help her. I need to do this, OK?"

A look of resignation spread across his face. "Look, I don't have the energy to fight about this anymore. So, do what you need to do."

A ripple of relief ran through Fabiola's body. "Thank you," she said.

"For the record, I'm not excited about it," he warned.

"I know," she said. "But thank you." She leaned forward to kiss him. He tensed for an instant, then softened and leaned into her, gripping her waist. As he pressed her to him, the doorbell rang. They drew back and looked at each other, both remembering at the same time.

"It's Monday," she said.

"Your dad," Aron said, releasing her.

Fabiola's father had been coming to dinner every week since Vivi was born. She'd been a needy baby, so at first this involved him walking around jiggling Vivi in his arms and singing softly to her while Aron and Fabiola collapsed greedily onto whatever takeout they'd ordered, thrilled to enjoy a meal without handing the baby back and forth. These days they all sat around eating while the kids fought for their grandfather's attention, talking over each other about their newest obsessions, from Olivia Rodrigo to Fortnite, staying at the table longer than they ever would on a normal night.

Sometimes Fabiola felt sad that Leonard was the kids' only grandparent. Aron's parents had been much older when they'd had him and had passed away before Vivi was even born. So, for the kids, Leonard was the only grandparent game in town—but he was a great one.

"Hi, Papa." Fabiola ushered in her father and kissed him on his cheek.

"Hello, sweets," he said, handing her a brown paper bag she knew contained dessert and pulling her in for a hug. She felt her shoulders relax as she inhaled his familiar scent of after-shave, shea butter, and a hint of the cleaning chemicals he used at work. He'd smelled the same as long as she could remember. He felt slighter than usual when she put her arms around him, and when she drew back, he looked more tired than normal. He was getting old. They were all getting old.

In the kitchen Aron greeted him with a handshake hug. "Leonard, wah gwaan?" Long ago he'd insisted Fabiola's dad teach him some Jamaican patois phrases and now used them with an entitlement Fabiola found deeply embarrassing.

Leonard smiled and shrugged. "Nutten nah gwaan, Aron."

"Grandpop!" Liam and Ben hurtled into the room and

wrapped themselves around Leonard. "What did you bring for dessert?" Ben asked.

"Yeah, what'd you bring?" Liam echoed.

Leonard laughed and took the paper bag from Fabiola, letting the boys peek inside. "You have choices tonight. Black and white cookies or coconut drops. The best of New York and the best of Jamaica." He smiled at Fabiola and ruffled the boys' hair.

At dinner they refrained from mentioning Vivi's incident, instead sticking to topics like soccer, the kids' new teachers, and who would win in a battle between Black Panther and Wolverine.

"Obviously Black Panther," Vivi said. "I mean, he can teleport and make himself invisible. And Wolverine doesn't technically have any superpowers. Everything he can do is just because he's a mutant."

"But Wolverine could definitely cut through Black Panther's Vibranium suit," Ben pointed out.

"And Wolverine has already fought, like, everyone," Liam said. "He has, like, a lot of experience."

"I'm with Vivi." Leonard winked at her across the table. "My money's on T'Challa."

After dinner Leonard helped Fabiola with the dishes while Aron looked over the kids' homework.

They worked in comfortable silence for a while, and then Leonard cleared this throat. "Everything OK, sweets? You were very quiet at dinner."

Fabiola looked down at the sink as she rinsed the baking sheet she'd washed. "I was thinking about Mom," she admitted. "About how I was around Vivi's age when she came back."

Leonard nodded. "You were, yes. I remember."

Fabiola's mother had left for the first time when she was three, so she didn't remember anything about her before then. The memories started when Fabiola was ten. It had been fall then, too. Fabiola remembered the scent of rotting leaves and the chill on her cheeks as she climbed the stairs to their apartment. At the kitchen table sat her mother and father, both teary-eyed. Her mother had turned to her, arms outstretched. Her thick, dark hair hung loose and wavy down her back and her face, while still beautiful, had more lines than in Fabiola's hazy memories.

"Mi niña," she'd said, rising from the table. "I'm back."

"Did you really believe she was home for good?" Fabiola handed the baking sheet to her father to dry.

Leonard's face drooped. "I hoped so. But she was your mother. How could I keep her from you?" Fabiola gave a sad smile, remembering how she'd refused to come out of her room for two days when her mother left again three years later, the night before Fabiola's fourteenth birthday. "When we had you," Leonard continued, his voice warm and steady, "it felt a lot like I was pushing my own heart around in the stroller, watching over it on the playground, making sure no harm ever came to it." He gave a small laugh. "It was terrifying at first. But eventually I realized my fear was actually love, and I came to enjoy it. To need it. But your mother... I think it was just always terrifying for her." He set the dishes he was holding in the sink and wiped his hands on his jeans.

"Oh, Papa." Fabiola's fingers tightened around the spatula she was holding and felt the familiar bitterness in her mouth that always accompanied thinking about her mother. "You never could come out and admit she was just selfish."

He shrugged and gazed at her with a thoughtful expression. "Maybe. But that's not for me to know."

Fabiola's mind went to Liz and Peter, and how to tell her father about what she was going to do for them. He'd always been the steadying force in her life. And while he might not fully understand her decision, he'd support her because he loved her and believed she had good judgment. But what if he didn't think it was a good idea? She realized, with a pang, that there was a chance he might have the same doubts as Aron.

She flushed, recalling that her dad was the only one who'd seen her teenage crush on Peter up close—an infatuation that, over time, had deepened into a close friendship that occasionally blurred into something more. But she also knew, in that instant, that she wouldn't change her mind now, even if he was concerned. She was going to do this—for Liz, and for Peter.

SIX

Fabiola and Liz sat across from each other in a small, dark wood-paneled restaurant. Liz and Peter had offered to come to Brooklyn for dinner to talk through a "broad strokes plan"—Liz's words—for the surrogacy, so Fabiola had chosen her and Aron's favorite Italian restaurant in Carroll Gardens. They'd started coming when they'd moved to the neighborhood ten years ago, and the place hadn't changed much since then. The food tasted like it was straight from an Italian grandmother's kitchen, and while Fabiola had always liked its complete lack of pretention and bare bones approach to décor, now she eyed the scuffed wood floor and worn red-and-white checked tablecloths, wishing she'd chosen somewhere more impressive, more like where Liz and Peter—mostly Peter—were probably used to dining.

Fabiola sipped the ice water the waiter had brought, trying to quell the pangs in her stomach that were part hunger and part nerves at the thought of seeing Peter for the first time since she'd agreed to be their surrogate. It was ridiculous—why was she so nervous now? They'd had dinners together, just like this, many times over many years. She wiped her palms over her white peasant blouse and navy-colored linen pants, wondering why she hadn't thought to at least put on something that made her look like she had a waist.

On the table next to Liz, her phone buzzed. "Ugh, sorry," Liz said, reading the message. "Peter's stuck in traffic. He's coming from the hospital."

"No problem," Fabiola said. "Aron is at least twenty minutes late to everything these days."

Liz picked up her menu and fiddled with the collar of her slate gray silk blouse. "Well, at least we get some time to catch up. I feel like we haven't talked at all since brunch two weeks ago."

Fabiola groaned. "I know, I've been way too busy. I mean, not Liz Connelly busy, but, like, busy for me."

Liz laughed. "Busy is good. Ooh, that puntarelle salad looks delicious."

"Mm," Fabiola said, flashing a grateful smile at the server as he deposited a basket of bread on their table. "Remind me what puntarelle is, Farmer Liz?"

"Easy, city mouse," Liz teased. The oldest of five, she'd grown up on a Christmas tree farm in rural New Hampshire and had been a competitive biathlete in high school. Despite Liz's polished Wall Street appearance, Fabiola had no trouble picturing her friend on skis with a rifle strapped to her back.

They were quiet for a minute, examining the menu while Liz continued to button and unbutton the collar of her blouse with one hand. "So," she said eventually. "Before they get here, you're still completely sure about this, right?"

"About having the baby?" Fabiola frowned and bit into a piece of focaccia. "Of course I am."

Liz nodded, her eyes downcast on the menu. "I just want you to know that I wouldn't hold it against you if you changed your mind."

"Liz." Fabiola set her bread down, her stomach dropping. "Do you still want me to have your baby?"

"What? Yes!" Liz looked up and nodded so quickly her chin blurred. "Yes, absolutely."

"Then what's going on? You're being weird." Fabiola's stomach churned faster. She'd already spent hours picturing her growing belly and imagining the joy on Liz's face at the first ultrasound appointment.

Liz sighed. "I'm sorry. This has nothing to do with you." She twisted the thick, diamond wedding band on her finger. "I think I'm just nervous. I mean, I don't know anything about being a mom. And I think we thought it would take longer to find someone... like I'd have more time to prepare."

Fabiola's stomach unclenched. "So, the good thing is that you don't have to prepare. It's one hundred percent on-the-job training."

Liz's face loosened a bit. "It's just a lot to think about, you know? Finding a nanny. Getting into a good preschool. Making sure they're cared for but not spoiled. And what about vacations—we always go skiing in March but how old does a child have to be to learn to ski? And should we raise them in the city? Peter mentioned New Jersey." She shuddered.

Fabiola reached across the table and placed her hand on top of Liz's. "Sweetie," she said. "There isn't even a baby yet. You don't need to worry about any of that. Who knows, maybe I won't even be able to get pregnant." She shrugged and immediately tried to rid her mind of the thought.

"You will," Liz said in a confident tone, as if she could will it into existence. And if anyone could make something happen, it was Liz.

"Can I ask you something?" Fabiola said, reclaiming her piece of focaccia and dunking it in olive oil. She flashed back to months earlier, when Liz had sat down at brunch and told her and Alice that she and Peter had decided to have a baby.

Alice had set down her cappuccino, confused. "You're going to have a baby? But what about your uterus? Or lack thereof?" Fabiola elbowed her. "Ow," Alice said. "Sorry, but I have *questions*."

Liz had shrugged. "We'll get a surrogate, of course, and hopefully we can use the eggs I froze a million years ago." She said it in the same tone she'd used a moment earlier to tell them about her new Italian stovetop, and Fabiola had been taken aback by her blasé nature.

"What changed your mind?" Fabiola asked now, reaching for a second piece of focaccia as her stomach rumbled. "I mean, you always seemed so sure about not having kids." Fabiola also knew Peter had never wanted them, either. He'd confessed this to Fabiola the night before he'd proposed to Liz, sitting across from her at a late-night diner sharing an order of cheese fries, the ambiguity of their decades-long relationship pressing in on them like a third wheel in their cozy booth.

Liz paused, considering Fabiola's question in the same way she would if Fabiola had asked her to calculate the value of the Brooklyn Bridge, her mind scanning for inputs to the question and constructing an equation that would lead to the answer. "Well," she said. "After my surgery, even though my eggs were frozen, I pretty much just put it out of my head. And it definitely wasn't compatible with my choice of career, at least early on. Peter and I... well, we have a great life, you know? But lately I think we're asking ourselves what's next. The time just feels right." She twisted her ring again.

"Well, hello ladies," Peter's baritone voice rang out. Looking up, Fabiola saw him approaching, grinning broadly, his hand clamped on Aron's shoulder as he steered him across the restaurant. "Look who I ran into outside." Aron offered a tired smile.

The foursome stood to exchange greetings. Peter brushed Fabiola's cheek with a kiss, his face smelling of fresh air and the tang of salt water, a familiar scent Fabiola knew wasn't manufactured by cologne. It was just Peter. She couldn't ignore the small zing the feel of his lips on her cheek sent through her. She tried to remember the last time she'd seen him; it had been a couple of months, at least. Despite the fact that he was her oldest friend—and married to her best friend—their paths didn't regularly cross. Deep down Fabiola knew this was probably for the best.

"Well," Peter said once they were settled at the table, menus in hand. "Here we are. I'd say this calls for a celebration. Bubbly?" He smoothed his short, sandy hair and signaled for the waiter with the confidence of a man who had never once questioned his place in the world. Fabiola remembered when he'd grown his hair long in high school to rebel against his parents. She'd liked the way it had fallen into his blue eyes and curled up slightly at the ends, and the way it felt to run her fingers through it on the nights when all their other friends had gone home for curfew and only the two of them were left.

They exchanged small talk, and Fabiola listened as Aron told Peter about the latest celebrity endorsements of Pivot, grateful that Peter knew how to ask all the right questions and sound so interested. When the bottle of champagne arrived, Fabiola covered her glass with her hand. "Oh, I probably shouldn't have any." She'd started reading about how to prepare for IVF, and one of the universal recommendations seemed to be avoiding alcohol. "Now that, well, you know." She suddenly felt shy saying it.

"Oh, come on," Peter urged. "One glass can't hurt." He winked at her and nodded at the waiter, who poured the fourth glass.

Peter took Liz's hand and raised his glass. "I think a toast is in order. To you, Fabi. For giving us the ultimate gift."

Fabiola blushed and raised her own glass. "To your family," she said, keeping her eyes on Liz instead of Peter. They all clinked glasses. Peter leaned over to plant a tender kiss on Liz's lips. Fabiola averted her eyes and leaned in to Aron as he put his arm around her. His hand around her shoulder felt warm and familiar.

"So," Aron said, taking a long sip. "How will this work, exactly?"

"Right down to business," Peter laughed. "I like it, man." He set his glass down and proceeded to unbutton his sleeves and roll them up, his movements slow and deliberate.

Aron's mouth turned up at the corners into something that wasn't quite a smile. "I just want to be sure that we're all comfortable with the... process. Especially Fabi." His arm tightened around her and she tried not to stiffen at his possessive tone.

Peter's smile flickered and was replaced with a serious expression. "Of course. We all do." He looked at Liz.

"I talked to my doctor today," she said, her eyes darting from Fabiola to Aron. "She said the next step would be for her to see you, Fabi, and to run a few tests."

"What sort of tests?" Aron asked. Fabiola tightened her grip on her champagne flute as he spoke for her.

"Just normal bloodwork, to make sure everything's working the way it's supposed to." Liz flushed and looked at Fabiola. "I'm sorry, it feels so weird to be sitting here talking about this over bruschetta." She gestured to the appetizer plates in front of them, then fanned herself and gave a small laugh. "I'm so nervous I'm actually sweating."

Fabiola smiled and reached across the booth to pat Liz's arm. "It's fine," she said. "I'm nervous, too." She was aware of Peter's unwavering gaze on her from across the table. She remembered the first time she'd seen him on her first day at Dalton. She'd been twelve years old with her brand new glittery pink backpack, which, with one look around at everyone else's weathered L.L. Bean bags, she knew was all wrong. She'd spent the whole morning waiting for the hand of a teacher or principal to appear on her shoulder and tell her there'd been a mistake, that she wasn't actually a Dalton student after all despite her dad's janitorial job there that offered her tuition relief. Then at lunch, just as she was considering fleeing the cafeteria rather than look for somewhere to sit in the sea of unfamiliar faces, she had spotted Peter, and felt instantly soothed by his blue eyes and bright smile, as he nodded at the seat next to him.

"OK," Aron said, forging ahead through the emotions on display, "let's talk about risks." Fabiola flinched at his brusque tone.

"Risks?" Peter asked.

"An ectopic pregnancy, hemorrhaging during delivery, uterine rupture." Aron sounded like he was reading from a Wikipedia entry on rare labor and delivery complications. Liz glanced at Fabiola, the faint worry line on her forehead deepening.

"Aron, there's no need to get ahead of ourselves," Fabiola said. She put her hand over his and tried to sound breezy and cheerful.

Peter caught her eye and flashed her a tender smile. Then he drained his glass and motioned for the waiter again. "Anyway, that stuff is really rare," he said.

Worry pricked at the edges of Fabiola's mind. Peter always drank more in times of emotional turmoil. Their freshman year of college she'd been the one to escort him home from the bar the night of his brother's funeral, dragging him out of the cab and up to his childhood bedroom, then undressing him and getting him into the bath after he'd thrown up on himself. She'd lain next to him all night to make sure he kept breathing.

"I didn't realize neurosurgeons had started delivering babies," Aron said now, his grip tightening on his wine glass.

Peter's eyes narrowed almost imperceptibly. "I'm just saying, there's no need to be dramatic—"

"Dramatic?" Aron brought his free hand down on the table with a loud *thud*. "This is my wife we're talking about."

Peter held his gaze, then his eyes strayed to Fabiola. "And my oldest friend," he said quietly. She felt her face grow warm.

"OK, OK." Liz held up her hands like a referee. She glanced at Fabiola and shot her a *let's just get through this* look. "We can all agree we want the best for Fabi."

Aron gave a tight nod.

"What's next after the test?" Fabiola asked, attempting to move the conversation forward. "How soon would we... try?"

"Well," Liz said, refilling everyone's glasses. "First there's some legal stuff to get through—we should probably have some kind of contract. But after that, well, we can start any time." She flashed a tense smile at Peter, who continued to signal for the waiter.

"Gin martini, please," he said. Liz raised her eyebrows at him and he looked away, but not before Fabiola caught an expression of annoyance on his face.

The server returned to describe the specials, including a grilled calamari appetizer which Aron ordered.

"But Fabi's allergic to shellfish," Peter said.

"Yeah, but she's not allergic to other people eating it." Aron shrugged, ignoring Peter's pointed tone.

"It's fine, really," Fabiola said, wishing she could fast forward through the rest of the evening. Having Peter and Aron in the same room was always an awkward collision of her past and present that made her feel caught in an uneasy swirl of what-ifs.

Fortunately, their food arrived, and the atmosphere at the table eased as they dug in and ordered another bottle of wine. Liz looked just as flustered as Fabiola felt, and Fabiola knew her nonstop small talk was her way of smoothing away the tension. Liz filled them in on their upcoming trip to Napa, and Peter and Aron talked about whether the Mets had any chance of making the playoffs. By the time dessert rolled around Fabiola had lost track of how many times her glass had been refilled and she was beginning to enjoy the evening.

"So," Peter said after they'd unanimously declined after-dinner coffee. "There is one other thing we wanted to talk about." His fingers drummed lightly on the table and Fabiola felt a little hint of unease kick in. "The issue of compensation."

"Peter," Liz began, her fingers going again to the collar of her blouse. "I don't know if this is the right time to—"

"Compensation?" Aron interrupted, raising an eyebrow.

Liz shot Peter a frustrated glance, then turned back to Aron with a forced smile. "We'd been planning to pay a gestational surrogate. It's a fairly substantial amount of money because, well, it's a substantial undertaking. We've talked about it, and we think it's only fair for that money to go to you. On top of any medical expenses, which of course we're covering. Call it compensation for any pain and suffering along the way." She laughed but the joke fell flat.

"Liz," Fabiola said, taken aback. Her best friend wanted to pay her to have a baby? Across the table she caught the apologetic look on Liz's face and realized what was happening. This was Peter's doing. He never liked to feel as though he owed anyone anything, and money had always been his way of evening the score. "That's really not necessary," Fabiola continued. "I want to"—she gestured to Aron—"*we* want to do this for you."

"And we couldn't be more grateful," Peter said, raising his nearly empty martini glass toward her and Aron. "Think of it as a kind of thank you gift."

"We don't need your money." Aron's voice was terse.

"Oh, we know," Liz interjected, holding her hands up. "We're just so thankful that— I mean, what you're doing is—"

"Money's never a bad thing," Peter said. "I mean, you've got three college tuitions to think about."

"Which we're more than prepared for," Aron snapped. This wasn't true, Fabiola knew. She'd seen the paltry amounts on the kids' 529 statements, and living solely on her income the past year meant their savings had taken a hit.

"Just take the money." Peter shrugged. "It's not a big deal."

"Because you've always worked so hard for yours," Aron said with a tight smile.

"I went to medical school." Peter's face hardened. "At Columbia."

"Remind me, isn't your dad on the Board of Trustees there?"

Peter half raised himself out of his chair. "I hope you're not insinuating that—"

"He's not insinuating anything." Fabiola flung her arm across Aron's chest as if they were in a car that had just stopped short. The quick movement tipped her off balance and she gripped the table with her other hand to steady herself. How much had she had to drink? She closed her eyes and wished for a power outage or a kitchen fire, anything to end the evening right then.

"We should go." Pushing Fabiola's arm away, Aron rose and tossed some cash on the table.

"Oh please, let us—" Liz began.

"I insist." Aron held up his hands, then grabbed Fabiola's arm and pulled her up next to him. She caught her knee on the table on the way up and the impact caused Liz's half-full wine glass to slide to the floor and smash.

Fabiola yelped. "Oh my God, I'm so sorry!"

"Hey, take it easy with her." Peter stood and pointed a finger at Aron. He was several inches taller than Aron. "Calm down."

"Calm down? God, you're such a prick." Aron tugged Fabiola's arm. "Come on, we're going."

"I'm a prick?" Peter replied. The dining room, which had

grown crowded since they arrived, had gone quiet, with everyone's heads turned toward them. Fabiola closed her eyes and wished to be anywhere but in that room. "You're the one who's delusional about how Pivot's going to be the next Bleacher Report while Fabi's working her ass off to subsidize your pipe dreams."

Fabiola wrenched her eyes up from the wine-stained tablecloth to Liz's face. She'd allowed herself to vent to Liz and Alice about their financial stress, but within the safe confines of their monthly brunches. Had Liz told Peter all that?

"And you ordered shellfish," Peter continued, his face creased with indignation. "Shellfish! Which could literally, like, kill Fabi." He shrugged and gave a harsh laugh. "But sure, whatever, I'm the prick." Fabiola's heart thudded in her chest. Peter had always defended her, right from the early days when her fake leather loafers and off-brand gym shorts made her an easy target among the rich, privileged Dalton students. Normally his protectiveness sent a pleasant charge through her body, but right now it was only making a bad situation worse.

"I have my epi pen," she offered weakly.

"We're trying to help you, man," Peter called after him as Aron stalked away toward the door. "You don't even know a good thing when it's staring you in the fucking face."

Fabiola locked eyes with Peter, then glanced at Aron's retreating figure. With a sigh, she followed her husband.

SEVEN

Fabiola struggled to catch up to Aron as he took long strides down the street. It had rained while they were inside, and while the skies were now clearing the water pooled on the uneven sidewalks in large, dark puddles, the depth of which was impossible to gauge until it was up over the tops of her feet. She'd had more to drink than she'd meant to, and her gait was unsteady in the heeled ankle boots she'd chosen. "Damn it," she said as she failed to avoid a puddle the size of a child's wading pool.

The water splashed up onto the suede material of the boots and dripped down inside to soak her socks. The boots were her favorite and she hoped they'd dry out OK. They were old and inexpensive, but Peter had once complimented them, saying how long they made her legs look. Right now, though, she had bigger problems than ruined footwear.

"Aron, wait!" she called out, and he glanced back over his shoulder and slowed his pace, allowing her to cross the street and catch up to him. "What the hell was that?" she demanded.

Aron jerked to a stop so fast she nearly slammed into him. "How can you stand him?" he asked.

The temperature had dropped after the rain and Fabiola

shivered, wishing she'd brought a jacket. "He's Peter," she said, flat and angry, knowing that there was no defense for what Peter had said, and no explanation that would mollify Aron right now.

"He's a prick, that's what he is." Aron's fingers were bunched into fists at his sides.

"Yes, you mentioned that. Loudly and to his face." Fabiola pulled out her phone to call an Uber and began to walk away.

"Trying to pay us off like that." Aron switched directions and strode alongside her, curling and uncurling his fingers. "Like we need his charity or something."

She rubbed her temples, trying to stave off the beginning of a headache. "He didn't mean it that way," she said, though the offer hadn't landed right with her, either. "God, you're always so paranoid and defensive around him."

"You told him, didn't you?" Aron pointed a finger at her. "You told him our private financial business." Fabiola bit her lip. "I knew it," he exclaimed. "God, Fabi, of all people—"

"I told Liz, not Peter." She stopped walking and crossed her arms in defense. "She's my friend, Aron. We talk about everything."

"You have no faith in me, do you?" he asked. The anger had drained from his face and he seemed to be trying to answer the question for himself. "You don't think Pivot will amount to anything. You think I'm a failure."

She looked away to gather herself before answering. "Look, you have to admit it's been hard since you left mainstream media. You're working a lot, and now I am, too, and with the kids..." She trailed off, uncertain of what she was trying to say. That he should quit? Give up his dream? Go back to doing what everyone else, mainly her, wanted him to do?

"So why would you want to add the surrogacy onto all that?" Aron asked, his jaw set.

Fabiola put her hands on her hips. "You agreed—"

"I know what I said." Aron ran his hand through his hair in frustration. "I just— Pivot... this is going to be big for me—for us." He grabbed her hand. "You have to believe me, Fabi. The company is so close, I know it. The payoff could be huge for us. *Will* be huge for us. I really want this."

"I know," she said. "And I have things I really want, too."

Aron dropped her hand. They stood in silence for a minute, weighing their next words. Then Fabiola wrapped her arms around herself. "I'm freezing," she said. "Let's go home."

EIGHT

Fabiola awoke feeling like her tongue was covered with sand. She checked the clock on her nightstand and groaned as she heaved herself out of bed.

Downstairs the boys were in the kitchen eating toast and Aron was at the stove. "Good morning," she said, her voice raspy.

Aron turned, holding a wooden spoon covered in scrambled eggs. "Good morning." His tone was cautious, as though he was feeling her out.

She kissed each boy on the top of his head, which they still let her do when they weren't in public. "Did you already do your run?" she asked Aron.

Aron shook his head. "No, I skipped it this morning. I thought you might, um, need a hand." He smiled. "But I did sprint to the bodega for you." He nodded toward the counter where a tantalizing blue box sat next to the toaster.

"No fair," said Liam. "Why does Mom get Pop Tarts? You never let us have them for breakfast."

"Because they'll stunt your growth," Aron said. "Mom, on

the other hand, is already fully grown. So she gets as many Pop Tarts as she wants."

"That's not, like, real science." Ben crossed his arms skeptically.

"Thanks," she said, giving Aron a grateful smile. Pop Tarts had always been her hangover food. After sixteen years together, he knew her almost better than anyone. The thought caused a small avalanche of guilt in her chest as she remembered how intoxicating it had felt to lock eyes across the table with Peter the night before. She blinked to erase the thought and looked around. "Where's Vivi?"

"She'll be down in a minute. I'm leaving to take the boys to school in"—he checked his watch—"five minutes, right guys?" The twins nodded.

"Oh. Thanks." Fabiola blinked at this unusual display of domestic support, then dropped her Pop Tart into the toaster.

She took a long shower while Aron got everyone out the door, then checked her phone. There was a missed call and three texts from Liz.

> I'm so sorry. Peter is an idiot. I asked him not to bring up $.

> Can we talk?

> Please call me. 🤍

She imagined Liz waking up next to Peter that morning. Did he snore? Talk in his sleep? Apart from the time she'd watched over him as he slept off his drinking, she'd never spent the whole night with him, though she'd imagined it plenty of times when they were younger. The closest she'd gotten was the night before Thanksgiving during their sophomore year of college.

She thought back to that evening, how she'd been changing into pajamas when her phone rang. The eleven p.m. news played in the next room while her father snored lightly in his recliner.

"Hey," Peter said. Her heart fizzed like someone had popped a champagne cork inside it. "Are you still on campus?" he asked.

"No, I'm at home with my dad for the weekend."

"Then can I see you?"

She went to him. She always did. Fifteen minutes later a cab had transported her from East Harlem to Peter's bedroom on the Upper East Side. She sat cross-legged on his familiar blue and green plaid bedspread while he went to make her a cup of tea.

"Here," he said, returning with a mug.

"Thanks." The water was only lukewarm, but she didn't care. It was the act of Peter making it for her that mattered.

"So, I'm leaving Princeton." He sat next to her on the bed, their knees touching. She stayed quiet, knowing there was more. "Actually, they asked me to leave," he said, clearing his throat.

The third generation of Princeton men in his family, Peter had been on academic probation since the end of freshman year. He lowered his face into his hands. "God, my dad is so pissed. He thinks I'm a failure, an embarrassment."

"You're not." She set her tea on the nightstand and reached for him. This was why she was here: to comfort him. He always needed her most when he was at his lowest, reaching for her as if he could be healed by her presence. The weekend he missed the penalty kick that would have won Dalton the varsity soccer championship. The day later that year when his parents told him they were getting divorced. The night he'd found out his older brother had been killed by a drunk driver. Being with him like this in these moments had always made her feel special, like she had a gift only she could give him.

After, they'd laid together under the sheets, his arms encircling her, her body curled around his. She woke later, the red numbers on the clock next to her abandoned mug of tea blinking 4:36 a.m.

She shook him gently. "I have to go."

"No," he'd mumbled, tightening his arms around her. "Stay."

"My dad will worry." She dislodged herself from his embrace and began hunting for her clothes.

"OK, fine." He sat up and rubbed his eyes, then began pulling on his own clothes.

"I can let myself out."

He gave her a sleepy smile. "As if I'd let you."

The doorman had hailed her a cab while Peter waited with her in the warmth of the lobby, squeezing her hand once before she pushed through the doors to the waiting car.

Now, Fabiola shook the memory of Peter's bedroom from her mind and pulled her wet hair into a tight bun. She opened Liz's texts to reply then stopped, unsure of what to say. The phone buzzed in her hand with an incoming call, and she jumped, startled.

"Hello?"

"Fabi, I'm so sorry. I was a complete idiot last night. Please tell me I didn't ruin everything." His voice poured into her ear like rain in the desert. "I called Aron, too. I got his voicemail, but I told him I wanted to talk, to apologize."

"Did Liz ask you to do that?" She opened her dresser and pulled out her oldest and softest sweatpants.

"Well, yes—initially. But I agree, obviously. I was a moron, and totally out of line. I've been under a lot of stress lately, I had too much to drink—that boring old story. Please, Fabi. I can't stand thinking you might be mad at me." He'd always been like this—unable to think straight whenever he feared he was out of favor with someone. Outwardly, he exuded confidence and bravado, but Fabi saw through it. She recognized the scars from years of trying to please his uninterested, impossible-to-satisfy parents.

"I'm not mad," she said. It was true. She wanted to be, but it never worked with Peter.

"Oh, thank God. Liz would kill me if I'd screwed this up."

Fabiola paused with one leg in her pants. "Screwed what up?"

"The whole surrogacy thing."

Something inside her chilled. "So that's what this is about? Not the fact that you acted like an entitled frat boy?"

Peter's sigh echoed through the phone. "Of course not. Though we both know I have a lot of experience with the whole entitled frat boy thing." She could hear him trying not to smile.

"Really, Peter?"

"Fabi, come on. Don't be like that." His voice was soft and pleading and she could picture him burying his hand in his thick hair like he did when he was agitated.

"I have to go," she said, though hanging up was the last thing she wanted to do.

"Fabi, please," he entreated, his voice taking on a warm, honeyed tone. "Can we meet so I can grovel in person? I have a window later this morning. Coffee? Bring Aron and I'll grovel for him, too."

"You're funny," she said, her voice flat.

"Please." His voice grew desperate. "I need to see you."

"When?"

His sigh of relief flooded her ears. "Ten o'clock? I'll come to wherever you are."

When she hung up and went back downstairs Aron had just walked back in the front door. Without the kids in the house a strained silence descended between them.

"Thanks for taking everyone this morning," she said in a neutral tone, trying to gauge his emotional state.

He gave a polite nod and walked over to the coffee maker to refill his travel mug. "No problem. How are you, um, feeling?"

She shrugged. "OK."

"So, last night..." He trailed off, his face unreadable.

"Peter said he left you a message," Fabiola said. "To apologize."

Aron's posture stiffened. "You talked to him? When?"

"He just called. To apologize."

"Ah."

"I think he's nervous about the whole becoming a father thing." She had no idea whether this was true. "He invited us to meet for coffee. To clear the air, in person."

"I have a full morning of meetings for my silly, failing company." Aron's voice was brusque and his grip on his coffee mug tightened. "And anyway, we're not some charity case. We don't need their money."

"They didn't mean it that way. And we don't have to take the money if that's what's tripping you up."

"Are you saying you want to?"

"What? No, I—" Fabiola pressed her lips together, knowing she needed to proceed carefully. "Look, I'm not going to lie, I've been feeling under pressure lately to make sure our bills are paid. But if you think Pivot is going to—"

"I *know* it will."

She closed her eyes for a split second and pictured Aron on their wedding day in the tailored gray suit he'd bought for the occasion. She'd thought herself lucky to be marrying a man who had his life figured out and who wanted what she wanted—a family. Later when he told her his dream was to start Pivot her first thought had been, *but I thought we were grown up now and done with chasing our dreams.* Now, standing next to him in the kitchen, she let reality settle over her. Maybe he was right, maybe it wasn't a good time for her to rock their delicately balanced boat with a pregnancy.

She opened her eyes. "We don't have to do this," she said, and though a lump of sadness formed in her throat at the thought, she meant it. Her family came first. "*I* don't have to do this."

Aron's face softened and a mixture of resignation and regret came over it. Slowly he reached out his hand and laid it flat against her stomach. "You always put other people first. That's one of the reasons I fell in love with you." He drew closer and tipped his head down until his forehead met hers. "I can see how much this means to you," he murmured. "And I don't want to be the one standing in the way of you doing this for Liz."

She pressed her face into his until she found his lips and kissed him, long and deep. "Thank you," she said when she drew back. "I love you."

His arms encircled her waist, and he pulled her in against his warm chest. She could feel his heartbeat against the side of her face. "I love you, too."

NINE

The whine of the espresso machine pierced Fabiola's skull like a spear. She closed her eyes and inhaled over her Americano, willing her body back to life.

"Hi." She opened her eyes to see Peter standing next to her. He smiled. "Sorry to interrupt your meditation."

"You mean my hangover?" she asked. His smile widened as he slid into the seat across from her, the skin around his eyes crinkling. A familiar tingling spread through her at his proximity. Even with slight bags under his eyes and a five o'clock shadow at ten a.m., he was still insanely handsome. His pale blue eyes and square jaw made her stomach flutter.

"You and me both." He winced.

"Do you want something?" Fabiola nodded toward the counter.

He shook his head. "No. The amount of caffeine I've had already today is probably illegal."

She laughed and his eyes crinkled again, then his face grew serious. "Fabi, I'm really sorry. I was completely out of line with Aron last night. I hope you can forgive me."

She took a sip of her drink. She couldn't exactly tell him that she hadn't been angry with him in the first place. That everything he'd said about Aron was something she'd also thought. That she *was* tired of supporting them while waiting for his gamble with Pivot to pay off. That his dogged confidence in his decision to trade job security and a 401(k) for equity in a company that was always only weeks away from not making payroll felt selfish and immature. But that every time she brought up their slowly diminishing savings, he accused her of not supporting his dreams or having an old-fashioned mindset about work and careers. Also, why *did* he always have to order the calamari?

She bit her lip. "Of course I forgive you. But you should really be talking to Aron."

"I will." He nodded, his forehead creased with determination. "I sent him an email on the way here. I have a friend from UPenn who's pretty high up at *SB Nation*. I told him I'd make an introduction."

Fabi's eyebrows drew together. "I could be more impressed if I had any idea what you were talking about."

Peter laughed. "It's the sports news division of Vox Media. I thought they might be interested in Pivot."

"Oh," Fabiola said, sitting up straighter. "Thanks." This introduction actually sounded promising—and of course it did, because it came from Peter. Thanks to his family, he moved in circles far beyond most people's reach. Yet he'd never once lorded this over her. Whatever he had, had always been hers, too, from the family chef who'd learned to make grilled cheese exactly the way teenage Fabiola liked it, on white bread with a slice of tomato, to the wealthy friends he'd referred to her as clients when she started her business.

She looked up to find him gazing at her, and her stomach dropped. Looking away quickly, she tried for a joke. "You might recall I don't exactly keep up with sports news."

Peter cocked his head and smiled. "Remember when I tried to teach you to play tennis?"

Fabiola rolled her eyes. Her second year at Dalton, Peter had encouraged her to go out for the school's tennis team. He claimed it didn't matter that she'd never picked up a racket before—or even that she lacked both athletic ability and hand-eye coordination—and that with his coaching she'd be playing Wimbledon in no time. He gave up on her after the first lesson when she'd finally gotten so annoyed with his constant barking of instructions that she'd drilled the ball across the court into his solar plexus, temporarily silencing him as he gasped for breath. It was the first and only time she'd gotten the ball over the net.

"I still maintain that I could have been great if only I'd had the right coach," she said.

Peter laughed, then reached across the table for her hand. Heat shot through her body. "Fabi, please don't back out. It would kill Liz. You know how she gets when she's set on something." He closed his eyes and rubbed the creases in his forehead that had recently appeared.

Fabiola felt a flash of annoyance at the guilt trip, but it swiftly dissipated, and she nodded. She did. During finals season at Vassar, Liz's bed had gone largely unslept in as she haunted the library and study lounges in pursuit of her goal of being number one in their class—which she was three years out of four.

Peter rubbed his thumb over the top of her hand, which he still hadn't released. Fabiola's heart raced to what felt like a dangerous speed. She wanted to pull away before she passed out or had a stroke, but she couldn't bear to sever their touch. Instead, she stared at his fingers cradling hers, wondering how he felt when he touched her. Did he experience the same fizzing sensation throughout his body that she did? Did he, like her, relive the memory of his skin against hers on that one night they had never spoken of since?

"Just imagine what it would be like to tell the baby that his Aunt Fabi had helped bring him into the world," Peter murmured.

Feeling stung, Fabiola pulled her hand back. *Aunt Fabi.* The words felt like a second-place trophy. She turned to look out the window so Peter wouldn't see the tears that had welled in her eyes. She wanted so much more than the consolation prize.

"Of course I'll do it," she said, forcing a smile as she turned back to him. "When have I ever said no to you?"

Her phone buzzed in her purse. Eager for a distraction she reached for it. An unfamiliar number flashed across the screen.

"Hello?" she said, holding one finger up to Peter in apology.

"Is this Fabiola Fernandez Butler?"

"Yes." She frowned and her shoulders tensed in response to the brisk, official tone of the caller.

"I'm calling from Lenox Hill Hospital. We have your father here."

TEN

Fabiola hurried after the doctor through the maze of fluorescent lit hallways. She kept her eyes on the back of the woman's long white coat as she tried to keep up with her long strides. She was grateful for the antiseptic tang of cleanliness that stung her nose and acted as a kind of modern-day smelling salt to keep the swimming of her head at bay.

Finally, they arrived at a room with her father's name scribbled on the white board mounted on the door, Leonard Butler.

"We gave him a sedative during the stent procedure, so he'll be groggy," warned the doctor, pausing with her hand on the doorknob. She had a short, natural afro and looked to be around Fabiola's age, mid-thirties. "We'll keep him here overnight and then he'll need to rest at home for at least another week. No strenuous activity. Apparently, he'd been experiencing symptoms for weeks—fatigue, pressure in the chest—but ignored them. He can't do that anymore; he needs to rest when he's tired. Then slowly he can return to normal activities."

"But he'll be OK, right?" Fabiola couldn't hide the quaver in her voice. Her father meant everything to her. She fought to keep the worst-case scenarios from filling her mind.

A flicker of sympathy flashed across the doctor's face. "Your father had what some people would call a 'mild' heart attack." She made air quotes with her fingers. "I don't like that word because any kind of heart attack is serious. We've got him on a beta blocker and an ACE inhibitor, and we put in the stent. But a lot of his long-term recovery will depend on him. Diet changes, exercise, stress reduction." She ticked the items off on her fingers.

Fabiola nodded as the doctor's instructions washed over her. She wished she had somewhere to write them down, but she'd left her bag in the waiting room with Peter. "Can I go in?" she asked. She felt an urgent, visceral need to see her father, to breathe in his familiar scent, touch his face, and reassure herself that everything would be all right.

The doctor nodded and pushed open the door. "Mr. Butler," she said in a crisp but friendly tone. "You have a visitor."

"Hi, Papa." Fabiola tried to mimic the doctor's upbeat tone, but her voice came out like the crunch of gravel. Her father's eyes fluttered open and a smile spread across his face. His normally warm, sepia-colored skin had an ashy undertone.

"Hi, sweets," he murmured.

Fabiola's chest clenched like a belt had tightened across it as she took in the various wires protruding from under his blanket and what looked like a NASA command center's worth of machines surrounding his bed. "How are you feeling?" she asked.

"I just need a little rest," he said. "Then I'll be back on my feet."

"Rest is a good idea." The doctor nodded. "You can visit for a few minutes." She stepped out of the room.

Fabiola perched on the chair next to her father's bed and reached for his hand. She remembered the feel of that same hand on her back when he'd taught her to ride a bike in Marcus

Garvey Park, the gentle, comforting pressure of his fingers between her shoulder blades as she pedaled past the crowded basketball courts toward the watchtower. It was the same hand that had brushed and braided her hair every morning before school after her mother left, clapped for her when she walked across the stage in her cap and gown at Vassar, and guided her expertly around the dance floor during the father-daughter dance at her wedding thanks to the lessons he'd taken on the sly.

Now, though, the hand looked wrinkled and felt lighter than she remembered, like the hollow bones of a bird.

"Papa," she said, blinking back tears. Her insides felt like they were caving in, and she worried she might collapse. He made a tsking noise in his throat.

"It's all right, sweets," he said, using the childhood nickname he'd given her. "I'll be back on my feet in no time." He struggled to push himself upright in the bed and winced.

"I know, Papa." She squeezed his hand. "But why didn't you tell me you weren't feeling well?"

He shrugged. "I just thought I had a little heartburn. Maybe Mami's chicken finally catching up with me." Fabiola had grown up blocks away from Mami's Luncheonette, which served roasted chicken seasoned with jerk seasoning and, seemingly, molten lava. Fabi couldn't eat more than two bites without her tongue swelling and tears streaming down her face, but her father often ordered an off-the-menu version that was even spicier.

She squeezed his hand again. "It's just, if anything happened to you..." She broke off, the thought too horrible to speak aloud.

"As if you could get rid of me that easily!" he scoffed. "You worry too much, sweets. You heard the doctor. I'm going to be fine."

"You need to take some time off work. Maybe take a vacation, or even think about retiring." She began formulating a mental checklist of rest and relaxation for him, all the while blinking back her tears.

He sighed. "Fabi, I'm only fifty-six years old. What am I going to retire for? To sit around all day waiting for the Scorpions game to come on?" he said, referring to Jamaica's cricket team.

"You could help Aron and me with the kids."

He smiled and patted her hand. "You know I love the kids. But they're getting so big. Vivi is in high school now, and the boys are busy with soccer and all the other things you have them doing." He raised his eyebrows. He'd never understood why his grandchildren had such crowded calendars, running from place to place like they were practicing to be stressed-out adults. "The last thing the kids want is their old Grandpops hanging around all the time." He leaned back against his pillow and closed his eyes, smiling. "Remember when Ben and Liam were born? It was like a hurricane hit."

"How could I forget?" Fabiola said with a soft laugh. "I didn't sleep for months." She remembered the chaos of having two babies and five-year-old Vivi, someone always hungry, the diaper pail and laundry hamper always overflowing. Every afternoon when he finished work at Dalton her father rode the subway to Brooklyn. She remembered the relief of handing him the babies and collapsing onto the couch for a few minutes of rest before she had to pick Vivi up from kindergarten. He'd stay until late in the evening, helping her with bathing the boys and rocking them to sleep while Aron fed Vivi dinner and put her to bed.

"I loved that time," he murmured, eyes still closed. She could see he was tired. She should leave, let him rest, but suddenly the words leapt into her throat, determined to escape.

"I might be having another baby," she blurted.

His eyes flew open. "A baby?"

"Not my baby," she hurried on. The excitement that had

begun to spread across his face turned to puzzlement, his lips pausing mid-smile. "Remember my friend, Liz?"

"Of course I do." He frowned.

"It's her baby. Hers and Peters." Once Fabiola and Peter had become friends at Dalton Peter would sometimes take the subway several stops north to walk with her to the market on her corner that sold the Jamaican sweets she'd introduced him to, hard candies made from wet sugar, coconut, ginger, and lime juice that weren't available at the Citarella on 75th Street where his family shopped. Often after he'd end up in her living room watching the soccer match with her father while she sat flipping through issues of *YM* and *Real Simple*. Every once in a while, Fabiola would feel a flash of jealousy when her father and Peter cheered and high fived each other or argued over a referee's call. Mostly, though, she was happy to see how much fun they had together. *Maybe this is what it would be like to have a brother,* she'd thought once. Except her feelings for Peter had never been entirely sisterly.

Her father's eyes widened in confusion from his hospital bed. "It's called surrogacy," Fabiola explained, speaking quickly. "Remember Liz's surgery in college?" Her father nodded. "Well, because of it she can't get pregnant. But she froze her eggs, and now she and Peter want to use them to have a baby. And I might help them by carrying the baby."

Her father squinted at her as he digested this information. "So they'll put their baby... inside you?"

Fabiola nodded. "Yes. I mean, a doctor will."

"And you just give it to them when you're done?" She nodded again and he was quiet for a minute before asking, "And Aron is fine with this?"

Fabiola stiffened but kept the smile on her face. "We're working out the details, but yes."

"And *you're* fine with it? Just handing over a baby that you... for so long... just like that?" Fabiola paused. In all her fantasies about being Liz and Peter's surrogacy, she hadn't actually stopped to consider what that moment would be like. A small bubble of unease formed in her stomach.

"Yes," she said. "Of course."

"Well. This all sounds very... modern."

Fabiola laughed. "I suppose it does."

"But it's Peter..." he continued.

Fabiola felt a heat rise in her cheeks. "What do you mean?" She cocked her head.

He closed his eyes again and tipped his head back into the pillow. "You two were such good friends." His voice slurred drowsily. "It always seemed like you would be good together."

Fabiola's face flushed and she was grateful her father's eyes were closed.

She stayed until he was asleep, then wound her way back through the hallways to the waiting room and exit. She pushed through the door to the low-ceilinged room with its rows of scuffed, teal-colored couches and chairs and two men rose to greet her.

"Hi," she said to Aron as he crossed the room to her. He folded her into her arms.

"Fabi, I'm so sorry," he said, speaking into her hair as he kissed the top of her head. "How is he?"

"He's doing OK." Her eyes strayed over Aron's shoulder to where Peter hung back, concern written on his face. "The doctor says he'll be OK."

"Thank God." Aron pulled back and squeezed her shoulders, smiling.

"How did you know to come?" she asked, remembering suddenly that she'd been so focused on getting to her father in the cab Peter had hailed for them that she hadn't even thought to call Aron.

"Peter called me." His smile slipped a fraction as Peter stepped forward.

"You're still here," Fabiola said, feeling a swell of guilt at how relieved she was he hadn't left. She had no idea how long she'd been at the hospital.

"Of course I am. You know how I feel about Leonard." In college Peter had once confessed that growing up, he'd fantasized about having Leonard for a dad instead of his own father, who spent most of his time at regattas and on the golf course.

Fabiola nodded. "He needs to rest, but he's going to be OK. He'll be OK." She repeated it, as if convincing herself, and then suddenly fat, sloppy tears were rolling off her cheeks onto the front of her shirt. She saw Peter's arms instinctively reach for her, but they quickly dropped as Aron pulled her close again.

"You're probably in shock, honey," he said. "Let's get you home."

They were silent in the car as Aron pulled onto the FDR. Out her window Fabiola stared out the window as they passed Roosevelt Island, then the white, curved wall of the UN Headquarters, then the bridges, Williamsburg, Manhattan, then the Brooklyn Bridge which Aron exited onto.

Aron broke the silence when they were over the water. "So, Peter and I talked while we were in the waiting room."

Fabiola glanced at Aron. "That's... everything's OK?"

He nodded, though she saw his grip on the steering wheel tighten. "Yeah," he said, glancing over at her. "Everything's fine."

ELEVEN

Fabiola and Aron agreed not to tell the kids about the surrogacy until they were sure it would move forward. In the meantime, the weeks raced by, with Halloween coming and going followed by Thanksgiving, which they celebrated at their house with her father. He was looking stronger, and his color had improved, but Fabiola still refused to let him have whipped cream with his pumpkin pie.

Now, after nearly two months of medical screenings and insurance forms, Liz's fertility doctor had cleared Fabiola to move forward. She'd begun taking estrogen supplements to prepare her uterus for what the doctor had called a "mock cycle."

"It's a kind of test run," Liz had explained to Alice during one of their regular brunches. "Like, they do all the same injections and monitoring to make sure Fabi's uterus responds appropriately, but we don't actually transfer an embryo. Then if all goes well, the next month we do it all over again with the embryo."

"Injections?" Alice's eyes widened.

Liz winced and flashed an apologetic look at Fabiola. "Yeah."

"In my butt, apparently," Fabiola offered cheerfully.

Alice paled and waved her hand. "OK, new topic." She cast a sidelong glance at Liz and Fabiola. "We can even talk about the stock market or, like, ways to organize your pantry. Anything but needles." She shuddered.

Fabiola shared a smile with Liz. The day before they'd sat together in the fertility doctor's office as Dr. Paulsen explained the same mock cycle process to them. Fabiola had liked Dr. Paulsen immediately. She appeared to be in her early fifties and wore her chin-length blonde hair in the feathered style of a 1970s gym teacher. Behind her thick glasses she was friendly, with an endearing edge of social awkwardness. Her confidence while speaking in medical terms gave way to nervous smiles and awkward hand gestures when making small talk.

"Oh my God," Liz exclaimed. "Next month." She looked over at Fabiola and gestured to Dr. Paulsen. "She said we could try as soon as *next month*."

"It's happening." Fabiola nodded. She placed a hand on her belly as if there was already something growing inside. Both women broke into nervous giggles and Dr. Paulsen smiled.

Now, though, it was time to tell the kids. Fabiola felt a lot less giddy about that.

"So, your mom and I have some news," Aron said that night at dinner. He glanced at Fabiola, then looked back at the kids.

Ben froze, his forkful of eggplant parmesan halfway to his mouth. "You're getting a divorce?" The panic on his face knocked Fabiola off balance.

"What? No? Why would you say that?" she asked.

He shrugged. "Zeus and Annabelle's parents just got a divorce," he said, referring to a pair of twins in his class. "And I hear you fighting sometimes."

"We're not getting a divorce," she said, with what she hoped sounded like certainty. "And Dad and I don't always agree on everything, but that's normal in a marriage." She and Aron had been bickering a lot lately, though. He was putting in more hours than ever at Pivot, even on the weekends. This left her with little time to catch her breath after juggling the kids and work all week. Plus, Hayley's social media marketing efforts had been paying off and she'd never been so busy with client requests.

"Then is it cancer?" The panic did not fade from Ben's face.

"Dude, shut up." Liam punched his brother in his arm.

"Don't say shut up, Liam," Aron said. "And Ben, buddy, we've got to work on your optimism."

"Are we finally moving to a bigger house?" Vivi asked. "I'm soooo tired of sharing a bathroom with them." She cast a withering glance at her brothers.

"We're not moving," Aron said.

"You're finally getting us the PS5?" Ben interjected.

"Ooh, can we get the new Spider-Man game?" Liam asked. "Or Gran Turismo?"

"No—just, can you all stop guessing and let me talk?" Aron said.

"I'm having a baby," Fabiola blurted out. A brief silence descended on the table, broken by a shriek from Vivi.

"What? Are you serious? You can NOT do this to me!" She flung her napkin down on the table. Aron shot Fabiola a dark look.

"A baby?" Ben scrunched up his forehead. "But aren't you, like, old?"

"Plenty of people much older than thirty-six have babies," Fabiola said defensively. She turned to Vivi. "And why is this such a bad thing?"

"Because where will the baby sleep? The house is too small already! It's not sharing a room with me, that's for sure." She crossed her arms over her chest.

"We're not keeping it," Aron said.

Vivi's eyes widened. She looked at Fabiola. "You're having an *abortion?*"

"What's an abortion?" Liam asked.

"No one's having an abortion!" Aron said. "Not that there's anything wrong with that, of course," he backtracked, holding up his hands. "It's a personal choice between a woman and her—"

"What he means is that I'm having someone else's baby," Fabiola said, trying to calm the frenzy building in the room.

"You *cheated* on Dad?" Vivi pushed back her chair and stood up, pointing an accusing finger at Fabiola.

"No. NO!" Aron bellowed. "Just, calm down, everyone. Sit." He pointed at Vivi, who glowered at Fabiola but sank back into her chair. "No one cheated on anyone." He sighed and rubbed his temples. "What your mom and I are trying to say is that she's going to be a surrogate."

"What's a surrogate?" Ben asked.

"And I still want to know what an abortion is," Liam said.

"We'll talk about that later," Aron said through gritted teeth. He turned to Ben. "A surrogate is someone who has a baby for another couple who can't have a baby on their own."

"Like, why wouldn't they be able to do that?" Ben asked.

"Some people can't get pregnant for medical reasons," Fabiola explained. "Like my friend, Liz. She had some surgery when she was younger that means she can't grow a baby inside her, so I'm going to grow it for her."

"And then you just... give her the baby?" Liam asked, echoing the question Fabiola's father had asked.

"Yes." She nodded.

"So I don't have to, like, learn to change poopy diapers." Ben looked at her for confirmation.

"No," she said.

"Not unless it's yours," Liam tittered.

Ben punched his arm again.

Fabiola grinned at the boys and fought the urge to giggle. She looked at Aron. The twins had clearly moved on. Vivi, however, was still staring at them as if they'd just announced they'd be locking her in a tower with only a loom and a spindle until she was eighteen.

"You're ruining my life," she said.

"Vivi, we're not trying to—" Fabiola began.

"You don't understand *anything!*" Vivi yelled, before standing and stomping out of the room and up the stairs.

"Can I be excused?" Ben asked. "I don't really like eggplant." He gestured to his mostly still full plate.

"Yeah, me neither," Liam said. "Can I be excused, too?"

"Fine," Aron said, defeated. "So," he said, once the room was empty of their children. "I thought that went well, didn't you?" Fabiola paused for a minute, then laughed. Then he did, too, which made her laugh harder, and soon they were both wiping tears from their eyes.

Once they'd composed themselves Aron reached for her hand under the table and squeezed it. "She'll be OK. We all will. I love you," he said.

"I know," she said, squeezing back.

TWELVE

Fabiola shivered, pulled her knit stocking cap down on her head until it almost covered her eyes. She cursed the red light that kept her from crossing the street and making her later than she already was. When it finally changed, she dodged puddles of slush, courtesy of an early December snow dump, and pushed open the door to the restaurant. Across the room she spied Alice and Liz in their usual booth which was half hidden behind a Christmas tree covered exclusively with small Buddha statues.

"I'm sorry I'm late," she said, unwinding a dark pink scarf from around her neck as she slid into the booth. She unbuttoned her black wool peacoat but left it on as she tried to warm up. "I tried to squeeze in a client consult this morning but of course it ran long, then Ben couldn't find his Tae Kwon Do belt because it turned out Liam had used it for his science project and—" She took a breath and looked at her friends. "Never mind, just, sorry."

"Don't worry about it," Liz said, pushing a mug across the table toward her. "We already ordered for you. An Americano and huevos rancheros."

"Thanks." Fabiola gave her a grateful smile and lifted the steaming mug to her lips. "You look casual," she said, eyeing Liz's leggings and sneakers. "Did basketball season start?"

Liz gave an excited nod. "You bet it did. And this year I've got some really good kids. This one girl can drain three pointers all day long." In the winter Liz coached basketball for girls at a YMCA in the Bronx. The age group was thirteen and fourteen year olds, and the team was usually a mix of girls who were committed to the sport and others from the neighborhood who'd been signed up by their parents or caregivers purely to keep them out of trouble. All of them adored Liz.

"Since when do you work on the weekends?" Alice asked Fabiola. "You're not going all Liz on us, are you?" Liz laughed.

"I don't usually," Fabiola said, cupping her hands around the mug to warm her frigid fingers. "But things have been bananas lately. I had four clients last week—two at the same time."

"How'd you manage that?" Liz asked. "Even I haven't figured out how to be in two places at once yet."

Fabiola sipped her coffee. "Hayley's gotten to where she can handle smaller jobs mostly on her own. I started off with her, then went to the other client, then came back to help her wrap up."

"That sounds exhausting." Alice frowned and smoothed the front of her black and white striped turtleneck.

"But it's great that Hayley's working out," Liz offered. "You should have hired an assistant a long time ago."

"It is," Fabiola said. "And she's good, she really is. But sometimes her ambition is just... exhausting."

"What do you mean?" Alice held her mug up to the passing waiter to signal for a refill.

"She has so many ideas, all the time, about how we should try to get more media placements, start our own product line, expand into new business lines like interior design or fashion consulting—capsule wardrobes, things like that. She wants me to be on TikTok, for God's sake. I mean, who has time for any of that?" Fabiola threw her arms up, sending a spoon flying off the table.

"All those sound like good ideas to me," Liz said, tugging at her smooth blonde ponytail. "Things have really taken off for you, so why not capitalize on that? You could be the next Martha Stewart, but, like, Brooklyn. With, like, kombucha and composting and all."

Fabiola made a face. "I don't know. I don't want to be working all the time and not seeing my family. Honestly, I don't think I want to be the next anything. I'm not like you guys." She looked down and swirled the coffee in her cup.

"What does that mean?" Alice raised an eyebrow.

Fabiola bit her lip. "I don't have these, like, big dreams. I never have; you guys know that. Remember that career interests quiz we had to take at Vassar?" Liz and Alice nodded. "You got doctor, Alice, which is pretty close to dentist, right?"

"Not if you ask a doctor." Alice rolled her eyes.

Fabiola turned to Liz. "And you got CEO."

Liz snorted. "I can only dream."

"It's just a matter of time." Alice raised her refilled coffee mug toward Liz in salute.

"And what did I get?" Fabiola asked.

Her friends looked at each other. "Hairdresser," they said in unison, then burst out laughing.

"Exactly." Fabiola slapped her open palm on the table. "And the guidance counselor was horrified! Like, almost embarrassed. She kept going on about how she'd never seen this result for a Vassar student, and how I should retake the test. And the three of us laughed about it, remember?"

"You have to admit it was pretty ironic considering you

didn't even know how to operate a curling iron," Liz pointed out.

"OK, fair," Fabiola admitted. "But I never told you guys what I was really thinking when that happened." She looked down at the table again and shrugged. "I was thinking how hairdresser sounded fine."

"Oh, come on, Fabi," Alice interjected. "You've always sold yourself short—"

"No," Fabiola said, raising her eyes to meet Alice's. "I haven't. I've just never wanted a big career. I've tried to want it, mainly because everyone tells me I'm supposed to, but I just don't. And I'm sick of feeling bad or guilty or like I'm letting down feminism or something because I don't want what everyone tells me I'm supposed to."

"What do you want, then?" Liz asked, her voice gentle.

Fabiola closed her eyes. "I don't know," she said. But she did. She thought about how she felt each night when she stood outside the kids' rooms in a silent vigil for their eternal health and happiness. If the lights were out, she'd slip inside and stand next to their beds, bearing witness to the miracle of their chests rising and falling as breath filled the lungs that had grown while floating inside her own body. They'd needed her then for their own survival. Now, though, Vivi's life revolved around her friends instead of Fabiola, caught up in the whirlwind of adolescence. And although the boys were a few years behind, she knew they were heading there, too. It was only a matter of time before the primal need for her that had defined their lives since birth began to fade.

Alice reached out and touched her hand. "It's OK, Fabi. Figuring out what we want is a never-ending pursuit." She paused. "For most people, that is. I already know."

"Oh?" Liz raised an eyebrow. "And what's that?"

"Just, like, ten million dollars and a house in Nantucket." Alice shrugged.

"Oh," Fabiola said. "No big deal."

"So," Alice said, switching topics. "How are we feeling about all the baby stuff? And by we, I mean you two. No more babies allowed over here." She gestured to her stomach.

Fabiola glanced at Liz, who smiled and nodded. "Dr. Paulsen just cleared me—us—for an embryo transfer in three weeks, right after New Year's."

Alice clapped her hands. "Finally! That's great news. Are you nervous?" Fabiola and Liz spoke at the same time.

"No."

"A little."

Fabiola looked at Liz. "You're nervous?"

Liz laughed. "You're not?"

Fabiola shrugged. She wasn't nervous, exactly. The gentle flutter in her stomach was more a feeling of excited anticipation mixed with a nagging, underlying worry about the strain a pregnancy might put on her family—and her marriage, though right now things with Aron seemed to be on an upswing. He was still working all the time, but he'd been in a better mood lately when he was home, and they'd even had sex twice that week. As for the kids, after the disastrous dinner table announcement the twins seemed to have forgotten about it altogether, though Vivi still glowered at her and occasionally asked if she was knocked up yet.

"I think it's just starting to hit me," Liz said quietly. She folded her hands in front of her on the table. "That this time next year I could be sitting here with a baby. That my life will look completely different." Her face paled a shade and her smile was shaky.

"You bet it will." Alice nodded, spearing a last bite of omelet with her fork. "Bye bye, spontaneous nights out and hello, overpriced baby music class."

A look of anxiety spread across Liz's face and Fabiola nudged Alice. "Hey, don't scare her!" The trilling sound of a phone sounded and Fabiola grabbed for her purse. "Sorry," she said. "I meant to turn that off. But let me just check to make sure it isn't a client." She fished out her phone and an unfamiliar local number flashed across the screen. "Hello," she said, answering. "This is Fabiola."

There was silence on the other end of the line, then a woman's voice said, "Fabi? It's your mother."

The cold hit Fabi as she stumbled through the restaurant door out onto the street. "Mom?" she said, frustrated at the choke of emotion in her throat.

"My beautiful girl." The voice on the other end was throaty and warm. The intonation of her mother's Peruvian accent snaked into Fabi's brain, summoning memories she'd tried to bury. She was three, nestled in bed with her mother, who stroked her hair and sang softly in Spanish. She was ten, unwrapping a birthday present from her mother, freshly returned after a seven-year absence, pretending to love the doll that was meant for a much younger girl. She was thirteen, sitting beside her mother at a salon, their nails painted the same shade of pink, unaware that this was one of the last days they'd spend together before her mother disappeared again.

She fought down the memories. "Mom," she said, forcing the emotion from her voice. "Hi."

"How are you, Fabi?"

Fabiola bristled. "What do you want?"

There was a heavy sigh on the other end. "Fabi, niña, don't be like that, please. I know it's been a long time, and I know I haven't exactly been a great mother, but can we at least talk? Please?"

Fabiola gave a bitter laugh. "A long time? It's been *twenty-two years*, Mom."

"Exactly. And do you think it's easy for me to make this call after all that time?"

"Where have you been?" Fabiola's voice came out in a near whisper as the painful memory of her mother's last and final abandonment seared through her.

Her mother had been back for just over three years; long enough for Fabiola to relax and trust that maybe this time she would stay. The night before they'd eaten dinner as a family, not the homemade lomo saltado her mother had cooked when she'd first returned, spending all her time in the kitchen like it was penance, but empanadas from the Ecuadorian street cart down the block. Fabiola had fixed a salad so they'd have something green. She'd gone to bed excited for their shopping trip of the next day. Her mother had promised to take her to find a new outfit for her fourteenth birthday. In the morning, she was gone, her clothes missing from the closet, two notes on the table. *I'll always be with you, Fabi. Be good. Mama,* hers read. She never saw what was written on her father's.

"I've been a lot of places, Fabi," her mother said in a steady voice. "But the important thing is that I'm here now." She paused. "And I'd like to see you. See my grandchildren."

"How do you know you even have grandchildren?"

Her mother tsked. "Fabi, you think I haven't been following your life? You look very happy, with your husband and your three beautiful children."

Fabiola tensed, thinking of her social media posts for her business, which sometimes included pictures of Aron and the kids. Hayley had encouraged this, saying people wanted to see her authentic, whole self.

"You'll never meet my children." The words flew out of her

mouth like bullets. There was a sharp inhale on the other end of the line.

"There's so much I'd like to talk to you about." Her mother's voice was pleading. "Please, Fabi. Just give me five minutes."

Fabiola shivered and stepped back toward the warmth of the restaurant. "Don't call me again."

Inside Liz and Alice looked at her with alarm as she slid back into the booth. "Are you OK?" Liz asked. "Was it bad news?"

Fabiola let out a bitter bark of laughter. "It was my mother."

Alice's mouth dropped open. "*Paulina* called you? Holy shit." She'd known Fabiola's mother when she'd re-entered Fabiola's life at ten.

"Oh my God, Fabi," Liz exclaimed. "Was that the first time you've talked to her since...?"

"Since I was thirteen? Yep." Fabiola nodded.

"Did she call to tell you that she just escaped from twenty years of being kidnapped?" Alice asked indignantly. "Or that she recently recovered from amnesia? Or maybe that she's rich and dying and leaving you all her money? I mean, any of those would be acceptable reasons for leaving you hanging the last couple of decades, right?"

"She wants to see me. And the kids."

"What did you tell her?" Liz's already large blue eyes had widened to take up most of her face.

"I hung up," Fabiola said, suddenly wondering if it was possible she'd imagined the whole thing. It had happened so fast.

"Fuck me," Alice said, leaning back in disbelief. She had a tendency to lapse into profanity when words failed her.

"Alice!" Liz admonished. Despite the fact that she spent her days around testosterone-swollen bankers who dropped f-bombs like breadcrumbs, Liz had a 1950s housewife's sense of decorum. She turned to Fabiola. "Where was she calling from? And why now?"

Fabiola shrugged, her shoulders tense. "No idea."

"But don't you want to know?" Liz persisted. "I mean, part of you must want to talk to her after all this time."

"Liz, that woman is poison." Alice had recovered from her shock. "I mean, one moment of insanity where you leave your family, OK, I might give you that. But *twice*? That's next level cruelty."

"Of course," Liz said. "I'm not saying she deserves to talk to you, Fabi. But aren't you even the least bit curious about what she wants after all these years?"

Fabiola clenched her jaw. "No." She knew the danger of curiosity where her mother was concerned. Curiosity was the crack in the door through which the emotional hurricane of Paulina Fernandez rushed in, devastating everything in its path.

FOURTEEN

Fabiola watched as Vivi wolfed down the chicken tikka masala she had ordered for dinner. Sunday was usually her day to grocery shop for the week but after she'd left brunch with Liz and Alice, she'd felt slow and foggy, a bit like being drunk but without the benefit of the buzz. Instead of heading to join the masses of other Brooklynites at Food Bazaar she'd gone straight home and drawn herself a bath so hot it distracted her from any thoughts of her mother.

Now, though, as she watched her kids dig into the food she'd served them out of cardboard cartons, guilt prickled along the length of her spine. She checked her watch. The grocery store was open until ten-thirty, and though she wanted nothing more than to don her pajamas and sink into bed, she had plenty of time to go stock up for the week.

"Can I go over to Layla's now?" Vivi asked, taking a paper napkin from the pile on the table and swiping it over her mouth.

"Layla's?" Fabiola asked, frowning. In the past couple of months Vivi had been spending less time with her old friends Harper and Izzy and more time with Layla of the off-the-shoulder shirt. Layla was tall, wore thick, black eyeliner, and had rendered Liam speechless as his eyes followed her around the room the handful of times she'd come home from school with Vivi.

"Don't even try to say no." Vivi crossed her arms in front of her chest. "Dad already said I could go."

"On a Sunday night?" Fabiola turned to Aron.

"I guess they're studying for some big test tomorrow?" He shrugged. "I told her she could go for an hour."

Fabiola shot Aron a look of impatience and then turned to Vivi. "Fine. One hour only. I can take you on the way to the grocery store."

When she dropped Vivi off Fabiola had insisted on walking her to the door so she could meet Layla's parents. A petite woman with honey-colored hair and sweepingly long, dark eyelashes answered the door. She wore the same asymmetrical shawl sweater Fabiola had recently seen in the window of the Stella McCartney store in Soho and had the kind of glowing, unlined skin that usually came from a syringe. Except that Fabiola could tell hers was just because she was young. Very young.

"Hi, Jade." Vivi waved and disappeared inside.

"I'm Fabiola, Vivi's mom," Fabiola said after a beat of silence in which Jade stared at her like she was peddling bibles. "I thought it would be good to meet Layla's mom and dad, you know, since the girls are spending so much time together."

"Stepmom," Jade corrected. "And her dad's not here. He travels a lot."

"Oh." Fabiola nodded.

There was a sudden thundering of footsteps on the stairs and Layla appeared. Despite the chill she wore hot pink bike shorts and a matching bandeau top that showed off the generous swell of her chest where Vivi was only just beginning to round out. "Come on," she said, pulling on Vivi's arm. "Jade said we could try on her makeup."

"Vivi's not allowed to wear makeup," Fabiola said. "And hi, Layla."

"Oh, hey," the girl said as if noticing Fabiola for the first time.

"Mom," Vivi whined. "It's just, like, a little contouring."

"You're supposed to be studying," Fabiola reminded her. She looked at Jade. "They have a big test tomorrow."

"Sure, whatever." Jade shrugged. "I usually stay out of the school stuff."

"What do you think of Layla?" Fabiola asked Aron later as they stood in the kitchen unloading the bags of groceries she'd bought. She kept her voice low since Vivi was back home and upstairs—now actually studying, Fabiola suspected, since she doubted little of it had happened at Layla's.

"She seems like a nice enough kid," Aron said, reaching for a cabinet over her head. "A little more grown up than Vivi, maybe."

"A little?" Fabiola raised her eyebrows. "The girl looks like she's eighteen. I'm not sure I like Vivi hanging out with her so much."

"You're saying she's a danger to our child since she grew out of her training bra first?"

Fabiola flushed. "No, of course not. It's just, I met her step-mom, and I don't get the sense there's a lot of supervision going on at home."

"Vivi's a smart girl. We've taught her how to make good choices," Aron said. "I'm not concerned."

"It's just, when was the last time she asked to hang out at Harper or Izzy's? It's like they never see each other anymore."

Aron's face grew dark. "Well, Vivi chose to quit the swim team, so obviously she's going to see them less since they're actually committed to working toward a goal." Vivi's abandonment of the junior varsity swim was still a sore spot with him.

Fabiola let his pointed comment go and they continued unpacking in silence. "My mom called me today," Fabiola said after a few minutes. She was surprised how benign the words sounded aloud, like she'd mentioned that Food Bazaar was out of the couscous they liked or that Liam needed new shoes.

Aron was bent over moving things around in the refrigerator. Hearing Fabiola he straightened up in a sharp motion, banging his head in the process. "Ow, damn it," he said, rubbing the back of his head. "What did you say?" he asked in disbelief.

"My mother called me. Earlier today."

Aron's eyebrows raised. "Your mom. As in the one you haven't seen since you were fourteen."

"Thirteen, really," she said. "She left the night before my birthday."

"Right." Aron nodded. "Honey, why didn't you tell me she called? What did she want?"

"I'm telling you now. And she wanted... to talk."

"And?" He was still rubbing his head, but his brow was now crinkled in concern instead of pain.

"I hung up on her."

"You hung up?" Aron didn't even try to hide the judgement in his voice.

Fabiola turned to him, hands on her hips. "What? It's not like I want to talk to her."

Aron paused. "I get that. It just seems... extreme. I mean, what if you change your mind? Do you even know how to get in touch with her?"

"I won't need to get in touch with her because I won't change my mind." Fabiola jammed a box of cereal into the cabinet with such force that the cardboard buckled. Where did people get off thinking that she should want to talk to her mom? First Liz and now Aron.

"How can you be so sure?" He had stopped putting things away and was leaning against the counter, hands in his pockets. "I mean, I know things with your mom are complicated but maybe something has changed."

Fabiola let out a shrill laugh. "You mean like she's suddenly going to be able to make up for leaving me motherless most of my life?"

He ran his hand through his hair. "No, of course not. I just thought—the kids don't have much family. No cousins, no grandparents other than your dad."

Both Fabiola and Aron were only children, and his parents, who were older when they'd had him, had passed away from years of smoking and a sedentary lifestyle early in Fabiola and Aron's relationship. "Would it be so bad to have an open mind about your mom?" he asked. "Just, you know, feel things out a bit more?"

Fabiola was suddenly very tired. "I don't want to talk about this," she said. "I'm going to bed."

"OK, fine, I get it," Aron said, surrendering. "I'll leave it alone. But what about the kids' lunches for tomorrow?" He pointed to the three bento boxes Fabiola had set out on the table, awaiting their contents.

She pointed. "I just bought groceries. I'm sure you can figure it out." Then she turned and walked upstairs. As she did her phone buzzed with a text from Liz.

> Hey, you ok? That was a lot today. I'm sorry if I was pushy about your mom.

Tears pricked Fabiola's eyes as she replied:

> Thanks. And I get it. Pushy is kind of your brand.

> Lol. Love you and here for you.

Fabiola clutched the phone to her chest. She reminded herself how lucky she was. Sure, she didn't have a mother, but look at all she did have: Aron, the kids, her friends. So why did she still sometimes feel a hollow ache, like something was missing?

FIFTEEN

Aron stared down at his green and red knit sweater which featured a giant Christmas tree on the front under the words "Get Lit."

"Do I really have to wear this?" he asked.

Fabiola gave his shoulder a playful punch. "You ask that same question every year," she said. "Yes, you do. It's an ugly sweater party." She gestured at her own sweater, which included red and white candy cane striped sleeves, and a large gingerbread man and woman tap dancing across her chest.

"Just don't let Bruce corner me again to talk about fantasy football." Alice's husband was a fantasy sports nut and viewed Aron as something of an oracle due to his work at Pivot.

"Honey, you run a sports blog. Of course he wants to talk to you about football."

"It's an online publication at the intersection of sports and culture," he corrected. "And it's about real sports, not that fantasy garbage."

"Fine. If you need rescue just pat the top of your head, tug your ear twice, and stand in a tree pose. I'll come right over."

Aron grimaced. "Great plan."

She smiled back at him and he reached for her hand as they walked outside to the Uber waiting to take them to Alice's apartment on the Upper East Side. Things had been better between them lately, or maybe she'd just been better, she couldn't tell. Throughout the fall she had felt conscious of a near constant resentment simmering just beneath her skin at his insistence on having equal say in parenting decisions while leaving most of the minutiae—homework policing, school pickups and drop-offs, ensuring soccer uniforms were clean in time for games—to her. Since scheduling the embryo transfer, though, she'd felt calmer and more centered. It was the same way she'd felt during both her pregnancies, like she was floating along on a river of well-being, beatific and unperturbed by the annoying details and discomforts of daily life. "Pregnancy Zen," Aron had called it. Maybe there was such a thing as pre-pregnancy Zen? She giggled at the thought.

"What's funny?" Aron asked.

"Nothing," she said, squeezing his hand in the back seat of the Uber as the city sped by outside. "I'm just happy."

As usual Alice and Bruce had gone all out with the "tacky Christmas" party theme. Their apartment, which had a view of the East River, was awash in tinsel-covered garlands and strands of blinking Christmas lights. A life-size, animatronic Santa with a wide, slightly crazed smile greeted them in the foyer, startling Aron as it waved a hand in greeting and exclaimed, "Ho, ho, ho!"

"You made it!" Alice embraced them, her face flushed as it always was when she drank. She wore a 1950s style house dress that was blue with yellow dreidels all over it.

"Wow," Fabiola said, stepping back to admire her. "That dress is truly..." She waved her hands around, at a loss for words.

"Isn't it awful?" Alice said, giving a gleeful clap of her hands. "I ordered it months ago from a site that was selling it totally unironically." She looked them up and down and pointed at their sweaters. "Speaking of awful, you two will fit right in. Let me get you a drink."

Alice steered them through the crowd toward a folding table draped in a white cloth set up near the upright piano in a corner of the living room. A tall, gangly boy in a black T-shirt and a serious case of bedhead stood pouring wine into cups.

"Um, is he old enough to serve alcohol?" Fabiola asked. Alice waved her hand.

"It's fine," she said. "He's Bruce's nephew. If anyone asks, I told him to say he's eighteen."

Aron procured two glasses. "Yours is non-alcoholic cider," he said, handing one to Fabiola. It was the closest he'd come to acknowledging the procedure that was happening in less than two weeks. Ever since they'd told the kids about the surrogacy, they'd spoken about it only once, when they signed the lengthy contract Liz and Peter's lawyer had drawn up.

Dr. Paulsen had recommended they formalize the surrogacy agreement to ensure all parties were clear on their individual rights and to plan for all possible medical situations. It had felt strange to hold the thick legal document knowing Liz and Peter were on the other end of it.

"All this just for a tiny baby," Fabiola had said ruefully as she flipped through the pages without reading them.

"It's better this way," Aron replied, reading every page carefully. "Just to be sure."

She took the glass of mulled cider from him. "Thanks." They stood for a moment, surveying the room. A long strand of chili pepper lights was draped on the back of the couch and the coffee table had been covered with a vinyl tablecloth featuring frolicking reindeer with bright red noses. Elvis's *Blue Christmas* played from the speaker and a six-foot inflatable snowman grinned out from the corner of the room.

"Aren't Alice and Bruce Jewish?" Aron asked.

Fabiola shrugged. "Yup. But she's never been able to resist a good party theme. And growing up her family still always had a Christmas tree." She and Alice had spent many Friday nights in junior high lounging in front of the ornament laden tree drinking hot cocoa and watching anything with Ryan Reynolds in it.

Aron laughed and squeezed her shoulder. "Want me to grab us some food?"

She nodded, grateful. They'd rushed to order pizza for the kids before getting themselves out the door. They'd left the kids alone with Vivi in charge for the first time. Vivi, thrilled, had taken their decision as confirmation that she was now a grown-up and immediately began bossing her brothers around. Still, even after strict instructions not to answer the door or the phone under any circumstances, Fabiola was nervous. She pulled her phone from her back pocket to check in with them.

"Hey!"

Fabiola looked up to see Liz. They embraced. "Hi!" she said, feeling a rush of warmth at seeing her, despite the cold from outside that still lingered on Liz's cheek. While Liz had always been a regular part of her life, they'd spent more time together than ever during the past couple of months, both at the appointments with Dr. Paulsen and then rehashing them after. They'd also taken to sending each other links to the most outlandish baby gear they could find.

You'll definitely need this, Fabiola had texted, including an image of a seven-hundred-dollar highchair complete with massaging seat and Bluetooth speakers.

Does it also feed the baby? Liz replied. Then she sent a link to a Swarovski studded potty training seat.

Fabiola sent back the brain exploding emoji.

"I'm so glad I found you before one of Alice's dentist friends started talking to me," Liz said now, glancing around the party.

"What, you're not in the mood to hear any molar-themed jokes?" Fabiola joked.

Liz snorted. She wore a dark green, cashmere sweater dress and suede, knee-high black boots. In a sea of polyester and garish holiday colors she looked like the main character from a Hallmark Christmas movie about a beautiful city girl who goes home for the holidays and has her icy heart slowly melted by the handsome local boy. "Nice outfit," Fabiola said, raising an eyebrow.

Liz made a face. "You know I hate costume parties. Is that the bar?" She pointed.

Fabiola nodded. "I'm pretty sure the bartender is Vivi's age."

Liz laughed. "Leave it to Alice to run a sweatshop—which is not in any way going to stop me from taking advantage of it. Don't move, I'll be right back."

While she waited for Liz to return, Fabiola tried to keep her eyes from sweeping over the crowd, searching for one face.

"Where's Aron?" Liz asked when she returned holding a plastic cup with a clear liquid and three olives. "Also, I just taught that kid how to make a martini. I may have completely changed his life trajectory."

Fabiola laughed. "Lucky kid. Aron went to get food, but I think he's been waylaid." She motioned toward her husband in the far corner of the room, nodding as an animated Bruce talked very close to his face.

"You're here!" Alice came up behind them and hugged Liz. "But no Peter?" Fabiola sent out a silent message of gratitude that she hadn't had to ask the question.

"He got held up at the hospital," Liz said, twisting her mouth. "Which means I don't get to be mad at him because it's literally a life-or-death emergency. I swear, being married to a neurosurgeon really makes me feel like a bad person sometimes."

"Well, maybe he'll make it in time for Christmas karaoke," Alice chirped.

"Karaoke? Seriously?" Liz groaned and held up her glass. "I better drink faster." At Vassar Alice had regularly dragged them out to karaoke bars where they consumed seemingly endless bottles of cheap champagne and worked their way through the entire catalogues of Gwen Stefani and Bruno Mars.

"Where do you store all this stuff?" Fabiola looked around at the decorations that were hanging from every piece of furniture and light fixture.

"In our basement storage unit next to the pasta maker, bread machine, juicer, and the set of weights Bruce bought during the pandemic but never used."

"It's so cute that you married a fellow hoarder," Liz said.

Alice swatted her arm. "You know kitchen appliances are my weakness." She glanced around their modest apartment. "I keep telling Bruce we should move to Long Island purely for the counter space."

"You're not going anywhere." Fabiola gave Alice a skeptical look. "Your body would shut down without a weekly dose of rugelach from Eli's." Both Alice and Bruce had been born and raised on the Upper East Side. And though Alice looked at real estate in Oyster Bay and East Hills the way some people looked at porn, Fabiola knew she'd part with every kitchen appliance she owned before she'd leave the city.

"You're probably right," Alice admitted. "But you can't fault a girl for fantasizing about a four bed, three bath open floorplan."

"Speaking of bathrooms," Fabiola said, holding up her empty cider glass. "I'm going to go find yours."

She made her way across the room to find the hall bathroom occupied, and so slipped into Alice and Bruce's bedroom to use the ensuite bathroom. When she came out, Peter was shrugging out of his coat, about to add it to the pile of outerwear on the bed.

"Oh," she said, taking a half step back as her heart pushed a rush of blood through her body. "Hi."

"Hi," Peter said, his smile broad at the sight of her. "Sorry, I didn't know anyone else was in here."

She nodded. "Liz said you got stuck at the hospital."

"Yes, well, hospitals are easy to get stuck at seeing as how they never close." He gave a rueful laugh. "But I'm here now."

"I'm glad." Her voice came out low and husky. Despite being in touch with Liz nearly daily, she hadn't seen Peter since the morning after their disastrous dinner when he'd apologized. Now, standing before him, she felt that familiar, forbidden ache. It was the same feeling she'd had in high school, watching him walk through the halls with his arm around his latest thin, swishy-haired girlfriend. She had bottled up those feelings long ago, determined not to let the past interfere with her future, and that had worked for years. But now, maybe because she was about to carry his child, it felt as if the door where she'd locked those emotions had cracked open just enough for them to begin to seep out.

He took a step toward her. "Me too." There seemed to be a spotlight on him, as if all the light in the dim room sought him out. "How are you, Fabi?" he asked. His eyes searched her face for the answer to a very different question.

"I'm fine," she said, unable to draw in enough breath to form any additional words.

"I worry about you, you know?" As if in slow motion he reached out to place his hand on her shoulder, a light, tentative touch that nearly knocked her off balance.

"About me? Why?"

He gave a soft laugh. "A million reasons. I mean, it's got to be a lot to manage. The kids, your dad's health, the pressure of financially supporting your family." He frowned and dropped his hand back to his side. Fabiola became aware of how close they stood to each other, their hands nearly brushing. "Look, I know Liz really wants this, really wants it to be you, but if it ever feels like too much—"

"It's not," she interrupted. "I mean, it won't be. I really want it to be me, too."

"So do I," he said in a low voice, and suddenly their lips were touching, pressing against each other, and his hand gripped her waist and pulled her toward him. The familiarity of his taste and smell overwhelmed her and she let herself tumble into the sensation of his tongue greeting her mouth, his hand on the back of her head.

SIXTEEN

The screech of feedback from a microphone jolted them apart. "All right!" she heard Alice say, her laugh amplified down the hallway. "I guess this thing is on!"

"Oh!" Fabiola stepped back, her hand flying up to cover her mouth.

Guilt hit her so hard it felt like running full tilt into a brick wall. She stepped back from Peter so fast she lost her balance. Only his hand still gripping her waist kept her from tipping backward onto the mountain of coats on Alice's bed.

Peter also stumbled as he struggled to keep them both upright, and for an instant his face was close to hers again. For a split second she thought he might kiss her once more and her mind pinballed between the desire to cling to him and the instinct to flee the room. Then he righted himself and drew back from her, his face flushed.

"Fabi, I didn't mean to—" He drew in a shuddering breath and covered his face with his hands. She smoothed her hair, her body still ablaze from his touch. Without thinking she brought her fingers to her lips. It had been years since they'd touched his. So long, in fact, that she'd often wondered if he still had any of those old feelings for her.

"It's OK," she said, shifting on her feet. Awkwardness rushed in to fill the space between them. "I should probably, you know, get back." She nodded toward the party on the other side of the bedroom door.

"It's time for some Christmas karaoke!" Alice bellowed into the microphone from the living room.

"Wait." Peter lifted his face from his hands and reached toward her, stopping short of touching her. He dropped his arm back to his side and cleared his throat. "I'm sorry. I shouldn't have done that. It was a mistake."

The formality of his tone felt like a slap. But what had she expected? He was married—to her best friend. Peter and Liz had met at *her* wedding, for God's sake. Speaking of which, she had a husband in the next room who was probably looking for her at this very moment. She glanced toward the bedroom door and pictured how things would look to Aron if he walked in right now; her and Peter standing together near the bed, the room charged with tension.

"It's fine," she replied, tugging her sweater lower over her hips. "A mistake, I get it." She gave a forced smile and turned to go.

"Fabi." The softness in his voice stopped her. "You know that's not what I meant."

"Oh?" She couldn't keep the bite out of her tone despite knowing her place in his life.

"Hey," he said, taking her shoulders and turning her to face him. "Talk to me."

She shook her head. "I'm fine. Really. These hormones I'm on really take a toll, you know?" She forced a laugh she didn't feel.

He hesitated, then he shook his head. "You know, it's too much, the whole surrogate thing..."

"It's not too much," she assured him, hoping she was right.

"Are you sure?"

"Now you just sound like you're trying to get out of it." She kept her voice light and teasing, trying to shift the mood in the room. Peter's face froze as though she'd turned a floodlight on him in a dark room. She eyed him. "Peter? You OK?"

He ran his hand through his hair and fiddled with the buttons on his cuffs. "It's just, sometimes I wonder who I'm kidding with the whole fatherhood thing. Like, what the hell do I know about being a dad?"

"Well, you'll have some time to figure it out," Fabiola said. "Even if the transfer works, it's going to be a while until the baby needs a dad. Nine months to be exact."

Peter gave a small smile. "I know. It's just, I didn't exactly have the best role model." His smile faded.

"I know." She nodded. In all the time she'd spent at Peter's house in middle school and high school, watching movies and ordering Chinese food on his parents' credit card, his dad was rarely around. And in high school Peter confessed to her that he'd known for years his father saw women other than his mother.

"He doesn't even try to hide it anymore," he'd said. "He talks to them in his study without closing the door and some nights he doesn't even bother to come home. Then he walks back in while the rest of us are eating breakfast like it's not at all unusual to be coming home at seven a.m."

Fabiola had been aghast. "What does your mom do?"

"Nothing." Peter shrugged. "I'm not even sure she cares. She just wants to be out at the stables, anyway, or out east at our Hamptons place."

"Who's up first?" Alice demanded, the microphone letting out another small screech. "Whoa, sorry about that. What's that? Yes, come on up! Ladies and gentlemen, I give you Charlene singing *All I Want for Christmas.*" There was a smattering of applause and some hooting over the low hum of conversation.

Peter sank down on the edge of the bed and slumped forward, his elbows on his knees. "I don't know the first thing about how to be a parent. And Liz is so confident about everything, all the time. Sometimes I feel like she should be doing this with someone else—someone who knows what he's doing."

Fabiola looked at her old friend as he dropped his head into his hands, and felt a wave of sympathy for him. She perched next to him, careful to leave a generous amount of space between their bodies. "First of all, no one knows anything about how to be a parent until they become one. And second, yes, Liz is confident about everything. That's part of why you fell in love with her. But I guarantee she's nervous, too. And honestly, if the two smartest people I know can't figure out how to raise a baby, then no one can." She shrugged. "They should just call off the whole human race."

She felt his body relax next to her. He looked up and smiled, shaking his head. "How do you always know just what to say to make me feel better?" he asked.

"Well, you're not *that* complicated." She rolled her eyes. He laughed and the sound fizzed through her body.

"Seriously, though. You've gotten me through so much, Fabi. Shit with my parents, the Princeton debacle, my brother —" Peter's voice caught.

Fabiola reached over to squeeze his hand. She kept her voice light. "And don't forget about the fact that you would have failed the SATs without me dragging you out of bed every Saturday morning for prep class."

"That, too." He grinned, then looked serious. "I mean it, though. Thank you. I wouldn't have made it through any of that without you."

They sat in silence for a minute and Fabiola felt the air

between them begin to buzz again, like an electric current gathering strength.

"Should we get back to the party?" she said, releasing his hand and jumping up from the bed.

"You go," he said. "I have to send a quick message to the hospital. Then I'll be right out." Fabiola nodded, grateful to leave the room separately from him. She knew Aron would be looking for her.

"Where were you?" Liz asked when she returned. "I've been stranded here forced to listen to this." She waved her hand at the man across the living room swaying out of time with the music as he fumbled his way through *Last Christmas*.

"Sorry, the bathroom line took forever," Fabiola lied. She waved at Aron across the room, still talking to Bruce, and beckoned to him.

"Oh, thank God," he said when he reached her side. "Where have you been?"

"Bathroom."

"And how much longer do we have to stay?" he whispered, slipping his hand up inside the back of her sweater to her bra line. Fabiola tensed at his touch, her mind snaking back to the feel of Peter's lips against hers only moments earlier.

"I'm pretty sure Alice isn't going to let us leave until we sing." She made a face.

Once Peter emerged from the bedroom, Fabiola steered Aron toward another couple she knew. They made small talk as she watched Liz and Peter get swept up into the conversation of a separate group of partygoers. Then an hour later they managed to slip out unnoticed by Alice.

Back at home in Brooklyn the house was dark and silent, though the kids had left the kitchen a mess of sticky ice cream bowls and empty microwave popcorn bags. Too tired to deal with it, Fabiola washed her face and climbed into bed.

"You looked so hot in that sweater," Aron said, turning to her.

"It was warm in there," she agreed.

"No," he laughed. "I mean hot as in sexy." He leaned forward and kissed her, running his hand up her thigh, their signal. She felt a flash of guilt remembering Peter's body pressed against hers.

"We can't." She pulled away and put her hand over his. "The transfer." He stared at her blankly. "The doctor said no sex one month before, remember?" Saying this, she realized it had been nearly a month since either of them had even initiated lovemaking.

He groaned. "Come on, you can't be serious!"

She kissed him and placed her hand on his chest. "It's only two more weeks. You'll survive."

"Oh, all right," he said, rolling over. Less than a minute later Fabiola heard his breath deepen into sleep.

She rolled over onto the cool side of her pillow, but her mind whirred too fast for sleep to catch up. Instead, she cycled through all the same old questions. What if Peter had chosen her all those years ago? What if she'd ever been brave enough to confess her true feelings? What if she'd never married Aron? Then her hand strayed down to rest on her belly as a new question formed in her mind. What would it be like if this was their baby? She turned over onto her side and banished the thought. Some things she'd just never know.

SEVENTEEN

For New Year's Eve Aron made paella. It was the kind of cooking he favored; elaborate with lots of clean up required, usually by Fabiola. Her father came for dinner and Fabiola asked Vivi if she wanted to have Harper sleep over as she had in past years.

"Can you stop, like, asking me about Harper?" Vivi had snapped. "It's not like she's my only friend."

"Well," Fabiola said, "then is there anyone else you'd like to invite over?"

Vivi scowled. "Everyone else is actually doing something cool for New Year's Eve, OK?"

Yet despite Vivi's dark mood, dinner had been surprisingly fun. They had a heated debate about which was more New York, a cronut or a bagel, made banana splits for dessert, and then argued over which movie to watch.

"Let's do *Back to the Future*," Aron suggested.

"Not *again*," Vivi groaned. "Dad, don't you ever want to watch something new?"

"It's a classic!" Aron defended himself.

"I agree with Vivi," Fabiola said, happy to be on the same side as her daughter about something. "No *Back to the Future*."

"*Goonies*?" Aron tried again.

"Noooo!" all three kids chorused. Leonard laughed.

Fabiola flipped her list of age-appropriate movies open on her phone. "What about *Harry Potter*? Or *Inside Out*?"

"Mom, we're not six," Vivi complained.

They finally settled on *Wonder,* which had them all sniffling at the end. By ten-thirty the boys were yawning so they did a countdown and a toast with sparkling grape juice, then said goodbye to her father and ushered the kids upstairs.

Aron was already in bed with his book when Fabiola returned from tucking the boys in. They'd always agreed on how overrated New Year's Eve was, preferring to ring it in snuggled up in bed, or better, already asleep.

"Reading anything good?" she asked, prepared to tune out the answer. These days Aron mostly read books on entrepreneurship with aggressive titles like *No Rules Rules* and *How to F*ck Up Your Startup,* with the occasional sports biography thrown in.

"Yeah, maybe." He held it up so she could read the cover, *How to Disrupt Disruption.*

"Mm." Fabiola went to the closet, pulled her shirt over her head and unhooked her bra. Before pulling on her pajama top, she glimpsed herself in the mirror. Her breasts hung lower than they used to, but they were still round and reasonably firm after three kids. There was more flesh on her hips than there had been when she was younger, especially now with the hormones she was taking. But the deeper curves weren't exactly unappealing, were they? She wondered what Peter would think of her body after all these years. It was so different than Liz's taut, athletic form.

Ever since their kiss at Alice's party Fabiola had found her mind turning to him whenever it wandered, like when Hayley was explaining to her once again what a Net Promotor score was, or when Aron began talking about investor pitches or Series A funding, whatever that was. She shivered. Just thinking about the kiss caused a dizzying rush of brain chemicals and wetness between her legs. How embarrassing. He'd probably forgotten about the whole thing by now.

She closed her eyes and inhaled deeply. She needed to get back to focusing on what she was doing for him and Liz. The intimacy of the situation was stirring up old feelings with Peter, but she reminded herself that they were just that—old. It was time to set them aside.

She climbed into bed with her phone and flipped open her group chat with Liz and Alice.

Happy New Year! she wrote, adding a champagne bottle and fireworks.

You're not seriously going to bed already, are you? Liz replied.

You know how I feel about NYE, Fabiola wrote, including a green puking face.

Lol that's me tomorrow if I have another drinhjk, Alice chimed in. *But I mighft also die of boredom if i don't.*

Bruce's annual family party? Liz asked. Every year Alice, Bruce and Abigail went to Westchester to his parents' house to ring in the New Year with them, his three brothers, their wives and a platoon of their various children.

I sdfuggested charades, Alice wrote. *But I wasdf votwesd down. INstead were sitgfn aroudn talkding abut golf and proerepty values.*

Maybe don't have another drink, Liz wrote. *Or if you do at least turn on autocorrect.*

What are you and Peter up to? Fabiola asked, trying to breathe normally.

We're at a wedding at the Rainbow Room. A former patient of Peter's who's now endowing a wing of the hospital.

Trade you, Alice said.

Liz sent through the shrugging emoji. *I wanted to go to the Caymans. But at least the food's good.* She sent through a picture of her and Peter in a cheesy pose pretending to feed each other oysters against the backdrop of the Rainbow Room's floor to ceiling windows that were framed in a pale, lavender light for the occasion. Peter was laughing, his head thrown back and his eyes half closed. Fabiola touched her finger to his face on the screen.

You offsdiaclly win new years, Alice said.

Lol. HNY! Liz wrote. *Love you guys.*

HNY. Love you too, Fabiola wrote, then clicked off her phone.

"So," Aron said, "*SB Nation* is seriously interested in Pivot."

Fabiola cocked her head at him. "Is that the contact Peter introduced you to?"

Aron cleared his throat. "Well, yeah, he made the intro, but it was my pitch that got them interested."

"Oh, OK."

Aron set down his book, annoyed. "You could show a little more enthusiasm, you know? This could be a big deal."

Fabiola tried to craft her expression into something more excited, but the problem was she'd already used up all her enthusiasm on Pivot's other "could be" big deals. "That's great, really," she attempted.

Aron picked up his book again. "Forget it."

"I'm sorry," she said, and she mostly was. She slid lower in the bed. "I'm just tired. And I have a lot on my mind."

"The transfer?" he asked. She nodded. After months of preparing, the embryo transfer was scheduled for January second, two days away. "Are you nervous?"

"A little, I guess." Nervous wasn't it, exactly, but she couldn't think of a better word to describe the fizziness in her body that grew stronger as the days counted down. Sometimes it was pleasant, like champagne bubbles running through her veins, and other times it was mildly irritating, like low grade static electricity.

"Are you sure you don't want me to come?" Aron had offered to accompany her, even to be in the room with her if she wanted him to be.

"No, it's fine," she said. She could imagine few things more awkward than having her legs up in stirrups while her husband watched someone implant Peter's DNA in her. "But thank you." She reached over and squeezed his hand. "Happy New Year."

EIGHTEEN

Fabiola had never been one for New Year's resolutions, which she viewed as superficial attempts at change that usually did nothing to address the root problem of people's self-loathing. Still, the New Year was good for business. It was astonishing how many people sought her help without realizing that their cluttered closet was not the source of the chaos in their life, or that the piles of paper threatening an avalanche in their home office were not causing their emotional distress. While a decluttered closet or a new filing system would help, what these people usually needed was a divorce, or rehab, or a therapist with whom to work through their unhappy childhoods. Still, Fabiola helped them. She saw herself as a waypoint along the path to true happiness. By organizing their pantries and alphabetizing their bookshelves, she helped them see that really, their problems lay elsewhere, and cleared a path for them to get to the root of whatever was holding them back.

This year, however, her jaw clenched with anxiety thinking about all the new business that would surely come her way in the next few weeks. She was already operating at capacity, even with Hayley taking over some of the smaller jobs. Then there was all the other stuff—Hayley's friend with the home design podcast who was badgering her for an interview, the blog Hayley had started for her that Fabiola had promised to post to weekly, the emails from Hayley that kept landing in her inbox with subjects like, *this brand ambassador opportunity is so up your alley!!!* and *this might be crazy but what about doing a coffee table book???*

She'd even had heartburn after Aron's paella, a sure sign her body was under stress. And stress, she knew, was not good for conception. So, on New Year's Day she woke up relieved to have the day to herself thanks to their annual tradition of Aron driving the kids to New Jersey for a stop at the outlet mall (for Vivi) and to see the new Marvel movie (for the twins) so that Fabiola could unwind by performing her annual deep cleaning of the house.

In the silence of the house, she felt her ears drop away from her shoulders. She donned her comfiest sweatpants, the baggy ones that had been washed so many times there were tiny holes in the knees, and an old Brooklyn Half Marathon T-shirt of Aron's. She began with the boys' room, pulling all their clothes out of the dresser and weeding out those that had grown too small or too stained. Next, she sorted through their toys, merciless in her culling of headless action figures, light sabers that no longer illuminated, and science kits with most of the ingredients missing.

Though Vivi had given her explicit instructions not to touch anything in her room, Fabiola couldn't resist going into her daughter's closet and at least turning all the hanging clothing to face the same direction. On her way out she noticed a shirt hanging out of one of Vivi's dresser drawers and went to tuck it back in and close the drawer. As she folded the shirt to place it back into the drawer, she spotted the edge of a photo frame peeking out from under a pile of clothes at the bottom of the drawer. Pulling it out, she saw it was the framed photo of Vivi, Harper, and Izzy that used to sit atop the dresser. Fabiola hadn't noticed it was missing. The picture had been taken at a swim meet a couple of summers ago, the girls sitting side by side on a lounge chair in their swimsuits, towels draped over their narrow shoulders as they grinned for the camera. But what was it doing buried in Vivi's drawer?

In the pocket of her sweatpants her cell phone buzzed with a call. When she pulled it out, she saw Peter's name on the screen and a small shiver ran over her body.

"Hello?"

"Hi." Peter's voice washed over her. In the background she heard the discordant symphony of New York City traffic.

"Where are you?" she asked.

"On a run." And she knew. After all these years she was so attuned to the small shift in the tenor of his voice, the note of distress so slight it might go unnoticed by anyone else.

"Peter, what is it?"

"It's nothing, I'm just..." The air brakes of a bus sounded frighteningly near him.

"Peter."

"Could we talk? Where are you?"

"At home."

"Is Aron there?"

"No."

"I'm grabbing an Uber now."

Fabiola paced her house, trying to quell her racing thoughts, for the ten minutes it took him to arrive. He stood in her foyer in jogging pants and a fleece jacket, his cheeks flushed from the cold and his hair mussed from the stocking cap he pulled off.

"I'll make us some tea," she said, leading him to the kitchen.

"So where is everyone?" He looked around.

She averted her eyes. "Aron took the kids for the day. They won't be back until later. Sit." She motioned to one of the bar stools and he slumped onto it. "Talk to me."

"I'm fine, really."

Fabiola laughed as she set the water to boil. "You never call when you're fine."

"That's not true." His voice was defensive and hurt, as if she'd poked him somewhere tender.

"Of course it is." She turned to face him and gave a small smile. "But it's fine. That's what friends are for."

"Friends." He nodded as though considering the word.

"So...?" she prodded. Rifling through her box of tea she selected a comforting chamomile for herself and a deep, rich chai for Peter.

He ran his hand over the stubble on his chin. "I was up all night."

"Well, it was New Year's Eve. The wedding looked amazing, by the way."

"No, I mean after that. I couldn't sleep thinking about tomorrow She regarded him, noticing the bruise-colored circles under his eyes for the first time.

"Tomorrow?"

"The—you know, the whole transfer thing."

"Ah." Reflexively she placed a hand on her belly. "What were you thinking about? Are you nervous?"

He gave a rueful laugh. "I guess so, but it feels like more than that. It's the same stuff I mentioned to you at Alice's party." Fabiola flushed, remembering their kiss. "It just won't go away," he continued. "This voice telling me I don't know what I'm doing. That I'll be a terrible dad."

Fabiola handed him a steaming mug. "You'll be great, Peter." She could picture him as the kind of dad who gave piggyback rides and did all the voices when he read stories.

He stared down into his tea. "That's easy for you to say, Fabi. I mean, you had the shittiest mother of all, and yet somehow you managed to become supermom. But I'm not like you. I wish I was, but I'm not. I'm not cut out to be a parent. Things never should have gotten this far."

"My mom called me, you know," she blurted out, looking down into the amber swirl of her tea. Fabiola was twelve when she started at Dalton and met Peter, during the three-year period from ages ten to thirteen when her mother had been back. Paulina had been charmed by Peter's prep school manners and easy confidence.

"He's a good boy, Fabi," she'd said once after Peter had come by their apartment to study with Fabi.

Now, Peter's face registered surprise. "What? When?"

"A couple of weeks ago."

"What did she want?" His forehead creased.

Fabiola shrugged. "To talk."

"And?"

"And I hung up on her." She looked at him. The shocked expression on his face somehow struck her as wildly funny and she began to laugh. He laughed, too, then looked concerned.

"Why didn't you tell me?"

"I didn't want to give her the satisfaction of me thinking about it for even one more second." Except she had thought about it, every day since then. Each time replaying the conversation in her head, wondering if she'd done the right thing. Her voice rose in anger. "She knows about the kids. Says she wants to be in their lives. As if she deserves that." Tears stung her eyes, and she wiped them away with the back of her hand.

"Fabi, I'm so sorry. That's a lot to process."

She gave a rueful laugh. "Wait, aren't I supposed to be the one comforting you?" She set crossed her arms and leaned against the counter next to him.

His eyes locked on hers for a long moment. "You were the only person who could ever make me believe things would work out, you know that?" he said in a low voice.

A shiver went through her despite the hot tea and over-heated apartment. *Don't do this*, said a faint voice in her head.

He stood and pulled her toward him. Instead of pressing his lips to hers, he began with her neck, making his way slowly down to her collarbone. She sucked in a breath and tried not to moan.

"Peter," she said. She tried to push him away, but her limbs felt useless.

"I've missed you so much," he murmured.

"We can't—" she tried, but then his lips were on hers and her protests dissolved into the feeling of his hands buried in her hair and his body pressed against hers. She tugged at his jacket until he pulled it off along with his T-shirt. She slid her hands against his bare chest, thrilling at its broadness and the tuft of soft hair in the center that she'd watched grow in over the years. Then her shirt was off, too, revealing the wholly unsexy sports bra she'd opted for that morning. Then that was gone, and Peter's hands were cupping her breasts, his lips traveling down to her nipples made darker by her pregnancies. She had a flash of self-consciousness about the changes to her body, both from age and the hormones.

Peter paused and drew back, his eyes raking her. "You're so beautiful," he murmured. A wave of dizziness came over Fabiola as he tugged at the waistband of her sweatpants and underwear and she fell against him, limp in her desire. He touched her between her legs and brought his hand away soaking, smiling at her before thrusting his fingers inside her and kissing her face and neck again. She bucked against him, wishing she could get closer, close enough to crawl inside his skin. She gasped, shocked at the strength of her desire. At the last second, he moved his fingers away and she helped him tug his waistband down and pulled him to her until he was inside her, filling her and thrusting as his hand gripped her backside.

"Fabi," he moaned, matching her crescendo. She was pressed up against the kitchen island, the concrete surface digging into her back, the pain mixing with her pleasure until the wave crested and she cried out with no thought to who might hear. He gave one final thrust and gave his own cry, then shuddered and wrapped his arms around her, squeezing so hard she could barely breathe, but not for a second did she want him to let go.

They stood there, leaning against the island, their heads touching and their breathing heavy. He shifted inside her and Fabiola felt a twinge deep in the space above her pelvic bone. Panic rose in her and she pushed Peter away.

"Fabi, what—?" He jerked his head up to look at her in surprise.

"How did— how could we—?" He saw the fear in her eyes and pulled her back to him.

"Shh, it's OK." He stroked her hair. "It's OK."

"Oh my God," she breathed.

"Fabi, please," he pleaded. "God, I'm sorry—no, not like that," he said, seeing her face. "I just mean, I know you and Aron... and me and Liz..."

She placed her hand on her forehead. Aron and Liz had been the furthest thing from her mind, which only made her feel worse. She stepped away from him and pulled on her sweatpants, then Aron's T-shirt, leaving her bra on the floor where it had landed. She was aware of Peter as he dressed beside her, of his eyes on her the whole time. An explosion of guilt rocketed through her. What kind of person did what she'd just done?

"Look," Peter said, wringing his hands, "I got carried away and I shouldn't have. This doesn't have to change anything."

"Right," she said, crossing her arms. She was his mistake, again.

"Hey," he said tenderly. He reached out and put his hand under her chin, tilting it upward until their eyes met. "But I don't regret it. I could never regret you."

"Me neither," she said, looking at his familiar face, so dear to her. But for the first time, she wondered if maybe she would.

NINETEEN

There was a cold snap the next day and three Ubers canceled on Fabiola before she found one that would shepherd her to the Tribeca fertility clinic. Liz was already there when she arrived, pacing the waiting room in three-inch nude heels under a dark blue suit and creamy silk blouse.

"I'm sorry I'm late." Fabiola rushed up to her.

Liz gave a short laugh and pulled her into a side hug. "Oh, don't worry, I'd be pacing regardless. How are you feeling?" She stopped and looked at Fabi, whose skin crawled under Liz's probing gaze.

"Fine. Great. I feel great." She smiled.

"Fabiola Fernandez Butler?" called a nurse with a clipboard at the front of the waiting room. Both women raised their hands. The woman looked back down at her clipboard, confused.

"Sorry, I mean her." Liz pointed.

"I'm Fabiola." Fabiola said. "But she's coming in with me." She looked around, then back at Liz. "Is, um, Peter...?"

"Oh, he couldn't come—I'm sorry, I forgot to tell you. He got called into surgery; I should have told you. He's devasted he can't be here." Liz's face fell. Relief shot through Fabiola's body.

"I understand." She nodded.

"Fabiola?" the nurse called again.

Liz gave Fabiola a bright smile. "OK," she said with a small fist pump. "Let's do this."

In the small exam room adjacent to the procedure room Fabiola was given a large bottle of water to consume. "A full bladder changes the angle of the uterus and makes the transfer easier for the doctor," explained the nurse. "Just let us know when you've finished it."

"I feel like we should play a drinking game," Liz said with a nervous laugh after the nurse had left and Fabiola began to chug the water. "Like back in college."

Fabiola groaned. "I was terrible at those."

"I know. You were always such a lightweight."

"Which was a lot to live down, especially since my roommate was the unofficial Vassar beer pong champion."

Liz smoothed her hair. "I've always been a little competitive."

Fabiola snorted. "A little? Remember when Ashton Montgomery from the boys' basketball team challenged you to a game of HORSE? You practically lived on the basketball court for a week before, practicing every trick shot in the book."

Liz gave a sly smile. "But I creamed him, didn't I? Speaking of, do you think Ben and Liam would want to go to another Nets game this year? I can get tickets through work."

"Are you kidding?" Fabiola asked. "They only just stopped talking about the game you took them to last year." She took another sip of water, guilt tightening around her as she realized how easily she slipped back into her usual rapport with Liz, only a day after... She shook her head sharply, refusing to let her mind linger on the memory of Peter in her kitchen. She already knew she'd spend the rest of her life trying to make it up to Liz. Statistically, she knew there was a good chance this first embryo transfer wouldn't work, but right then and there she vowed she would do as many as it took to give her best friend a baby. This was her chance to make things right.

The nurse popped her head in the door. "How are we doing in here?"

Fabiola held up the nearly empty jug. "Almost there."

Once her bladder was full the nurse escorted them both to the procedure room. She instructed Fabiola to undress from the waist down and hop up on the table. Liz averted her eyes as Fabiola climbed onto the table and arranged the paper blanket over her lap. It was warm in the room, and she wished she could have some more water, but was afraid her bladder might burst if she did.

"Do you want any particular music?" Liz asked, holding up her phone. "Like soothing classical or a guided meditation or something?"

Fabiola stared at her friend. "Did you also bring me some essential oils or healing crystals? Who even are you?"

Liz rolled her eyes. "Ha ha." Then her eyes grew soft. "Look, I really appreciate this, Fabi. It's not a small thing you're doing, and I just want you to be comfortable."

Fabiola looked down at her feet in stirrups. "I can promise you comfort is not possible," she said. "But thank you. And I'm happy to be doing it. You know I'd do anything for you." *Except refrain from sleeping with your husband.* A flush of guilt swept over her face, and she placed a hand on her belly where she'd felt the twinge the day before.

A parade of medical professionals swept through the room. First the embryologist, a stocky, curly-haired woman with a wide smile who showed them the embryo, invisible in its tiny dish, and asked if they had any questions. Then the ultrasonographer, who squirted warm gel on Fabiola's abdomen and showed them the picture of her insides. Then the nurse again with some additional questions. Finally, Dr. Paulsen entered the room dressed in purple scrubs and a jaunty surgical cap.

"So nice to see you both again," she said, waving. She washed her hands and then lowered herself onto the wheeling stool near the surgical table. "How are you feeling today?" she asked.

"Good." Fabiola nodded, hoping her nervousness didn't show.

"And you?" Dr. Paulsen addressed Liz.

"Me? Oh, good, I guess. Excited." Liz's voice rose on the last word like it was a question. Her eyes had a wild look, like a cornered animal.

Dr. Paulsen nodded. "Excellent. Well, everything looks good, so I'd say let's get started." She glanced up at Fabiola. "I'm going to start by feeding the prep catheter up through your cervix. Then we'll place the embryo and perform the transfer. Ready?" Fabiola nodded. Dr. Paulsen picked up a thin, clear plastic tube from the tray of equipment. "This may pinch a bit," she said. "But I understand you've already given birth to three children, so I'm sure you can handle it." She smiled at Fabiola and then bent forward between her legs.

Fabiola gripped the edge of the table and gasped as the catheter was inserted. "Pinch a bit" had been an understatement. Liz looked pale and kept her eyes fixed on the floor.

Dr. Paulsen examined the ultrasound picture. "Looks perfect," she said. "Now, if you want, keep a close eye on the screen." She beckoned over her shoulder to the embryologist who had re-entered the room. "The embryo is too small to see, but if you watch closely, you'll see a small flash which is the air bubble that flushes the embryo into the uterine lining. It's subtle, but it's there." She nodded to the embryologist who came forward to load the embryo into the catheter. Dr. Paulsen's eyes remained fixed on the screen. "OK, here we go." Fabiola held her breath and watched the screen, but all she saw were the shifting light and dark blobs of her own insides. "There." Dr. Paulsen smiled up at her. "All done."

"Did you see it?" Liz rushed forward and gripped Fabiola's hand. "I was too nervous to watch." Her voice caught Fabiola by surprise; she'd been so focused on watching the screen she'd forgotten Liz was in the room. But Fabiola had felt nothing, seen nothing. A feeling of sadness came over her. It hadn't worked.

Fabiola squeezed Liz's hand and forced a smile. "I think so," she said.

"I feel terrible," Liz said once Fabiola had dressed and they were in the elevator headed back down to the street. "I wish I could take you out for a coffee or something, but I need to dash back for a client meeting." She lowered her voice. "No one at my office knows we're trying."

"I understand," Fabiola said, smiling. "Don't worry about it." The elevator deposited them into the building's small lobby.

"Can I at least get you an Uber back to Brooklyn?" Liz asked.

Fabiola shook her head. "Actually, I'm going to walk for a bit."

"In this cold?" Liz knit her eyebrows together. "Intrepid." She paused. "So, I guess now we wait two weeks? God, that sounds so long." She rubbed her forehead. "But you'll tell me if you feel anything—any pregnancy symptoms?"

"I promise." Fabiola forced Liz into a hug, then they stepped outside, waved to each other and walked in separate directions. She couldn't bring herself to tell Liz that she didn't think it had worked.

The cold air rushed into Fabiola's lungs and made her cough. It stung her ears, and she yanked her hat out of her coat pocket and jammed it down over them. As she headed in the direction of the Hudson River she placed her hand on her belly again.

With both of her pregnancies she'd known the second they happened. Each time, she'd felt the same thing. Once lying in bed with Aron at a hotel in Santa Monica the morning after his college roommate's wedding, and the second time on the couch in their old apartment in Carroll Gardens, the one they'd brought Vivi home to, surfacing from their working parent exhaustion long enough to take an intermission from binging *Mad Men*.

She knew any doctor would tell her it wasn't possible to feel the moment of conception. But both times she'd felt the same snap of a tiny rubber band somewhere deep inside her, followed two weeks later by tender breasts and a heightened sense of smell.

Yet when the embryo was implanted, she'd felt nothing.

PART TWO

TWENTY

"We ordered you the usual," Alice said as Fabiola slid into their regular booth next to her and across from Liz. "Huevos rancheros and an Americano—decaf." Fabiola's stomach lurched and she tried to smile.

"What is it?" asked Liz quickly. "Are you feeling OK?"

"I'm fine," Fabiola said, waving her hand. "Just a little queasy this morning. I'll have oatmeal or something bland instead. The smell of eggs..." She shrugged.

She'd thrown up nearly every day for the past six weeks, something that had never happened with her first two pregnancies. The nausea had begun just a week after the shock of seeing the positive pregnancy test.

Liz gave a sharp wave to get the server's attention. "Cancel the two omelets and the huevos," she said. "We'll take three oatmeals instead."

Fabiola groaned. "Oh, come on, it's not like you guys have to suffer with me. Enjoy your omelets, please."

"As if." Alice frowned. "Friends don't let friends throw up at brunch."

"Has it been bad?" Liz asked. "The morning sickness?"

"It's been fine," Fabiola lied. "Totally manageable." Aron kept urging her to take the anti-nausea medication her doctor had offered but she waved him off. "Once I throw up, I feel much better," she told him, which was mostly true. The fatigue, however, was on a whole different level. Most mornings it felt like her body was made of cement as she struggled to drag herself out of bed. Multiple times she'd caught herself nodding off at a client's house—including once while standing up, rearranging someone's closet.

"It's March third," Alice said, consulting her watch. "So you're eleven weeks now, right?" Fabiola nodded. "Almost into the second trimester, which should be better."

"I feel terrible," said Liz. "It's my fault!"

"Well, technically it is," Alice pointed out. "Yours and Peters. You guys must have some nausea-inducing DNA." Liz rolled her eyes.

"Seriously, though, Fabi, is there anything Peter and I can do to help?" Liz asked.

Fabiola tried not to react at the mention of Peter's name. Since that day in her kitchen, she'd managed to have very little contact with him. On the day she'd told Liz about her positive pregnancy test he'd called her later, but she'd let it go to voicemail and he hadn't left a message. Instead that night he'd sent a text:

Liz told me the news. Wow.

Beyond that they'd exchanged a few texts here and there about how she was feeling, but neither of them had mentioned what happened. This did not, however, keep Fabiola from thinking about it constantly—at least until her morning sickness had started. Since then, she'd been too tired and sick to think about anything but just getting through the day.

"You're sweet," she said to Liz. "But I promise I'm fine. It's not that bad, really."

Alice looked at Liz, who nodded. "OK." Alice rubbed her hands together. "Well, we happen to have something we think will make you feel better." Liz hefted a large gift basket from the seat next to her onto the table.

"What's all that?" Fabiola exclaimed.

"Happy birthday, babe!" Liz smiled.

"You guys," Fabiola protested. "You didn't have to—"

"Of course we did," Alice said. "So don't even go there." She began pulling things out of the basket and pushing them toward Fabiola across the table. "Maternity leggings from Hatch, Le Labo lotion and body wash, macaroons from Lauderée—"

"Alice," Liz chided, "you're ruining the presentation!"

"Oh, whatever," Alice said, "it's not like she wasn't going to crack it open immediately anyway."

"You guys." Fabiola's eyes filled with tears.

"Oh my God, what is it?" Liz asked, concerned. "Are you OK?"

"It's probably just the hormones," Alice said. "Right?" She glanced at Fabiola, who nodded through her tears.

"You guys are too good to me," she sniffled. "And this —" She gestured to the basket, the contents of which were now scattered across the table. "It's too much." She dug her fingernails into her palms in an attempt to stop the tears. She didn't deserve this. Not after what she'd done to Liz.

"I hope not," Liz said. "Because if you think that's too much then you'll definitely hate this." She pulled an envelope out of her purse and slid it across the table to Fabiola.

"Tell me you didn't go buying another birthday present behind my back to make me look bad," Alice demanded in mock anger.

Liz laughed. "This one is from me and Peter," she said. "And it's not a birthday present, exactly. More of a thank you."

"Liz," Fabiola said, her tone worried. "We agreed not to—"

Liz waved her off. "Just open it. You'll like it, I promise."

Fabiola slid her finger under the envelope flap and pulled out a piece of thick, cream-colored stationery with an elaborate dark green crest stamped on it bearing the name The Sagamore. She cast a questioning look at Liz.

"It's a gift certificate to our favorite hotel upstate in Lake George," Liz explained. "We figured with everything you have going on—work, Aron's job, the pregnancy—you guys could use a weekend away, just the two of you."

Fabiola pulled the piece of paper the rest of the way out of the envelope and gasped when she saw the figure written on it in calligraphy. "Liz!"

"Hush," Liz said. "It's not a cheap place and we wanted to include enough for spa treatments for both of you. Their spa is to die for. Peter used to act like he was too manly to put on a robe and let someone put hot stones on his back, but then I dragged him to The Sagamore. Now he gets mad if we don't have time to go to the spa every day we're there."

Fabiola tried to will away the image of Peter naked on a massage table. "I don't know what to say." She brought her hands to her heart. "Thank you, both of you." She looked at Alice. "I'm so lucky I had to line up behind you in the school lunch line." Her eyes crowded with tears again.

"Borowitz, Butler," Alice crowed, pointing at her chest and then Fabiola. "Friends for life."

Fabiola turned to Liz, wiping away the tears that had spilled over onto her cheeks. "And Alice and I are both so lucky you got stuck with us freshman year."

"Though in fairness I didn't think that initially when your basketball gear took up half our living room," Alice said. "But I came around."

"At least I didn't need an air raid siren to wake up every morning," Liz shot back. "I swear I have permanent hearing damage from your alarm clock."

"Remember that first weekend?" Alice asked, a gleam in her eye. "I wanted to go to that frat party over at Marist College but neither of you wanted to go."

"I was on scholarship," Fabiola protested. "I had to study."

"And I had practice the next morning," Liz said.

Alice rolled her eyes. "When did you not have practice? Anyway, good thing I convinced you both to go."

"Why, so I could narrowly escape a fist fight with a bunch of frat guys?" Liz asked.

"You got us *kicked out* of our first college party!" Alice dissolved into giggles.

"Not just kicked out, banned for life from their fraternity," Fabiola reminded them.

Liz huffed. "It was totally their fault! I mean, they weren't letting girls pour their own drinks—"

"So you started bartending." Alice mimicked Liz's square-backed posture and spoke in a commanding voice. "Ladies, line up here for your roofie-free cocktails!" She waved her arms as if beckoning to a crowd. "One hundred percent safety guaranteed! Did some rando just hand you a drink? Well, put it down and come get one from me!"

"Oh my God," Fabiola said, remembering. "I mean, did you really think they were going to roofie someone?"

"Nah." Liz shrugged. "They seemed like decent guys, actually. But it was the principle of the thing."

"Anyway," Alice said, resting her elbows on the table and tenting her fingertips together, "as I was saying, you guys have me to thank because that's the night we became friends."

Fabiola smiled. It was true. Something in Liz's chilly New England veneer had cracked that night and the three of them had ended up back at their dorm suite ordering pizza and re-enacting the whole episode while laughing hysterically.

"Well," Liz said, smoothing her hair, "look at us now." She raised her mug of coffee in a toast. "Cheers to us. BFFs."

Fabiola raised her own in return, then caught Liz's eye and a knife of guilt pierced her chest. She gave Liz a weak smile. "BFFs," she said.

TWENTY-ONE

Fabiola sat at the kitchen table in the light-filled Brooklyn loft while Hayley ran a makeup brush over her face.

"Nothing dramatic, right?" Fabiola confirmed for the third time.

"Girl, I got you," Hayley said, hovering close to Fabiola's face. "I'm a pro at the no-makeup look. Now close your eyes."

Obediently Fabiola did so. "Wouldn't the no-makeup look be exactly what I walked in with?" she asked.

"Nope," corrected Hayley. "That's just no makeup. This is the no-makeup *look*."

"Mm," Fabiola said, trying to act like she was following.

"There." Hayley sat back. "Perfect. Take a look." She pulled a small handheld mirror out of her oversized bag and handed it to Fabiola.

Fabiola had to admit she looked pretty. Really pretty. Hayley had curled and then brushed her hair out into soft waves and had used various other brushes on her face in some kind of alchemy that made her look several years younger and like she regularly slept eight interrupted hours a night—though maybe those were one and the same.

"Wow," she said. "Thanks."

"Hi, ladies, ready when you are." Hayley's friend, Bianca, called to them from across the loft where she was settled in an off-white, oversized bucket chair, her long legs pretzeled underneath her. Her dark hair was cut in a sleek, asymmetrical bob, and though the April day was warm her compact body was ensconced in a thick, gray cable-knit turtleneck sweater several sizes too big. She looked, in short, like someone who ran a design blog.

Bianca motioned for Fabiola to sit across from her on an exquisite blond leather couch which looked so expensive that for a moment Fabiola questioned whether she was worthy of sitting on such a thing of beauty. "Oh, don't worry," Bianca said, seeing her hesitation. "It's vegan leather."

"Oh," Fabiola said. "OK." As she settled onto the couch, she was grateful for the olive-green jumpsuit she'd chosen for its forgiving waist. Her midsection had begun to expand in a way that was only noticeable to her when she tried to zip her jeans, and she hadn't yet mentioned the pregnancy to Hayley or anyone else beyond her immediate circle. Her thoughts drifted back to that moment in the kitchen when Peter had reached for her. Shifting on the vegan leather couch, she placed a hand over her stomach, as a small, pebble-sized worry surfaced in the back of her mind.

"Thanks so much for fitting us into the pub schedule, Bianca," Hayley gushed, snapping Fabiola back into the moment. "It's perfect timing because Fabiola is just about to *blow up* on the design scene." She gave Fabiola a thumbs up.

Bianca nodded. "We'll get some photos after the interview," she said, hitting record on her phone. "Ready?"

After, Fabiola was grateful to head back down the creaking elevator to the street. She'd arranged for Liam and Ben to ride home from soccer practice with a friend's mom and, despite her better judgement, had given Vivi permission to go home with

Layla until dinner. This meant that Aron had to pick Vivi up by quarter past five in order to get home when the boys were dropped off at five-thirty. Normally this is something they would have argued about—he often stayed at Pivot's offices until well after six p.m., arriving home just as she and the kids were finishing dinner. This morning, though, he'd accepted her reminder about the evening's schedule with a nod and a smile.

"Hello?" she called as she opened the front door, hoping Aron had remembered to order pizza. "I'm home." She hung her bag and jacket on her designated hook and lined her shoes up on the rack before heading into the kitchen. "Is anyone—"

"Happy birthday!" Fabiola gave a small jump to see her whole family, including her father, gathered around the kitchen island smiling at her. On the island sat several wrapped gifts and cards, a bouquet of spring flowers, and a telltale pale pink box from her favorite pasty shop, Betty's Bakery.

"Oh!" she cried. Joy flooded her body like a sugar rush. They'd remembered.

Ben jumped up and down. "Are you surprised? Are you? Are you?"

"Yeah, are you? Dad said you would be," Liam chimed in.

Fabiola looked over at Aron who was smiling at her. "Yes," she said, stretching her arms out for the boys to come hug her. "I am *very* surprised."

"It was my idea to get Thai because it's your favorite," Vivi said. Her statement was devoid of excitement and accompanied by a blasé shrug.

"Thank you, honey," Fabiola said, her eyes filling with tears at her daughter's uncharacteristic thoughtfulness. "That was very sweet of you." She gazed at her beautiful daughter, her heart swelling with gratitude for the privilege of being her mother.

"Whoa, Mom, it's not, like, a big deal or anything," Vivi said, seeing Fabiola's watery eyes.

"I know." Fabiola wiped her eyes. "It's just been a long day."

"You're working too hard, sweets," her father said, stepping forward and squeezing her into a hug. "You should be resting in your condition."

"I'm fine," she said, giving him a weak smile. Aron moved in to embrace her and swept his lips across hers.

"Happy birthday," he said softly.

"Thank you." She smiled and leaned in to kiss him again.

"Gross!" Liam declared.

"Can we eat already?" Ben asked. "I'm starving."

"Yes," Aron said. "Everyone can make their own plate and take it to the table."

Perhaps everyone was on their best behavior because it was her birthday, but it was the most pleasant family dinner Fabiola could remember in a long time. Even Vivi smiled and laughed at Ben's stupid jokes, and her father looked better than he had in a while. His color was back and the tiredness around his eyes had diminished.

"Open your presents now," Liam said once they'd finished dinner and cupcakes.

"Yeah," Ben said. "Maybe you got a VR headset. Then I could borrow it."

"No, *I* could borrow it," Liam retorted.

"No, *I*—"

"OK," Aron cut in. "That's enough. I promise Mom did not get a VR headset for her birthday."

Fabiola selected a card in a pale green envelope that had come in the mail to open first.

"BOR-ing," Liam said. "You're supposed to open the big stuff first!"

"Oh my God." Vivi rolled her eyes. "Just let her open it already."

Fabiola flashed her daughter a smile of thanks, which Vivi ignored. Using a slim copper letter opener, Fabiola slit open the top of the envelope. The handwriting on it was vaguely familiar, but it had no return address. For a minute she pictured Peter writing out and addressing a card to her, and she wondered if she'd be better off opening it when she was alone—but it was too late now.

On the front of the card was a simple pale yellow sun shining over a bed of pastel tulips. "You are my sunshine" was printed in a looping font. Inside was printed "Happy Birthday" with another handwritten word tacked on. Daughter.

Fabiola froze as the rest of the note rushed up to meet her eyes before she could look away.

Mi querida Fabi,

While you may not want to hear from me, I couldn't pass up the chance to wish my darling daughter a happy birthday. I've missed many of them, I know. But I hope that can change. There is a lot I'd like to explain to you. I'm here whenever you are ready to talk. Until then I'll be thinking of you every day, as I always have.

Love,
Mama

A phone number was included under her signature.

Fabiola tossed the card onto the table like it had stung her. "What's wrong?" Aron asked, reaching for it. Scanning the message inside, he blanched.

"Fabi?" said her father. "Are you all right?" Silently Aron passed him the card. A cloud passed over her father's face as he registered the sender and gave a small sigh.

"How dare she?" Fabiola breathed. "How does she know where I *live*?" Her breath felt shallow, and her heart raced with anger.

"Who's it from?" Vivi asked. "What's going on?"

Fabiola stood up and took her plate to the sink, then gripped the counter with both hands as her heart raced.

"It's from her mother." Leonard's voice was soft and even. "Your grandmother."

"But I thought Mom didn't have a mother," Liam said, confused.

"Everyone has a mother," Leonard replied.

"Wait, I have a grandmother?" Vivi asked. "But you told me she was dead." Fabiola turned around to face Vivi's accusatory look.

"I never said that," Fabiola admonished. "I said she wasn't with us anymore."

"Yeah, which means dead, duh." Vivi crossed her arms. "But apparently she's alive and well and *you've* been keeping her from me."

"Is she coming to our birthday? Like, with presents?" Liam asked. The twins' birthday in two weeks had become a nonstop topic of conversation.

"I want to see her." Vivi set her jaw and glared at Fabiola. "I want to meet my grandmother."

"Yeah, me too!" Ben said. "Especially if she's getting us presents."

Fabiola stomped her foot, causing everyone to jump. "No one is seeing her. No one is getting presents from her, and no one is talking about her ever again, understand?"

"That's not fair!" Vivi spat. "She's *my* grandmother. Why should you get to decide?"

"Because I'm your *mother*," Fabiola said. "And I know what's best."

TWENTY-TWO

Fabiola transferred the leftover pad thai and papaya salad to glass containers while her father rinsed their plates and placed them into the dishwasher. Normally the dishwasher was Vivi's job, part of how she earned her allowance, but she'd disappeared upstairs behind a slammed door. And for once Fabiola didn't have the strength to go argue with her.

She and her father worked in silence until the kitchen was spotless; the counters buffed and shiny, the floor crumb-free. The only thing out of place was the small stack of unopened birthday presents that remained on the table, the bright ribbons and wrapping paper mocking her dark mood.

"Aren't you going to open them?" her father asked once they'd surrendered their dish towels and cleaning spray.

Fabiola shook her head. "Maybe later. I'm not really in the mood right now." He sighed, his breath so deep and heavy she looked up at him in alarm. His face drooped with sadness. "Oh, Papa," she said, "I'm so sorry. This has got to be so painful for you, to have her turn back up like this after so many years. I could kill her for being so selfish and hurting you all over again." She moved to hug him, but he held up his hands.

"Fabi," he said. "I've long since let go of everything that happened with your mother. But I should have talked to you about it more, I know that. I'm sorry." He shook his head. "Do I still think about her? Yes. Do I wish you could have grown up with a mother, that we could have remained a family? Absolutely. But I don't carry any anger anymore. If I'd kept carrying it around, it would have crushed me. I only wish, sweets, that you could let it go, too, so it doesn't crush you."

"Let it go? Ha." Fabiola crossed her arms and felt her blood begin to pump faster again. "She destroyed both our lives. I'm sorry, but I'm not letting her off the hook for that."

He swept his arms open wide. "Destroyed my life? Look around. I have a beautiful, successful daughter, three amazing grandchildren, my health. You have all this and more. So, what did she destroy, really? You've lived through the pain, yes, but the suffering is optional, Fabi. Maybe it's time to make your peace."

His words deflated her anger like a leaky balloon. Her dad had always known how to make things OK—he was her safe harbor. She turned away to fill the electric kettle and get two mugs down from the shelf.

"Your mother never held a grudge," he said. "I loved that about her. She had a temper, sure, but just as fast as she got angry, she'd be hugging you and making you laugh. You, though," he laughed. "She could never get angry with you." He settled onto a bar stool at the island while she got out the ginger tea he liked. "I remember when you were around four years old you were so naughty. You'd hide your shoes in the morning so you didn't have to go to school, or splash in the fountain in the park on the way and soak your clothes. But she'd never let me reprimand you." He laughed and shook his head. "*Our daughter knows her own mind, Leonard,* she'd tell me, *and we're not ever going to take that away from her.*" The lines on his face softened as he spoke, and his eyes seemed focused on something off in the distance that Fabiola couldn't see.

She handed a steaming mug to her father and held her own in front of her face to disguise the tears that had gathered in her eyes. "But see, you have all those memories," she said. "And I barely have any. She took that from me." Anger gripped her chest. She hated that thinking about her mother's abandonment still brought up so many emotions. She wanted to be done with it, already.

He blew on his tea, then raised his eyes to meet hers. "Well, she wrote to you, which is more than I can say. So maybe this is your opportunity to make some new memories."

There was a movement in the corner of the room and Fabiola turned to see Aron leaning against the door jamb. She narrowed her eyes and turned back to her father. "No," she said. "That will never happen."

TWENTY-THREE

Fabiola shifted on the exam table, the paper sheet crinkling underneath her, and checked her phone again.

Traffic's finally moving so maybe 10 more min? so sorry! Liz wrote. *I hope I don't miss it!!*

I'm still waiting for the doctor so no worries, Fabiola reassured her. Liz was coming on her own because Peter had a conflict at work, or so he said. Fabiola wondered if the real reason was that he didn't want to be trapped in a room with both her and Liz.

Her phone buzzed again, this time with a message from Alice. *AHHH, so excited for both of you today! Send me ultrasound pics IMMEDIATELY! Xo*

Fabiola smiled and added a heart to Alice's message.

She glanced around the exam room, which was painted a soothing terracotta color with tasteful, abstract art hung throughout. On the counter next to the sterile jars of cotton swabs and gauze was a magazine rack filled with up-to-date issues of magazines like *Architectural Digest* and *Vogue*, and a rubber plant, the leaves of which Fabiola had already squeezed. It was real. All of it was a far cry from her normal Brooklyn OB/GYN, whose office had fluorescent lighting, cracked linoleum, and sometimes smelled like the pizza shop next door. But while she loved her doctor, for this pregnancy she and Liz had agreed to find one in Tribeca so it would be more convenient for Liz to attend appointments.

The only fault Fabiola could find with the new practice so far was that it was warm—hot, even, in the room. Sweat had gathered on the back of her neck and she pulled her hair up into a knot on top of her head and fanned herself with a copy of *Vanity Fair* with Simone Biles on the cover. Just as she felt moisture gathering between her breasts there was a perfunctory knock and the door swung open.

"Hello, I'm Dr. Acharya." A slim Indian woman about Fabiola's age with flawless skin and hypnotically shiny hair extended her hand. "Nice to meet you."

"I'm Fabiola."

Dr. Acharya flipped open the chart she was holding. "I understand this is a surrogate pregnancy? And that you're about twelve weeks along?"

Fabiola nodded. "Yes, I'm carrying for a friend of mine. She's on her way, actually. She wanted to see the ultrasound." She felt shy, suddenly, talking about her situation. She wondered if surrogacy was something the doctor saw all the time—it was Tribeca, after all—or if she was unusual.

"Sure." The doctor scanning something in the folder. "So, you've had previous pregnancies?"

"Yes, two."

"Any complications?"

"No."

"Vaginal births?"

"Yes." Fabiola nodded. "Even the twins."

Dr. Acharya made a noise of understanding, her eyes still on the chart. Already Fabiola missed the warmth of Dr. Paulsen.

Her phone dinged in her hand and she glanced down at a text from Liz.

> Here! Waiting for the elevator.

Fabiola looked at the clock. She had two minutes at the most before Liz got there. Two minutes to ask the question that had been nagging at her. It was a question that hadn't even occurred to her early in the pregnancy; she'd been too sick to think straight. Now, though, the pea-sized worry that had sprouted in the back of her mind last week had grown into a large marble that barreled recklessly around in her brain, smashing through her concentration when she was at work, with the kids, or thinking about anything else, really.

Fabiola swallowed and summoned her courage. "So," she said, clearing her throat, "I wanted to see if it was possible to do a DNA test on the baby."

Dr. Acharya flipped through the chart and then glanced up at her. "It looks like you already did the standard panel of genetic screening for abnormalities with your fertility doctor—Dr. Paulsen."

"Yes." Fabiola nodded. Her words tumbled out. "But I mean another kind of test. To know who the baby's parents are."

Dr. Acharya's eyebrows came together in confusion. "You mean a paternity test? With a surrogacy, everyone already knows who the father is."

"I'm not talking about the father," Fabiola said. Her underarms were clammy with sweat now and she fanned herself again. "Is it hot in here?"

Dr. Acharya peered at the thermostat on the wall. "No. Oh, wait." She stepped toward the exam table and pressed a button. "It looks like someone left the exam table heater on. Sorry about that, it can get warm."

"Oh, thank God," Fabiola breathed.

"So, if not the father," Dr. Acharya continued, "then you mean..."

"The mother, yes." Fabiola averted her eyes. "I'd like to know if it's... me." She swallowed the enormous lump of guilt that had formed in her throat.

"Oh," Dr. Acharya said. Her eyes widened. She cleared her throat. "Well, um, ordering a DNA test for maternity would be highly irregular—"

"Trust me," Fabiola said, biting her lip. "This is all highly irregular. I just want to know if it can be done." An embarrassed flush covered her face. She couldn't believe she was even having this conversation.

"Well, yes. It's a simple blood draw. I'm not sure insurance will cover it, though, given the... situation." Dr. Acharya cleared her throat again.

"That's fine." Fabiola glanced at the clock again. "And we have, um, doctor-patient confidentiality on this, right?"

"Yes, of course." Dr. Acharya's mask of professionalism returned. "I'll submit the lab order and you can do a blood draw on your way out."

There was a knock on the door. "Hello?" Liz called. "Fabi? It's me." The doctor looked at Fabi, who nodded, then walked over to open the door. Liz tumbled into the room, breathing heavily. "I'm so sorry," she said. "Traffic, then the elevator, then—"

"It's fine," Fabiola said, taking a deep breath to slow her racing heartbeat. "I think we were just about to start the ultrasound."

The doctor introduced herself to Liz, then had Fabiola pull up her shirt and roll the waistband of her leggings down to her hips before lying back on the table. She squirted warm gel onto Fabiola's midsection and began running a wand over her puffy skin. Fabiola watched as on the screen next to them white blobs rippled against a dark background until Dr. Acharya slowed the wand and pressed against one spot on Fabiola's belly.

"Oh my God," Liz gasped. "It looks like an actual baby."

"It is an actual baby," Fabiola teased, but she knew what Liz meant. The baby was in profile, the curve of its forehead, nose, and lips clearly visible. Its arms were tucked in by its sides and its legs were drawn up close to the belly. A rush of emotion swept through Fabiola's body. *That's my baby*, she thought. Tears filled her eyes. She looked at Liz, wondering if she was having the same reaction, but Liz's face had paled, and her shoulders moved up and down rapidly with her breath. "Liz, honey, are you OK?" Fabiola asked. Without a word Liz leaned over and thrust her head between her legs.

"Whoa, now," the doctor said, pulling the wand away from Fabiola's belly. "Let me get the nurse."

"I'm fine." Liz's voice was weak as she held up a hand, her face still hovering near the floor. "Just a little light-headed, that's all."

"Keep your head down," the doctor said. "Do you want some water?"

Liz shook her upside-down head. "I just need a minute." Several seconds later she slowly drew her head up and leaned back in the chair. "I apologize," she said. "Seeing that"—she gestured to the screen—"I just..."

"Some people can find it overwhelming," Dr. Acharya said.

"Overwhelming, yes." Liz nodded. "That's the word."

"Oh, honey," Fabiola said, wishing she could get up off the table and put her arm around her friend. Her heart ached for Liz, who'd waited so long for this moment. "It's a lot."

"Mm hm." Liz kept her lips pressed together and her skin looked ashen.

"I'll just take some quick measurements and then we'll listen to the heartbeat," the doctor said. "From what I'm seeing everything else looks as it should." She placed the wand back onto Fabiola's stomach and the baby reappeared on the screen. "OK," Dr. Acharya said after clicking around for a minute. Fabiola held her breath, praying for good news. She remembered this feeling from her visits to the doctor while pregnant with Vivi and the twins. Never a religious person, she'd bought rosary beads and took them with her to every appointment despite not knowing the prayers that were supposed to accompany them. Instead, she'd run her fingers over the smooth wood in her pocket, whispering her own pleas to God for a healthy baby.

"Everything looks good. You're measuring at twelve weeks and two days, right on target." Dr. Acharya looked up at Fabiola, then at Liz. "I forget, did you want to know the sex?"

Liz twisted her mouth. "I do but Peter doesn't."

"So that's a yes?" Fabiola asked.

Liz hesitated, then shook her head. "No, he'd find out somehow, I know it. Or I'd slip up and tell him."

Dr. Acharya nodded and adjusted the volume on the monitor. Loud static played, then the sound morphed into a quick, pulsating beat. "Strong heartbeat," she said. "One hundred forty beats per minute. You have yourself a healthy baby. Great work, Mom," she said to Fabiola. "I mean—" She looked toward Liz, whose eyes had glazed over. The color had still not returned to her face after her dizzy spell.

"Thank you," Fabiola said, feeling a pang of guilt. Dr. Acharya nodded and pulled a lavender scented hot towel out of a nearby metal bin for Fabiola. While she wiped the gel off her stomach, Dr. Acharya printed several ultrasound photos.

"In case you want these," she said. She seemed unsure whether to look at Liz or Fabiola and so stared at the wall somewhere in between them. Liz was frowning at her phone, which was buzzing in her hand. She let out a frustrated groan.

"I'm so sorry, I have to take this. I'll be right back." She pushed open the exam room door and disappeared.

"Thank you," Fabiola said to Dr. Acharya, reaching out her hand for the photos. "I'll take them."

TWENTY-FOUR

After they left the exam room Fabiola found Liz waiting for her in the hallway. "Hey," she said. "Everything OK?"

Liz nodded. "Yeah, sorry. I don't know what happened in there." She gave a shaky laugh. "I mean, obviously I knew there was a baby in there, but..." She trailed off and pointed to Fabiola's stomach. "I think it just, like, hit me. That it's *my* baby in there."

Fabiola's breath caught in her throat. "I understand," she said, trying to keep her voice even. "It's a big deal." She pointed to the lab down the hall. "I just have to do one more blood draw." She held her breath, wondering if Liz would ask what it was for.

"I'll wait with you," Liz said. She waved her phone. "That was my next meeting canceling on me. A meeting with a potential client I worked for months to get." She rubbed her temples. "Michael and the other partners are going to be furious."

Fabiola eyed her. "Are you sure you're OK?"

Liz squared her shoulders and straightened up. "Yes, just stupid work stuff. I've been under a lot of pressure lately." She smiled. "But I guess the good news is I don't need to rush back to the office. Want to grab a coffee when you're done?"

"Depends," Fabiola said. "How much caffeine have you had already today?" Liz drank coffee like it was a sports drink. In college their apartment had been littered with her empty Starbucks cups, all bearing smears of her cherry ChapStick on them.

Liz laughed. "Only two espressos so far, so I'm definitely undercaffeinated."

After the blood draw they stopped at a coffee shop and, drinks in hand, settled at a table. At the next table were two nannies, nursing drinks and feeding bites of muffin to their small, drooling charges. Fabiola smiled at one of the curly-haired toddlers who gave her a crumb-covered grin in return.

Liz nudged Fabiola. "How old are those kids? Like, three? Four?"

"What? No," Fabiola said. "They're definitely not even two yet. She doesn't even have that many teeth." She nodded at the smaller girl.

"And when do they get teeth?"

"All my kids got their first ones around six months. That's when nursing becomes a lot less fun." Liz winced. "Sorry," Fabiola laughed. "TMI. Anyway, you won't have to worry about that."

"I bought a bunch of books," Liz said. "*What to Expect the First Year*, *Happiest Baby on the Block*, that one about raising your kid to be French. But I haven't read them yet." She cast a guilty look down at her drink.

"I never read any of them," Fabiola offered. "So I wouldn't worry about it."

Liz looked aghast. "But how did you know what to do?"

Fabiola shrugged. "It's not that hard to figure out after a while. When they cry the main options are that they're hungry, tired, or need a diaper change." She smiled, remembered the satisfied feeling of deciphering her kids' needs when they were babies. She'd been far better at it than Aron.

"You should write your own book," Liz said, sipping her cappuccino.

"I could call it *Benign Neglect*," Fabiola said, only half joking. Lately she felt stretched far too thin to be present at home with her kids in the way she wanted to be. Just thinking about them made her acutely aware of her exhaustion and the overwhelming longing to be back home with her family.

Liz laughed. "Seriously, you always made it look easy with Vivi and the twins." Fabiola flushed with pride at the compliment. "I mean, I feel like I'm OK hanging out with older kids," Liz continued, "but I'm not sure I'll know what to do with a baby."

"You'll figure it out," Fabiola promised, trying to ignore the turmoil inside and focus on her friend. "And, honestly, I think older kids are harder in a lot of ways. But you sure have mine wrapped around your fingers." Liz gave a half smile. She had a special bond with all three kids. Liam and Ben loved how she could talk sports with them and Vivi was obsessed with Liz's shoe collection, which was far superior to Fabiola's. "So, how's Peter?" Fabiola did her best to sound casual. "Sorry he couldn't make it today." Liz twisted her mouth and Fabiola's heart gave a small stutter. "Everything OK?" she pressed.

Liz shrugged and looked down at her drink. "We're just going through some stuff lately. Nothing new, honestly. We just get in these cycles where everything turns into an argument." She looked up, her eyes weary.

Fabiola swallowed. "I'm sorry."

"It's fine. At least, it usually is. This cycle seems to be lasting longer than normal." Liz sighed. "He just seems more on edge than usual, and even small things blow up. Like the other night he got mad when I suggested going hiking in Spain this summer because we might not get to do another long trip for a while. 'Of course we will,' he said. 'Unless you've decided we should become one of those pathetic couples whose lives revolve around their kids.' He was so *mean* about it. Then it turned into an argument about how much time I'll take off when the baby's born and how much time he'll take... I mean, we don't even have a baby yet and we're already arguing about it." She gave a rueful smile.

Fabiola felt a pang. She wondered what Peter thought of her and Aron. They were most certainly one of those couples whose lives revolved around their children. She couldn't remember the last time they'd had a vacation alone; probably before Liam and Ben were born.

"I'm sorry," she said to Liz, and she truly meant it. She wanted this to be a time of joy and excitement for her best friend. Pushing away the uneasy thought that Peter's edginess might be linked to what had happened between them, she added, "I think it might just take men a little longer to adjust to the idea of having kids."

Liz placed her palms on the table. "Right. Anyway, it'll all be fine. He does this sometimes, gets moody and distant. But it's all cyclical." She glanced at her phone. "I should get going. I guarantee Michael's been blowing up my email about this canceled client meeting."

"Of course." Fabiola nodded and rose to her feet. She put her hand in her jacket pocket and fingered the ultrasound photos. She should take them out, give them to Liz, who could share them with Peter and maybe that would help. She pressed the photos between her hands, feeling the smoothness of the paper they were printed on. "Here," she said, "you should take these." Then she withdrew the photos from her pocket and handed them to Liz—all except for one.

TWENTY-FIVE

Fabiola woke slowly as the gentle morning light filtered through the window. She was sleepy but in a pleasant, lazy way, like she'd nodded off at the beach. Her limbs felt loose and her head clear, free from the heavy blanket of exhaustion under which she usually woke. The mattress cradled her and sheets as soft as a baby's cheek whispered against her bare skin. Her bare skin. With a jolt she realized she was naked. Sitting up, she held the sheet against her and looked around, her eyes landing on a thin, folder-sized leather book on the nightstand. *Room Service Menu*, it read on the front. *The Sagamore*.

She gave a satisfied sigh and sank back down into the bed, her head resting on a deliciously plump pillow. Next to her, Aron rolled over and opened his eyes. "Hi," she said.

"Good morning." He smiled and the night came back to her. Her midnight craving for a grilled cheese. Kisses that tasted like French fries. His tongue exploring places on her body it hadn't ventured to in quite some time. The freedom of moaning as loud as she wanted to without worrying about the kids hearing. The kids, who were currently all off at separate sleepovers and would then spend the day with their grandfather at the

Brooklyn Museum, then watching movies at home and having their every whim indulged for another twenty-four hours until she and Aron got home.

Aron rubbed his eyes and sat up. "God, I can't remember the last time I slept in," he said. Fabiola bit back a snarky comment. Vivi now slept as late as they'd let her, and Fabiola was the one who got up and made the boys toaster waffles on the weekends. Aron reached for her hand. "I also can't remember the last time we were so..."

"Acrobatic?" Fabiola filled in.

He laughed. "I was going to say passionate, but I guess acrobatic also applies."

She flung the covers off and stretched her arms over her head, aware of his eyes on her breasts as she did. "I'm starving," she announced. "Let's go explore the buffet. Liz said it's to die for."

"Are you sure you can't wait just a little while longer?" Aron slid close to her and slipped his hand under the sheets onto her thigh.

A loud gurgle came from her midsection, and she pointed. "My stomach waits for no one," she said.

His hand inched higher on her thigh. "Just give me five minutes," he murmured.

Afterward they lay on the bed, entangled and panting. Fabiola remembered this as one of her favorite pregnancy side effects: her ability to become aroused as fast as a teenager. They lay on their backs, and she peered down at her belly, which had become visibly convex now that she was four months along.

"Wow," Aron said, his hand resting on his heaving chest. "Remind me why we don't do that more often?"

Fabiola poked him. "I'll give you three reasons. Now come on, I'm seriously starving."

The late April morning was warm enough to sit on the restaurant's terrace, where their table overlooked an expansive green lawn with an ornate fountain and reflecting pool. The lush grass was scattered with white Adirondacks, all facing the stone wall at the bottom of the hill and the fields beyond.

"They're for viewing the sunset," their server said when he saw them looking at the chairs. "I wouldn't miss it if you're staying with us—it's a spectacular view."

"Then we'll definitely make time in our busy schedules for it," Aron said, squeezing Fabiola's hand across the table.

"I can never eat breakfast again," Fabiola said when she finished. She pushed her plate away and leaned back in her chair. "That was too perfect. Nothing will ever live up to it."

Aron laughed and pulled her to her feet. "Come on," he said. "Let's go explore."

After a walk around the grounds, they returned to their room to prepare for their spa appointments. Fabiola donned the white robe and slippers she'd been asked to wear and slipped her phone into one of the pockets.

"Just leave it for once," Aron chided her. "I thought we could relax in the spa solarium after and it's not like you can use it there, anyway."

"But what if one of the kids—"

He stepped forward and removed the phone from her pocket, placing it on the nightstand. "The kids are fine. They're having more fun with their friends than they would be with us right now, anyway. And then they'll be with your dad the rest of the weekend, where they'll get to eat as much junk food as they want, and Ben and Liam will play video games until their eyes cross. Trust me, everything is fine."

"Fine." Fabiola gave a playful eye roll. "Let's go be footloose and child-free."

Nervous about the risk of a massage while pregnant, Fabiola had opted for a facial. Lying on the table, she felt a warmth toward Aron that she hadn't experienced in a long time. She realized, with some surprise, that she hadn't thought about Peter at all since they'd arrived at The Sagamore. It felt good. Maybe all she and Aron needed was to get a babysitter more often and spend more time together.

When she emerged to the solarium an hour later feeling scrubbed and glowing, she joined Aron on a lounge chair near the indoor pool in front of floor to ceiling windows that looked out onto the side lawn where croquet and bocce ball were set up.

"How was your massage?" she asked.

He moaned. "As good as your breakfast."

They napped and read for another hour until Fabiola began to feel restless. She'd never been good at sitting still, especially when her life offered so few opportunities for it. "Want to go for a walk?" she asked.

Aron roused himself enough to open one eye. "I'm pretty comfy," he said. "Would you mind if I stayed here just a little longer?"

She smiled. "Of course not." The thought of wandering around on her own for a bit was appealing. Alone time was something she rarely got. "I'll see you back in the room in a little while."

She took the elevator and the long hallway back to their room, nodding to the two other robe-clad guests she passed. She imagined having the money to come here whenever she wanted. What a life that would be. For a brief moment, she allowed herself to imagine Aron's fantasies about Pivot getting bought coming true. Maybe they'd have enough money to buy a home in Lake George, and she could pop into the spa at The Sagamore whenever she wanted.

Once in the room she sank onto the bed and automatically reached for her phone. The screen told her it was 1:52pm and that she had seven missed calls and thirteen unread texts. Her heart leapt into high gear as she swiped to unlock her screen. The calls were from Noah Parker's family, where Liam and Ben had slept over, Layla's stepmother, where Vivi had been, and finally Vivi herself. The texts were all various versions of the same thing.

> Hi Fabiola, just wondering if there was some kind of mix up? We're at your house with the boys waiting for your dad but haven't heard from him.

> Hey, I'm at your house with Vivi. She said her grandpa will be there soon so it's ok to leave her right?

> Hi Fabiola, it's Noah's dad again. Still no sign of anyone. Everyone's hungry so I'm taking the boys (and your daughter, who was dropped off by someone's nanny) to lunch in the meantime. Please get in touch when you can.

> mom where's grandpop? u said he was meeting us at our house this is so embarrassing. i tried calling him but he's not answering

A chill ran through her body as she pulled up her father's contact. The phone rang and then went to voicemail. She tried again with the same result. Her brain spun like a slot machine, trying to come up with a satisfying explanation. He was stuck on the subway somewhere with no cell service. But even the most far-flung stations now had coverage. He was taking a nap and had forgotten to set his alarm. But her father was not a napper. He'd mixed up the date. But her father was as reliable as New York's four seasons.

She pressed one hand to her chest as if she could keep her galloping heart from bursting out of it that way, and with the other she pushed the button to call Noah's dad back. "Hi, yes, I'm so sorry," she said, trying to keep her voice from shaking. "I'm not sure what's happened, I'm trying to get in touch with him now. I'm so sorry for the inconvenience. Thank you, I really appreciate it. I'll call back as soon as I can."

Then, biting her lip, she placed another call. *Please pick up,* she prayed. *Don't ignore me.*

"Fabi, hi." Just hearing his voice flooded her with relief.

"Peter," she said, her voice sounding strangled.

"What's wrong? Did something happen? Is it the baby?"

"No," she said. "It's my dad. This is our weekend at The Sagamore, and he was supposed to be at the house with the kids almost two hours ago, but I can't get hold of him. He's not answering his phone." She let the fear flood into her voice. With Peter there was no sense pretending.

"I'm getting an Uber now," he said. "I'll call you as soon as I'm at his apartment."

"Thank you," she whispered, then dropped the phone on the bed next to her.

The door beeped and opened, and Aron walked in. His face paled as he looked at her. "What is it? The kids?"

She forced herself to speak. "No, they're fine. It's my dad. He's... missing."

"Missing?" Aron's brow creased with concern. "What do you mean, missing?"

"He never showed up at the house."

Aron sucked in a breath. "OK," he said, loosening the tie on his robe. "I'm sure there's an explanation. We'll just—"

"Peter's on his way to my dad's apartment."

"Peter?" Aron's voice was sharp. "You called him?"

"He and my father are close."

She watched Aron swallow something he was about to say. "Where are the kids?" he asked.

"Noah's dad took them to lunch and then said they could all go back to their house as long as they needed to."

Aron nodded. Fabiola's phone dinged and she scrambled to pick it up.

ur sending me to some stranger's house w/a bunch of 10 yr olds??? MOM. can't I just take an Uber back to layla's pleeeeeease

Fabiola tensed and Aron sat next to her and put his arm around her. "I'm sure it's just some sort of mix up," he said. "Everything will be fine."

They sat like that for minutes that felt like hours until Fabiola's phone rang and Peter's name appeared on the screen.

"Is he there?" she asked, straining to hear her father's voice in the background or the sound of the soccer game on TV.

"Fabi." Peter choked on the word. A faint siren wailed in the distance.

"No." Her body went cold.

"Fabi, I'm so sorry."

TWENTY-SIX

The next several hours unrolled in fragments. One minute she was lying face down on the hotel's thousand thread count sheets, choking on her own sobs. Then the next she was waking up in the car, a crick in her neck from falling asleep with her head against the window as Aron drove. For a moment she wondered where they were going as fields and charming, ramshackle farm buildings rushed past outside. Then she remembered and the sobs returned.

As they neared the city hours later, she spoke briefly to Peter, the comfort of his voice flooding her nervous system. "I'm still with your dad at his apartment," he said, his voice swollen with grief. "The medical examiner is here... it was another heart attack—a big one." His voice caught. "Do you want me to— I mean, I can make arrangements to..."

"Yes," Fabiola choked out. "Just tell us where to meet you."

They parked outside the funeral home on Madison and 81st Street, its tasteful navy-blue awning blending in with the rest of the understated buildings that lined the block: a smattering of boutiques, a dry cleaner, the city's top public elementary school.

Inside, the anteroom resembled a furniture showroom, with

many heavily upholstered chairs and couches scattered about under soft lighting. Large vases of expensive looking flowers sat on end tables, their scent mixing with the aroma of coffee. Peter was waiting for them with Liz by his side, their fingers entwined. The light blue of his wrinkled button-down shirt made his reddened eyes stand out. As soon as he saw her, he dropped Liz's hand and moved forward to embrace her. She fell into Peter's arms without a thought for Aron trailing behind her.

"I'm so sorry, I'm so sorry," he repeated as he rocked her, and she felt the wetness on his face, too. When he pulled back Liz wrapped an arm around her other shoulder.

"Oh, honey," she said, her face grim. "I don't know what to say." Peter led Fabiola to a couch where she sat, Peter on one side, Liz on the other. Aron paced in front of them.

Fabiola gripped Peter's hand. "Thank you," she managed, "for staying with him."

He nodded. "They said it was fast," he said in a low voice. "He looked peaceful when I got there." He paused and swallowed hard. "I hope it's all right I had them bring him here. This is where... my brother..."

Fabiola nodded and squeezed his hand. "Thank you," she said again.

Aron glanced at her hand in Peter's and cleared his throat. He rose from the couch. "I'm going to call the kids," he said. He looked at Fabiola. "Should I tell them?"

She shook her head. "No, not yet."

"Why don't I go to your house and wait with them until you're back," Liz said. "I need to feel useful."

Aron paused, considering, and looked at Fabiola. She gave a small nod. It calmed her to think of Liz there with the kids. "Yes," he said. "Thank you. They're at a friend's house but I can call and ask for them to be brought home. Vivi has a key."

Liz stood. "I'll text you when I'm there," she said. She gave

Fabiola's shoulder a last squeeze and then wove her way through the couches to the door.

The funeral director came out to greet them just as Aron dialed his phone. He was younger than she expected, his thick, dark hair only beginning to gray around the temples, and his suit was so sharply pressed she wondered if he'd just put it on. If he kept one hanging in a bag nearby for occasions such as these. "Bert Thomas," he said, extending a smooth, pale hand in Fabiola's direction. "I'm so sorry for your loss."

His handshake was limp, as if he himself hovered closer to the dead than the living. But his smile was warm and his voice soothing. She brushed a tear from her cheek. "Can I— can I see him?"

"Of course," Bert said. "Right this way. You can spend as much time as you'd like. Then we'll have some decisions to make."

Aron lowered the phone from his ear. "Do you want me to come with you?" he asked. She shook her head and tried to smile to let him know it was nothing personal, but the corners of her mouth felt weighted down.

She followed Bert down a hallway into another, smaller living room. The walls were painted a dark, soothing green and the Persian rug felt thick and springy under her feet. Off to the side of the room sat a wheeled bed that resembled the one she'd seen her father in at the hospital. Her breath caught in her throat seeing him now.

Bert gave a small bow and backed toward the door. "I'll leave you alone," he said.

There he was, looking for all the world like he was sleeping. He wore his sneakers, the baggy jeans Vivi used to tease him about, and the tan windbreaker she'd bought him for Christmas. Fabiola wondered if he had been getting ready to leave when it happened, preparing to take the long subway ride from East Harlem down to Brooklyn. She wondered how many times he'd made that trip since she'd moved there. At least once a week for fourteen years—what would that make it? Numbers swam in her head as she approached him.

Up close it was clear he was no longer there in the body she knew so well. Though his face was arranged peacefully, the smile lacked the hint of a joke he always seemed to be on the verge of telling. For a split-second the room tilted and black spots began to fill her field of vision, then she took a deep breath and gripped the cold, metal rail of the bed.

"Hi, Papa," she whispered. He remained silent, unmoving. "Please don't leave me," she said, the tears breaking free. "Please."

She pulled a chair up next to the bed. At first, she was afraid to touch him, scared his skin would feel cold and clammy. But once she got up the nerve to take his hand, she found it still felt like his, the smoothness of his palms contrasting with the dry, roughness of his fingers.

How long she sat like that, her tears flowing unchecked, she had no idea. But no one bothered her. Finally, she ran dry and a sleepy peace overtook her. Her eyelids drooped and she forced herself to stand and stretch before she slumped over in the bed next to him. Tasks began to organize themselves in her mind, her brain defaulting to years of being wired that way. She'd need to cancel her clients for a while—a week? Two weeks? Two years? How long did grief take?

She pulled out her phone to email Hayley. She'd start with a week and then see where things were. Several new emails sat in her inbox but one jumped out at her. Sent from Dr. Acharya's office, the subject read **You Have New Lab Results**. For a second her thumb hovered over it, then she quickly scrolled past it and opened a new email to Hayley.

TWENTY-SEVEN

The next few days passed in a haze. The funeral was scheduled for Thursday and Fabiola was quickly overwhelmed by the number of decisions that needed to be made, and also the expense of everything. Death, it turned out, was not cheap.

Alice, having dismissed Fabiola's flimsy assurances that she didn't need any help, showed up Monday morning bearing two huge bags of food from Citarella. "I took the day off," she said, "so don't even try to send me away because I have nothing else to do." She strode into the kitchen and began unloading bagels, a tray of lasagna, and a bag of Tate's cookies. Seeing the distinctive green packaging, Fabiola burst into tears. "Oh, honey," Alice said, opening her arms. "Come here."

Tate's cookies had been a staple in Alice's pantry growing up, an after-school treat Fabiola had been unable to resist even during her brief diet phase in high school. When Alice had shown up to move-in day at Vassar with a small suitcase full of the green packages, Fabiola had teased her that they also had grocery stores in Poughkeepsie.

Alice offered to stay with the kids while Fabiola and Aron

went back to the funeral home. "Don't worry about anything here," she said. "We'll be fine, right, guys?" She turned to smile at the twins who'd stumbled into the kitchen seeking breakfast. They looked from the Tate's bag back to Alice, unsure whether to be excited or terrified. The last time Alice had watched them they'd been forced to clean their rooms, but she'd also proven to be excellent at Minecraft.

"Can I come with you?" Vivi appeared in the kitchen.

"Hi, sweetie," Fabiola said, surprised. "I didn't realize you were awake."

Vivi had changed out of her pajamas into flannel pants and a top that also looked like pajamas, but Fabiola knew better than to voice this. She ran to Fabiola and wrapped her arms around her waist like she'd done when she was small. "Please?" she said. "I'll bring a book and just read or something. I won't bother anyone, I promise."

When Fabiola looked down, she was surprised to see her daughter's eyes were filled with tears. "OK," she said, swayed by Vivi's uncharacteristic display of physical affection. It had been months since Vivi had hugged her voluntarily, a fact that felt like a sharp puncture to the heart if Fabiola stopped too long to contemplate it. "Sure, you can come." Vivi rewarded her with another squeeze around the waist and allowed Fabiola to kiss her hair.

"Hey, no fair!" Liam said.

"Yeah, I want to go, too." Ben crossed his arms over his wrinkled Avengers T-shirt.

"We'll be back as soon as we can," Fabiola said to them.

"And we're going to have more fun here anyway," Alice said, herding them toward the living room. "You can teach me how to play Donkey Kong, or whatever."

"Can you sit in the backseat with me?" Vivi asked as they walked out to the car.

"Sure, sweetie." Fabiola tousled her daughter's hair, touched by her newfound clinginess.

They rode in silence until Aron merged on to the FDR. "Did you get to see him?" Vivi asked in a low voice.

Fabiola turned her head from where she'd been staring into space out the window. "Yes." She nodded.

"What did he look like?"

Fabiola paused, considering. "He looked peaceful. But also like he was, you know, gone. Does that make sense?"

Vivi nodded and sat back in her seat. Fabiola's phone dinged and she looked down to see a text from Peter.

I'm at the hospital today but call if you need anything. If I don't answer call the main switchboard and they'll find me. I'm serious. I'll drop everything.

Thanks.

I can't believe he's gone.

Me either.

She rubbed the sudden tears from her eyes and felt a pang as she remembered the DNA test results, still unopened in her inbox. It was the last thing she could deal with right now. Her phone buzzed and she looked back down at Peter's reply.

He loved you so much.

He loved you, too.

Remember Medieval Times?

Ugh, I wish I could forget it.

She smiled, remembering their outing to the themed restaurant in New Jersey that featured a live jousting show with knights in armor and whole turkey legs that could be waved around by the spectators. It was the one thing Peter had wanted to do for his thirteenth birthday, but his parents refused, calling it "déclassé" and instead getting a box for him and his friends at Madison Square Garden for a Knicks game. The next weekend Leonard had borrowed a car from a friend and driven Peter and Fabiola to Lyndhurst, New Jersey for an afternoon at Medieval Times. They'd laughed, cheered themselves hoarse during the entertainment, and then had all gotten food poisoning on the way home, with Leonard pulling over every ten minutes for one or all of them to throw up.

"You OK?" Aron looked at her in the rearview mirror, puzzled at her smile.

"I'm fine," she said, blinking back the tears.

Once back inside the hushed, floral-scented funeral home, Bert escorted them to a small conference room where various books containing pages of flower arrangements and coffin finishes were spread out on the table. Vivi had refused to be left alone in the anteroom, but, true to her words, she sat quietly in a chair in the corner reading *The Hate U Give* for her English class.

Fabiola's father had left no will or instructions, but she remembered him once mentioning that he'd never want to be left to rot in some box in the ground.

"Cremation," she said, when Bert inquired. The funeral director looked exactly as he had the day before, not a hair out of place and the creases in his suit pants as sharp as ever. Fabiola wondered if he simply stood in place and closed his eyes to sleep.

He nodded at her response and placed a little checkmark on the leather clipboard he was holding. Seeing the list in front of him comforted Fabiola. She pointed to it. "What's next?"

With each item Fabiola felt herself drifting further away from the terrible reality of why they were doing this planning in the first place. She was in her comfort zone, swaddled by task lists and logistical challenges. The mental labor of making dozens of small decisions about the funeral service kept Fabiola's mind occupied and her grief at bay. Food: tea and coffee service, assorted finger sandwiches, and cookie platter. She'd wanted Caribbean food, but no outside catering was allowed at the funeral home. Flowers: minimal and no lilies. Her father had hated the smell. Eulogy: Fabiola would make remarks and each of the grandchildren would do a short reading from something that reminded them of Leonard.

"And then there's the topic of music," Bert said. "Did your father have any favorite hymns?"

"Hymns?" Fabiola asked. "No." Her father had not been a religious man. They had gone to church on Christmas and Easter when her mother was around, walking the five blocks to St. Cecilia's. When it was just the two of them, though, they'd opted for popcorn and a movie on Christmas Eve instead of midnight mass. "No," she said again.

"Then any songs that had particular meaning to him?" Bert pressed. Fabiola drew a blank.

"I mean, he likes reggae, obviously," she said. "But beyond that I'm not sure..."

"He really liked the soundtrack to Grease," Vivi piped up from the corner. All three adults jumped, having forgotten she was there.

"That's right, he did." Fabiola smiled, now remembering. "Though I guess I never knew why." She wished now that she'd thought to ask him.

"He always said there was something, like, so American about it. Like he imagined maybe that was what high school was like here." Vivi laughed. "I told him no way." She shrugged. "And sometimes he'd put on Whitney Houston. 'Whatta set of pipes,' he always said." Vivi imitated Leonard's deep, slow voice and accent. Aron laughed.

"Whitney Houston?" Fabiola asked. "Really?"

Vivi nodded. "He loved that old movie, *The Bodyguard*. We'd watch it sometimes when you guys went out to dinner."

"You *did*?" Fabiola said. "Wait, isn't that rated R?"

Vivi shrugged. "Yeah, but, like, in the nineties. That's, like, PG today."

Fabiola felt a wave of sadness at these details about her father coming from her daughter. They were inconsequential, of course, but they were things she herself had never known about him. She squared her shoulders. "All right, so we'll do Grease, Whitney Houston and reggae for music."

Bert's eyebrows moved up almost imperceptibly. "Uh, that's rather... unconventional, but if you're sure..."

"We're sure," Aron said.

On the drive back to Brooklyn, wrested from her cocoon of planning, Fabiola felt the fog of grief closing back in around her. To keep it at bay she took out her phone and focused on calculating and recalculating the number of mourners they'd agreed on with Bert, double-checking the figures he'd quoted for food and chair rentals.

"Do you have any pictures of my grandma?" Vivi asked.

"What?" Fabiola jerked her head up from her phone.

"Pictures. Of my grandma." Vivi chewed the inside of her cheek. "I was wondering what she looks like."

Fabiola closed her eyes and pictured her mother. The image was fuzzy, but she could see long, dark hair, almond-shaped eyes and a beauty mark on her left cheek—or was it her right? "I don't want to talk about her," she said, reopening her eyes.

"But why not?" Vivi pressed. "I mean, I still have a grandmother out there. Don't I at least deserve—"

"She is not a grandmother." Fabiola turned to face her daughter in the backseat. Her voice had a hard edge to it. "A grandmother is someone who was a *mother* first."

"Fabi." Aron put his hand on her thigh and squeezed, in compassion or warning, she wasn't sure.

Fabiola ignored him and swallowed hard to stifle the ache she felt in her chest. He could never understand the cold, painful shock of waking up to find her mother gone—not once, but twice. "She was never a mother to me," she continued. "So, no, Vivi. You don't have a grandmother."

TWENTY-EIGHT

The day of the funeral was cold and windy and felt more like January than early April. While they were planning the service Fabiola had fretted about empty chairs, but it turned out her father had had a fuller life than she'd realized. During the service she'd stumbled through her eulogy, clenching her page of notes to keep her hands from trembling and avoiding looking at the enlarged photo of her father in the back of the room. It was one she'd taken at Christmas, catching him in a moment of relaxed joy as the kids opened their presents around him and the mound of wrapping paper on the floor grew.

She'd pinched the insides of her arms to keep from crying while the boys read passages from *The Giving Tree*, and the *Velveteen Rabbit*, books her father had read to them over and over. Then Vivi had plugged her phone into the speaker to play Whitney singing *I Will Always Love You*, and the non-denominational pastor wrapped things up by blessing her father's ashes and inviting everyone to stay to "celebrate Leonard Butler's life."

Fabiola exhaled, hoping the worst was over.

She was oddly hungry, and she had to pee, but before she

could make a move, she found the gravity of the room had shifted and people surged toward her. A gray-haired Jamaican man with rheumy eyes clasped her hand. She'd often seen him sitting on one of the stools in the luncheonette near her father's apartment, where his adult daughter, who worked handing out menus and taking orders, could keep an eye on him. "I'm sorry, love. Dat Leonard was a good mon," he said, his accent far thicker than her father's had been.

His daughter stood behind him, holding his elbow and tugging at the floral dress she'd worn for the occasion. "Leonard was always so sweet to my dad," she said to Fabiola, her accent more Queens than Caribbean. Her jaw gave small pulses as she worked at a wad of gum between her back teeth. "He'd talk soccer with him, sneak him tamarind balls even though I'd tell him not to, what with my dad's teeth and all." She wiped her eyes and patted Fabiola's hand. "I'm sorry for your loss."

Her father's chess friends were next, men he'd started playing against in Marcus Garvey Park over a decade ago. "Your father was a man of integrity," said one of them, a man with a graying Afro and a Hawaiian shirt despite the cold weather. "He never cheated. Not like some people." He glowered at the portly, red windbreaker-clad man next to him, who rolled his eyes.

"We're all gonna miss Leonard," windbreaker man said. "He was a class act." Fabiola nodded her thanks.

Reggae played in the background and the somber atmosphere lifted somewhat as people began to chat amongst themselves and fill their plates with the catered sandwiches and cookies on offer. Liz and Alice cut through the crowd gathering around Fabiola.

"You OK?" Alice asked, eyeing Leonard's chess friends like a mobster about to order a hit. "You don't have to talk to anyone if you don't want to," she said.

"It's OK." Fabiola nodded. "Really."

Liz handed her a plate of couscous salad and two miniature crab cakes.

"Oh, thank God," Fabiola said. "Is it weird that I'm starving?"

"It would be weird if you weren't," Alice said, eyeing her rounded stomach.

"Need anything else?" Liz asked.

"A stiff drink?" Fabiola suggested, smiling through her tears. "An escape hatch?"

"Ms. Fernandez Butler." She turned to see Mr. Flowers, the Dalton headmaster, in his signature tweed jacket, which he wore no matter the season. His hair, dark brown when she'd been a student, had long since turned white. Along with his beaky nose and glasses it gave him the look of a disapproving owl. Back in the day he'd never missed an opportunity to remind Fabiola that she was only at Dalton due to the school's generosity in waiving tuition for school employees—never mind the fact that she'd still had to apply and be accepted just like everyone else.

Still, she was touched he would take the time to come to her father's funeral. "I'm so sorry for your loss," he said now. "Leonard was an institution at Dalton. Everyone loved him." He motioned to the side of the room where Fabiola recognized several Dalton teachers standing together, some of whom raised a hand in shy greeting.

"Thank you," Fabiola said. Vivi had sidled over and stood next to her. The headmaster smiled at her.

"Vivian, yes?" he said. Vivi nodded. Fabiola pictured him flipping through some kind of file on Leonard in his town car on the way to the funeral, refreshing himself on Fabiola's name and the names of her children. His eyes flitted to the curve of Fabiola's stomach, then back to Vivi. "And it seems you're about to be a big sister. Congratulations."

"Oh, we're not keeping the baby," Vivi said. A strained

noise escaped the headmaster's throat. Fabiola elbowed her daughter. "What?" Vivi's face was a mask of innocence.

"Thank you for your kind words," Fabiola managed. "And for coming today." The headmaster shifted with discomfort, then nodded and backed away. "Vivi!" Fabiola hissed, but Vivi had dissolved into giggles.

"Oh my God, did you see his face?" she asked. Fabiola tried to glare at her daughter but instead gave a snort of laughter. She clapped her hand over her nose, which only made her laugh harder.

"I'm sorry, Mom," Vivi said, trying to keep a straight face. "I'm sad, really, I am."

"Me, too," Fabiola said, trying to compose herself. "So sad."

"Excuse me, ma'am?" Fabiola looked down to see a short, Latino looking man with a bike messenger vest holding an insulated bag. She smelled the jerk seasoning even before he opened the bag to reveal a large, clear plastic container of glistening chicken wings. "Where would you like this?"

"I'm sorry, I didn't order—"

"Right over there, please." Peter stepped up and pointed to the table where the rest of the food sat. Across the room Bert frowned at the container of forbidden "outside food."

"Are those—" Fabiola started to ask.

"Your dad's favorite jerk chicken wings? They are." Peter winked at her.

She shook her head, a smile spreading across her face. "Bert's going to kill you," she warned. Peter shrugged.

"For Leonard, that's a risk I'm willing to take."

Her eyes flooded with the tears she'd been working so hard to keep at bay. "Thank you," she said in a hoarse voice.

"Oh, Fabi," he said. He reached out to take her hand and her fingers tensed as she thought of the email from Dr. Acharya's office, still sitting unopened in her inbox. Overwhelmed by her sadness and the swirl of funeral logistics she'd had no energy to face it.

"Is everything OK?"

Fabiola dropped Peter's hand as Aron appeared at her side. "I think it's all just hitting me," she said, wiping the tears from her face with her sleeve. Aron nodded and took hold of her arm, his grip firm as he steered her away from Peter toward him.

"It's going to be OK," he said and tried to hug her close. But her body had gone rigid as if exposed to the cold. A shiver swept down her spine and the hairs on her forearms stood as if the barometric pressure had dropped. The murmur of voices in the room faded into a tuneless static sound and her field of vision narrowed.

There, standing across the room next to the photograph of her dad, was her mother.

TWENTY-NINE

When Fabiola didn't yield to Aron's embrace, he turned his head to follow her gaze across the room. "Oh my God," he said, his voice low and stunned.

Though she couldn't possibly have heard Aron over the music and chatter, Fabiola's mother turned toward them. She was shorter than Fabiola remembered, and rounded through the hips and bottom in the same way Fabiola was. She stood erect, her narrow shoulders squared as if balancing an invisible crown on her head. Her hair, the same burnt cinnamon color as Fabiola's, hung thick and heavy past her shoulders. In a sea of dark, muted clothing her scarlet dress stood out like a warning flare.

"Mom?" Fabiola heard her voice as though someone else had spoken. Her mother glided toward her like a boat on calm water and Fabiola found herself face to face with her own strong brow and high cheekbones. Up close there were fine lines around her mother's eyes and mouth, but her tawny skin was otherwise plump with no signs of sagging. How old must she be? She'd been a year older than Fabiola's father, a running joke between them about his "older woman" so that would make her fifty-seven? Fifty-eight?

"Fabi." Her mother's eyes filled with tears, and she stretched her arms toward Fabiola. "Querida."

"No." Fabiola stepped back in a sharp motion, jostling the people behind her. "Don't." Aron put his hand on her shoulder like a buttress holding her upright. In her peripheral vision Liz and Alice appeared, closing ranks around her.

Hurt flickered across her mother's face, but it was quickly replaced by a placid, closed-off expression, like the deep, cold water surrounding an iceberg. Her eyes moved to Vivi, who stood next to Fabiola, her mouth agape. "And you must be Vivian," she said, smiling.

Vivi blinked. "Are you my grandmother?"

Fabiola's mother laughed, a tinkling sound that stirred a frisson of pleasurable recognition deep inside Fabiola. "Yes, I am. And you have no idea how wonderful it is to finally meet you. Your brothers, they're here?"

Vivi nodded. "Over there." She pointed to the corner of the room where Ben and Liam, bored and uncomfortable in the new dress shirts Aron had made them wear, were tossing cubes of cheese into the air to see who could catch them in their mouth.

"Ben, Liam," Aron said sharply. "Come here." The boys froze and cast guilty looks at each other.

"Sorry, Dad," Liam said as they shuffled over. "We'll knock it off."

"Boys," Aron said, putting a hand on each of their shoulders, "this is your grandmother." His voice was stilted, like he was onstage and had forgotten his lines.

Liam's eyes widened. "Whoa," he said.

Ben's eyes, in contrast, narrowed as he regarded the strange woman before him. "How come we've never, like, met you?" he asked.

"That's a great question," Fabiola said, her voice tight. Aron brought his hand up to squeeze her shoulder and she shrugged it off.

Fabiola's mother continued to gaze at the twins as if she hadn't heard Fabiola. "What handsome grandsons I have," she said. "What strong young men you're becoming." Liam smiled and even Ben stood a little taller. Her head swiveled from her grandchildren to someone approaching on the other side of Fabiola. "And Peter," she said. "How nice to see you again." She extended her hand and Peter took it, clasping it briefly before letting go. As Peter gripped Paulina's hand he caught Fabiola's gaze, his face both protective and sympathetic.

"And you as well, Mrs. Fernandez."

Fabiola's mother clucked her tongue. "Call me Paulina, please. You always had such nice manners, even when you were a little boy. Didn't he always have nice manners?" She turned to Fabiola, who had grown light-headed from the competing waves of grief, fury, and a surprising sensation of longing that crashed over her.

"I need to sit down," she murmured, looking around for a chair.

Liz stepped forward and steered her toward a nearby loveseat. "Are you OK?" she whispered.

Fabiola flinched as her mother followed her and sat down beside her. "I had no idea you were pregnant," her mother said softly, eyeing her belly. "I was always dizzy when I was carrying you." She smelled of damp earth and sandalwood, and an image of her leaning in to kiss Fabiola goodnight flashed though her mind.

Fabiola fixed her mother with an icy stare. "What are you doing here?"

"Attending my husband's funeral." Paulina straightened her shoulders.

Fabiola gave a bitter laugh. "Your husband? Who you last saw, what, twenty years ago?" The crowd in the room had grown thin now that late afternoon had given way to evening, and most of the people who remained were being gently escorted to the door by Bert. Alice had taken the twins to the other side of the room and was showing them something on her phone, and Liz stood a respectable distance from the loveseat, her eyes trained on Paulina as if ready to dive in front of Fabiola and shield her with her body at a moment's notice.

Paulina gave a small shrug. "He was still my husband, all that time."

Tears blurred Fabiola's vision. "How dare you come here?"

Paulina stiffened. "But I thought you wanted—" Her eyes strayed to Aron, who watched them with a stricken look. "Ah," she said, nodding slowly. "I see. It seems I misunderstood." She rose from the loveseat, regal in her movements. "I'll leave you." She took a step toward the door, her gaze sweeping around the room at the twins, Vivi, and then back to Fabiola. "I know you don't want to, but I really hope we can talk someday," she said with a sad smile.

"That," Fabiola said, "will never happen."

THIRTY

Liz rushed to her side the minute Paulina walked out. "Are you OK?" she asked, scanning Fabiola's body as if checking for bruises and abrasions. "What was she doing here?"

"I think I might know," Fabiola muttered, casting a dark look at Aron, who would not meet her gaze. She closed her eyes and leaned back against the loveseat as exhaustion enveloped her. "I just want to go home."

"Of course." Liz jumped up and returned with a pile of jackets and began doling them out to Fabiola, Aron, and the twins. Then she stood holding the puffy lavender North Face jacket Vivi hadn't wanted to wear. "Has anyone seen Vivi?" she asked.

"I'll check the bathroom," Alice said. The rest of them filed out into the funeral home lobby, trailed by Bert whose sympathetic smile hadn't faltered the entire afternoon. As they stood waiting, Vivi came in through the front door, her arms wrapped around her to ward off the chill.

"Vivi, where were you?" asked Aron, annoyed. "We're ready to go."

"I was outside waiting for you," Vivi said, shifting her eyes away from his.

Liz and Alice hustled them outside to the car like body-guards. Liz squeezed Fabiola's hand as she climbed into the passenger seat. "Call me," she said. Fabiola nodded.

She closed her eyes as Aron pulled out onto Madison Avenue and then made a left on 79th street. Her body ached as though she'd been in a car accident, which, she supposed, was an apt metaphor for her mother. They rode in silence all the way to Brooklyn, and once home the twins and Vivi filed word-lessly off to their rooms. Fabiola knew she should go to them; that they were grieving, too. This was the first funeral any of them had ever been to. But right now, she was in too much pain to mother anyone. With an ache she realized she longed for someone to mother her. Without removing her jacket, she walked upstairs and climbed into bed, pulling the comforter up to her eyes.

Aron followed her and stood a safe distance from the bed, shifting on his feet. He cleared his throat. "Fabi, I'm so sorry."

"Did you invite her?" she asked, refusing to look at him.

"No." He held up his hands. "Absolutely not. But I... called her."

Fabiola remembered the phone number on the birthday card from her mother, written in small, tidy printing so the numbers couldn't be mistaken.

"But I threw the card away," she said. Aron stared at the floor with a guilty expression.

"I kept it," he said. "I worried you might regret it, that you might want to get in touch with her after all and, well, then when Leonard... I thought she deserved to know, you know?"

Fabiola shivered, whether from cold or fury she wasn't sure. "She doesn't deserve anything."

He took a tentative step toward the bed. "But I didn't invite her. I didn't even mention the funeral."

Fabiola pressed her lips together. It didn't take a genius to search for Leonard's name online and find the funeral service information. And now the genie was out of the bottle. Her mother was back. She'd taken Fabiola's hand in hers and triggered a slew of memories Fabiola had worked for years to forget. She'd seen that Fabiola was pregnant. She'd met her children, for God's sake. None of this could be undone.

"You had no right," she whispered. She wanted to yell, to break things, to fly at Aron and smash her fists into him. How could he stand there comforting her at the funeral, his hand on her back, the murmured inquiries of "Are you OK?" at regular intervals, when all the while he'd betrayed her by calling her mother. Her mother, the one person in the world she despised—something he was well aware of.

She felt all her pent-up resentment of him boiling to the surface. She hated the way he blindly followed his interests; triathlons, brewing beer, the pickle ball league he kept insisting she'd love if she just gave it a chance, oblivious that the space and time he used to pursue these things was furnished by her—by the laundry she folded while he sat next to her on the couch, researching hops and malt extract, and the lunches she packed in the morning while he ran laps in Prospect Park. If she'd been able to spend less time making sure the kids did their homework, remembering which soccer uniforms needed to be clean for which days, staying on top of summer camp registration, and all the other things she did while carrying the entire mental load of their relationship, she might have had more energy to make sure her dad was staying healthy. That he was doing everything the doctor had told him to do, eating the way he was supposed to be. If she'd been paying attention—been there to support him more—maybe he'd still be alive.

All these things ran through her head, her rage sizzling like drops of water on a hot skillet, as she cast around for something that would pierce the bubble of Aron's inflated sense of self, the perfect poison dart to cut him down.

"I slept with Peter," she said, raising her head to look at her husband dead on. The color drained from his face, and all at once she saw her life for what it was: nothing more than a pile of tinder; her words a match she'd just tossed at it.

Panic rushed in like a cold rain, squelching her fury. What had she done? The hormones must be getting to her—or the stress or the grief or the guilt or the sheer overwhelming too-much of it all. She'd wanted to wound Aron, not slash and burn her own life to the ground. She'd already lost her father; she wasn't ready to lose anything else. Not yet.

"When?" Aron asked. His voice was calm, but he gripped the dresser to steady himself.

"Back in high school," she backtracked, to toss a bucket of water on the flames she'd just stoked. But the guilt and confusion still burned her up inside. She thought again of the unopened test results, of the possibility she hadn't yet fully let herself consider.

"You told me there was nothing between you," he said, his voice faltering. "That there was never anything. You *swore*."

"You always seemed so insecure around him," she said, her body suddenly heavy with exhaustion. She didn't have the energy for this conversation, not right now. "I didn't want to make it worse." This was true. She'd always known it was too complicated, that it would drive an unnecessary wedge between them. And having to explain it to Aron the way she was now, as a meaningless teenage fling, would cheapen what she and Peter had—then and now. Plus, Aron would inevitably have questions about what Peter meant to her now, how she felt about him. Questions she couldn't answer. She wished desperately that she could make up her mind about her feelings for Peter, but she was as uncertain as ever.

"Does Liz know?" Aron asked.

Fabiola nodded. Liz knew most of it, anyway. When she'd met Peter at Aron and Fabiola's wedding, she'd asked Fabiola about their history before agreeing to a date with him.

"Oh, Peter and I kind of had a thing a long time ago," Fabiola had said, a painful fault line cracking open on her heart. "We were just kids. It's ancient history."

"So I'm the only one who didn't know?" Aron asked now, gripping the bedpost. Fabiola was sweating, still in her jacket under the comforter. She never usually sweated; her hormones were definitely out of whack. Everything was.

"I'm sorry," she said, wishing she could close her eyes and sleep for days. "It seemed easier that way."

Her mind wandered back in time four years, to the day before Peter proposed to Liz. Fabiola had recognized the panic and self-doubt in his voice when he called her.

"Can you come?" he'd asked. Her pulse quickened. He hadn't called her like this since she'd married Aron nearly nine years earlier. She'd thought they were done. She'd meant to be done.

Checking her watch, she'd seen she had an hour before she needed to pick the twins up from their half-day preschool. Peter was pacing his apartment when she arrived, which was still furnished with the leather and dark wood furniture of his bachelor days. "I can't do this," he said. "She's too good for me. And I'm not cut out for this. I'll be a terrible husband."

"She's definitely too good for you," Fabiola had agreed, trying to make him laugh. "But she loves you and you love her, which is as good a reason as any for getting married."

"No," he said, sounding resigned. "Marriage isn't for people like me."

"You have to stop that." Her voice was firm. "Stop acting like you're broken. Plenty of people with fucked up parents get married. I mean, look at me." She put her hands on her hips.

"My mom didn't even love me enough to stick around. But I still get to be happy." And at that time she was.

His expression had softened as he stepped closer to her. Moving in slow motion, he put his hands on either side of her face, cradling her cheeks. "You're so strong, Fabi." His voice was hoarse. "And you're so... good. Why do you even put up with me?"

"Peter," she'd said, starting to protest, but then he'd kissed her, and she hadn't wanted him to stop.

She'd known it was wrong, of course. She was married, for God's sake, and he was about to be—to one of her best friends. But it was just a kiss. And it was Peter. Her Peter. The boy she'd grown up with, the one who knew her better than anyone. And together they existed in an alternate plane that had nothing to do with anyone else.

Now, her eyes shifted back to Aron, who'd been standing, quiet, for a long time, hands still gripping the dresser. She could almost see the gears turning in his head, the scales of justice balancing. "Was it really just the one time?" he asked.

"Yes," she lied, feeling sick to her stomach. What had she done? There was no way to ever make this right.

His jaw tightened. "Well, you certainly picked a great time to tell me. Right after your dad's funeral so I don't even get to be mad at you."

"You can be mad at me." She shrugged and gave him a sad smile. She deserved the worst.

He held her gaze, the anger on his face softening. "Let's take it a day at a time, OK? Just promise me no more lies."

She nodded and pulled the covers tighter around her, the sick feeling threatening to consume her. "No more lies."

THIRTY-ONE

"How are you?" Alice asked. She asked with such tenderness that Fabiola wanted to lay her head down onto the table and sob. Around them the restaurant buzzed with the usual Sunday morning crowd. Liz was running uncharacteristically late, but Alice had intimidated the hostess into seating them anyway.

"I'm OK." Fabiola shrugged. "Still nauseous a lot of the time, if you can believe it." She gestured to her plate of dry toast. "I mean, I'm twenty-two weeks, well into the second trimester. I should be feeling great. It was never like this with Vivi or the boys. I always felt good, even right up until the end."

"I remember," Alice said, stirring her cappuccino and then licking the foam off the spoon. "You were, like, radiant and glowing all the time, like you were playing a pregnant woman on a prenatal vitamin commercial or something." She rolled her eyes.

Fabiola raised an eyebrow. "Are you saying I'm not glowing right now?" She already knew the answer. She saw her own reflection every day, the bags under her eyes and her dull, dry skin. Along with the nausea, it was like the baby was punishing her. Her stomach lurched as she thought about the unopened

DNA test results. Fabiola stared at the unopened email, her finger hovering over the screen, paralyzed. It was the definition of Pandora's box—something she both desperately wanted and feared to open.

The test results inside would unravel everything. If the baby wasn't hers, she would have to hand it over to Liz and Peter, knowing it would be raised by the man she still loved in so many ways. But if the baby *was* hers, the consequences were even worse. What was she supposed to do? Keep the secret forever, watching her own child grow up in another woman's arms? It was unthinkable. Or tell the truth, knowing it would shatter her friendship with Liz and likely her own marriage. Either way, her world would never be the same.

Every day, she promised herself that today would be the day she'd finally look at the test results. And every day, she found herself paralyzed by the impossibility of any scenario they could reveal. And so, every day she gave herself over to grief and exhaustion and allowed herself to do nothing.

Alice gave her a sympathetic smile. "You look tired, Fabi. I'm worried about you. Liz and I both are. I know it's only been a couple of months since your dad—"

"It's been seven weeks and two days since the funeral."

"Yes, and since then I've barely even talked to you." Alice twisted her mug in her hands. "You don't answer my calls or my offers to come by to help with the kids. Liz says it's the same with her. I know this must be awful, Fabi, but we're your best friends. We want to be there for you."

Alice looked truly distressed, and Fabiola was caught off guard by the display of emotion from her usually flippant friend. Fabiola buried her face in her hands as tears filled her eyes. The truth was, she *had* been avoiding her friends. She'd been avoiding anyone she didn't expressly have to interact with, like her clients or her children. She'd been spending her days trying to outrun a fog of grief, staying mere inches ahead of it thanks to the frenetic pace of her work and the end of the school year crush with the kids; Spirit Days that necessitated last minute silly hats or socks, Field Day where she was expected to spend a Tuesday morning cheering for the boys as they ran relay races and drank Gatorade, the Thursday night production of *Into the Woods* that Vivi had helped paint scenery for. Liz and Alice, she knew, would force her to sit still and talk about how she was feeling, which was the last thing she wanted to do. Because it wasn't only grief she was trying to outrun, it was also guilt.

Now, though, as she peeked through her fingers at Alice's concerned eyes boring into her across the table, Fabiola felt her defenses faltering.

"I told Aron about Peter," she said. Alice's eyes widened in disbelief.

"God, Fabi, he still didn't know? After all these years?"

Fabiola lifted her head. "I told you I wasn't going to tell him."

"Yeah, like thirteen years ago when you got married. I figured it had come up by now." Alice exhaled a sharp puff of air. "Seriously, Fabi?"

Fabiola sighed and slumped in her chair. "You don't know Aron like I do. He's already jealous of Peter without adding all that on. Anyway, telling him did not go well." She'd felt forgiven initially, like they'd been given a fresh start, never mind the part she'd left out, the huge lie that still existed between them. But then as the weeks passed and put distance between her father's death and their day-to-day existence, she'd felt Aron pull away and recede back into his work.

Alice crossed her arms and cleared her throat. "Perhaps it didn't go well because you lied for over a decade about sleeping with the man whose baby you're now growing inside you." Her lips were pressed together in a thin line.

"Perhaps," Fabiola said with a feeble smile. She felt small

and weak in the face of Alice's judgment, like a vase with a hair-line crack in it, afraid one wrong move would shatter her. What would Alice think if she told her what had happened with Peter all those weeks ago in her kitchen? She repressed a shudder as she imagined her friend's reaction.

"I'm so sorry I'm late!" Liz rushed up to their table and slid into the booth next to Fabiola, her hair pulled back into a perky ponytail, but her eyes looking tired.

"Is everything OK?" Alice asked. "I mean, Liz Connelly, late? Was there an earthquake down in Tribeca? A global financial crisis? An Uber strike?"

Liz laughed, then her face fell. "I wish," she said.

"Hey, honey, what's wrong?" Fabiola reached over to give Liz's arm a gentle squeeze.

Liz pressed her lips together. "Just a stupid fight with Peter," she said. "Not even worth talking about." She blinked rapidly and tried to smile.

"Um, no," Alice said. "You don't get to do that with us. Spill it."

Liz put her fingers to her temples. "I feel silly talking about it. In the grand scheme of everything it doesn't even compare to what you're going through." She looked at Fabiola.

"Believe me," Fabiola said. "I'm really sick of thinking about everything I'm going through." Her father's face flashed through her mind, followed by the unopened lab results email.

"We're just both stressed right now. Working too much, the same old story." She gave a firm shake of her head. "It's fine, really." She took a sip of water. "Anyway, sorry again to be late. What did I miss?"

Alice gave Fabiola a quick glance, her face twitching almost imperceptibly. Then she turned to Liz. "You didn't miss a thing."

THIRTY-TWO

"Are you OK?" Hayley asked. They were seated at their usual coffee shop where Hayley had been walking Fabiola through the mechanics of the online store she'd finally convinced her to open on their website. They were starting small, partnering with a Brooklyn-based start-up that made organic cleaning products and room sprays, but Hayley had visions of adding things like ethically sourced woven storage baskets, bamboo shoe racks, and organic cotton tote bags.

Fabiola rubbed her abdomen and smoothed the grimace from her face. "Fine, sorry. Just a cramp, I think."

Hayley's eyebrows shot up in alarm. "Is it the baby? Do you need to go to the hospital?"

Fabiola smiled at the younger woman's concern. "No, it's just a Braxton Hicks contraction, it's fine. I've had them before."

The worried look on Hayley's face deepened. "A contraction? Oh my God, who should I call? Like, an ambulance?"

Fabiola held up her hand. "No, seriously, it's fine. It's false labor—Braxton Hicks, it's called. Lots of women get them for weeks, sometimes months, before actually going into labor. I had them in the second trimester with both my other pregnancies. It can hurt but it doesn't mean anything is wrong."

Hayley looked skeptical. "So, you're just, like, practicing being in pain before you go into labor and actually are in pain."

"Well, yeah, I guess."

"Crazy." Hayley shook her head. "No offense but being pregnant sounds awful."

Fabiola started to say no, that being pregnant was an amazing experience, that there was no greater honor than nurturing the miracle of a new life inside her own body. Except that this particular pregnancy was not amazing. While it was still thrilling to feel the baby's movements inside her, she was plagued by nausea, heartburn, and a cloud of guilt that followed her everywhere. This morning she'd stood in the shower staring down at her now undisguisable bump and thinking about the day she told Liz she'd be her surrogate. She'd felt like a different person then.

Then there was the email with the test results she still hadn't opened. It sat there in her inbox like a bomb ready to detonate. At first, she'd been desperate to confirm what her body suspected. Then reality set in: there was no scenario in which she'd escape unscathed. Viewing the results would either shatter her heart or blow her entire life up. She wasn't ready for either.

She focused back on Hayley and the laptop. "The store looks great, Hayley. You've done a fantastic job with the website, the branding, everything. Thank you." Hayley beamed. In January Fabiola had bumped her up to full-time, which meant they could now accommodate more clients. But this also meant that Hayley was juggling client work with all the assistant duties she'd been hired for—answering emails, scheduling appointments, and updating the website and social media. Fabiola leaned toward Hayley. "Look, I know it's a lot, everything you're balancing. I really hope maybe by the fall we can afford to hire someone else to take some of the administrative stuff off your shoulders."

"That would be ah-mazing," Hayley said. "Maybe then we could talk about the whole capsule wardrobe consulting line as a natural brand extension."

"Sure." Fabiola nodded. While it was exhausting to try and keep up with all Hayley's ideas, she had to admit that most of them so far had been good ones. She just wished there was someone else around to execute them. She checked her watch. "Hey, I'm sorry, I have to head out to pick Liam and Ben up from practice."

"No problem." Hayley saluted her. "See you tomorrow."

Despite Aron's promise to be home by six-thirty, by six forty-five he still wasn't there. She stood in front of the fridge, staring blankly at the leftovers, her mind wandering back to her confession about having slept with Peter. A knot of regret tightened in her chest. Why hadn't she just laid it all out on the table? She was exhausted from tiptoeing around Aron's feelings, trying to downplay what Peter had meant to her—what he still meant to her. But how could she tell Aron that the old flame she thought had burned out had suddenly roared back to life? What would that do to their marriage? Not to mention to Liz and Peter. Fabiola knew they'd been arguing more than usual lately —was that her fault, too?

Her thoughts swirled as she reheated two-day-old spaghetti and called the kids to the table, all the while trying to ignore the dull ache in her heart that appeared every Monday night. Because every week she still held out a tiny, irrational hope that the doorbell would ring, and there on the doorstep would be her father, a bag of tamarind balls in one hand and a box of black and white cookies in the other.

"How was soccer?" she asked the twins once they were all seated, willing the tears to leave her eyes.

"Liam had to run extra laps because he was talking to his

girlfriend during warmups," Ben replied, his mouth full of noodles. Liam's face turned a deep scarlet.

"Dude, she's not my girlfriend."

"Whatever." Ben rolled his eyes. "But he had to run extra laps."

"Anyone I know?" Fabiola asked, trying to sound casual. Her heart clenched as she thought of how the boys' eyelids had fluttered in their sleep when she used to stand over their cribs watching them. How could those sweet babies be talking about girls?

"No," Liam said.

"Olive Hopkins," Ben said at the same time.

"Isn't that Izzy's little sister?" Fabiola turned to Vivi. Vivi nodded, keeping her eyes fixed on her plate.

"She's *not* my girlfriend," Liam said, stabbing a meatball with his fork.

Fabiola nodded. "Speaking of Izzy," she said, focused on Vivi. "I have to send in the final payment for Camp Timberlake this week. I know you, Harper, and Izzy have always requested the same cabin, but I wasn't sure if this year..." Fabiola trailed off and Vivi stared at her as if she'd begun babbling in Klingon.

"I'm not going to camp this summer, obviously," Vivi said. For the past three summers she'd spent a month upstate at Camp Timberlake with Harper and Izzy, learning to construct baskets out of birchbark, identify poison ivy, and many other skills that were irrelevant to a Brooklyn teenager the other eleven months of the year.

"Yes, you are," Fabiola said. "We've already paid for most of it."

"You can't make me." Though Vivi's voice was calm she had rolled her napkin into a tight coil between her fingers.

"Can't make you what?" Aron breezed into the room and planted a kiss on the top of Fabiola's head before ruffling the twins' hair.

"Go to camp." Vivi crossed her arms.

"But you love camp." Aron frowned as he slid into his seat. "Leftovers again?" he asked Fabiola, eyeing his plate.

"I said I'm not going." Vivi's voice rose.

Fabiola placed a hand on her belly as if to protect the baby from her daughter's wrath and tried the logical tack. "Vivi, it's a lot of money that we can't get back."

"So?" Vivi glared at her. "Dad says we're going to be rich soon anyway."

Aron held up his hands, but he was smiling. "Whoa now, don't blame this on me."

"Well, are we, or aren't we?" she asked.

"Are we what?" Aron asked.

"Going to be rich." Vivi rolled her eyes as if she couldn't bear her parents' stupidity.

"Well, nothing is guaranteed," Aron said, still smiling as if he'd just been gifted the secret recipe for Coca Cola. "But I'd say that yes, our financial situation will be changing. Soon."

"So, see?" Vivi gestured to Fabiola. "The money doesn't matter."

"Being rich doesn't mean you get to waste money," Fabiola said, wishing Aron wouldn't get the kids' hopes up like this. "Especially if you're not rich *yet*." She cast a dark look at Aron who was loading his plate with sweet and sour pork.

"As always, thanks for your vote of confidence, Fabi," he shot back, narrowing his eyes. They glared at each other.

"Can I get a go-kart when we're rich?" Ben asked.

"And can we go to Antarctica?" Liam chimed in. "I want to ride a polar bear."

"They don't live in Antarctica, stupid," Ben said. "They live at the North Pole. And you couldn't ride it, it would just eat you."

"Don't say stupid," Aron said.

"Well, it would never eat you because you'd taste like BO," Liam shot back.

"Well, you'd taste like—"

"Enough." Aron held up his hand. "Give me a break, guys." He pinched the bridge of his nose. "It's been a long day."

"You're going to camp, end of story." Fabiola stood up to clear her plate.

"No!" Vivi's voice was shrill and carried such a note of desperation that Fabiola sat back down.

"Sweetheart, what's wrong? Why don't you want to go?"

"I'm not, like, friends with Harper and Izzy anymore. It would be so weird to be there with them. Please don't make me go." Fabiola felt a sudden ache in her chest and wished she could wrap Vivi in her arms and rock her to sleep. Fourteen was so hard. She tried to beam compassion to her daughter with her gaze.

"Why aren't you friends anymore?" she asked.

Ben snickered. "Vivi doesn't have any friends," he said in a singsong voice.

"Shut up!" Vivi snapped. "I don't know, we're just not."

"Don't tell your brother to shut up," Aron said, but his heart wasn't in it.

"Well, tell him not to be so annoying." Vivi tossed her hair.

"OK, fine." Fabiola shrugged, defeated. "If your dad really isn't worried about the money"—she shot Aron a pointed look—"then you don't have to go." Vivi bounced in her seat and smiled. "But don't think you can just lie around the house all summer," Fabiola warned. "You have to do something productive. Get a job."

"A job?" Vivi wrinkled her nose. "I'm fourteen. Who's going to hire me?"

Fabiola paused to consider the question. "You know," she said. "I just might know someone who would."

THIRTY-THREE

When Fabiola came downstairs Vivi was already dressed and eating a bowl of cereal. Her daughter wore cutoff jean shorts, a white T-shirt and a long, oversized black blazer. Her hair was pulled back into a tidy bun. Fabiola blinked at her daughter's transformation from sulky teen to something closer to Gen Z power broker. The outfit looked so familiar. Then she realized where she'd seen it: Hayley had worn something nearly identical yesterday.

"No way am I spending the summer working for my mom," Vivi had insisted when Fabiola gave her the ultimatum of going to camp or working for her for the next ten weeks. Then Vivi had met Hayley. She'd listened with laser-like focus during their first meeting while Hayley taught her how to update the website and manage their shared calendar, hanging on her every word.

"Hayley is so cool," Vivi had said to Fabiola after her first day. "Why is she working for you?"

Now, two weeks later, school had let out and Vivi was handling their inbox, tracking orders from the online store, and even making her own suggestions about their social media.

"What about a before and after series?" she suggested, her head bent toward the computer where Hayley had Instagram pulled up. "Or some time lapse videos?"

"I love it!" Hayley said, and Vivi grinned wider than Fabiola had seen in a long time.

"You're up early," Fabiola said, popping a Nespresso pod into the coffee maker. Vivi shrugged, trying to hide her excitement. She was going along with Fabiola and Hayley on her first client engagement that day. "I've got to get the boys to soccer camp and then we'll head out, OK?"

Vivi nodded. "Hey, can I make a coffee?" she asked.

"Um, sure," Fabiola said. "But do you even like coffee?"

"Hayley said it's an acquired taste," Vivi said, getting her own mug out.

Fabiola fought back a smile. "Indeed."

Once her coffee was brewed Fabiola woke the boys and herded them into the kitchen for breakfast, then into their soccer gear. She had just gotten them out the front door when Aron jogged up, sweaty from his run.

"Have a great day, guys!" he said, high fiving them. To Fabiola he said, "You have their water bottles?"

"Of course," she said, annoyed. After all, she was the one who'd printed out the daily camp checklist and made sure their bags were packed with everything on the list.

"And sunscreen?"

"Yes," she snapped, pushing the boys forward toward the car.

Aron held up his hands. "I was just trying to help."

Fabiola spread her arms wide, gesturing to the boys and their bulky gear bags. "As you can see, everything's already been taken care of. Hope you had a good run." The snark in her voice made even her wince. But she was so tired of Aron's charade of helping, when really she took care of everything.

Aron had already left for work by the time she returned

from dropping off the boys. She and Vivi then took the subway to an apartment near Columbus Circle, where they were scheduled to meet Sheila Houser. Sheila had recently moved to the city from Scarsdale with her husband.

"The kids are all out of the house and settled," Sheila had explained during the intake call. "So Roger and I decided to sell the house and buy a place in the city. He's been commuting for years, and we thought it'd be fun to finally live in Manhattan again—go to shows, try new restaurants, walk in Central Park, all that. The problem is..." She hesitated. "I thought we'd downsized enough, but the apartment looked so much bigger without all our things in it! Now we can barely move because there's so much stuff everywhere. It's driving us both nuts, and I don't even know where to start."

Hayley was already there when they arrived, chatting with Sheila in the cramped kitchen, where an oversized dining table had been shoved into the corner, making it impossible to pull out the bar chairs at the high counter. Books were piled on the living room floor, and a china cabinet stood in front of the fireplace, blocking the bottom of the television mounted above it. "We didn't have anywhere else to put it," Sheila said, wringing her hands.

Fabiola nodded. "Don't worry," she said in a soothing tone. "It's a beautiful space. We just need to create some breathing room."

Hayley nodded. "Absolutely. Open up some space for you and Roger to start living the life you want."

Vivi trailed Hayley as she guided Sheila through the apartment, pausing at each piece of furniture and décor to hear its origin story and gauge Sheila's willingness to part with it. Fabiola hung back, snapping pictures and estimating how much Sheila could get for the table, china cabinet, and other items that would need to be sold to free up space. She was crouched down, moving a stack of books to get a better shot of the over-sized couch, when she felt it.

A sharp cramp in her abdomen was followed by a sudden wetness between her legs. A lot of wetness. Fabiola rushed to the bathroom, squeezing past a file cabinet wedged in the hall. Pulling down her pants, she saw a dark stain on her underwear, and when she sat on the toilet, the water turned bright red. Another cramp hit, stealing her breath, as the lights above the medicine cabinet began to blur.

"Vivi?" she called, pressing her hand against the wall to steady herself. "Vivi!" She used all her strength to call her daughter's name as black dots swam before her eyes

"Mom?"

"In here," Fabiola said weakly.

"Why are you in the—oh my God, Mom!" Vivi's voice sounded like it was coming from far away as Fabiola faded into blackness.

When she woke, the lights blinded her, and she threw an arm over her eyes, bumping something clamped to her face. Panicking, she tugged at the straps holding whatever it was in place.

"No," said a firm voice, bringing her hand back to her side. "You need to leave the oxygen mask on. We're almost there." A sharp turning motion jostled Fabiola and she realized she was in the back of an ambulance. Vivi crouched nearby.

"Hi, Mom." She waved. "Are you OK?" Her small face was creased with worry.

But before Fabiola could answer the vehicle came to a sharp stop and the back doors flew open. The stretcher she was on bumped down onto the pavement and Vivi ran alongside as two burly EMTs pushed her forward. A Mount Sinai sign flashed by and then she was inside.

"Female, thirty-six years old... twenty-five weeks pregnant...

loss of blood..." Voices swirled around her as people in scrubs and white coats hovered above her.

"Can I go with her?" Vivi asked as they continued to wheel her forward.

"The baby!" Fabiola cried, finally succeeding in ripping the oxygen mask from her face. "Is the baby OK?"

"Shh, we're going to get you checked out and taken care of," said a woman in pink scrubs. She had a soothing voice and Fabiola tried to focus on it as the lights flashing by above her blurred and blackness descended again.

THIRTY-FOUR

Fabiola fluttered her eyes open and saw Aron's face. "Hey there," he said, smiling. Fabiola inhaled the tang of antiseptic.

"I'm in the hospital," she said, confirming.

Aron nodded. "You were bleeding."

"Like, a *lot*." Vivi's voice came from the corner and Fabiola turned to see her daughter sitting on a chair, her knees curled into her chest.

"Vivi," Aron said sharply. "Not necessary. Everything's fine."

"The baby—" Fear caught in Fabiola's throat, and she raised herself up on her elbows to look down at her stomach.

"The baby's fine." Aron took her hand. "And more importantly, so are you."

Fabiola exhaled and flopped back against the pillow.

"Hello there." A tall, angular man with thinning hair and a white coat walked in. He held up a hand in greeting. "I'm Dr. McAllister," he said. "You gave us quite the scare."

"What happened?" Fabiola asked.

"Placenta previa," he said. "Did you have it with either of your other pregnancies?"

"No," Fabiola said. "What is it?"

The doctor took off his glasses and rubbed the bridge of his nose. "It's when the placenta covers the cervix. It can cause bleeding, as you experienced, along with pre-labor contractions."

"But the baby's OK?" Fabiola asked.

He replaced his glasses on his nose and nodded. "Baby is fine. And in the second trimester the placenta previa isn't something we need to be overly concerned about, provided it doesn't cause excessive bleeding or continued contractions. Often it corrects itself. However, it's something you'll want to keep an eye on with your doctor. If it persists then you would need a C-section."

"But everything's going to be OK?" Fabiola asked again.

"It should be, yes." The doctor nodded.

"Is this, like, a bedrest situation?" Aron asked, concern on his face.

"It shouldn't be, no," the doctor said. He looked at Fabiola. "We're going to keep you overnight for observation to ensure the bleeding and contractions have stopped, but I anticipate you'll be free to go tomorrow—provided you rest and minimize your stress."

"My stress?" Fabiola thought of her packed client schedule, strained marriage, and increasingly unhappy daughter. And of the unopened email that loomed in her inbox, becoming more unavoidable as the weeks ticked by. She wanted to laugh. "My stress," she repeated.

"Yes," the doctor said. "Get plenty of fluids and try to stay off your feet as much as possible the next couple of weeks. Assuming you're discharged tomorrow you should schedule a follow up with your doctor in a week."

Fabiola nodded.

"OK then." Dr. McAllister gave a kind of salute with his fingers. "I'll be back to check on you later."

"Liz and Peter are here, too," Aron said once the doctor had gone. "In the waiting room. I felt like I should let them know so I called them once you were stable."

A nurse with long braids and forest green scrubs breezed into the room. "Hi, mama," she said. "Let's see how you're doing." She pulled out a blood pressure cuff.

"I'll go get Liz and Peter," Aron said.

"Only two guests at a time," the nurse said, not looking up as she fastened the cuff around Fabiola's arm.

Aron hesitated. "OK, Vivi, let's go," he said. He leaned over and kissed the top of Fabiola's head. "We'll just be in the waiting room if you need us."

Liz appeared in the door seconds after the nurse finished her checks and left. Peter was close behind her. "Come on in." Fabiola waved, trying to sound energetic and healthy.

"Fabi." Liz rushed to her side. "How are you feeling?"

"I'm fine," Fabiola said with a weak smile. "And the baby's totally fine. I'm so sorry to scare you."

"I don't care about the baby!" Liz exclaimed. "I was so worried about you." Fabiola stared at her and Liz's face reddened. "I mean," she said, "of course I *care* about the baby, but you're the most important thing, obviously."

Peter lingered a step behind Liz, and Fabiola looked away quickly after glancing at him, aware of his eyes on her. There was something about the way he looked at her—intense, almost protective—that made the rest of the room fade into the background. The DNA test results flickered in her mind, and for an instant, she indulged in the fantasy she'd been mentally avoiding all this time—what if this baby were hers and Peter's? A testament to all they'd shared, wrapped in a tiny being with Peter's blue eyes and her tawny skin. The idea warmed her, offering a brief escape into a world where Peter was by her side, caring for her and the baby—his family—with the same unwavering loyalty and protection he had always shown her.

"What did the doctor say?" Liz asked, bringing Fabiola back to reality. "I kept asking them about you in the waiting room, but no one would tell me anything."

"I thought they were going to take out a restraining order on her," Peter said, tugging on the sleeve of his button-up shirt.

Liz shot him a glare. "I was *worried.*"

"Placenta previa," Fabiola said, and Liz immediately googled it, then looked up, alarmed.

Fabiola waved her hand. "I'm fine, really. I'm just supposed to rest, I guess." She stifled a yawn, suddenly exhausted. "But everything's OK."

"You have to promise you'll slow down." Liz's voice was firm.

Fabiola tried to smile but she was so tired. "Message received," she murmured. Her eyelids felt droopy.

"Let's go." Peter nudged Liz. "She needs to rest." He stepped forward and brushed his hand across Fabiola's forehead. "Take care of yourself, OK?" She nodded and slid into sleep.

A soft beep from one of the machines nudged her awake sometime later. She had no idea how long she'd been out, but her first instinct was to scan the room for Peter. When she realized she was alone, a sharp pang of guilt settled in her chest. Why was he the one she'd hoped to see?

She reached for her phone on the nightstand and pulled up the email from Dr. Acharya. She knew she should face it now—detonate the nuclear option and deal with the fallout, whatever it might be. But as she gripped the phone it buzzed with an incoming call from Alice.

"Fabi, oh my God, Liz just called me—are you OK?" Alice's voice was full of worry as Fabiola picked up the phone.

"I'm fine," Fabiola sighed, touched by her friend's concern. "It was just a blip, really."

"You need to slow down," Alice said.

"So I've heard," Fabiola replied wryly.

"No, seriously," Alice pressed. "Not like someone who thinks grocery shopping alone counts as a break." She made a disapproving sound. "I'm sending you my housecleaner."

"Alice, you don't have to—"

"Too late, I already texted her."

Fabiola let out a small laugh, her heart aching with gratitude. "Thank you."

They chatted for another minute until Alice's next patient arrived. After hanging up, Fabiola again found herself staring at the email with the DNA test results. Her finger hovered above the link. But then she pictured Aron's devastated face and Liz's anger. She set the phone back on the nightstand. Not yet. Not until she had a plan. It was too huge. She still had time.

THIRTY-FIVE

> I scheduled dinner delivery for the next two weeks.

You didn't have to do that, Fabiola replied to Liz. *But thank you.*

Now you don't have any excuse not to take it easy. And you better be texting me from bed, Liz wrote. Fabiola took a quick picture of her feet up on the couch and sent it. *OK fine,* Liz replied. *Next best thing. Xoxo*

Fabiola drummed her fingers on the coffee table before grabbing her laptop. It was ten a.m., the day after her overnight hospital stay, and she was already restless. Aron had dropped the boys at camp, and Vivi had only surfaced to make a cup of generously sweetened coffee, her new morning ritual, then disappeared upstairs. With the house spotless thanks to Alice's cleaner, Fabiola had no excuse but to stay put on the couch.

She pulled up her weekly calendar. She needed to discuss with Hayley how they'd manage while she "rested." Fortunately, they only had two clients booked, but Fabiola was also set to record an interview for a *New York Magazine* article on

"21 BIPOC-Owned Businesses That Make NYC Tick"—a huge opportunity, according to Hayley.

Her phone dinged and she tossed her laptop aside to pull up her texts.

> How are you feeling?

Her heart accelerated as she replied:

> I'm fine. Honestly.

> Did you know people who say "honestly" are usually lying?

She laughed.

> I promise I'm OK. Really.

Three dots appeared on her screen, and she wondered where Peter was as he typed. Was he working today? Maybe at home, just waking up after an overnight surgery? She imagined him in the bed she'd seen at their apartment, always perfectly made with a smooth, white comforter. Their apartment was full of white—the enormous orchid in the foyer, the Italian-made dining chairs. That would have to change once the baby arrived. A chill of dread shot through her, and she pressed her free hand to her round stomach.

Don't ever scare me like that again, he wrote. *Seriously. I don't know what I'd do without you.*

She blinked away thoughts of the baby and returned to the image of Peter in bed—stubble on his chin, hair tousled, sheets wrinkled, and the pillow scented with him. She inhaled, imagining him beside her, but all she smelled was the lingering scent of the toast Aron had burned earlier.

The house was quiet around her as she typed her response, then hit Send before she could take it back.

> Do you ever think about it?

> About...?

> You know.

She sucked in her breath as she waited for him to respond.

> What if I'm thinking about it right now?

A tingle of joy spread through her body and she rubbed her midsection.

The doorbell rang, snapping her out of her daydream. Vivi thundered down the stairs. "I'll get it!" she yelled. Fabiola hoisted herself up as Vivi dashed by. Moments later, Hayley appeared in the living room with Vivi close behind.

"Hiiii!" Hayley cried, stepping forward to wrap Fabiola in a hug. "Oh my God, how are you?"

"Hayley! What are you doing here?" Fabiola asked, confused, but delighted for the company. Hayley and Vivi exchanged a smile.

"Vivi invited me," Hayley said. "I wanted to check on you. Oh, and I brought sustenance. I know they're your fave." She held up the bag from Court Street Bagels.

Unexpected tears welled up in Fabiola's eyes. She was surrounded by such wonderful people. Her mind flashed to Peter's hands in her hair, her back pressed against the kitchen counter, and she shivered. She didn't deserve them. "Thank you," she said to Hayley. "You didn't have to do that."

"It's so cute in here!" Hayley sank into one of the armchairs and looked around the living room at the whitewashed molding, mid-century modern furniture, and vintage floral rug. "This would feature really well in a shoot. We should pitch that somewhere: Fabiola Fernandez Butler at home."

Fabiola laughed, pulling an everything bagel from the bag. Lately, no amount of carbs seemed enough to satisfy the baby. "I doubt anyone cares where I live."

"Not true," Hayley insisted. "You've developed quite the following!"

"Thanks to you." Fabiola raised her bagel in salute before tearing into it. "So," she said between bites, "since you're here, I have some ideas for handling the next couple of weeks until I'm back to full strength."

"Oh, don't worry, Mom," Vivi chimed in. "We've got it covered."

"What do you mean?" Fabiola raised an eyebrow.

Vivi straightened up. "Hayley and I made a plan." Fabiola turned to Hayley, who shrugged.

"It's true," Hayley said. "Vivi called me earlier, and we mapped it all out."

Vivi pulled out her phone and opened her Notes app. "I'm handling the wrap-up interviews from last week's clients," she said. "Hayley will do the first one with me, just in case."

"But she's totally got this," Hayley added, pumping her fist at Vivi, who gave a wide grin.

"Hayley's also leading the two client projects this week," Vivi continued. "She'll handle new client intakes, too—I've scheduled four so far. Oh, and I prepped this brief for your *New York Magazine* interview." She handed Fabiola a printout.

Fabiola scanned the well-organized bullet points on the podcast's history, the host's background, previous guests, and recent media mentions. "This is really good, Vivi," she said, looking up at her daughter. Vivi beamed.

"Thanks. Hayley gave me the format, but I did the rest."

"I should be there at the client sites." Fabiola turned to Hayley.

"You should be right there." Hayley pointed to the couch. "They're not big jobs. Vivi and I can handle them."

"You're taking Vivi with you?" Fabiola asked, glancing between them.

"She'll be a huge help," Hayley nodded. Vivi's smile grew even brighter.

Fabiola looked back at Vivi. "Sweetheart, could you grab the cream cheese from the fridge?" Vivi nodded and headed to the kitchen. "I don't expect you to babysit Vivi," Fabiola murmured to Hayley.

"She wants to help." Hayley shrugged. "And she's a fast learner."

Fabiola pressed her lips together. "She's also a moody fourteen-year-old girl."

Hayley laughed. "She's not that bad. Just trying to figure herself out. I get it—I was fourteen once, too."

"Here you go," Vivi said, holding up the cream cheese as she reentered the room.

Hayley's watch beeped. "I've gotta dash to my aerial yoga class," she said, turning to Vivi. "You should come sometime."

"Oh my God, like, for sure," Vivi gushed. Hayley winked at Fabiola.

"Thank you," Fabiola mouthed, holding her hands in a prayer position.

After Hayley left, Fabiola was surprised when Vivi stayed in the living room with her and had a bagel.

"Check out this reel I made of me organizing the pantry," Vivi said, showing a timelapse video on her phone. "Of course, I had to un-organize everything first to film it." She rolled her eyes. Fabiola kept the pantry meticulously organized with clear glass containers and handwritten labels. "But I thought it would be good for our Instagram."

Fabiola smiled at Vivi's use of the word "our." "It's great, sweetheart," she said.

"Hey, I'm up to date on our inbox, so can I go over to Layla's?" Vivi changed the subject. "I can just walk or take the bus."

Suppressing a sigh, Fabiola nodded. Layla seemed to be the only friend Vivi had around this summer. It was only late June, and Fabiola had already run out of excuses to keep Vivi from seeing her. Besides, all the parenting blogs warned that discouraging the friendship would only make Vivi more determined.

"Sure," Fabiola said, biting her lip. "But text me when you get there, OK? And remember, family dinner tonight." A sharp pang hit her as she mentioned this; Monday nights still felt empty without her father.

After Vivi left, Fabiola turned on the television and dozed on the couch, realizing maybe this slower pace wasn't so bad after all.

She woke to the doorbell ringing again. Wiping drool from her mouth, she struggled to her feet, her limbs heavy with sleep.

"Hello?" she said, opening the door. Standing there was a tall, sturdy blonde woman dressed in white, holding a folded-up contraption.

"I am Natasha," the woman said with a slight Eastern European accent. "I am here for prenatal massage service."

"Massage?" Fabiola rubbed the sleep from her eyes. "Sorry, I think you have the wrong—"

"It is a gift from—" the woman checked her phone, "—Mr. Peter Worthington."

Fabiola's face softened. "Peter," she repeated. "Of course." She glanced at her watch—one p.m. She didn't need to pick up the boys until four. She opened the door wider. "Come on in."

Fifteen minutes later, Fabiola slid onto the massage table Natasha had set up in her living room. Her phone rang just as

Natasha reentered the room. "Sorry," Fabiola said, embarrassed. "If you could hand it to me, I'll just—"

Natasha passed the phone to her. Fabiola was about to mute the call when she saw the caller ID: NYPD.

She swiped to answer. "Hello?" She sat up, clutching the sheet.

"Is this Vivian Butler's mother?" asked a voice.

"Yes." Fabiola's breath caught.

"Ma'am, we have your daughter."

THE PEDESTRIAN

THIRTY-SIX

The police station smelled like greasy takeout and cleaning spray, a combination that assaulted Fabiola's nose and roiled her stomach.

"I'm here for my daughter," she told the woman at the reception window who sat behind a panel of smudged plexiglass. "Vivian Butler."

The woman typed something into her computer. "Sit," she ordered, gesturing to a row of vinyl chairs in the hall. Once orange, they had faded to a dirty peach.

Fabiola's first reaction to the police call had been panic, imagining her daughter lifeless in a crosswalk or alley. But her panic quickly turned to rage when the officer explained why Vivi was at the station. Now, she lowered herself into one of the faded chairs, taking deep breaths to calm the stress coursing through her. She rubbed her stomach in small, gentle circles, trying to reassure the baby, *Everything's going to be OK.*

Aron hadn't answered any of her calls or texts, a habit that had become increasingly common when he was at work. *Fuck him,* Fabiola thought, surprised by her own harshness.

"Who's here for Vivian Butler?" a police officer called out, holding a file folder at the end of the hallway. Fabiola hurried toward him, trying not to focus on the gun at his hip.

"I am," she said.

"Come with me, please."

She followed him down a fluorescent-lit hall that smelled of stale coffee to a small, windowless room. Vivi sat staring at the table, her eyes red.

Fabiola stood beside her. "What happened?" she asked curtly.

"Your daughter and her friend were caught with unpaid merchandise," another officer said as he entered. "Lucky for her the store declined to press charges since it's a first offense."

Fabiola nodded in relief, then turned to Vivi, who still hadn't looked up. "What did you steal?"

"A shirt," Vivi whispered. "It wasn't even that cute."

"Then why, Vivi?" Fabiola crossed her arms.

A tear slipped down Vivi's cheek. "Layla said she'd done it lots of times before."

Layla, Fabiola fumed. Of course, this was her influence. "You're done with that girl, understand?" she said sharply.

"But Mom—" Vivi looked up, desperate.

"Done," Fabiola repeated. She turned to the officer. "What happens now?"

"She's free to go," he said, then added, "Your daughter seems like a good kid, but you might want to be careful who she spends time with."

Blood surged hot in Fabiola's veins. How dare this man judge her? She noticed his ringless finger and assumed he didn't have kids—or if he did, he was probably divorced, leaving his ex to do the hard work while he showed up with ice cream and age-inappropriate video games every other weekend.

Fabiola gave him a curt nod and grabbed Vivi's arm, pulling her to her feet. She silently pushed Vivi out the door and down the hall to reception, where Jade stood.

She wore a distressed denim halter top over white cutoffs and leather sandals that wrapped halfway up her toned calves. Her blonde hair fell perfectly into her eyes, and as she brushed it back, she spotted Vivi and Fabiola. "Hey," she said, giving a small wave.

Fabiola closed the distance in two strides. "Did you know about this?" she demanded. "Did you know about Layla's shoplifting?"

"Mom," Vivi hissed.

Jade threw her hands up. "Whoa! I wasn't even home today."

"Then who was with them?"

"They're fourteen," Jade said. "They don't need a babysitter."

Fabiola whirled toward Vivi. "Did you know there were no adults home when you asked to go?" Vivi nodded slightly without looking up, and Fabiola clenched her teeth.

"So Layla's allowed friends over with no supervision?"

Jade shrugged. "Like I said, they're fourteen. Independence is good for kids, right?"

"Oh, because you have so much experience with kids," Fabiola scoffed.

Jade bristled. "Look—"

"Forget it," Fabiola said, grabbing Vivi's arm. "We won't be seeing you again, anyway."

THIRTY-SEVEN

"How could you?" Vivi demanded as they stood across the street from the police station, where Fabiola had miraculously found a parking spot. The air reeked of hot asphalt and baking trash. Fabiola cupped her hand over her nose, trying to block out the smell and quell her nausea. "That was so humiliating," Vivi continued, her voice rising as she pointed accusingly at Fabiola.

"Get in the car," Fabiola said, as beads of sweat formed on her neck under the harsh late June sun.

"No!" yelled Vivi. "You can't do this. You can't tell me who I can or cannot be friends with."

"Vivi," Fabiola lowered her voice, glancing around. "We'll talk about this at home." A man across the street had stopped to watch, and a woman scooping up her dog's poop was listening in.

"You're ruining my life!" Vivi shouted. A police officer exiting the station turned toward them, and Fabiola gave a limp wave, hoping to signal control.

"I'm ruining your life?" Fabiola put her hands on her hips.

"You're the one shoplifting! Stealing, Vivi! What's wrong with you?"

"What's wrong with me?" Vivi sneered. "You think you're so perfect, but all you care about is that stupid baby that's not even yours." She jabbed a finger toward Fabiola's stomach.

"That's not true." Fabiola pressed a hand to her belly, as if to shield the baby. Sweat trickled down her back, pooling in her underwear. "And in case you've forgotten, I'm doing this to help give two people what they've always wanted." At least that was the plan.

"Oh, I forgot you were such a saint." Vivi rolled her eyes.

Fabiola glared at her and opened the car door. "Layla's a bad influence, and you're not seeing her again." She slid into the driver's seat and slammed the door behind her.

Aron declined to come home early despite Fabiola's repeated SOS texts. *I can't*, he wrote. *I'll explain later.*

Fabiola spent the rest of the afternoon oscillating between anger and despair. After yet another call to Aron went to voicemail, she called Liz.

Liz answered on the first ring. "Are you OK?" she asked in a hushed voice. "Is it the baby?"

"No, I'm fine," Fabiola said, cringing. "It's not the baby—God, I'm sorry, I shouldn't be bothering you at work."

"Well, I've already stepped out of my meeting," Liz said, her voice returning to normal. Fabiola heard the sound of a door closing. "What's going on? You sound upset."

Fabiola sighed. "It's Vivi," she said, then filled Liz in.

"Oh, wow, that's intense," Liz said. "What can I do?"

Tears filled Fabiola's eyes. "I just wish I knew what I'd done to make her hate me," she choked out.

"Fabi," Liz said gently, "Vivi doesn't hate you. Well, maybe a little, but that's normal for a teenage girl. I've worked with plenty of them at the Y, remember? Every girl on my basketball team has issues with their mom."

Fabiola managed a shaky laugh. "I just feel like a terrible mom. Like Vivi only got the best of me before Ben and Liam were born. For those first five years, I took her to baby music classes, toddler yoga—I even made her baby food from scratch. Then the boys came, and I couldn't keep up. I started feeding them all the store-bought pouches you can't even recycle."

Liz sighed. "Vivi is a good kid, Fabi, even if you dared to feed her mass-produced food. She's just going through something."

"Thanks for listening." Fabiola wiped her eyes. "I'll let you go."

"Call me later, OK?" Liz said.

"I will."

Liz's words offered momentary comfort, but soon Fabiola's thoughts spiraled back to the DNA test. What if she was about to become a mother again? She closed her eyes, picturing a pudgy, smiling baby nuzzled in her arms. At least one of her kids would love her. Then she shook her head and opened her eyes with a sinking feeling. How on earth would she manage a baby when her oldest child hated her, just as Fabiola had hated her own mother? And Fabiola hadn't even been absent like her mother had been. Unlike her mother, Fabiola hadn't missed a single recital or school program, attending them like it was her job—which Aron had assured her it would be once Pivot took off. Any day now. How naive she'd been to believe that.

Not anymore. She was done trying to do everything she could to make his life run smoothly. Let him see what it felt like when things got bumpy.

She went to the kitchen, opened the refrigerator to consider dinner, then slammed it shut. Forget it. They'd have takeout again. Standing there, her gaze fell on the photos stuck to the fridge with magnets. She focused on one of toddler Vivi in her arms, their noses touching, both smiling like they were the only two people in the world. She grazed her finger over Vivi's cheek in the photo, remembering her skin, as soft as rose petals.

Fabiola buried her face in her hands. How could she allow herself to imagine a baby in their lives? This was meant to be Liz and Peter's baby. It was insane; if the baby was in her life that would mean she had imploded Liz and Peter's, ended her marriage irretrievably and probably traumatized her children. She would be worse than her own mother, and Vivi would be justified in hating her. She had to fix things with Vivi. The last thing she wanted was a grown daughter who refused to take her calls.

Upstairs, Vivi's voice drifted out from under her door. Fabiola knocked and turned the knob. Vivi, lying on her bed with the phone to her ear, sat up abruptly. "I have to go," she said, then dropped the phone onto the bed.

"Who was that?" Fabiola asked. Vivi was allergic to talking on the phone. If Fabiola ever called her, she'd let the call go to voicemail and then text *Yeah?*

"No one." Vivi closed her hand around her phone. "Just a friend."

"Layla?" Fabiola raised an eyebrow.

"No." Vivi stared down at the bedspread, flicking off an invisible piece of lint.

"You're sure? I can check your phone, you know."

"Be my guest," Vivi replied, holding out her phone with a glare.

Fabiola hesitated, not wanting to push her daughter further away. "I trust you," she said.

Vivi laughed. "Yeah, right."

Fabiola sat on the edge of the bed, and Vivi scooted as far away as possible. "I do, Vivi. You made a bad choice today, but I think it was because of Layla. When it's just you, I trust you." Vivi kept her arms crossed, eyes fixed on the bedspread. Fabiola cleared her throat. "Look, I was fourteen once, too, just wanting to fit in with the popular kids." She thought of Peter's easy confidence at Dalton and how she'd tried to emulate it, using phrases like "It's all good" and "No worries."

Vivi snorted. "Layla's not exactly popular."

Fabiola pressed on. "Your choice of friends says a lot about you. What do you see in Layla, anyway? And why aren't you friends with Harper and Izzy anymore?"

Vivi drew her knees into her chest. "You wouldn't understand," she muttered.

"Try me."

They sat in silence until the front door slammed. "Fabi?" Aron called. "Honey, are you home?" Fabiola tilted her head, surprised—he usually came in quietly and disappeared into his laptop before she could ask him to block his calendar or remind him of the boys' soccer tournament.

Fabiola rose from the bed and searched her daughter's face for something—love, remorse, forgiveness? But Vivi remained motionless, chin on her knees, her expression blank.

"Hey," Fabiola called as she headed downstairs. "I'm here." Aron met her in the living room, a crazed grin on his face. Without warning, he picked her up and spun her around. "Oh!" she cried. "Aron, what in the—"

"It's happening," he said, setting her down and grabbing her hands like they were about to dance. "It's finally happening." He twirled her out and caught her as she spun back.

"What's happening?" She clung to his arm, dizzy from the spinning.

"Remember when I told you we had meetings with Vonic Media Group?"

Fabiola vaguely recalled it—something about Vonic considering adding a sports news site to their portfolio. "Sure," she said.

"Well, when they heard SB Nation might be interested in us, they jumped."

"Jumped?" She was still confused.

"Pivot is being acquired by Vonic Media Group." Aron was practically vibrating with excitement.

"That's great," she said, trying to muster enthusiasm, knowing this was his goal. But all she really felt was exhaustion.

"Guess how much?" he asked gleefully.

"How much?" she asked, playing along.

His eyes gleamed as he gripped her shoulders. "One hundred million dollars."

THIRTY-EIGHT

An unusual silence settled around the dinner table as the kids processed Aron's news. He hadn't mentioned the exact figure, but he told them Pivot was being acquired, which would change their lives. Finally, Ben asked, "Are you going to lose your job now that someone else owns Pivot?"

Aron laughed. "No, but my job will change. They'll bring in a new CEO with more experience in bigger companies, but I'll stay on as President and COO."

"What does that mean?" Liam asked, piling more tempura shrimp onto his plate.

"I'll handle the company's day-to-day operations."

"I want to change schools," Vivi announced. "And I want my own bathroom."

"Wait, what? Why?" Fabiola asked her daughter.

"Because those two are gross," Vivi said, wrinkling her nose at Ben and Liam.

"No, I mean, why switch schools? You're in a great one."

"I just want to, OK?" Vivi glared at her. "And we can afford private school now, right?" She looked at Aron, who nodded. "See?" she said to Fabiola.

Fabiola opened her mouth to argue with Vivi, then closed it. If this really was happening, then they *could* afford private school now. They could afford a lot of things. Her stomach fluttered with excitement, followed quickly by a wave of nerves as her thoughts began to race. What were the actual logistics of suddenly becoming very rich? How would she get Vivi accepted into a new school mid-year? Could she outsource that? That was what rich people did, right?

"If Vivi gets to change schools, then I want a hoverboard," Liam said.

"And I want an e-scooter," Ben chimed in. Aron laughed and Fabiola shot him a look, feeling suddenly overwhelmed. He cleared his throat.

"We will have more money, it's true," he said. "But that also comes with more responsibility." He looked at Fabiola to ensure he was on the right track.

"What do you mean?" Liam asked.

"Like that having money isn't just about getting a lot of new stuff," Aron said. "It's about taking care of our future."

"And of other people," Fabiola prompted. "Having money means you can help other people, too."

"Like Martin?" Liam asked. Martin was the mostly toothless homeless man who hung out in front of the bodega, greeting everyone who passed. Occasionally, they bought him a sandwich and his favorite Dr. Pepper. At Christmas, Fabiola always had the kids wrap presents for him—mostly warm socks and toiletries.

"Like Martin." Aron nodded. "And other people like him."

"I want to donate to Planned Parenthood," Vivi said. Fabiola smiled.

"We can definitely do that," Aron said.

"But after helping people I can still get a hoverboard, right?" Liam asked.

"We're not, like, leaving New York, right?" Vivi interjected.

Aron shrugged. "Who knows? Pivot might open a West Coast office eventually."

"No," Vivi said, her eyes widening. "We can't leave. What about my—um, friends?"

"But you don't have any friends now that you can't see Layla," Ben pointed out. Vivi glared at him.

"We're not moving," Fabiola said firmly.

Later that night in bed, her head spinning, Fabiola turned to Aron. "If this is really happening, we need to find a way to keep the kids from becoming spoiled."

He looked up from his laptop, annoyed. "Why would you say that?"

"I don't want them to become entitled—"

"No, I mean, why say it like, 'If this is really happening?'" he repeated.

"I just don't want to get ahead of ourselves—"

"Fabi, it's done." He closed his laptop with a thwack. "They've signed the letter of intent. Due diligence starts tomorrow, and it should only take a couple of weeks. Are you ever going to stop doubting me?"

She bit her lip. "I'm sorry. It's just a lot to process."

He stared at her, then softened and took her hand. "I understand. I've been working on this for years, but I get how it feels sudden for you and the kids. But it's happening, Fabi. Something good is happening to us. I wish you'd just let go and enjoy it." He squeezed her hand.

She scooted over next to him and rested her head on his shoulder. He was right. Why was she so reluctant to believe good things could happen? "Congratulations," she said. "You did it."

He kissed her forehead. "What do you want first? A new car? A trip to Bermuda? A penthouse apartment?"

"I want one of those really expensive cordless Dyson vacuums," she said.

Aron gave a playful groan. "Come on, dream big!"

She paused. "OK, and maybe someone else to do the vacuuming. A chef so I don't have to cook anymore. And a pair of Proenza Schouler Chelsea boots." She'd admired Liz's pair for ages.

"Better," Aron said, snuggling her closer.

Leaning against his warm body, she imagined having all the help she needed and amazing footwear. She realized she wouldn't have to keep working. Her whole life could change if she wanted it to. The question was, did she?

THIRTY-NINE

"How could you wait a whole week to tell us?" Alice stared at Fabiola, gripping her mug, her eyes wide behind the steam. Alice was a firm believer in hot drinks no matter the weather, and just looking at her mug made Fabiola sweat.

Liz let out a low whistle from across the booth. "A hundred mil is a serious valuation these days in the online media world."

"You can buy a brownstone," Alice said. "Hell, you can buy a whole block. Will you even stay in Brooklyn? I could see you in the mountains, maybe the Adirondacks. Or—"

"It hasn't even happened yet," Fabiola said, raising her hands.

"But they're in due diligence," Liz pressed.

Fabiola nodded. "Aron says they're making good progress."

Alice squealed, drawing a glance from the white-haired couple in the next booth. "What's the first thing you'll do? Quit your job? Buy a Birkin?"

"Send Vivi to boarding school?" Fabiola added, only half joking.

"Oh, right." Liz grimaced. "The petty theft issue."

"It's her new friend," Fabiola said, pursing her lips. "She's sad news. I wish Vivi would go back to her old friends. She still won't tell me what happened between them."

"Whatever." Alice waved her hand. "You'll be able to hire Vivi a very expensive therapist. She'll learn to blame everything on you, her mother, and she'll be fine."

"Alice, she stole something."

"Teenagers do stupid things. Remember when we snuck out to see Maroon 5 at Madison Square Garden in eighth grade?"

"Oh, I remember." Fabiola raised an eyebrow. She and Alice had each told their parents they were going to a movie in Lincoln Square—a perfect plan except for the freak blizzard that hit the city. Ever the worrier, Alice's mom trekked across town to pick them up when the movie let out. When Alice got home two hours late, her mom had already reported her missing, and Fabiola's dad was beside himself. They were both grounded for a month.

"If I'd known Adam Levine would turn out to be such a tool, I'd have just gone to the movie," Alice mused.

"Do the kids know yet?" Liz asked.

"About Pivot? Unfortunately, yes," Fabiola said. "I wanted to wait to tell them until it was official, but Aron couldn't hold back. And no matter how many speeches I give about staying grounded and giving back, the boys just keep asking when they're getting their own rooms and if they can get a drone."

"Can I get you anything else?" the server asked, eyeing Liz, Alice and Fabiola's empty plates. Fabiola glanced at Liz, feeling a familiar stab of guilt. *A world where I hadn't slept with Peter seven months ago?* She rested a hand on her rounded midsection. Lately, she found herself trapped in the murky space between regret and hope, more uncertain than ever about what she truly wanted—and whether her own happiness was worth the risk of hurting the people she loved.

"Just the check," Alice said to the server. She pointed to Fabiola. "She's paying."

"Alice!" Liz admonished, leaning closer to Fabiola. "Have you thought about security?"

"Security?"

"You're about to be very wealthy. The deal will be covered in the major financial press. Weird things can start happening."

"Weird things like what?" Fabiola frowned.

"Oh, you know, long-lost relatives showing up, people trying to scam you, following your kids, that kind of thing," Liz said.

"People following my kids?" Fabiola had been imagining an easier life now that they would have more than enough money, but she hadn't considered the darker implications of this.

The server walked by and tossed their check on the table without stopping.

"I've seen it happen." Liz gave a rueful smile. "I can send you the names of a couple of security firms we recommend to our clients."

"Um, sure," Fabiola said, her mind still stuck on the image of her children being tailed by shadowy men in trench coats. "That would be great." She glanced at her phone. "Sorry, I have to go. I'm meeting Hayley and Vivi at a client's."

Alice groaned. "Shouldn't you be headed to a very exclusive spa instead of working?" Fabiola rolled her eyes as she pulled out some cash.

"How's it going with Vivi working for you?" Liz asked.

"Good, actually," Fabiola said. "She has a knack for it. And work is the only place she'll talk to me right now, so..." She shrugged.

"She'll come around." Liz smiled sympathetically.

"Wait, I need to talk to my godchild before you go," Alice said, scooting closer and leaning down toward Fabiola's belly. "Hello in there," she cooed. "It's Auntie Alice. Remember this voice—it's the one that'll always tell you how perfect you are and that you can eat all the sugar you want. I can't wait to kiss you, squeeze you, and spoil you rotten." Alice straightened up and waved her hand. "OK, on your way."

Fabiola laughed and looked at Liz. "Um, did you want to..." She pointed to her belly.

Liz made a face. "Um, no, thanks, I'm good, thanks," she laughed.

The client project was a straightforward pantry organization in a newly renovated Park Slope brownstone. Hayley and Vivi could've handled it alone, freeing Fabiola to relax or catch up on errands. But Fabiola enjoyed watching Vivi work. She appreciated how her daughter stepped back, scanning every inch of the space from different angles, just like she did. She also liked how Vivi sang along to Hayley's playlists, filled with songs Fabiola had never heard.

"I think each kid needs their own snack bin," Vivi said, eyeing the empty shelves. The client had four kids under ten, which, in New York City, was practically showing off. "That way they can grab them themselves."

"Encourages independence and saves Mom time—I love it," Hayley said, snapping her fingers. Vivi smiled and did a little shimmy to the music.

After they finished, Fabiola and Vivi drove home in silence. Vivi spotted it first. "What is that?" she asked, eyeing the silver Mercedes G Wagon in their usual parking spot. Fabiola circled the block to find another spot. When they reached the front steps, Aron opened the door.

"Please tell me that's not ours," Fabiola said quietly, nodding toward the street. Aron grinned.

"Of course it is. It's for you. I'm looking for something sportier for myself." He kissed her cheek and tried to spin her, but she held out her arm to stop him.

"Holy shit," Vivi said, mouth agape. "That's our car?"

"Don't say shit," Fabiola corrected.

"Can you drive me to school in it on Monday, Mom? Please?"

"I don't need a new car," Fabiola said to Aron. "And if I did, it definitely wouldn't be that." She pointed at the hulking SUV.

"OK, no problem," Aron said breezily. "You'll get something different."

"You didn't even ask me. We agreed to consult each other before major purchases." Vivi's gaze darted between them like a tennis match.

Aron laughed. "Things are different now, Fabi." He beckoned them inside. "Come on, I ordered Nobu."

She watched Aron and Vivi disappear inside, then glanced back at the car. Aron had tried, she reminded herself, but guilt crept in, cold and unwelcome. How different would things be if she'd told him the truth about Peter when she'd had the chance? A rapid slideshow of their history played in her mind: Peter locking eyes with her in the Dalton lunchroom, his grin framed by wire braces. Peter meeting her at Grand Central that first Christmas home from college, holding a grease-spotted bag with a bacon, egg, and cheese from her favorite bodega. Peter's reddened eyes at her father's funeral. They'd never put a name to what they were to each other, how they always gravitated toward one another like magnets, even in the most crowded room. There was so much she hadn't told Aron.

Fabiola drew in a series of deep breaths to dispel the thoughts. She needed to relax. Good things were finally happening.

FORTY

Before climbing onto Dr. Acharya's exam table, Fabiola made sure the heater was off. It was her twenty-eight-week appointment, two weeks since Aron had announced the Pivot deal. Due diligence was progressing well, he'd mentioned the night before while opening a bottle of wine far pricier than their usual thirteen-dollar Cabernet. Despite Fabiola's protests, he'd already bought the boys hoverboards, and a new laptop for Vivi, which she claimed was for "work." Fabiola found it hard to remain annoyed, however, when she came home to find a Proenza Schouler shoe box on her bed.

Fabiola's body tensed as Dr. Acharya entered, wheeling her mobile laptop. It dawned on Fabiola that the doctor likely had the DNA test results in her file. Would she have noted them? Knowing this was a surrogacy, was Dr. Acharya legally bound to inform Liz? And if she hadn't said anything, did that mean it really was Liz's baby? Fabiola shivered.

Dr. Acharya looked up from her screen. "Are you cold? Let me turn on the heater."

"No!" Fabiola exclaimed. "I'm fine, thank you."

"Will your friend be joining us?" Dr. Acharya asked.

Fabiola shook her head. When she'd texted Liz to schedule the appointment, they couldn't find a date that worked. "I'm sooooo sorry," Liz had replied. "That week is terrible for me. Raincheck for the next appointment?" Liz's casual tone made it seem like she was rescheduling brunch, not missing a chance to see her baby. Well, maybe her baby.

The doctor nodded and glanced back at her laptop. "OK, twenty-eight weeks. Third trimester. How are you feeling?"

"Good," Fabiola said, and she was. The nausea that plagued her second trimester had finally faded. She was beginning to feel a hint of the goddess-like state she'd experienced when pregnant with Vivi and the twins. She felt ripe and curvy, like a mango ready to be devoured. Her body hummed with sensual energy, and her dreams were filled with sex. Sometimes it was Peter, but often it was anonymous men who licked and stroked her, making her beg for more. That morning she'd woken up wet and breathless. Instead of reaching for Aron, she'd masturbated in the shower, muffling her cries in her elbow.

"Good." Dr. Acharya nodded. "We're doing an ultrasound today to check on the placenta previa. Ready?"

Fabiola nodded, leaned back, and felt the warm goo on her stomach. Then there it was on the screen: the curve of a perfect little nose and a set of lips. Two tiny hands pressed together, with the baby's cheek resting on them as if sleeping. Two miniature feet tucked up close to a round belly, and the dark line of the umbilical cord snaking upward, connecting this small being to her.

One of the legs kicked, and a rush of joy shot through Fabiola. Without thinking, she reached out toward the screen, as if she could touch the baby's cheek.

"Everything OK?" Dr. Acharya asked. Fabiola realized her cheeks were wet and nodded, embarrassed. What must Dr. Acharya think of her—a woman getting emotional over a baby that wasn't even supposed to be hers?

All at once, the question mark of what to do about the DNA results vanished, and for the first time in months her head felt clear. She'd spent too long hiding in the deep canyon of her uncertainty. But now, the distant rumble of a river was growing louder, gaining strength. It was only a matter of time before the truth came barreling toward her, unstoppable. She had to face reality on her own terms before its raging waters swept her away.

On the monitor beside her, her heartbeat momentarily spiked. She could ask the doctor right now. Fabiola shifted on the exam table, glancing around the sterile room—the glass jars of gauze and band-aids, the bright orange biohazard needle disposal container, and her chest tightened. This wasn't where she wanted to be when her world turned upside down.

She'd wait until she was home, locked in her bedroom alone, a pad of paper and a pen beside her. Then she'd open the email and make a plan.

"Everything looks great," Dr. Acharya said, pointing to the squiggly lines on the screen. "The heartbeat is strong, and your placenta previa has cleared up, which is great news, though we'll keep monitoring it. Just keep taking it easy and stay hydrated." She removed the ultrasound wand from Fabiola's belly.

"Wait," Fabiola said. "One more thing."

"Yes?"

Fabiola cleared her throat. "I know Liz—my friend, the, um, mother—doesn't want to know the sex..."

"But you do?"

Fabiola nodded. "I do."

Dr. Acharya nodded. "I'm not privy to your agreement with her, so I'll let you handle that, OK?"

"Yes, of course."

Dr. Acharya smiled. "It's a girl."

FORTY-ONE

Fabiola's thoughts dipped and twirled like a flock of sparrows as she sat on the Brooklyn-bound train.

It was a girl. She was having a girl. Whose girl, she was about to find out.

In her mind, a split screen emerged, as if she'd stepped into a Wes Anderson movie. On one side, her life continued as usual —or as usual as it could be when she and Aron were on the verge of becoming multi-millionaires, and she was still carrying a torch for her high school on-again, off-again, maybe soulmate. She saw herself on the hospital bed, Liz on one side and Peter on the other, all of them shedding tears of joy as the baby was lifted from between her legs and placed in Liz's arms. On the other side, it was only Peter with her, gripping her hand as she cried out from the contractions, his eyes shining with pride as he urged her on.

She strode home from the subway so quickly that by the time she opened the front door, sweat glistened on her forehead. "Vivi?" she called. Fabiola had let Vivi stay home alone on the condition that she clean her room and stay off her phone. As Fabiola padded upstairs, she heard Vivi's voice.

"Yeah, it's so dumb... for sure... I'll try. K, bye."

Fabiola poked her head around Vivi's door and saw her daughter toss the phone onto the bed, sprawled out next to a pile of wrinkled clothes. "Who was that?" Fabiola asked. Vivi's eyes flicked to her phone.

"A friend." She shrugged.

Fabiola raised an eyebrow.

"Not Layla, I promise," Vivi added, rolling her eyes. "What? You told me to find other friends, right?" She shot Fabiola a defiant look.

Fabiola crossed her arms, biting her lip, debating her next move. Sighing, she pointed to the clothes on the bed. "Looks like you still have work to do in here."

Vivi tossed her head. "I'm Marie Kondo-ing. You're not supposed to rush it."

"Fine." Fabiola put her hands up and continued down the hall to her room, nerves fluttering in her stomach. Once inside, she locked the door and walked to the dresser. From the back of the top drawer, she pulled out a small lavender blanket with white satin edges, worn and ragged in places. It had been Vivi's, and though Fabiola had long since parted with most baby items, she couldn't let this go. Before it was Vivi's, it had been hers, a gift from her mother and one of the only remaining remnants from that time of Fabiola's life.

Fabiola put the worn fabric to her nose as she had so many times. When she was little, she always thought she could still make out a hint of her mother's scent, long after her mother had left. Now she swore she could still smell Vivi's baby powder.

She rubbed the satin edging between her fingers and sank down on the bed with her laptop. Would there soon be another of her daughters clutching this blanket in her tiny fist as she slept? Her body buzzed like there were a thousand moths inside, beating their wings to get out. She sat down and opened her laptop. This was it. It was time.

Holding the blanket in one hand, she opened her laptop. The unread message stared back at her. She clicked the link to the test results, and a page filled with numbers and confusing headers like "Percent Fetal DNA in Plasma of chDNA" and "Paternity Inclusion" appeared. But at the bottom, a bold blue box caught her eye.

Probability of Maternity: 99.999999999%

It was her baby. Hers and Peter's.

The breath rushed out of her lungs, and she had the sensation of falling, even though she was sitting down. She gripped her phone with one hand, the other feeling for the mattress beneath her, as if to confirm she hadn't plunged into freefall.

A part of her had always wanted to be with Peter, had always nurtured the glimmer of a fantasy that one day they would find their way back to each other—somehow without leaving a trail of collateral damage. Had that dream finally come true? But what about Liz? Fabiola's stomach twisted at the thought of her friend's anguished face. And what about her kids? And Aron? Sweat gathered at her temples and under her arms. The cocktail of emotions made her queasy. She closed her eyes, pressing the baby blanket to her face, seeking comfort in its familiar softness against her cheeks. *It was her baby.* She wanted this so much. And yet, there was no way...

A hot bubble of anger welled up in her stomach. It wasn't fair. She'd wanted so many things in life—a mother who loved her enough to stay, a husband who supported her and shared the weight of parenting, a daughter who didn't look at her with disdain. She'd tried so hard to do everything right, to be good, believing that somehow it would lead to the life she deserved. But nothing had come of it. Nothing, until now. And yet, now that she finally held what she desperately wanted in the palm of her hand, it came with a price that was unbearably steep.

The doorknob to the bedroom rattled. "Fabi?" came Aron's voice.

"Just a sec." A bolt of adrenaline shot through her as she slammed her laptop shut and scrambled to her feet. "Sorry," she said, opening the door while hiding the baby blanket behind her. "I didn't realize it was locked." Her face was flushed, and she wondered if he noticed. But then she saw his own face was drained of color, and he was breathing heavily, as if he might pass out. "Fabi," he said, propping himself up against the doorframe. "We have to talk."

FORTY-TWO

Aron lurched into the bedroom and sank onto the bed, his face in his hands. Fabiola's heart raced. He must know. But how? Her mind spun in panic. She didn't have a plan. Would Aron still want her, knowing she was carrying Peter's baby? Did she still want him? And what about Liz? How could she explain this? She needed to talk to Peter first. They could make a plan and break the news to Liz together.

She took a step toward the bed. "Aron, before we talk about this—"

He jerked his head up. "So you know about the money?"

Fabiola blinked. "What money?"

"Oh God," he groaned, burying his face in his hands. After a deep, shuddering breath, he straightened up and faced her. "The Pivot deal's off. Vonic Media backed out."

"Oh. I'm really sorry," Fabiola said, confused. It was a blow, but Aron looked as if he'd been sentenced to the gallows. "What happened?"

"God, I'm so stupid." Aron's body tensed, and he slammed his fist into the bed. Fabiola yelped, jumping back. Then he crumpled forward, burying his face in his hands again. "I'm so fucking stupid," he muttered, rocking back and forth.

"I'm sure it'll be fine," she said, trying to keep her voice even, but a flash of anger surged. Of course the deal was off. That was just like Aron—getting ahead of himself, raising their hopes. She didn't have time for his drama right now; she had enough of her own.

He looked up at her, fear in his eyes. "No, it won't be. The money's gone."

Fabiola frowned. "What money?"

"Remember the money we invested in Pivot last year?" She nodded. Last summer, Aron had said Pivot needed a cash infusion—a bridge loan, he called it. They'd make it back tenfold. They'd argued, Fabiola accusing him of being selfish and irresponsible, asking why he couldn't just get a real job. Aron had yelled that she'd rather see him miserable and working for the man than support his dreams. In the end, she'd given in, and they cashed out a small IRA in her name to invest in the company.

"I lost it, along with everything else," he whispered.

A dull ache of dread settled in Fabiola's bones, like a sudden drop in barometric pressure. "What do you mean, everything else?"

"My 401(k). Your main retirement account. The kids' college funds." His tone was flat, as if he were ordering a pizza and listing his desired toppings.

The breath rushed out of Fabiola's lungs. "What did you do with it?" she choked.

He kept his eyes fixed on the rug. "I put it into Pivot."

"Without asking me?" He nodded. "But how?"

"Remember all the surrogacy paperwork we signed?" Fabiola nodded, recalling the stack of legal documents she'd signed without reading. "I slipped the withdrawal forms in there. Then, on Pivot's end, I made it look like the money came from different investors." Fabiola gasped, and he gave her a pleading look. "Companies like Vonic Media were finally interested, and I needed to show we had other investors."

The room tilted, and any thoughts of the DNA test results flew out of her mind as panic set in. "So, what you're saying is…"

He lifted his eyes to meet hers, hollow and hunted. "We have nothing."

She slid down the wall until she was sitting on the floor. "Nothing, as in—"

"Literally nothing."

She stared at him, grasping for a solution to keep her alarm at bay. She had to fix this. "The apartment," she said, gesturing and talking fast. "We'll sell it. The market's crazy, and we've paid off a chunk of the mortgage, so we have some equity—"

"No," Aron interrupted. "There's no equity." He curled up on the bed, his voice dropping to a whisper. "I took out a second mortgage."

A ringing began in Fabiola's ears, growing louder until it was nearly unbearable. She closed her eyes, white fireworks of fury exploding in her mind. Her whole body vibrated with rage. She scrambled to her feet. "When?" she demanded, grabbing his shoulder and wrenching him around. He sat up, taking a deep breath.

"Six months ago. I told you it was a life insurance form, and you signed it." Fabiola remembered that morning—racing around, packing the twins' backpacks, yelling for Vivi to come down for breakfast. Aron had thrust papers at her, babbling about Pivot providing life insurance to all employees. He'd high-lighted where to sign, and she'd done it without a glance, her eyes scanning for Ben's missing gym shoes.

"How dare you?" She wanted to scream, but the breath had been sucked from her lungs, and all she could manage was a whimper. Aron jumped up and grabbed her arm.

"Fabi, I'm so sorry," he pleaded, pressing his hands together. "I'll fix this, I promise."

"You've never fixed anything in your life," she said, shaking off his touch as her rage built. "You wouldn't even know where to start."

"Believe me, I feel—"

"I don't give a shit how you feel." She held up a hand to cut him off, then pressed her hands to her ears as if to block him out. "I'm so *sick* of talking about how you feel. I can't do it anymore." She ground her teeth. "Get out."

"Fabi, calm down, let's—"

"Do not tell me to calm down." She pointed a trembling finger at him. "Get. Out."

"If we could just—"

"Get out!" she shrieked, her voice exploding up through her chest.

"OK, OK, I'm going." Aron held his hands up in surrender and edged toward the door. She followed him down the stairs, and only when she turned back did she see Vivi standing in her doorway, watching.

FORTY-THREE

Liz paced the living room, processing everything Fabiola had told her. "So he falsified Pivot's financials?" Fabiola, lying on Liz's couch, nodded, a cream-colored cashmere blanket pulled up to her nose as if to shield herself from her own life. Liz let out a low whistle. "That's a serious crime."

"Fucking asshole," Alice muttered, perched on the arm of the couch near Fabiola's head.

It was nearly nine p.m., the kids finally in bed, when Fabiola texted Liz and Alice. Aron had vanished after their fight, but by the time she picked up Ben and Liam from camp, he was back, buzzing around the kitchen making dinner, as if one night of Arroz con pollo could erase his deceit. They endured a stilted family dinner, and sitting across from Aron, it took everything in her not to hurl her plate at him. Rage simmered just beneath her skin. Another mess for her to clean up, and this time, she had no idea where to start. So, she turned to the people she knew she could count on. After the kids were asleep, she called an Uber to Tribeca, walking past Aron, who was bedded down in the living room, without a glance.

Now, lying swaddled on Liz's couch, Fabiola studied her

friend's grim face and tried to imagine how Liz would look at her once she knew the truth about the baby. That's what she should be telling Liz, not unloading her own problems. But she hadn't known who else to call. If she had any chance of getting through this, she needed her friends. Then she would tell Liz the truth.

"Do you have any accounts in your name alone?" Liz asked. She'd just come home from the office, dressed in a slim black dress with leather piping. As she paced, she stood out against the mostly white room.

"Just my business account and credit card," Fabiola said.

"Fabiola!" Alice chided. "Don't you watch Dateline? You always need your own account with your own money in case you need to disappear."

Fabiola burrowed deeper under the blanket. "I was so young when we got married," she said quietly. "I didn't have any money, so we just shared everything." God, she was so stupid. She'd let Aron handle all their finances. If she'd even glanced at her retirement account in the past year, she would have noticed something was wrong. Some independent woman she was.

"Vonic Media could sue to recover their vetting costs, maybe even launch a criminal investigation. This is financial fraud. We need to make sure you're protected. I know a lawyer who owes me a favor. I'll call him first thing tomorrow," Liz said, her work persona taking over. Her face became a mask of concentration as she whipped out her phone to make notes. Fabiola could see how intense she must be with her clients.

"A criminal investigation? You mean Aron could go to jail?" Fabiola shivered under the warm blanket. Despite her hostility toward Aron, she wasn't sure she wanted him to become a felon. What would that do to the kids? Would she have to visit him in prison? And who would want the wife of a felon cleaning out their closets?

"It's possible." Liz nodded curtly. "New York isn't exactly lenient on white-collar crime."

"White-collar crime?" Fabiola repeated, feeling dizzy. She was already lying down but wished she could escape further.

"You need to get divorced immediately to protect your assets," Alice said, snapping her fingers. "That's what they do on *Real Housewives*." Fabiola expected Liz to roll her eyes and chastise Alice for watching too much reality TV. Instead, Liz pursed her lips.

"It's not the worst idea," Liz said.

Fabiola's stomach churned. She knew in that instant that she wanted it. The marriage was over. She hated Aron right now. But she'd been angry with him for years, really, and somehow that had always seemed kind of normal. Didn't everyone with kids hate their spouse at least a little? Besides, Aron would definitely seek a divorce once he discovered what she'd done—and Liz likely would, too. The knife of guilt embedded in Fabiola's chest twisted.

"You can discuss that with the lawyer, too." Liz's voice jolted Fabiola back to reality.

A new thought struck Fabiola. "Where will we live?" she wondered aloud. "We'll have to sell the apartment, right?"

"One step at a time, hon," Alice said, gently brushing Fabiola's hair from her forehead. "We'll make sure nothing bad happens to you and the kids. Wait, do the kids know?"

"Vivi heard us fighting but not everything," Fabiola said. Her heart ached at the memory of Vivi's shocked face peering from her bedroom, watching her mother tell her father to leave.

"What's going on?" Vivi had asked, her voice trembling.

"Everything's OK," Fabiola had replied instinctively.

"But you yelled at Dad."

"I did," she admitted. Fabiola and Aron rarely raised their voices; passive aggressive comments and simmering resentment were more their style. "We had a fight," she told Vivi. "Just grown-up stuff. It'll be OK, I promise." What else could she say?

Liz stopped pacing and sat on the other arm of the couch near Fabiola's feet. "How long have you been married? Twelve years? Thirteen?"

"Fourteen years next month."

"Jesus." Liz clucked her tongue. "You think you know someone." She looked at Fabiola and shook her head. Shame rose in Fabiola's throat, and her chest began to heave.

"I don't deserve you guys," she said, pressing her face into a throw pillow, struggling against sobs.

"Hush," Alice said, waving her hand. "Of course you do. Sisters before misters. Chicks before dicks. Besties before testes—"

"OK, we get it." Liz cut her off with an eyeroll.

Fabiola tried to laugh but it came out as a sob. "No," she said. "I really don't."

PART THREE

FORTY-FOUR

"I want a divorce," Fabiola said.

Aron sat in the spot on the couch where he'd been for most of the past two weeks since their life had imploded. His face was unshaven, and he'd been wearing the same Flight of the Conchords T-shirt for days. For a moment she felt a wave of sympathy for his pathetic state.

"A divorce?" He straightened up out of his slumped position. "But why?"

Her sympathy vanished. *Because you ruined our life!* she wanted to scream. *The life I built for us while you were off chasing your stupid dream of being the next Jeff Bezos, which, by the way, turned out to be a colossal fraud.*

In truth, the only part of her life that offered any clarity was her anger. Every morning, she jolted awake to the harsh reality of the DNA test, her tired mind picking up where it had left off, endlessly cycling through her future options. Sometimes, depending on the day—or even the minute—she'd glimpse a moment of clarity about what to do next: how to tell Liz and Peter, how her life would change, and what it might become. But those moments were fleeting and unreliable, always followed by waves of confusion. Plus, with her growing belly as a constant reminder, time was running out. She needed to have a plan in place before the baby arrived.

The only thing cutting through the agony of her indecision was the cold fury she felt toward her husband and the unshakable clarity that she was finished with their marriage. She gripped the back of the couch, willing herself to remain calm, and stuck to the script she'd rehearsed on the phone with Liz the day before.

"Legally it's the best option for me and the kids," she said. "If we can push it through quickly, we'll have some protection from Vonic's lawsuit. You don't want Vivi and the boys to be left with nothing, do you?"

After another epic argument, they'd agreed to tell the kids that the acquisition had been canceled but to withhold the news about their impending financial ruin until they had a plan. There was no reason for the kids to bear the burden of an adult problem, Fabiola had reasoned. *An adult problem caused by you*, she thought, glaring at Aron.

Aron swallowed hard. "Obviously that's not what I want," he said. "But a divorce? Right now, when I need your support more than ever? How could you do that to me?"

"How could *I* do that to *you*?" she asked, her body rigid with anger. "Last time I checked you were the one who lied, cheated, and stole because you couldn't deal with your own failure. The only reason we're in this mess is because you needed to preserve your ego above everything else."

"My ego?" Aron narrowed his eyes. "You think that's why I did it? Jesus, Fabi, you're blind. I did it for you. Because all you do is complain about working so hard."

"I do not complain." Fabiola's spine stiffened. Though her inner monologue simmered with resentment toward Aron, she had mostly kept it to herself—hadn't she?

"Oh, please." Aron's voice was sharp. "You don't have to say a word. Your whole attitude is a complaint. The way you look at me when I come home late, how you slam the dishes when you clean up, and the way you make a point to mention every podcast or blog that interviews you."

"You're jealous," Fabiola said, her eyes widening with the realization. "You can't stand that I've been more successful than you." She wondered why she hadn't noticed it before—the way he never mentioned her growing contributions to their joint account or celebrated her achievements.

Aron snorted. "Come on, give me a little more credit than that. You can't even compare the two. You're cleaning out people's closets and I'm—"

"Defrauding potential investors and bankrupting your family?"

"Whatever." Aron pushed himself to his feet, holding up his hands. "I know how this goes. You're so perfect, right? At least that's what you want everyone to think." He gestured toward her stomach. "Look at Fabi," he said in a mocking tone. "A wife, a mother, and the owner of one of Brooklyn's hottest businesses. How does she do it all?" He quoted from the *New York Magazine* article. "Not to mention she'll be canonized any day now for being a surrogate for her poor, barren friend."

She flinched at his harsh tone, picturing the DNA result, and managed a strained laugh. "I'm far from perfect, I promise."

"Well, you sure as hell act like you are."

Fabiola closed her eyes and took a deep breath. "I want a divorce," she repeated. "The lawyer said—"

"Fine," Aron snapped, his face softening slightly as he sank back onto the couch. "I get it. I want the kids and you to be protected, too. It's just a piece of paper. After this is all over, we can—"

"Not just on paper." Fabiola forced herself to be clear. It was time for honesty. "I want a real divorce. The kind that lasts forever. I don't want"—she gestured between them—"I don't want this anymore." Her stomach dropped as she spoke, but she didn't waver. Amidst all her confusion, it felt grounding to be certain about at least one thing.

The skin around Aron's eyes flushed a blotchy red. "Fabi, please," he gasped. "Don't do this. I'm begging you."

She pressed her fingernails into her palms, forcing herself to hold firm. "The lawyer says you should move out as soon as possible to make it clear we're living separate lives."

"But the kids..." His voice cracked.

"We'll tell them together tonight," she said, biting back her tears. "You can see them whenever you want. Trust me, I'm not going to keep them from you. I wouldn't do that."

Aron's expression hardened. "Trust you? Right." His tone was cold. "I don't know who you are anymore."

Fabiola flinched and opened her mouth to respond, but the words didn't come. She pressed her lips together in a grim line. *I'm not sure I know who I am anymore, either*, she thought, blinking back tears.

FORTY-FIVE

Fabiola's phone pinged with a text from Liz as she sat in the art deco lobby of her client's Chelsea apartment building, her fingers tracing the polished arm of the leather chair.

How are you? Like, for real?

Fabiola bit her lip, considering how to respond. She rubbed her increasingly swollen belly, feeling the reassurance of the life growing inside her. Everything had shifted now that she knew this child was hers. She had become hyper-attuned to the tiny life inside her, each kick or flutter sending a thrill through her, reminding her that amidst the chaos, something extraordinary was happening. For the first time in a long while, she felt at peace.

I'm strangely OK, she typed back to Liz. It was true. Yes, her world was unraveling, but there was a new thread, one of hope and life, stitching her back together. There was something profoundly comforting about that, like the steady rhythm of a heartbeat in the dark.

I'm here if you need me, came Liz's reply.

I know, Fabiola wrote back, adding a heart emoji, feeling the warmth of her friend's support.

"You don't have to be here, you know." Hayley's voice interrupted the quiet as she stepped into the bedroom where Fabiola was sorting through the neatly organized piles of clothes on the bed. They'd been hired by a Broadway producer to help downsize his elderly mother's Chelsea apartment before her move to a senior living community in Florida. His wife had forwarded him a brief profile of Fabiola from *New York Magazine*—a not-so-subtle hint that she had no intention of helping with this project. The article had sparked enough interest to keep Fabiola and Hayley booked for the rest of the year.

"I know," Fabiola replied. "But staying busy helps." She moved a heavy wool jacket from the Sell pile to Donate. "There's a stain on the collar," she noted.

"Oops, sorry," Hayley said. "I didn't notice." She hesitated. "How's, um, everything?"

Fabiola cupped her belly with her hands. At thirty weeks, it was hard to see her feet or reach certain parts of her body in the shower. She remembered how, with Vivi and the twins, she and Aron had eagerly checked the size chart each week—a plum, then an onion, later an eggplant, then a pineapple. She hadn't done that earlier in this pregnancy. But this morning, she'd confirmed her baby was the size of a large cabbage. Because that's what she thought of it now: her baby. A daughter, who would be raised alongside Vivi and the twins, whatever that looked like. Once she had broken her best friends' hearts with the news.

"Aron and I are getting a divorce," she told Hayley.

"Oh my God," Hayley murmured. "Fabi, I'm so sorry." She paused. "How is Vivi taking it?"

Fabiola offered a wan smile. "Not well." They had told the kids two nights ago, gathering them in the living room after dinner. Ben had immediately started crying, and even Liam was too shocked to speak. Vivi, true to form, had lashed out at Fabiola.

"It's your fault, isn't it?" Vivi had narrowed her eyes, pointing an accusatory finger at Fabiola. "You told him to get out. I heard you."

"Sweetheart," Fabiola had said, trying to keep her tone steady, "these things are complica—"

"And I bet it's also your fault we won't be rich anymore." Vivi had glared at Fabiola, then looked to Aron for confirmation.

"It's not your mom's fault," Aron had said, his eyes fixed on his lap.

"I hate you!" Vivi had whipped her head back toward Fabiola, then slammed her fist against the arm of the couch before storming out of the room. But not before Fabiola had seen the tears streaming down her daughter's face. Later, when Fabiola went upstairs to check on her, she'd been met with a locked door and silence.

"Vivi thinks it's all my fault," Fabiola said, pushing the clothes aside and sinking onto the bed. "She hates me."

Hayley shrugged. "Every girl hates their mom at fourteen. Didn't you?"

Fabiola blinked, recalling how her mother hadn't even been there when she turned fourteen. She hadn't hated her mother then—not yet. While her friends complained about embarrassing moms, all Fabiola had wanted was to have hers back. "No," she said quietly. "Not then, anyway."

"Well, consider yourself lucky," Hayley said, checking the label on a cashmere cardigan. "I couldn't stand my mom, and now we talk three times a day." She patted Fabiola's arm. "Vivi will come around. It's just a lot for her right now, you know?" She glanced at Fabiola's stomach. "Speaking of a lot, do we need to talk about work coverage after you have the baby? I know you're not taking maternity leave since you're giving the baby up, but will you need time to recover? September is crazy busy for us."

A spike of anxiety pierced Fabiola, shattering the calm she'd felt moments earlier. *Giving it to someone else.* That was what she was supposed to do. But now that she knew this baby was her daughter... Yet, how could she possibly raise another child when she had no idea how to support the three she already had? She didn't even know where they'd live once the apartment was sold. A clammy sweat sprang up on the back of her neck.

"Oh my God, Fabi, are you OK? I'm so sorry, I shouldn't have brought it up. You've got enough on your plate." Fabiola lifted her eyes from her stomach and saw Hayley looking stricken. She quickly brushed away the tear sliding down her cheek.

"I'm fine," she said, shaking her head. "Really."

Fabiola left Hayley at the producer's mother's apartment and walked south along Ninth Avenue, which soon turned into Hudson Street, leading her into the West Village. It was one of those rare, perfect July days in the city, made even more unusual by the fact that she had nowhere to be for the next hour. The humidity had lifted overnight, and the temperature had dropped just enough that stepping into the shade of the cafés and brownstones lining the street sent goosebumps over her bare shoulders.

She'd always loved this neighborhood, despite the tourists. Maybe, after they sold their Brooklyn place, she and the kids—and the baby—could move here. They could stroll to Saint Ambrose for brunch, and Ben could learn to play chess with the regulars in Washington Square Park. She paused, gazing up at a charming three-story brownstone with wide stone steps leading to an antique door with a brass knocker, then snorted. As if. Only tech moguls and twenty-somethings with trust funds could afford the Village these days.

"Fabi?" She turned quickly toward the familiar voice and

saw Peter jogging toward her in shorts and a T-shirt that hugged his broad shoulders. She quickly clapped a hand over her mouth and nose. Had he heard her snort?

"Peter," she managed. "Hi."

"What are you doing in the Village?" he asked, stopping beside her, slightly out of breath.

"I had a client on 18th Street," she replied. "It's such a beautiful day, I thought I'd take a walk."

He nodded. "Mind if I join you?"

"Of course."

He placed a hand on her back, guiding them forward. Her skin glowed hot where he touched her. He cleared his throat. "Um, Liz told me about you and Aron. God, Fabi, I'm so sorry. What a mess. The thought of him doing that to you." Peter's hands balled into fists, his jaw clenched. "It makes me want to punch him in the face."

"That makes two of us." Fabiola tried to sound light, but the bitterness seeped through. Her anger had come in waves over the past week, especially when faced with Aron's shoes left in front of the door instead of on the rack, or the sight of him slumped on the couch watching endless WWII documentaries. It had been over a week since she'd told him to leave, yet nothing had changed. She was still cleaning up his messes while he remained absent, physically or mentally. The same life, except now they were teetering on the brink of bankruptcy. Sometimes she'd search Aron's face for the man she'd married, but all she saw were hollow eyes belonging to someone she no longer recognized.

"He was never good enough for you." Peter's face darkened. "I should have said something a long time ago."

Yes, Fabiola thought. *You should have. And so should I.* Her hand instinctively moved to her stomach, where her secret— their secret—rested. She took a deep breath. "Peter, I—"

"I just want you to know I'm here for you, whatever you

need," he interrupted. "I'll always take care of you, Fabi. Under-stand?" He stopped walking and turned to face her, cupping her cheek. To her surprise, his eyes were misty. "You know I've always loved you, right? Sometimes I wish we could go back."

"Me, too." She breathed in the musky scent of his sweat as their bodies drifted closer. Her belly bumped against him, and he quickly stepped back, clearing his throat.

"I, uh, heard there's going to be a criminal investigation into Pivot," Peter said. The sudden shift in topic caught Fabiola off guard, and she nodded. Aron had learned of the investigation just hours before *Business Insider* tweeted the news, which was quickly amplified by Pivot's former competitors. She wondered if Vivi might see it and finally understand that their life falling apart wasn't solely Fabiola's fault.

"Are you selling your place?" Peter asked. "Do you need money? A realtor? Anything, Fabi, just ask." His eyes were so earnest they left her breathless. Words struggled to escape her mouth, and she resisted the urge to reach out and take his hand.

"Well," she began. "There is one thing."

FORTY-SIX

The paper on the exam table crinkled as Fabiola reclined, her tank top hiked up and her linen pants pushed below her navel to expose her swollen belly. She watched Peter's face as Dr. Acharya moved the ultrasound wand over her gel-covered skin.

"You're measuring at thirty weeks and five days, right on target," the doctor said. Peter stared at the ghostly outline of the baby on the monitor, his expression not what Fabiola had hoped for.

She had asked him to come when they ran into each other in the West Village.

"Your ultrasound? Doesn't Liz usually go with you?" Peter had asked, puzzled.

"She's busy," Fabiola lied. She hadn't even told Liz about the appointment. It was just a quick check to peek at the baby and ensure the pregnancy was progressing normally and that her placenta previa hadn't returned.

She stopped telling Liz about her appointments once they became so frequent because each time she did, Liz treated it as an inconvenience, responding with *Yikes, big client meeting that day*, or *I'll try to move some things around*. In the end, there was always a reason she couldn't come. Liz's absence at the appointments began to trouble Fabiola. She wondered if it was too painful for Liz to see her carrying the baby, knowing she couldn't herself. Her heart ached for her friend, made worse by knowing she was about to deepen Liz's pain even further with her news.

Fabiola tried to envision the conversation where she'd have to break Liz's heart on two fronts: telling her that not only was Fabiola keeping the baby, but she had also betrayed her with Peter. A wave of nausea tightened her stomach. Yes, Fabiola wanted the baby, and she wanted Peter, but how could any of that ever be worth losing Liz?

The ultrasound monitor beeped, and Fabiola forced herself to focus on Peter, who sat just inches away, staring at the outline of their baby on the screen. The baby's hands were crossed over her chest, and as Dr. Acharya pressed the wand harder, the baby wiggled and extended an arm toward them.

"Aw, baby gave you a wave," Dr. Acharya said. Fabiola's heart swelled with joy at the sight of her daughter, and she looked at Peter, hoping to see him falling in love with their baby the way she had, to see his eyes mist over with the realization that he had created the life growing inside her. It would make telling him the truth—that they had created this baby together—so much easier once he felt the significance himself.

"Amazing, right?" Fabiola smiled at Peter, but his face didn't reflect amazement. His jaw was clenched, and the vein in his forehead bulged. "Peter?" she prompted, touching his arm. He pulled back as if her touch burned him.

"Yes, great," he managed. "Wow."

He remained silent for the rest of the appointment, his expression tense as Dr. Acharya played the baby's heartbeat and printed out photos, which Fabiola pressed into Peter's hands.

"So, what did you think?" she asked as they stepped into the elevator. She searched his face, hoping for a sign that he shared her joy.

"Great, yeah," he replied, staring straight ahead. When the elevator dinged on the lobby floor, he held the doors for her.

"Do you have time for coffee?" Fabiola asked, her voice shaky as she forced herself to continue. "There's something I wanted to talk about."

Peter glanced at his watch. "I wish I could, but I've got to get to the hospital."

"Oh, OK." The bubble of anticipation inside her deflated.

"Talk soon?" He bent to kiss her cheek, eyes already distant. Tears filled Fabiola's eyes, and by the time she wiped them away, he had already turned to walk away.

As Fabiola stood alone on the sidewalk, her phone buzzed with a text from Alice to her and Liz.

How was the appointment??

Fabiola smiled ruefully. While Liz had been absent from the doctor visits, Alice had them all marked in her calendar and faithfully texted after each one for an update.

All good! Fabiola replied, hesitating as she considered whether to mention that Peter had come along.

Alice sent back a champagne bottle and a baby bottle emoji, making Fabiola laugh despite the tight, anxious feeling in her chest. With a sigh, she dropped her phone back into her purse.

Fabiola arrived home to find their stoop crowded with a duffel bag and the rolling suitcase Aron had given her for her thirtieth birthday, promising her a beach vacation once his new venture paid off. He'd already been working on Pivot part-time then, operating from their living room desk when he wasn't at his day job.

"Hey," Aron said, stepping through the open door onto the

stoop. Fabiola looked up from the suitcase. "I'm leaving some stuff here until I have more space. I hope that's OK."

"Where are you going?"

He looked down, scuffing the concrete stairs with his sneaker. "I'm crashing with Jer and Kristina for now. The kids are at camp, so they have an open bedroom. I wanted to stay close so I can help with the kids and stuff."

Jer and Kristina's daughters were nine and eleven, and Fabiola's heart tightened at the thought of Aron tucked into a child-sized bed in a room decorated with unicorns and rainbows.

"OK," Fabiola said, shifting on her feet and clearing her throat. "Well, I'm just going to..." She gestured awkwardly toward the front door.

"Oh, yeah, sure," he said, stepping aside so she could maneuver around the luggage.

She paused. "Since you'll be nearby, could you drop the boys off at camp in the morning?"

"Tomorrow morning?"

"Every morning," she said with a shrug.

Aron's mouth twitched. "That's not, um, ideal for me."

Fabiola put her hands on her hips, exasperated. "You said you wanted to help with the kids."

Ben and Liam were already anxious about how often they'd see their dad, making Fabiola promise every night at bedtime that he wouldn't move to California without them—as if Aron had the money to do so. The boys had been heartbreakingly kind, clearing their plates after dinner and even filling their own water bottles in the morning. These small gestures tugged at her heart, but not as much as hearing them whisper to each other at night, long after they were supposed to be asleep, their small voices tight with worry.

"Yeah, and I do want to help," Aron said, holding up his hands defensively. "But Jer and I are training for a half marathon, so I'll be running or cross-training in the mornings."

Fabiola narrowed her eyes. "Why can't you run later in the day? It's not like Jer has anything else to do."

"It's too hot later. It's late July in New York—the city's like a sauna."

"Yes, I'm aware," Fabiola said, her voice rising. "I'm aware because I spend my nights washing sweaty soccer uniforms and then driving the boys to Greenpoint for camp in the morning, getting home just in time to sprint to the subway for my first client."

"Then take an Uber," Aron said. "Or don't schedule clients in the morning."

"We don't have any money!" Fabiola tried, unsuccessfully, to keep her voice from becoming a yell. She put a hand to her belly, reminding herself that stress wasn't good for the baby. "That's why I'm taking the subway and cramming in as many clients as possible." She pointed at Aron. "And you're training for a half marathon."

"You think this is easy for me?" Aron's voice matched hers. "I'm unemployed, basically homeless, and drowning in legal fees."

"And whose fault is that?"

They stood in a standoff, her hands on her hips, his arms crossed.

"Hey," Vivi said through the open door behind them.

Damn it, Fabiola thought. How much had Vivi heard? Probably all of it. She glanced around—likely the whole neighborhood had heard. She and Aron needed to learn to fight in private.

"Can I go over to Harper's?" Vivi asked, her eyes flicking to the suitcase.

Fabiola blinked, surprised. "Harper? But you and Harper—"

"We made up." Vivi shrugged, pulling her hair into a ponytail.

"When? That's wonderful," Fabiola said, reaching out, but Vivi sidestepped and leaned against the doorway.

"Yesterday, over text. So, can I go?"

"Of course. You don't know how happy it makes me that you two are friends again. There's nothing like old friends." Her thoughts drifted back to Liz, and a wave of anticipatory loneliness washed over her at the thought of losing her.

Vivi's eyes lit up. "Cool. Bye!" She waved and hopscotched past Aron and the bags.

"Give Harper a big hug for me!" Fabiola called after her.

"So," Aron said once Vivi was gone, "you'll take the boys tomorrow?"

Fabiola's joy evaporated in the summer heat. She shot Aron a withering look and went inside, slamming the door behind her.

FORTY-SEVEN

The next two weeks passed in a blur, even though each day felt like pushing a boulder uphill. Mornings were a whirlwind of getting Ben and Liam up, fed, and off to soccer camp before racing home to shower and dress. In past years, summer had been slow for Fabiola, with her clients fleeing the sweaty subway platforms and smell of garbage baking in the hot sun for the Hamptons or the Hudson Valley. But this year, thanks to Hayley's PR magic, her calendar was booked solid.

Fabiola did her best to keep up, dividing and conquering client projects with Hayley. Vivi still refused to go anywhere with Fabiola, so she tagged along with Hayley, putting in nearly full-time hours. And as much as Fabiola worried about burdening her daughter, she knew they couldn't have managed the frenetic pace without Vivi's help.

I'm doing this for you, she'd murmured more than once in the direction of her belly, giving it an affectionate pat. *For you and for your big brothers and sister, so we'll have a roof over our heads.*

Despite his half marathon training, Aron was proving helpful. On days Vivi didn't go with Hayley, he'd take her to a museum or a movie. Other days, they'd just hang out at home, and as much as Fabiola loathed coming home to find Aron lounging on the couch beside the pile of unfolded laundry she'd left the night before, she needed his help so she bit her tongue.

When Fabiola returned home after camp drop-off, Vivi was usually already at the kitchen island, sipping coffee and sorting through their inbox. Vivi now managed their email, the master calendar, client projects, meetings, and even ran their social media. Under Vivi's direction, they were on TikTok, where her before-and-after timelapse videos were gaining a growing following.

"Hey, Mom," she said one morning as Fabiola raced in the door.

"Good morning, sweetie," Fabiola said, squeezing her daughter's shoulder as she passed. For once, Vivi didn't pull away. Fabiola had let Vivi go to Harper's nearly every day that week, and as a result, Vivi's poisonous glares had eased into a tentative détente. Last night, Harper's mom hadn't dropped Vivi home until nearly ten, but Fabiola said nothing, not wanting to upset their fragile truce. "So I was thinking about LEGOs," Vivi said.

"Mm hm." Fabiola listened with one ear as she refilled her travel coffee mug.

"Actually, I was thinking about the LEGO incident."

Fabiola groaned at the memory. Both twins were LEGO fanatics, spending hours building Star Wars ships and Harry Potter scenes. Steadily creations took over every inch of floor space, leaving just a narrow path from their bunk beds to the door. One day, while delivering laundry, Fabiola had tripped and sent a basket of clothes crashing onto a three-foot Death Star model. There had been yelling and tears from both her and the boys. Afterward, she installed floating shelves and a Lazy Susan with transparent doors in their room, so they could rotate displaying their projects without cluttering the floor.

"What LEGO incident?" Fabiola widened her eyes in mock innocence. "I've completely repressed all memories involving LEGOs. Doesn't ring a bell."

Vivi rolled her eyes, but Fabiola caught a hint of a smile. "Seriously, though, you should do that for other people. I remember Harper's brother's room was also a LEGO disaster zone. I saw some posts about organizing them, but none were as good as what you did for Ben and Liam. I could do a whole TikTok thing about it, maybe cross-post with some LEGO fan accounts."

Fabiola cocked her head. "What do you mean, you *remember* Harper's brother's room? Weren't you just over there?"

Vivi's eyes flickered. "I mean, from when he was younger. I doubt he plays with LEGOs anymore."

Fabiola took a sip of coffee. It was going to be a long day. "You're right, though. It's a good opportunity for expansion. Mock up a service description for the website and find some stock photos of LEGOs. If not, we can take pictures of the twins' room." Vivi nodded. "Oh, and Dad's coming over around lunchtime, so you won't be alone all day. There's leftover—"

"—pizza in the fridge, I know. And I don't need Dad to babysit me."

"One, he's your father, so it's not babysitting," Fabiola said. "And don't ever let a man tell you otherwise. Two, I thought he was the parent you actually liked."

"I don't really like either of you right now," Vivi said matter-of-factly.

"Ouch," Fabiola said, shaking her head. "On that note, I'm headed to the Upper East Side. Text me if you need anything and don't—"

"—don't answer the door, I know." Vivi waved a bored hand and turned back to her laptop.

Uptown, Fabiola spent most of the day with a widow in the basement storage locker of a condo building.

"He was always a pack rat," the woman said, sniffing with distaste. "I was saddled with him long enough. I don't need his stuff hanging around, too."

"Understood," Fabiola replied. "We'll get this sorted."

The woman sniffed again. "Good riddance."

By the time Fabiola got home, it was after dinner. She felt grimy from her hours in the storage locker, her throat dry from the dust. Vivi and the twins were in the living room, eating pizza off paper plates and watching *Drive to Survive*. The boys were still in their dirty soccer uniforms, but Fabiola didn't have the energy to yell. She was starving and needed a shower.

"Is your dad still here?" Fabiola asked, but the kids didn't respond. She grabbed the remote and hit pause, greeted by a chorus of protests. "Hello?" she said, waving her hand. "I asked if Dad was still here." Aron had promised to pick up the boys and stay until she got home, but who knew if he'd followed through.

"Upstairs, I think," Liam muttered, reaching for the remote. She let go and headed upstairs.

Aron's back was to her as she entered the bedroom. He sat at the small desk crammed into the alcove, papers spilling over it —papers she still needed to organize. She sighed. When the organizer's life needed organizing, things were officially bad.

The floor creaked, and Aron swiveled to face her. Her laptop was open in front of him, and her blood turned to ice as she saw the columns of numbers and percentages on the screen. Her DNA test results.

His face was blotchy with anger and his eyes blazed as he rose from the chair. "It's your baby," he said, his voice tight. "Yours and Peter's. You lied to me."

FORTY-EIGHT

Fabiola stood frozen, her heart pounding in her ears.

"What are you doing at my computer?" she asked, struggling to keep her voice steady. "Why are you—"

"I needed a tax form for the lawyer and knew you'd have it since you're so 'organized,'" Aron sneered, making air quotes. He had her laptop and phone passwords, she realized. He always had.

"You were reading my email," she said, trying to breathe. "Snooping."

"Turns out you have a lot to hide." Aron stepped closer. "When were you planning to tell me? God, you're a shitty person." He let out a bitter laugh.

Fabiola flinched. "You had no right to—"

"To what? To know my wife slept with someone else and is secretly having his baby? Jesus, it's like a bad daytime talk show." He ran his fingers through his hair. "How long has this been going on?"

Fabiola gripped the dresser to steady herself. "Aron—"

"How long?" He was yelling now, his face twisted into a mask of rage. "How long have you been fucking him?"

Clammy sweat formed on the back of Fabiola's neck. "It was the first time in a long time," she whispered. Aron was right. She was a shitty person. She should have confessed immediately—or better yet, never done it at all.

The baby kicked, and her hand flew to her belly as a sudden wave of clarity came over her. She realized she didn't regret doing it. Yes, she regretted the pain she was about to cause, but her actions had resulted in this baby, her daughter, and she couldn't regret that. *I'm sorry,* she thought, directing the words to her child, who'd had no say in her mother's choices and now would have to live with them.

Aron pressed his palm to his forehead. "I'm so stupid," he muttered. "I knew something was going on between you two. But whenever I asked, you lied. You lied right to my face."

Fabiola swallowed the hard lump in her throat. She couldn't deny it. "I'm sorry," she whispered.

"Did you ever even love me?" Aron asked, bitterness seeping into his voice.

Fabiola thought back to when she'd fallen for Aron and his tousled hair, steady job, and an apartment with plants and actual artwork, not bongs and movie posters like the others she'd dated. Then she thought of Peter's arms around her, his mouth on hers.

"I did," she said. "Just not enough."

"Does Liz know she's not getting a baby?" Aron asked. Fabiola felt a knife twist in her chest. Tears trembled on her lower eyelids as she shook her head. Aron let out a bitter laugh. "Wow," he said, shaking his head. "You're even more of a cold-hearted bitch than I thought. And my divorce lawyer is going to have a field day with this—backing out of a legal surrogacy contract at the last minute because, oops, you slept with the father and it's actually your baby. Maybe I'll go for custody." He raised his chin, daring her.

Anger surged through Fabiola. "At least I'm not a white-collar criminal who lost all our money," she snapped. "And don't pretend you want the kids—you'd actually have to take care of them."

"At least they don't hate me," he shot back.

A strangled noise came from the hallway, and Fabiola turned to see Vivi standing outside their bedroom, her face pale. She stepped into the room, her eyes fixed on Aron. "You don't want us?" she asked. "And you lost all our money?"

"Honey, that's not—" Aron began.

Vivi spun to Fabiola. "And you cheated on Dad? That's your baby?" She pointed to Fabiola's stomach, her face twisted in disgust.

Fabiola reached out to her. "Vivi, I—"

"Don't touch me," Vivi snapped. "Neither of you. Just tell me the truth. Did you cheat on Dad?" She glared at Fabiola.

"Yes, but—"

Vivi cut him off, turning to Aron. "Did you lose all our money?"

Aron lowered his gaze. "Yes."

Vivi's eyes widened. "Do we have to move?"

"Vivi, everything will be OK, I promise." Fabiola took a step toward her daughter, hoping that holding her close would make everything right.

"You're lying," Vivi said, her voice rising in pitch. "You're lying," she repeated, shouting so loud that Fabiola recoiled. "You're both liars and I hate you!" Her face was red from screaming, her hands clenched into fists.

"Vivi, please," Aron begged.

"Leave me alone!" Vivi shouted, running from the room and down the stairs. Moments later, the front door slammed shut.

FORTY-NINE

"She'll be back soon," Aron said. "You'll see. She just needs to cool off."

Fabiola glared at him, her phone pressed to her ear as Vivi's voicemail greeted her for the fourth time. Out of habit, she began dialing her father. Even after all these months, it was his support she craved. She knew he would have dropped everything and come to Brooklyn to help find Vivi without hesitation. And though she recognized the futility of her action, she let it ring until an unfamiliar voicemail message came on, sending a sharp pang of grief through her.

The minutes stretched into an hour as Fabiola and Aron remained in the bedroom, as though remaining at the scene of their fight would somehow summon their daughter back. Finally, Aron cleared his throat. "Can we at least wait downstairs so I can have a beer?" he asked, his voice low and pleading.

Fabiola followed Aron into the kitchen, pacing while he opened an IPA from the fridge. Despite how irritating she found his presence she was reluctant for him to leave. The idea of facing the mess she'd made of her life alone was overwhelming. She checked her phone again, hoping for a missed call from Vivi, and thought about Liz. Vivi and Liz had always been close, thanks to Liz's knack for connecting with teenage girls. Had Vivi gone to her?

Fabiola's palms itched as she typed a text.

> Hey, odd question, but is Vivi with you?

The response came quickly.

> No, why?

Fabiola grimaced as she tried to condense her worry.

> We had a big fight, and she left about an hour ago. She's never done this before, and I'm really worried.

Her phone rang abruptly, Liz's name flashing on the screen.

"Hey," Fabiola answered.

"What's going on?" Liz's concern was clear. "Are you OK? Do you know where Vivi went?"

"No." Fabiola's voice trembled as she fought back tears. "She just walked out, and she's not answering her phone."

"Oh, honey," Liz said softly, "I'm so sorry. I'm sure she's fine. Have you tried her friends?"

"She doesn't really have any," Fabiola admitted, her voice quaking. "Can you let me know if you hear from her?"

"Of course," Liz said firmly. "Call me back in a bit, OK? Let me know if she's back. Love you."

"Love you more." Fabiola hung up to find Aron watching her with a raised eyebrow.

"Your dear friend Liz?" he asked, his expression mocking.

Liam wandered into the kitchen. "Can I have ice cream?"

"It's bedtime," Fabiola replied.

"Sure," Aron said, glancing at Fabiola before turning back to Liam. "But then it's off to bed, OK?"

As Liam headed to the living room with his bowl of Rocky Road, Fabiola and Aron's phones dinged simultaneously.

I'm staying at Harper's tonight, Vivi's text read.

Fabiola exhaled sharply with relief and grabbed her purse from the counter.

"Where are you going?" Aron asked.

"To Harper's," Fabiola said, tossing him an impatient look.

"Whoa, hold on." He raised his hands. "She doesn't want to talk to you."

"Excuse me?" Fabiola crossed her arms.

"I mean, she doesn't want to talk to either of us. Just leave her alone for now."

"I'm her mother. It's not my job to leave her alone. That's your move, not mine." She shot the words at him like daggers.

"Whatever." Aron's eyes narrowed as he finished his beer and slammed the bottle on the counter. "That's why she hates you, you know. You won't give her space."

"Oh, now you're giving me parenting advice?" Fabiola scoffed.

Aron's jaw clenched as he headed toward the door. "Careful, Fabi. You don't get to pretend you're perfect anymore. I know the truth now, remember?"

Once Aron left, Fabiola realized she couldn't go to Harper's without leaving Ben and Liam alone. And she wasn't about to call Aron to come back and watch the boys. Though she tried to ignore it, a small voice in her head suggested Aron might be right—maybe Vivi needed space.

I love you, Fabiola texted her daughter. *Just say the word, and I'll come get you.* But no reply came.

Fabiola awoke later than she meant to the next morning after a night of restless sleep punctuated with checking her phone for non-existent messages from Vivi. Throwing on shorts and an old T-shirt of Aron's that barely covered her bulging stomach, she flew into the boys' room. "Time to get up, we're late." She shook Ben's shoulder on the bottom bunk and tugged Liam's foot on the top one. Both groaned in dismay. "Get dressed," she instructed. "Breakfast in the car this morning." She was halfway down the hall to Vivi's room, hoping against hope she'd find her daughter asleep in her usual position of face buried in the pillow and both hands tucked up under her, when she heard the lock on the front door click open.

"Vivi?" she called, nearly tripping down the stairs in her haste. She barreled into the kitchen at the same time Vivi walked in with someone else behind her. Fabiola gasped and came to a stop so quickly she rocked back on her heels, planting her hand on the wall to keep from toppling over.

From over Vivi's shoulder Fabiola's mother nodded at her. "Hello, Fabi," she said.

FIFTY

"Vivi, thank God," Fabiola said, pulling her daughter into a tight embrace. Vivi remained stiff until Fabiola gently released her and turned to her mother. "What are you doing here?" she demanded.

"I'm bringing Vivi home," Paulina replied. "She stayed with me last night." Her lipstick was freshly applied, her dark hair pulled into a smooth, low ponytail. The sleeveless yellow sundress she wore made her olive skin glow.

"She stayed with you?" Fabiola's eyes widened. "You said you were at Harper's. You mean this whole time you were—" She glanced sharply at her mother. "And you didn't think to tell me you had my daughter?" She felt simultaneously limp with relief at seeing her daughter and rigid with anger.

Paulina raised her hands defensively. "I didn't know she'd lied to you about being with a friend." She gave Vivi a disapproving look. "I thought you knew she was with me. It only came out this morning when I decided to bring her home."

"I'm sorry," Vivi said in a small voice.

"It's all right, querida," Paulina said, wrapping her arm around Vivi, who leaned into her.

"Mom, Ben took my... whoa." Liam burst into the kitchen with Ben on his heels, halting so quickly Ben crashed into him. "Grandma?" Liam stared at Paulina with wide eyes.

"Good morning, mi amor." Paulina smiled at him.

"Amor means love," Ben explained to Liam.

"Dude, duh." Liam elbowed him.

Paulina raised her eyebrows. "You speak Spanish? Que bueno."

"We had it once a week at school," Ben explained. "But we didn't really learn much."

"I learned how to say balls," Liam said, brightening. "Huevon."

"We're going to be late," Fabiola said, looking at the wall clock.

"Go," Paulina said. "I'll wait here with Vivi until you're back." She shooed the boys toward the door. "Ándale, now. Go with your mama."

Fabiola hesitated, then nodded. Walking to the car she dashed off quick messages to Aron, Liz and Alice, letting them know Vivi was back safe. As she buckled her seatbelt and pulled away from the curb, her mind raced, trying to grasp that she had just left her mother at home with Vivi. She felt a surge of anger —she was undeniably furious—but it was tempered by a deep, surprising relief that someone had her back. She just wished it wasn't Paulina.

The boys were uncharacteristically quiet in the backseat as she drove. Then, after a few minutes, Ben asked, "Why does our grandma know so much Spanish?"

"She's from Peru," Fabiola replied. "They speak Spanish there." A pang of guilt pierced her. While the boys were familiar with Jamaican slang and customs, they knew little about her mother's heritage. Fabiola herself knew scant details. For a moment, she envisioned an alternate reality where she had grown up with her mother speaking Spanish to her, teaching her to salsa, like she remembered her parents dancing together in the living room. Perhaps they would have traveled to Peru, where she might have met her grandparents and cousins—she must have cousins, right?

"Will she be here when we get back?" Liam asked, pulling Fabiola from her thoughts. "I want her to teach me some Spanish swear words."

"No," Fabiola said, her grip tightening on the steering wheel. "She won't."

When Fabiola returned home, she took a deep breath before opening the front door. The aroma of coffee and something frying greeted her, and her stomach growled in response. In the kitchen, Vivi sat at the island with a mug, laughing at something, while Paulina stood at the stove, flipping bacon with tongs. Vivi's smile faltered when she saw Fabiola.

"You're back," Paulina said, setting a plate of bacon and toast on the counter. "Here, eat. That baby needs protein."

Fabiola took the plate, her hunger momentarily overshadowing her anger. She didn't usually eat bacon—Aron made it for himself and the kids on weekends—but right now it smelled irresistible.

Paulina cleared her throat. "Vivi, your mama and I need to talk for a minute." Vivi hesitated, then nodded and got up to leave.

"And then you and I need to talk," Fabiola said to her daughter, her lips pursed. Vivi gave a guilty nod, grabbed one last piece of bacon, and slipped out of the room.

"Don't be too hard on her," Paulina said softly once Vivi was gone. "She's going through a tough time."

"That doesn't excuse lying about where she was for an entire night," Fabiola replied sharply. "What was she doing with you?"

"She called me," Paulina explained. "Said she'd had a fight

with you and her dad and asked if she could come over. I said of course. Anytime."

"And you didn't think to ask my permission?" Fabiola took a bite of bacon and tried to keep from cramming the whole, delicious strip into her mouth.

"She said you knew where she was," Paulina said. "From the first time I saw her after the funeral, I always thought you knew when—"

"The funeral?" Fabiola choked on a crumb of toast and coughed.

"Yes." Paulina nodded. "I was relieved when she called. You were so angry with me—" Her voice caught. "But Vivi, I hoped at least I could build a relationship with my granddaughter."

Fabiola began to speak but choked on the crumb still lodged in her throat. Paulina quickly filled a glass with water and handed it to her.

"She said you didn't want to see me," Paulina said softly, her eyes welling up with tears. "But that you were fine with her visiting. I was so grateful I didn't question it. I should have. I'm sorry."

"So you've been seeing her for..." Fabiola calculated in her head. "Six months now?"

"More or less, yes."

Fabiola fell silent. What else didn't she know about her daughter? Exhaustion washed over her, erasing her anger and replacing it with a profound, bone-deep fatigue. It all felt overwhelming—work, motherhood, life itself—a relentless tsunami that left her gasping for air, never reaching the shore.

"I need to talk to Vivi, and then I have to get to work," Fabiola said, glancing at the clock with a heavy sigh. She wondered how she'd muster the energy to drag herself to Soho for her client meeting. Her limbs felt as if they were weighed down, and she was so exhausted she could have collapsed on the hard kitchen floor and slept.

"Vivi was supposed to come with me today," she remembered. But now, she didn't want to let Vivi leave the house. She wanted her safe at home, possibly for the rest of Vivi's life. And Aron wasn't scheduled to come over; he had a full day of meetings with his lawyers. But leaving Vivi alone felt out of the question.

"I can stay with her," Paulina said, as if reading Fabiola's thoughts. "I know Aron isn't... here anymore. Vivi told me." She glanced at Fabiola's stomach. "She told me everything."

Fabiola flushed, then felt a surge of anger at herself. Why should she care what her mother thought? Given her absenteeism, Paulina had no right to an opinion. Tension coiled in every muscle in her body at the thought of her mother being in her house with Vivi, intruding on her life. But what choice did she have?

"Fine," Fabiola said curtly. "You can stay."

Paulina raised an eyebrow. "Don't you mean thank you?"

Fabiola pressed her lips together. "Thank you," she muttered.

FIFTY-ONE

Upstairs, Fabiola found Vivi curled up on her bed with her AirPods in. Vivi pulled them out and sat up as her mother entered.

"Mom, it's all my fault," Vivi said quickly. "Please don't be mad at Lita."

"Lita?" Fabiola raised an eyebrow.

Vivi blushed. "She said 'Grandma' made her feel old, and that in Peru she called her grandmother Lita."

"I see." Fabiola struggled to keep the bitterness out of her voice. Her daughter now had a nickname for the woman who had abandoned Fabiola twice. She sat on the edge of Vivi's bed. "Vivi, you can't just run off like that."

"But I didn't run off; I went to Lita's."

"After lying to me about where you were," Fabiola reminded her. "And now I find out you've been sneaking around and lying for months."

"Um, you mean visiting my grandmother?" Vivi crossed her arms.

"Whom I expressly told you I didn't want you to see."

Vivi rolled her eyes. "Do you even hear how messed up that sounds? That I'm not allowed to see my only grandparent?"

"She's not part of our lives," Fabiola said, trying to keep her anger in check.

"Well, she's part of mine," Vivi shot back. "So she was a bad mom a long time ago. Can't you just get over it?"

"She wasn't just a bad mom, Vivi," Fabiola said softly. A wave of sadness washed over her, pulling her back to their old apartment, where the smell of Caribbean spices mingled with whatever the downstairs neighbors were cooking. She remembered waking early on her fourteenth birthday to an empty silence and finding her father at the kitchen table, his face buried in his hands, his shoulders heaving.

"She *left* me," Fabiola continued, her voice thick with emotion. "Do you understand? She left me and Grandpops all alone. One day I had a mother, and the next day I didn't."

"Well, she hasn't left me," Vivi retorted. "She might have been a bad mom, but she's a good Lita."

"Vivi, please," Fabiola pleaded. "We don't need her in our lives. You have me, your dad, your brothers, and your friends."

"My friends?" Vivi's laugh was bitter. "I don't have any friends. Or maybe you've been too busy posing for *New York Magazine* and cheating on Dad to notice."

Fabiola gripped her left hand with her right to keep it from reaching out in anger. "You have no idea what I—" she started, then stopped. "Wait, what do you mean you have no friends? You've been spending so much time with Harper lately."

Vivi stared at the bedspread. "I never made up with Harper," she muttered.

"What do you mean, you never made up?"

"I just said that to go see Lita," Vivi confessed. "I knew how much you wanted me and Harper to be friends again, so I figured you wouldn't question it." Tears began to stream down her face, sudden and heavy. Fabiola's heart ached; there was no worse pain than seeing your child suffer.

"So all those times you said you were going to Harper's..."

Vivi nodded, pulling her knees to her chest and burying her face in them. "Harper's forgotten about me now that she has her varsity swim team friends." Her voice was muffled.

Fabiola knew she should be angry about Vivi's lies, but seeing her daughter's pain was like a bucket of cold water on hot coals. She reached out, rubbing her daughter's back as it shook with quiet sobs.

"I'm sure that's not true," Fabiola said gently. "You and Harper have been friends since kindergarten."

Vivi shook her head and looked up with tear-filled eyes. "Everything's different in high school," she said. "It's like everyone got sorted into groups right away, like in *Harry Potter*. But I missed the day everyone got their assigned friends. So now I'm just... drifting. I don't fit in anywhere."

"But you made friends with Layla," Fabiola said, feeling a pang of guilt for dismissing Vivi's only seeming friend.

"Layla didn't have any friends either," Vivi replied. "We just ended up together by default. Everyone thinks she's a bi— as, you know. She lies about everything to make herself look good."

"Oh?" Fabiola asked. "Like what?"

"Like, she told everyone she was moving to California to be with her mom because it's better there, but really her dad sent her because he was mad about the shoplifting thing." Vivi's mouth twisted. "Too bad, because Jade was cool."

Fabiola suppressed an eye roll and continued to gently rub her daughter's back. "Sweetheart, anyone would be lucky to have you as a friend." She felt a pang as she thought of Liz and Alice, still unaware of her betrayal. When she'd texted to tell them Vivi was home they'd both responded immediately, their relief palpable.

Clearing her throat, Fabiola said, "I'm sorry I haven't been around more. I could make up a lot of excuses, but that wouldn't help. I'm also sorry about... this." She gave an awkward gesture toward her stomach. "I know it must have been a lot to process yesterday, hearing your dad and me talking about... it." The weight of guilt pressed heavily on her, making each breath a struggle. She was out of time now—she had to come clean with Liz, though the thought churned her stomach with nausea. She focused on the comforting warmth in her chest at the prospect of telling Peter. She pictured the smile spreading across his face, the way his arms would open to embrace her. But then doubt seeped in, erasing the image. What if his reaction didn't match her daydream? There were no guarantees. What would she do then? She didn't have a backup plan yet.

"You mean screaming at each other?" Vivi said, crossing her arms and jolting Fabiola back to their conversation.

Fabiola winced. "Yes, neither of us handled it well."

"So you really did cheat on Dad?"

Fabiola gave a deep sigh. "I really did." She offered a rueful smile. "I know I should tell you how wrong I was and how I'm not proud of my behavior. That's all true. But what's also true is that I would never let anything bad happen to you or the boys. Even though everything seems awful right now—and believe me, it is—you will always be safe, loved, and taken care of. I will never leave you. I need you to know that, Vivi."

Vivi blinked and met Fabiola's gaze. "I do understand," she said. "I mean, I hate you right now, but I know you're doing your best."

Tears welled up in Fabiola's eyes as she leaned forward and enveloped Vivi in her arms. "Thank you," she whispered into her daughter's hair. She wished she could stay there forever, cocooned with Vivi where nothing bad could reach them.

Vivi returned the hug, then yawned and pulled back. "So, what happens next?"

Fabiola swallowed and tried to inject confidence into her voice. "We'll figure it out together, OK?"

Vivi nodded and yawned again. "I'm tired. Lita's cat kept waking me up."

Fabiola stared, stunned. "My mother has a cat?" Growing up, her mother had always considered animals dirty, never even entertaining the idea of anything but a goldfish.

Vivi nodded, rubbing her eyes and slumping down on the bed. "Yeah. She wants a dog but says her shifts are too long."

"Her shifts?"

"She's a nurse."

Fabiola blinked in disbelief. Her mother of the red lipstick and salsa clubs was now a nurse and a cat owner?

Vivi sat back up as she remembered something. "You can't tell me not to see her. I won't let you."

Fabiola's jaw tightened, but she forced a smile. "Get some sleep, sweetheart."

FIFTY-TWO

Fabiola's thoughts darted through her mind like a school of fish trapped in an aquarium, forced to swim in circles for eternity. How had she missed what was happening with Vivi? She knew she needed to be home more for the kids, but how could she manage that while working to keep them afloat? Was Aron really going to contest custody? It seemed almost surreal that her long-absent mother was with Vivi while she was left sorting through scarves and costume jewelry from a deceased elderly woman on the Upper East Side.

She thought of her father and how unprepared she'd been to go through his apartment, despite the fact that she'd made a career of doing it for other people. But that was what people paid her for—the emotional distance to perform otherwise impossible tasks.

She held up a Burberry silk scarf, its geometric print marred by a small stain. As Fabiola stared at the brown mark, tears blurred her vision and her breath grew ragged. The biggest question of all burned inside her. How was she going to face Liz with the truth? She pressed her face into the scarf, which smelled faintly of mothballs and violets, unable to stop the tears.

How is this my life? How did I make such an enormous mess of everything?

Fabiola had always been a fixer, but in that moment, slumped against the wall and clutching a vintage scarf, she felt utterly unfixable. Her life had been a carefully mapped route toward goals she believed would bring happiness. Yet, a single misstep had left her entangled in a thicket of mistakes with no clear way out. Her whole life had been about being good at things—about being good. But now, all she could see was how badly she had failed: as a mother, a wife, a friend.

Her phone dinged and she located it on the bed under a pile of scarves. She wiped the tears and snot from her face with the Burberry scarf—the stain would have killed its value anyway—and peered at the screen.

Checking on you, read Liz's text, followed by a heart emoji. *Still breathing? I got you in with Maggie Liu, the divorce attorney I was telling you about. Her husband's company was a client a couple of years ago. She's a killer. Next Tues at 4pm. Lmk if you want me to go with you.*

Fabiola's stomach churned as she barely made it to the bathroom, retching into the toilet. She was such a fraud. Sitting back to wipe her mouth, she caught a glimpse of herself in the full-length mirror and looked away. She could hardly bear her own presence, so deep was her self-loathing.

Later that evening, she trudged back through the front door, relieved that the boys had been able to catch a ride home with another mom. The aroma of spices and roasting meat greeted her, mingling with the sound of music from the kitchen. There, she found her three children at the counter, watching Paulina sway to the tunes playing from Vivi's phone.

"Wait, what did he just say?" Ben asked, a notebook open in front of him. "Mi cortisone sees through you?"

"Mi corazón se estruja en tu mano," Paulina repeated, talking over the music. "It means 'my heart beats in your hand.'"

"Corazón equals heart," Ben muttered, writing something down.

"But what does that even mean?" Liam asked, his face screwed up in confusion. "Like his actual heart?"

Vivi gave him a light punch on the shoulder. "No, dummy, he's, like, in love."

"Lita, play us something else," Liam said as the sound faded out. "Something with bad words." The eagerness in his voice sliced through Fabiola like a scalpel. "Oh, hey, Mom," he said, noticing her.

"Lita's teaching us Spanish," Ben explained, pointing to his notebook.

Paulina shrugged. "They were interested. And I learned English from listening to the radio and watching TV, so I thought—"

"And she taught us how to say..." He paused, concentrating. "El burro sabe más que tu." He turned to Paulina. "What does it mean again?"

"A donkey knows more than you," Paulina replied. "But I only taught you after you promised never to say it to each other, OK?" She wagged her finger at Liam and Ben.

"What are you drinking?" Fabiola asked, noting the tall glass of purple liquid in front of each kid.

"Me and Lita made chicha morada," Vivi said. "Mom, it's so good. Try it."

"Lita and I," Fabiola corrected, taking the glass Vivi offered. The mellow sweetness of the liquid flowed down her throat like a river of memories. She recalled her mother's hand in hers as they strolled down 116th Street, lined with fruit and vegetable vendors and barber shops.

"Here," her mother had said, pushing open the door to a small, white storefront with a hand-lettered sign. "They have good chicha morada. We'll make it together sometime. It's easy."

They never had.

Fabiola choked down a swallow of the drink. "Thank you for staying with them," she said stiffly to her mother. She fumbled in her purse and held out some cash. "Here. I'm sorry it's not more. Do you have Venmo?"

Paulina's eyebrows twitched. "They are my grandchildren," she said. "You don't need to pay me."

"Fine." Fabiola shrugged.

If Paulina was hurt by Fabiola's dismissal, she showed no sign. "Let me at least get dinner on the table," she said, gesturing to the oven. "It's almost ready."

"Can't Lita stay for dinner?" Liam asked.

"Yeah, Mom, she promised to teach us how to salsa," Ben added.

Fabiola stared at him. "Since when do you want to learn how to salsa?" In an effort to be a gender neutral parent she'd tried putting the boys in dance when they were younger but they'd resisted so strongly she'd canceled them after just two sessions.

Ben's ears flushed red. "She said girls like boys who can dance," he mumbled.

Vivi giggled. "I'll set the table," she offered, heading to the cupboard for plates. The matter was settled.

Fabiola remained mostly silent during dinner, which, to her chagrin, was delicious. As she ate, she listened to the children quiz Paulina with curiosity.

"What's the weirdest thing they eat in Peru?" Liam asked.

"Well, it's not weird, as you say, in Peru," she explained. "It's a street food, anticuchos. It's made out of cow hearts."

"No way." Liam's eyes widened, impressed.

"Do you ever want to go back?" Vivi asked.

Paulina's smile grew wistful. "I came here at eighteen on a student visa and have lived here far longer than I ever lived there. Peru is more of an idea to me now. This is home. Besides, you're all here. How could I leave that?" She glanced at Fabiola.

"OK," Fabiola cut through the moment. "Time to clear your dishes everyone. Ben, Liam, you both need showers. Badly." She herded the boys upstairs and Vivi drifted toward her room. When she returned from refereeing the nightly routine—"Liam, the water needs to stay *inside* the shower. Ben, step away from the LEGOs and get in here to brush your teeth."—Paulina was pouring two cups of tea to steep. The kitchen was spotless and filled with the rich cooking smells of dinner and the scent of the lemon cleaner.

"Have some tea." Paulina lifted one of the mugs and pushed the other toward Fabiola. "It's good for digestion."

Fabiola crossed her arms. "Enough with the doting grandma act, already. You might have the kids fooled, but I'm done. Thank you for today, but we're finished here."

Paulina set her mug down. "Fabi, I know you're upset with me, and you have every right to be. I—"

"Upset?" Fabiola laughed bitterly. "You get upset when you lose your keys or spill coffee. What I am is..." She struggled for the right word.

"Angry? Furious? Am I close?" Paulina's voice wavered as she stood tall, almost eye-to-eye with Fabiola. "You hate me. I get it. I left you. I left my own daughter." Tears welled in her eyes.

"Twice," Fabiola said, her voice breaking. "You left me twice."

"I wasn't ready," Paulina pleaded. "I loved you, but I wasn't ready to be a mother or a wife. Your father—" Her voice faltered. "He was a good man, but we were so young. I was eighteen, my whole life ahead of me. I was supposed to go to school, to be a doctor. Instead, I became a mom. And your father, bless him, wanted a family. So we married. Then you came, and you were perfect." She smiled through her tears.

"But not perfect enough for you to stay." Fabiola's tears

began to fall as she clutched her sides, trying to hold back her emotions.

"I wanted to," Paulina said, reaching out as if to close the gap between them. "I wanted to, but I didn't know how. Your father could soothe you instantly. I couldn't. I was terrified of breaking you, of not holding you right, of not saying the right things. I'd get so angry if you cried while I brushed your hair, because how could you not see how hard things were for me?" She swallowed hard and blinked rapidly.

"I don't remember you being angry," Fabiola said. "I just remember you being gone." She was too tired to maintain her anger, which faded to a low hum of deep sadness within her chest. She wanted to laugh—here was the conversation she'd always wanted to have with her mother, and yet she felt too exhausted to fully engage.

Paulina's hands trembled as she fumbled for her mug. "Motherhood didn't come naturally to me, Fabi."

"So you left," Fabiola replied, heaving herself down onto a kitchen stool and wrapping her hands around the steaming mug. The ceramic was too hot, but she kept her hands there, trying to focus on the physical pain rather than the one inside her.

"Yes," Paulina said, her voice breaking. "I'm sorry." Her voice dropped to a whisper. "But I've come back. This time for good, I promise. Please. We've lost so much time already."

Fabiola closed her eyes for a moment, feeling like Dorothy in the eye of a cyclone, watching her chaotic life swirl around her, wondering where it would finally settle.

"Where did you go?" she asked when she opened her eyes. "What was better than being with Dad and me?"

"Miami," Paulina said, not refuting the implication of Fabiola's question. "I knew someone there who could get me a job. It was winter in New York and the gray just piled on top of the gray inside me, you know? I thought the sun would cure me and then I'd go back. And I did, it just took... longer than I thought." She lowered her eyes in shame.

Fabiola paused, then plunged ahead. She might as well ask all her questions—who knew if she'd ever get another chance? "Why did you leave again, then?"

Her mother was silent for a moment, as if searching for words. "You were already ten when I came back, and so mature and serious. You had these big eyes that watched everything, took it all in. I could tell you were really smart." A smile played around Paulina's lips and then vanished. Her shoulders slumped forward. "But by then, you and your father had figured out how to live without me. It felt like I had never been there. I tried to fit back in, but I didn't know how. You'd built a life without me."

"Because you weren't there." Fabiola's tone was sharp. "What were we supposed to do, wait for you to come back?"

"No," Paulina said, looking down at her mug. "But I thought you'd learn to need me again. You never did."

Fabiola set her mug down with such force that hot water splashed over her hand. Wincing, she wiped it on her shirt. "Of course I needed you. You were my mother! I needed you every day, but you were never there."

"I'm here now," Paulina said softly, her hope at odds with the pain in her eyes.

Fabiola shook her head. "No, it's too late."

FIFTY-THREE

When Fabiola woke the next morning there was a faint red blister on her hand where the hot tea had splashed onto it. She pressed on the spot, summoning pain. She deserved it, after all.

Downstairs there was a note near the coffee maker. Her mom must have scrawled it after Fabiola had gone upstairs, telling Paulina she could let herself out. Her hand hesitated over the paper. She pictured herself sweeping it off the counter into the trash, sweeping her mother back out of her life forever. But the smell of roast chicken still lingered in the air, and she thought of her children's excited chatter as they talked and laughed with their grandmother. Swallowing the lump in her throat she picked up the note and began to read.

Fabi,

When you were ten years old all you wanted was a pony. Your father and I tried to tell you a pony wouldn't like city life, that it needed space to run around, but you swore you would take good care of it living in our apartment and that you'd ride it to school and back every day to give it exercise.

*I was working as an assistant in a nursing home then, which
meant I did everything the nurses didn't want to do. I hated it,
but they gave me shifts that let me pick you up from school every
day. One of the nurses told me about a pony ride her niece had
gone on in Central Park. Your dad and I took you the next weekend. And let me tell you, there may have been a hundred other
little girls who rode that brown and white pony, but he belonged
to you. Even the people handling the horses noticed the way his
ears perked up when he heard your voice. His name was Buster,
and we took you to see him every Saturday until it got too cold
out. It was $20 for a ten-minute ride, but Buster's handlers
always let you go for longer.*

*Why am I telling you this? Probably because I'm selfish and
want you to remember something happy and good about me. But
also because you should know your happiness has always been
the most important thing to me. And for most of my life I thought
I would ruin that happiness if I was around.*

*You were born to be a mother, querida. Anyone who sees you
with your children can tell that in an instant. I was never like
you. I struggled and I let fear get the better of me. I'm sorry. I
know that doesn't mean a lot now, but it's important to say.*

*All my love,
Mama*

Next to the note was a small photo. It had been cut from a
larger one so that it was small enough to fit in a wallet, and was
worn around the edges. In it a little girl with a thick braid and
Fabiola's eyes sat on a brown and white pony. The girl's mother
stood next to the pony, her arms encircling the girl, enormous
smiles stretching across both their faces.

Fabiola crumpled the note in her fist and tilted her head

back. She closed her eyes, drawing in a deep breath. She knew what she had to do now. This was it. She smoothed the paper back out on the counter, folded it into a neat square and inserted the photo inside before slipping the whole thing into her pocket.

Fabiola dropped the boys at camp and Vivi off with Hayley to begin on a pantry makeover. Her next stop was a high-end Tribeca condo building with a gleaming marble lobby that smelled like a spa. As she walked in, her phone rang. Seeing Alice's name on the screen, her stomach tightened. What would Alice think when she learned what Fabiola had done to Liz? They'd been a loyal trio for decades, but now Fabiola was about to test the limits of that loyalty.

Her palms were clammy as she gave her name to the familiar doorman and was ushered toward the elevator. She stepped off directly into the spacious apartment with floor to ceiling windows on one side with a view out over the Hudson River. Across the foyer was a narrow table holding a large white orchid laden with blossoms.

"Hello?" she called. The apartment smelled like orange blossoms, Liz's favorite scent.

"In here!" Liz called.

Fabiola slipped her shoes off and stepped across the gleaming white floor tile onto a fluffy, eggshell rug. She found Liz in the open-plan kitchen dressed in leggings and a fitted tank top, her face damp and her hair pulled back into a ponytail. She took a sip of green liquid from a clear plastic bottle and made a face. "Why does being healthy have to taste so bad?" She grabbed a towel from the counter and swiped at her forehead, frowning. "Sorry I'm so sweaty. My trainer was brutal this morning."

"No problem," Fabiola said, acutely aware of the shift about to occur in their friendship. Every one of their shared experiences—impromptu dance parties in their dorm, confidences exchanged over brunch, inside jokes on their text chain—would now be labeled as Before. All future interactions would belong to the After. If there was an After.

"So, what's up?" Liz asked. "The divorce lawyer didn't try to reschedule, did she? I told her how urgent it was."

"No," Fabiola said, her voice barely a whisper. "It's nothing like that." She gripped the countertop, struggling to suppress a wave of nausea.

"Wait, do you want some coffee or fresh squeezed orange juice?" Liz asked, peering into the fridge. "I've got eggs—I could make you an omelet, the only thing I can cook thanks to you." She turned back to Fabiola with a smile.

"Stop it," Fabiola commanded.

Liz's smile faded. "Stop what?"

Fabiola put her hands over her ears as if to block out her friend's kindness. "Stop being so nice to me!" Her voice broke.

"Fabi, what—"

"Please." Fabiola held up her hand. "Please just let me— I just need to... I need to say something." Liz leaned against the counter, confusion on her face. Fabiola inhaled a shaky breath. "It's big, Liz. I'm so sorry. The baby isn't yours."

Liz scrunched her eyebrows together. "That baby?" she asked, pointing at Fabiola's stomach.

Fabiola bit the inside of her cheek and tasted blood. There was no turning back. "I slept with Peter. The night before the transfer. I did a blood test, it's my baby, not yours. Mine and Peter's." She forced the words out of her mouth so fast she nearly stumbled over them.

The color drained from Liz's face. The bottle of green liquid slipped from her fingers, crashing to the floor and sending an emerald river across the white tile. "Peter?" she gasped, the word a sharp inhalation. "And you?"

Fabiola nodded and closed her eyes as if the whole scene might disappear. "I'm so sorry," she said. And she was. Sorry she'd been awful enough to hurt her closest friend like this. Sorry for the pain she'd caused which could never be undone. But when she thought of Peter's body against hers, of his mouth on hers, she couldn't regret that. And as she felt the baby flutter and kick inside her, she didn't regret that either.

A heavy silence settled over the room, thick and suffocating, like smoke filling the air. Liz's face was a shifting canvas of shock, hurt, and anger, before it finally settled into a tight, closed-off expression. In that moment, Fabiola felt an impenetrable wall rise between her and her best friend of nearly twenty years.

"I'm so sorry," she said again, scrambling to find a crack in the new barrier, a way to get through to Liz. But the wall remained, unyielding.

"And Peter knows?" Liz's voice was low, carrying a cold, sharp edge that made Fabiola shiver.

Distraught, Fabiola ran her hands through her hair and instinctively reached down to cup her belly. She shook her head. "I wanted to tell you first. I thought it was only fair since it was supposed to be your—"

"Supposed to be my baby?" Liz asked. She eyed Fabiola's hand stroking her stomach, and Fabiola quickly dropped her arm back to her side. Liz closed her eyes and felt behind her for one of the white leather upholstered bar stools, sinking onto it.

Fabiola nodded, her stomach churning with adrenaline and self-loathing.

"So you're having Peter's baby," Liz repeated, her eyes still closed. "And I don't get to be a mother." Her eyes flew open, two icy pools of blue. "Do I have that right?"

"Yes." Fabiola's voice was a near whimper. She clutched the linen fabric of her pants in her fists, willing herself not to throw up. She'd just ruined Liz's life, she didn't need to also ruin her furniture. "Liz, I..." She hesitated. "I love him. I'm sorry. I don't know what else to say."

Liz blinked. "You love him?" She gave Fabiola a cold, appraising glance, then broke out in a high, mean laugh. "Of course you do. Because he's Peter." She planted her hands on the counter as if summoning her strength, then stood up. "You know what?" she said, her voice like cut glass. "You can have him. You deserve each other."

"Liz," Fabiola pleaded. "You mean the world to me. I never wanted to hurt you."

Liz pointed at Fabiola, every muscle in her body taut with rage despite the cold blankness of her face. "Get out," she said.

"We've been through so much together—" Fabiola began, her palms pressed to her chest as her heart pounded. Dark spots swirled before her eyes. How had she become such a monster? She'd tried to give her best friend the greatest gift, only to snatch it away at the last moment, taking Liz's husband along with it.

"Get out!" Liz roared, raw and guttural.

Fabiola flinched and stumbled backward, tripping over the sandals she'd discarded in the foyer. Her trembling hands fumbled as she tried to pick them up. For a moment she stood clutching her sandals to her chest, while Liz's icy glare pierced through her. When the elevator doors finally slid open, Fabiola turned, stepped inside, and averted her gaze from the tears streaming down Liz's face.

FIFTY-FOUR

The elevator seemed to grow smaller as Fabiola descended, closing in on her until finally the doors opened onto the lobby of Liz's building and she burst through them, gasping for air.

"Ma'am?" the doorman called, taking in her pregnant shape and white face. "Ma'am, are you all right?" But Fabiola shoved her sandals on her feet and fled past him as though she was being chased.

She pushed through the heavy, glass door and the soundscape of the street rushed to meet her: traffic noises, the steady beep of a reversing delivery truck, and the faint staccato of a distant jackhammer. Leaning against the building, she tried to steady her breath. She closed her eyes, sought calm, but the hurt on Liz's face was seared into the darkness behind Fabiola's eyelids.

And what had she expected? A pardon for her unforgivable actions? For Liz to embrace her and say, "Let's all be one big happy family"? Clearly not. But she hadn't been prepared for the twin icebergs of Liz's eyes or the anguished twist of her face as comprehension set in.

Peter. She had to tell Peter. That was the saving grace of the whole mess; that she and Peter were in it together.

Fabiola hailed a passing taxi. The driver rolled down his window and eyed her stomach. "If you have baby in my taxi, you pay cleaning fee," he said with an accent of indeterminable origin.

Fabiola's jaw dropped with indignation. "I'm not due for another seven weeks," she huffed.

"You pay for cleaning fee," he warned again, unmoved. Fabiola scanned the street, but no other taxis appeared, so she tamped down her annoyance and climbed in.

"Mount Sinai hospital," she said.

They could page Peter, the bored-looking woman at the desk on the surgery floor told Fabiola, but only if it was a true emergency.

"It is." Fabiola nodded. "Please." She paced as she waited, rubbing her stomach and whispering comforting phrases she told herself were directed at the baby. "It's going to be all right, you'll see. We're going to talk to your daddy."

"Fabi?" She whirled around at the sound of Peter's voice. He looked handsome in his white coat. "What are you doing here? Are you all right?" His gaze flickered from her stomach to her face. Without warning, she broke into tears and threw herself into his arms. "Hey," he said, his embrace tightening. "What's going on? Please, Fabi, you're scaring me." He kissed the top of her head and rubbed her back soothingly.

"It's the baby," she whispered into his chest. "Our baby. Yours and mine." Pulling back, she looked up at him, seeking his understanding. "That night in my kitchen... I took a test. I'm the mother, not Liz. We're having a baby." She searched his face for joy, but his expression went blank, like an animal caught in a trap.

"We— you and me— are..." He gestured to her stomach.

Fabiola nodded, smiling through her tears. "Yes," she managed, reaching for his hand. "I know it's a lot to take in. And it's not how I would have planned it. Liz is devastated—"

"Liz knows?" He jerked his hand away from hers and took a step back.

"I just came from your apartment," Fabiola said, confused by the panic in his eyes. "I feel awful, Peter, believe me. She must hate me. But—"

"Fuck," Peter said, running his hand through his hair and turning in a circle, then turning to face her. "How long have you known?" His tone was accusing, angry even.

Fabiola drew back from him and lowered her eyes. "A while," she admitted. A sharp pang of guilt shot through her chest. "I didn't know what to do... how to tell you..." She glanced back up at him, her eyes pleading for his understanding.

"Fuck," Peter repeated, then looked around as if realizing where they were. "We can't do this here. Why would you come here to tell me, of all places?"

The sharpness of his tone brought tears to her eyes. It was a shock, she rationalized. She'd caught him off guard. "I—I thought you'd be, I mean, I know it's not what you planned, but..." Through her tears she met his eyes, remembering how he'd cupped her face with his hand in the West Village and his tender words. "You said you'd be there for me," she said, struggling to get the words out as her mind swirled with hurt and confusion. "That you'd always *loved* me."

Peter stared at her in disbelief. "This isn't what I meant," he said, gesturing to her stomach. "Did you think I'd be happy about this?" His eyes were wide. "You just blew up my life, Fabi."

"I thought..." Tears streamed down her face, and she felt a flush of shame. What *had* she been thinking? That she could ride off into the sunset with Peter, sacrificing her closest friendship for true love? It had seemed so easy in her mind, so naively simple.

"I have to get back to work," Peter said, glancing around. "There are people who need me." Without another word, he turned and walked away, not looking back.

FIFTY-FIVE

Sleep eluded Fabiola. At thirty-three weeks pregnant there was now no position where she could rest comfortably for long. Still, she stayed in bed, tossing and turning in the darkened room. Whenever she woke, she was gifted a split second when it felt like just another day, but then her hands went to her belly and the scenes with Liz and Peter came crashing back. Each time she clawed through the sheets to find her phone, but there was never any reply from either of them, despite her repeated calls and texts. She'd even left a voice-mail for Alice, confessing everything and begging for her help intervening with Liz, but it, too, was met with silence.

Their distance was a vise around her heart, tightening with each hour. From Liz, she understood it. Fabiola had done the unthinkable, torpedoing her most precious friendship with a single encounter. OK, not just an encounter, but the culmination of years of longing for Peter to realize what she'd always known: that they were supposed to be together. And what could be better proof of this than a baby?

She barely made it home from Mount Sinai before collapsing in ragged sobs. She dragged herself upstairs, canceled her client meetings, and texted a fellow mom, begging her to pick up the boys from camp. When Vivi cracked open the bedroom door to ask about dinner, Fabiola could only mumble instructions to have cereal.

The next day she emerged to drive the boys to camp in the morning and then immediately returned to bed. Vivi appeared in her doorway again. "Mom?"

"Mm?"

"Hayley wants to know if we're still meeting later. She says she's been emailing and texting you."

"Not today, no." Fabiola tried to say more but her mistakes filled her mouth like sawdust. How wrong she'd been. How utterly stupid. She'd been a fool to believe she mattered to Peter. But her gravest error of all had been putting her friendship second.

On the third day, Vivi knocked on the bedroom door again and stood at the foot of Fabiola's bed. Her white T-shirt glowed in the dark room, giving her a ghostly appearance.

"We're out of milk," she said.

"Here." Fabiola fumbled for her phone. "Do an Instacart order. Whatever you need."

"Mom." Vivi's voice pitched high and frightened. "What's wrong with you?"

Fabiola struggled into a seated position, taking in the room's disarray. Crumpled tissues were scattered like flower petals, and an empty cracker sleeve and three cups of ramen noodles cluttered the nightstand. She had eaten them only because of the baby, though she felt far from hungry. She wrapped her arms around her stomach. Her child wasn't even born yet and already she'd failed her. Failed all of her children. She'd been so preoccupied with her own issues that she hadn't noticed Vivi's struggles. And what would the boys think of her when, like Vivi, they found out the baby would be a permanent fixture in their lives—and that Fabiola had no idea where they would all live once the apartment was sold.

"I'm sorry, I'm sorry, I'm sorry." She whispered the words like a prayer for all her children, born and unborn.

"Mom?" Vivi said again, panic in her voice. "Should I call Dad?" The lawsuit against Pivot had stalled for August as most of the lawyers on the case headed to the Hamptons. Aron had gone upstate with Jer for several days of "camping" at a boutique eco lodge, which Fabiola assumed Jer was paying for. They had signed the divorce papers the week before to stay ahead of Vonic's lawsuit, agreeing to joint custody.

"No," Fabiola said sharply. "I don't want him here." Not like this, when she was shattered and alone. She couldn't face Aron until she had a plan. She just needed some time to piece her life back together. "I just need to rest," she told Vivi, who was already retreating from the room.

Later, another knock came at the bedroom door. The curtains were still drawn, shrouding the room in darkness, and Fabiola wasn't sure if hours or minutes had passed since Vivi had been there. She squinted against the light that spilled in when the door opened, gradually making out her mother's silhouette in the doorway.

In an instant, Paulina crossed the room and sat on the edge of the bed. She took Fabiola's hand and began to stroke it gently. Fabiola stiffened, and then despite thinking she'd finally cried herself dry, new tears burst forth.

"Shh," her mother soothed. "It's going to be OK. We'll figure it out." Leaning forward, she kissed Fabiola's forehead. Fabiola clutched her mother's waist, her sobs rising from the deep well of heartbreak she'd carried for decades. Her mother's familiar smell overwhelmed her and the primal comfort of being near her battled with Fabiola's anguish.

"I don't know what to do," Fabiola managed through her

tears. "I can't— I'm not— I didn't..." Her body shook and she choked on her sobs.

"I'm here," her mother murmured into Fabiola's hair. "I'm here. Tell me."

So Fabiola did. She told her everything: from that first time in Peter's high school bedroom at seventeen to their recent encounter in the kitchen. She told her about the blood test and Aron's discovery of the results, Liz's icy gaze as she sent Fabiola away, and Peter's fury as he turned his back on her.

Her mother stroked her hair throughout, and as Fabiola finished, her sobs eased. She felt hollow, her heartbeat echoing through her empty body, yet lighter, as if the weight that had kept her pinned to the bed had dissolved. Sitting up straighter against the headboard, still holding her mother's hand, she said, "When Peter and I... I never thought..." She gestured to her stomach, then pressed her palm to her forehead. "I was so stupid. I should have known it would end like this, with everyone hating me."

"Not everyone," Paulina said, raising an eyebrow. "Vivi was worried enough to call me. And here I am."

"I'm a terrible person," Fabiola murmured, her shoulders slumping. The baby shifted inside her, but instead of joy, Fabiola felt a dull ache.

"Stop," Paulina said, holding up a hand. "You're allowed to be human. I made the mistake of thinking I had to be perfect. It's OK to make mistakes and fall apart. And it's OK for your children to see that, as long as they also see you putting yourself back together."

"But I don't entirely feel like it's a mistake," Fabiola whispered. "That's what makes me so terrible. I want this baby and wouldn't change that."

"Cariña," Paulina said gently, her face softening. "No child is ever a mistake. And as for what happened with Peter, well, it takes two to salsa." She wiggled her eyebrows, making Fabiola giggle despite herself.

"What about Vivi?" Fabiola groaned. "I can't imagine what she must think of me. And the boys, once they find out."

"Pfft, they probably already know," Paulina said with a dismissive wave. "Children aren't stupid. As long as they know you love them, they'll be fine."

Fabiola turned her face away. "And what you must think of me," she said, swallowing. It was hard to admit that after years of pushing any thoughts of her mother from her mind, Fabiola cared what Paulina thought of her.

"Fabiola Antoinette Fernandez Butler, look at me," her mother said firmly, using her full name. Fabiola obeyed, noting a fierceness in her mother's gaze she'd never seen before. "It doesn't matter what anyone else thinks, even me. I am your mother and will always love you. Now, get out of bed and on with your life."

FIFTY-SIX

The email from Liz's lawyer requested the DNA test results and stated that once it was confirmed that the baby wasn't biologically related to Liz, the surrogacy contract would be void and no further contact required. Its cold, business-like tone cut deeply, especially since Fabiola had received no response to the half-dozen messages she'd sent Liz over the past week. She'd apologized and raked herself over the coals. She'd offered to repay all the medical costs Liz had covered. And even though she knew what she'd done was unforgivable, she begged for forgiveness. All of it was met by silence.

Despite her anguish, after Fabiola sent the test results to the lawyer she felt a surprising, expansive sense of relief, similar to the sensation she had at the end of each day when she removed the tight band of stretchy fabric she wore about her midsection to keep the full weight of the baby from pressing down on her pelvis. It was done. The baby was hers, as recognized by the law and science. She was about to be a mother of four.

Liz wasn't the only one who'd cut her off. Alice had also gone silent. Desperate to explain herself, Fabiola called daily until Alice finally picked up. It was a short, stilted conversation.

"It's a lot to process, Fabi," she'd said, her voice cold and distant. "I mean, what you've put Liz through... and now what Peter's done..."

"What about Peter?" Fabiola couldn't keep herself from asking.

Alice was silent for a beat. "I would have thought you'd be the first person he'd have told," she said.

"Told what?"

"Peter left."

A million questions rushed to Fabiola's tongue, but Alice had already hung up.

The boys were unsettled by the news that they were going to have a little sister. "So Auntie Liz doesn't want the baby anymore?" Liam asked.

"Actually, turns out the baby is biologically mine, not hers," Fabiola said, trying to sound cheerful.

"Like from your egg?" Ben asked. "But how?"

Fabiola closed her eyes in deep regret that she'd followed the parenting blogs' advice to be "radically transparent" about reproduction. "It happened the usual way, with an egg and a sperm coming together," she explained.

"But whose sperm?" Ben asked.

"Uncle Peter's," Fabiola said.

Ben's eyes widened as he processed this. "So... sex? Like with the penis and the vagina and everything?"

Liam punched him in the shoulder. "Dude, you said vagina. Gross."

"Vaginas aren't gross," Fabiola said, rubbing her temples.

"But why would you do that with Uncle Peter? That's weird." Ben eyed her suspiciously.

"It is," she agreed. That afternoon, she came home with the latest Avengers video game, and any other questions were momentarily forgotten.

Aron came and went, picking up the boys from camp and

occasionally staying for dinner. Fabiola often retreated to the bedroom when he was there, citing work, while listening to the kids laugh and joke with him, including Vivi. Although she knew the kids needed these moments of normalcy, having Aron there was like staring down a firing squad. His resentful gaze followed her, waiting for the right moment to send a stinging comment her way.

"So, what's new with Liz these days?" he asked across the table one night. His eyes brimmed with spite.

"How is your apartment search going?" Fabiola asked, forcing herself to ignore the jab.

"Good." Aron nodded. He turned to the kids. "So, guys, I'm moving into a new place in September. It's a high-rise with great city views, a theater room for movie nights, and a game room with air hockey and foosball."

"Cool," Liam said.

"And no credit check for renters, I'm assuming?" Fabiola murmured.

Aron glowered at her. "There's plenty of room for all of you," he said to the kids. "Because you guys won't want to stay here once there's a loud, stinky baby around." He held his nose and Liam laughed.

"Joint custody, remember?" Fabiola reminded him in as pleasant a voice as she could manage. Provided she had somewhere to live.

The apartment would go on the market in two weeks at the beginning of September, but any new place with enough space for the kids and the baby would likely cost her as much as their mortgage. There would be no child support from Aron—she'd been lucky to escape without owing *him* money given that she'd outearned him for years.

Her head throbbed with the growing tally of expenses. She pushed her plate of half-eaten pizza away. After the baby was born, she'd need to return to work as soon as possible, but paying for a nanny was out of the question. Maybe she could bring the baby with her, she mused. After all, newborns slept most of the time and didn't take up much space.

She could ask Peter for help, and even force him with the DNA test. But she wasn't ready to beg, especially since he'd shut down communication. The only response he'd offered in response to her countless texts and emails was a terse, "I'm sorry, I can't right now."

"Mom?" Vivi's voice surfaced through the fog of Fabiola's thoughts. "What do you think?"

Fabiola realized her face had frozen in a grimace. She forced a smile. "Sorry," she said. "What did you say?"

"I asked if you'd had a chance to look at the social media posts I have queued up this week. I'm focused on the back-to-school campaign and the new virtual dorm room consultation offering."

"It's fine, I don't need to see them. I trust your judgement," Fabiola said. As she said it, she realized she did.

"Vivi's going to be finished helping you in a couple of weeks when school starts, right?" Aron asked, digging a piece of pepperoni out of his teeth with his finger.

"That's up to her," Fabiola said. "She's been a huge help this summer." Vivi perked up with pride.

Aron frowned. "Well, the rest of life comes first—school, friends, trying out for swim team again. It's not normal for a fourteen-year-old to be so involved in her mother's business."

"I don't swim anymore," Vivi said, annoyed.

"So pick another sport. You've got to commit to something and stick with it, Vivi. Otherwise, you'll never get anywhere."

"I want to keep working for Mom," Vivi said. "And was thinking about starting, like, an entrepreneurship club at school or something."

"The club is a great idea," Aron said. "But it's not your responsibility to help Mom anymore. She needs to figure out how to run her business without your help. Stand on her own two feet." He shot a patronizing glance in Fabiola's direction.

"But why?" Vivi asked. "Her and me and Hayley are a good team." Fabiola struggled to hide her smile before excusing herself before she said something to Aron she wouldn't want the kids to hear.

As usual, Aron left the dirty dishes and crumbs behind when he got up from the table. Later, when she heard the front door close behind him, Fabiola came back downstairs to clean up. Instead, she found Vivi directing Liam and Ben on how to load the dishwasher while she wiped down the counters.

"You're supposed to rinse the plates first," Vivi instructed Liam.

"Why do we have to do this?" he whined. "Dad never makes us."

"Because of the patriarchy," Ben said, looking at Vivi. "Right?"

Vivi nodded. "Exactly."

"What's patriarchy?" Liam asked, tossing pizza crust into the trash.

"It's when men think they're better than women," Vivi explained.

"But what if they are better?" Liam smirked.

In one swift motion Vivi put her brother into a headlock. "Say it again," she dared.

"I'm sorry," Liam squeaked. "Let me go!"

Fabiola choked back a laugh and slipped away before they noticed her.

FIFTY-SEVEN

In early September, cooler weather arrived along with a For Sale sign on Fabiola's front steps. During the initial walk-through, the realtor, whose son played soccer with Ben and Liam, took notes.

"I'd suggest re-staining the floors, painting the kitchen cabinets a lighter color, and updating the downstairs powder room," she said. "It will really boost the value."

Fabiola pointed to her swollen belly. "No time for that."

The realtor gave a sympathetic smile and tucked a strand of highlighted hair behind her ear. "When are you due?"

"Three and a half weeks," Fabiola replied.

The realtor clucked sympathetically. "I can't imagine what you're going through. I heard about your split with Aron." She glanced around and lowered her voice, as if someone might overhear her. "Did he just not want another?"

"Oh, it's not his," Fabiola said, enjoying the look of shock on the woman's face. "So, anyway, the apartment goes on the market exactly as it is."

Aron's new apartment in a Downtown Brooklyn high-rise boasted amenities like a movie theater and a game room, but the kids were reluctant to spend much time there. "It doesn't feel like home," Liam said. "And the building smells like a skunk."

Vivi laughed. "That's marijuana, idiot."

Despite the realtor's warning about the updates she should have made, Fabiola received a flurry of offers on the brownstone during the first week of school. She settled on the one that came in well over her asking price—provided she agreed to close and move out in three weeks. Now, every spare moment, of which there were few, was consumed by viewing potential new homes. So far, each place she'd seen was either too small for her and the kids or too quirky, like the two-floor unit with a skylight running from the kitchen to the master bedroom.

As time ticked down, her anxiety grew. A low-grade stress headache throbbed in her temples from the time she woke until the time she lowered her aching body back into bed at night. Her feet had swollen to the point where she splurged on a new pair of Birkenstocks because it was either that or a beat-up pair of flip flops. Her back ached if she was on her feet for more than fifteen minutes, which complicated work. Hayley had taken over as many of their clients as she could, but she only had so much room in her schedule and many of their clients specifically wanted Fabiola.

She had client projects lined up daily, including weekends, until her due date in three weeks, and she still needed a plan for after the baby arrived. She couldn't afford to slow down. Yet in the midst of the whirlwind, she still compulsively checked her phone, hoping for a text from Liz.

She woke one morning with a sharp twinge in her lower back. *No way*, she thought. *You can't fool me.* She'd made multiple false alarm runs to the hospital before both Vivi and the twins' birth. Not this time. Instead, she lumbered into the kitchen to make coffee and set out bowls of cereal. Though the kids usually ignored them, she felt less guilty tossing out the food than not trying to feed them at all.

Another twinge of pain doubled her over as she waited for the coffee maker to finish, staring at it with the intensity of a Formula One fan during the final lap.

"Mom?" Vivi appeared behind her, her voice gravelly with sleep. "Are you OK?"

"Fine, fine," Fabiola managed, exhaling through the pain. "Waffle?" She held up the box she'd pulled from the freezer for herself.

Vivi shrugged, which was as close as she ever got to an enthusiastic yes, so Fabiola added a second waffle to the toaster.

"Don't forget, you're going to Dad's after school tonight for dinner."

"Do we have to?" Ben lurched into the kitchen, his springy curls matted down on one side of his head. "His girlfriend, or whatever, is so annoying."

Fabiola froze. The toaster dinged and she made no move toward it.

"Ben," Vivi hissed.

"What?" He looked confused.

"Girlfriend?" Fabiola managed.

"Yeah, Clementine. She does something with lattés."

"Pilates," Vivi corrected with a stricken look toward Fabiola. "She teaches Pilates."

"Anyway, she made me a gross smoothie last time we were there. It was green." Ben made a face.

"I see," Fabiola said. Here she was, working herself to the bone while worrying about her children being left homeless, while Aron was making smoothies with a Pilates teacher named after a citrus fruit. And introducing said citrus fruit to their children without Fabiola's permission. She squared her shoulders. "Well, I promise there will be no more smoothies with Clementine." She'd make sure of it.

"I'm sorry," Vivi whispered to Fabiola, her face creased with concern. "Dad asked us not to mention her. But Ben's right—

she's, like, super annoying. She's always laughing at Dad's dumb jokes."

Fabiola raised her eyebrows. "I'm sure she is."

Fabiola's first client that day was near Lincoln Center. By the time she walked the four blocks from the subway, she was out of breath and desperately needed to pee as the elevator ascended to the fifteenth floor. A lean, middle-aged woman with unnervingly smooth skin greeted her at the door.

"You must be Fabiola." She beamed. "I'm Gwendolyn Reardon. I'm so happy to—"

"Could I use your bathroom?" Fabiola interrupted.

"Of course," the woman said, blinking. "It's just down there —" But Fabiola was already heading that way. She made it just in time and felt a wave of relief. As she flushed and pulled her maternity jeans back up, a rush of wetness surged down her legs. Fabiola gasped as the fluid pooled at her feet.

No, no, no, she thought. *It's fine. There's still time.* With the twins, her water had broken a full twenty-four hours before she delivered. But it also hadn't come three weeks early. As she stared at the fluid spreading toward the rug, a red-hot pain shot through her lower back and radiated outward. She crouched, gripping the bathroom counter for support, and a strangled moan escaped her lips.

"Fabiola?" Gwendolyn called. "Is everything all right?"

Fabiola held her breath as the pain eased, then pushed herself upright and splashed cold water on her face. "I'm OK," she called weakly. One contraction wasn't a big deal. She reached for the doorknob, but another wave of pain hit her, and she couldn't stifle her cry.

Gwendolyn pushed the door open, knocking Fabiola back against the wall. Her eyes went wide as she looked from Fabiola's contorted face to the wetness on the floor. "I think we'd better call someone," she said.

FIFTY-EIGHT

Fabiola lay in the back of the ambulance, flushed with embarrassment. "Really, I can just take an Uber," she said, but the paramedic, a squat, broad-shouldered woman, shook her head.

"Honey," she said. "No driver in his right mind is going to pick up a woman in labor."

"Is the siren really necessary?" Fabiola asked. "I mean, I'm not exactly dying." Even in the well-insulated back of the vehicle the wailing noise was loud enough to set her teeth on edge.

"George gets a kick out of putting it on—he'd do it even if all you had was a broken toe," the paramedic said, rolling her eyes. "Men."

Fabiola was about to ask whether they were in the habit of rushing people with broken toes to the hospital when another contraction gripped her. She let out a sharp cry. The paramedic grabbed her hand.

"Squeeze as hard as you need to," she said. "I once delivered a baby back here before we made it to the hospital. I thought they might name it after me, but I never heard from them again." She seemed genuinely disappointed.

"What's your name?" Fabiola gasped through the pain.

"Gladys."

When they arrived at the hospital, Fabiola allowed George and Gladys to carry her like a rag doll to a waiting wheelchair. Inside, she answered the nurse's questions through gritted teeth as the woman strapped a blood pressure cuff around her arm.

"Is there anyone you want to call to come meet you?" the nurse asked. "A partner or friend?"

A twinge shot through Fabiola's body, unrelated to her labor. Whenever she'd thought about the baby she'd never gotten this far, to the reality of being at the hospital about to give birth. She hadn't thought about who she'd call when it happened, or who would be there by her side.

Aron had been with her with Vivi and the twins, feeding her ice chips and sleeping on the short couch in the labor room. Despite the nurse's instructions not to eat anything after her epidural, he'd smuggled in potato chips when she complained of hunger, and then had held her hair back as she vomited them up later.

Now, there was no one to sit beside her, hold her hand, or offer words of encouragement. No one to stroke her hair and reassure her that she was doing great and that her baby would be lucky to have her as a mom. A sob shuddered through her.

"I know it hurts, mom," the nurse soothed her. "We're going to get you over to labor and delivery and do some pain management."

The nurse was right; it hurt. But no drugs or needles could ease the anguished loneliness Fabiola felt. "My phone," she said, reaching toward the tote bag at the end of the stretcher. The nurse handed it to her, and Fabiola fished out her phone. There was only one person she could think to call.

A different nurse took over once they reached the labor and

delivery floor. She kept up a steady stream of bright patter as she hooked Fabiola up to a series of complicated looking machines with blinking lights. "Is this your first?" she asked.

"Fourth," Fabiola said. Her eyes followed the wire from the electrode pads the nurse was affixing to her stomach back up to the machine it attached to.

"Oh, wow," said the nurse. "All normal deliveries?" Fabiola nodded. "Then I'm sure this one will be, too." She patted Fabiola's arm and turned to fiddle with the knobs on the machine. "Huh," she said after a minute.

Fabiola's heart lurched. "What's wrong?" she asked as the nurse adjusted an electrode pad, glancing between it and the machine.

The nurse's cheerful face faded into practiced neutrality. "I'm having some trouble picking up the baby's heartbeat," she said. "I'm sure it's just a matter of finding the right spot." She cleared her throat. "I'm going to page Dr. Acharya to get her here as soon as possible. We'll keep trying."

The room tilted before Fabiola's eyes as the nurse hurried out of the room. She gripped the metal rail of her bed. No. Everything was fine. She'd just felt the baby move that morning. Hadn't she? Or had it been the morning before? Shit. All the days ran together. But she would have noticed if something was wrong, wouldn't she? She'd been so busy the last few weeks that the baby's kicks had faded into the background like the rumble of the train from inside the subway car.

Where was the nurse? How long had she been gone? It felt like an hour. Cold sweat broke out on Fabiola's body. She reached for the call button but was hit by another contraction before she could press it. Nausea surged up, and she leaned over the bed, vomiting.

"Oh dear," the nurse said, bustling back in. "Let's get you cleaned up."

"What's happening?" Fabiola croaked.

Dr. Acharya followed the nurse and quickly attached three more electrode pads to Fabiola's midsection. The monitor flickered to life with faint static. "There it is," Dr. Acharya said, then frowned.

"Someone tell me what's going on," Fabiola demanded, but she felt weak and her voice came out in a whisper.

"The baby's heartbeat is significantly slower than it should be," Dr. Acharya said. "The best thing is to get her out as soon as possible. I'm going to prep you for an emergency C-section."

Fabiola's hands flew to her stomach protectively. "But she'll be OK, right?"

Dr. Acharya ignored the question. "Let's get her wheeled over to surgery," she said, addressing the nurse, who nodded, already unhooking and rearranging various wires trailing off Fabiola's body. The doctor turned back to Fabiola. "I'll see you in a few minutes."

"Is there anyone you'd like us to notify?" the nurse asked as Dr. Acharya's white coat disappeared out the door.

Fabiola tasted salt as her tears dripped down her cheeks to the corners of her mouth.

"I'm here!" came an out of breath voice from the doorway and Fabiola looked up with relief to see her mother hurrying in. Paulina crossed the room and took Fabiola's hand in hers. She wore a red and white polka dotted sundress, a few flyaway hairs escaping from her otherwise smooth chignon. "I just got your message," she said, panting. "I'm so sorry, querida, I was at the store and I'd left my phone at home." She smiled and squeezed Fabiola's hand. "This is so exciting."

"Something's wrong," Fabiola said, her voice trembling. "With the baby. They're taking me to surgery."

Her mother paled and turned to the nurse. "What's happening?"

"There are some complications," the nurse said. "We're about to get her over to surgery. If you want to wait in the—"

"What sort of complications?" Paulina demanded. Her eyes swept over the monitor attached to Fabiola and her face tightened. "The baby's heart rate..." she said.

The nurse stepped sideways to block her view of the screen. "I'm also a nurse," Paulina said, crossing her arms.

The nurse gave a tired sigh. "Then you know how important it is to get her to surgery right now. The waiting room is—"

"Waiting room? Pfft." Paulina's eyebrows shot skyward. "No. I'm coming with my daughter. Let's go."

FIFTY-NINE

The light was so bright that Fabiola quickly shut her eyes as soon as they'd fluttered open. An antiseptic smell itched her nose. She shifted slightly on the bed and felt a lightning bolt of pain through her abdomen. She remembered her mother beside her in surgical garb, the anesthesiologist on her other side, the sheet over her midsection. She remembered vomiting over the side of the bed, and the cry of a baby.

The baby. Her eyes flew open again. Squinting, she struggled to sit up but the pain in her abdomen flattened her. A low, melodic song filled her ears. Fabiola turned her head to see her mother facing away from her near the window, swaying gently. The soft light filtering into the room framed her like a Madonna.

Paulina turned, a small, wrapped bundle in her arms. Her face glowed with happiness. "She's beautiful," she said, moving toward the bed. She lowered the bundle gently onto Fabiola's chest. "She's perfect."

Fabiola pulled the pink and blue striped hospital blanket back from around the baby's face and stared down at her daughter's impossibly small, impossibly perfect lips. Below twin fuzzes of eyebrows her tiny, nearly translucent eyelids fluttered in sleep. One doll-like hand had escaped the blanket and was pressed against the side of her face as if to say, "Thank goodness that's over."

"Hi," Fabiola whispered, stroking her daughter's soft cheek. "Welcome." In response the baby moved her lips in a small sucking motion like a baby fish.

A nurse appeared at Fabiola's side. "How are you feeling, mom?"

"Everything hurts," Fabiola said.

The nurse nodded. "On a scale of one to ten, how much?"

"Seven?" Fabiola grimaced.

"Wow, you're tougher than most." The nurse grinned. "I'll get you something stronger than Motrin. Do you want to try to nurse her?"

Fabiola nodded and the nurse helped her sit up against a pillow. "I hope I remember how to do this," Fabiola said, untying her hospital gown.

"The body never forgets," Paulina said, her eyes shiny with tears.

The baby's lips found Fabiola's nipple and closed around it. Warmth tingled through her body, mingling with the pain. The baby suckled for a few minutes, then dropped back to sleep. Fabiola felt her own eyelids droop.

"Wait, the kids," she said, her eyes flying open.

"They're with Aron," Paulina said. "They send their love. Now rest."

Fabiola woke to the bustle of nurses in her room, her fingers searching for the baby she'd been holding.

"She's right here," said her mother, lifting the baby from the bassinet next to the bed and lowering her into Fabiola's arms. "I'm glad you rested."

"Congratulations," chirped one of the nurses. "You're graduating from triage. Everything looks good so we're moving you down to labor and delivery." She glanced at the chart she had pulled up on the computer. "Does baby have a name yet?"

Fabiola pressed her lips against her daughter's warm, wrinkled forehead and looked over at her mother. "Leonora," she said. Her mother smiled.

She cradled Leonora in her arms as the orderly wheeled her through the halls, her mother at her side. Around her people's faces lit up as they saw the baby, a beacon of life and health in the midst of everything else that went on in hospitals.

"Aw, so precious," cooed a woman in the elevator holding a stuffed animal and a Get Well Soon balloon.

"Ah, a fresh one," said an older man, flashing a grandfatherly smile. "Congratulations."

Fabiola was surprised when they wheeled her into a room with only one bed. Manhattan hospitals were notorious for their overcrowded labor and delivery wards. Private rooms were highly sought after and very expensive. With both Vivi and the twins Fabiola had been in a shared room with a thin curtain separating the two beds. With Vivi the other woman had farted constantly, and she and Aron had worked—largely unsuccessfully—to stifle their giggles. With the twins the other woman had loud phone conversations so incessantly that Fabiola had begged her doctor to release her a day early.

Fabiola looked up at the orderly, the medical bills already adding up in her head. "I'm not supposed to have a private room," she said.

The orderly consulted his paperwork. "It says here that you are."

"But I didn't request it," Fabiola pressed.

"No, I did," said a familiar voice.

Fabiola turned toward the person standing in the doorway. Her mouth dropped open and her heart gave a sickening leap halfway up her throat. "Liz," she said.

SIXTY

"Hi," Liz said. She gripped the doorframe with both hands as if anchoring herself. "Actually, it was Peter who requested the private room. I made him call in a favor."

Fabiola blinked, confused.

"So, you're staying?" the orderly confirmed, impatient.

"Yes, she's staying," Liz said firmly. She stepped fully into the room as the orderly left.

"How did you know I was here?" Fabiola asked.

"Your mom told me."

Fabiola gave Paulina a questioning look. Her mother kissed the top of Leonora's head and handed her back to Fabiola. "Your phone rang while you were in triage," she said. "It was Liz, so I answered." She hesitated, as if afraid of Fabiola's reaction. "I hope that's OK. I know you'd been... trying to reach her."

Yes, thought Fabiola. *A month ago when I ruined her life.* But she'd given up on ever hearing back.

She looked up at Liz, whose eyes seemed to have grown bluer since Fabiola had last seen her. The intensity of her gaze made Fabiola shiver.

"I think I'll get some coffee," Paulina said, shifting on her feet. "Can I get anyone anything?" Fabiola and Liz shook their heads. Paulina patted Fabiola's arm and disappeared out into the hallway.

Liz pulled the chair next to Fabiola's bed back a few feet before sitting down, maintaining some distance between them. There was an awkward silence. "How are you feeling?" Liz asked finally.

Fabiola smiled weakly. "Oh, you know. Like someone just removed all my organs, rearranged them and put them back."

Liz grimaced. "God, that sounds barbaric."

Leonora gave a faint grunt in Fabiola's arms and Liz leaned forward almost imperceptibly. "Do you want to see her?" Fabiola asked shyly. She felt tentative, as if one wrong word would send her friend fleeing. But Liz paused, then nodded and scooted closer. A small smile spread across her face.

"She has your nose," she said after a minute.

Fabiola examined her daughter. "Yeah, maybe." She looked back up at Liz, whose eyes were fixed on Leonora. She couldn't even imagine how Liz must be feeling right now, staring at a baby that was supposed to have been hers. "Do you want to hold her?" Fabiola asked.

"What? No." Liz jerked back so fast the chair almost tipped.

Fabiola flushed at her mistake. "Oh my God, I'm sorry, that was stupid, I shouldn't have—"

"I just, I don't think I can—" Liz held up a hand.

"It's fine, I understand," Fabiola said, chiding herself for being so insensitive. It was a miracle that Liz was even here; she didn't need to push things. Fabiola hesitated, looking from Leonora to the bassinet. "Would you mind just setting her down for me? I can't get up and it hurts to hold her for too long."

Liz bit her lip, then nodded. She took the baby, holding her as though she were a bomb ready to detonate. Placing her in the bassinet, Liz quickly stepped back.

Outside in the hallway soft lullabies played over the PA system, interrupted now and then by the crackle of announcements. *"Dr. Blair please report to triage." "Cleaning crew to room 246." "All visitors must check in at the registry desk."* Fabiola and Liz sat in silence for several minutes. The quiet wasn't exactly comfortable, but the weight of their shared history soaked up some of the tension that might have otherwise felt unbearable.

Fabiola searched her exhausted mind for something to say. "Thanks for asking Peter about the private room," she said.

Liz's jaw tightened. "It was the least he could do. He wouldn't even have known you were in labor if I hadn't called to tell him."

But now he knew, and yet he wasn't there with her. Peter was aware of his baby's birth, but it was Liz by her side, not him. As grateful as Fabiola was for her best friend's presence, Peter's absence felt like a hot poker searing her skin. Liz read the pain on her face.

"He's a selfish bastard," she said. "He always has been."

Tears leaked from Fabiola's eyes, and she hurried to wipe them away. She had no right to cry in front of Liz, given the pain she'd caused—what she'd taken from her.

"Why are you here?" Fabiola asked, her voice trembling. "You should hate me."

"Oh, I do," Liz said, her voice thick with hurt. "When you told me that day, it was so humiliating. My first thought was how embarrassing it was going to be when everyone found out what happened. For people to see how I'd failed—at my marriage, at becoming a mom."

"Liz, I'm so—" Fabiola began, but Liz held up her hand.

"I was furious at you for betraying me," she said. "But with Peter I was angry he'd betrayed our *plan*. That he'd taken a wrecking ball to what was supposed to be our future. It wasn't until after three days of fighting with him that I realized what I didn't feel." She swallowed and lowered her gaze to her lap. "I didn't feel sad about not having a baby." Her eyes darted back up to Fabiola's and her voice dropped to a whisper. "I felt relieved." She rubbed her shirtsleeve between her fingers and closed her eyes as if gathering strength. "I think I never really wanted to be a mom," she said. "But it just made sense to try, you know? Peter and I had reached a point where our lives were kind of running on parallel tracks. But trying to have a baby was something that united us. It put us on the same team again, working toward the same goal."

Fabiola lay back, absorbing Liz's words, feeling their truth sink in. She'd never once seen Liz cast a wistful glance into a passing stroller or voice any regret at her biological situation.

"Plus," Liz continued, opening her eyes and turning a frank gaze on Fabiola, "I'd gotten to the age where, as a woman, people start to judge you because you don't have kids. Like, oh, she must be too selfish, or career-focused, or whatever." She gave a rueful smile. "So I thought, OK, maybe just one kid. I can handle that. One kid doesn't change things too much, right? It was like an assignment I gave myself. Like, do one thousand crunches in a month. Close that client deal. Have a baby." She made a motion like she was checking things off a list.

Fabiola thought of the night she and Aron agreed to start trying for a family, a month after their wedding. She'd tossed her birth control pills in the trash with a flourish as Aron stood by and applauded, then pulled her down onto the bed, both of them laughing and giddy with possibility.

"Peter moved out," Liz said, snapping Fabiola back into the present. "Three days after you told us the truth." She laughed. "Three days! It was like he'd been waiting for an excuse. Like, 'Oh, you mean we're not permanently connected because we combined our DNA to make a tiny person? Right, see you later then.'"

"Liz, I'm really—"

"Don't." Liz held up her hand again. "I mean, you don't have to. I read all your emails and texts. I didn't come here to make you apologize again. I believe you're sorry. And I didn't come here to forgive you. I'm not ready for that."

Liz's words stung and Fabiola sank back against the pillow in defeat. She knew she had no claim to forgiveness after the hurt she'd caused. Still, when Liz had showed up, she'd dared to hope. "Then why did you come?" she asked, her voice weary.

Liz shook her head, her face a mix of pain and confusion. "Because even though I hate you, I also love you. It was unfair to drag you into all of this to begin with. When you offered, it just seemed like the perfect plan. I thought if it was you, Peter wouldn't be able to say no." Her shoulders sagged. "What really pisses me off is that he left first—that he beat me to it, the asshole. That's the worst part, really."

"Not the part where I slept with your husband?" Fabiola asked, biting her lip.

Liz gave a sharp exhale. "Yeah, that was bad. Really, really bad. But Peter and I were finished long before that. I was just so drained from work and the constant fighting that I didn't see it. It took this mess for me to finally realize it."

"Knock knock." A woman in green scrubs pushed a cart through the door. "Dinner time." She placed a tray on the night-stand between Fabiola and Liz.

"Do you think they'd let me check in here?" Liz said. "I could use a few days of rest and people bringing me meals."

"And really good drugs," Fabiola added. "Though I'm posi-tive you could find a place with better food." She glanced at the plastic containers of pasta, overcooked vegetables, and Jell-O on the tray with distaste.

Liz laughed softly. "I should let you rest," she said, standing and pausing to look down into the bassinet. She studied Leonora for a moment before adding, "Yep, definitely your nose." Then she gave Fabiola a half-smile, a little wave, and left, closing the door softly behind her.

SIXTY-ONE

"Good morning, querida." Her mother's voice filtered down through Fabiola's layers of exhaustion. The pain from her surgery had kept her awake the night before, and when she slept, she did so fitfully, one ear open to Leonora's grunts and whimpers.

She'd been dozing with Leonora nearby in the bassinet, and now she opened her eyes to see Paulina standing there. Behind her stood Vivi, Ben, and Liam, all eyeing her warily.

Fabiola's heart expanded and she opened her arms. ""Hi, my loves."

Liam was the first to barrel toward her.

"Take it easy," Paulina warned him as he wrapped his arms around his mother.

"It's fine," Fabiola said, hiding a grimace of pain as she buried her face in Liam's hair. After a beat Ben joined his brother at her bedside and she wrapped her arms around both of them. They smelled like little boy sweat and something musky; Aron's bodywash, she realized. "I've missed you," she said.

"It's only been, like, a couple of days," Ben said.

"That's too long," she said. "I mean, you've gotten taller!"

"Really?" He grinned and straightened his shoulders.

"I swear." She ruffled his hair.

Vivi had stopped at Leonora's bassinet and was staring down at the small, swaddled bundle. "She has your nose," she said.

Fabiola smiled. "That's what Liz said."

Vivi's gaze shot up. "Liz was here?"

Fabiola nodded. "She was."

"Are you, like, friends again?"

Fabiola paused. "Too soon to tell, I think," she said. Vivi nodded, and Fabiola's heart tightened as she saw how, almost overnight, Vivi had shed her little-girl look. It wasn't just the new hairstyle in imitation of Hayley—parted in the middle and loose around her face—or the subtle curve of her chest beneath her loose T-shirt. It was the confidence in her posture, the way she held her shoulders back and her head high. "Come here," Fabiola said, gesturing to Vivi, who stepped into the family hug. "Tell me everything. How's school? What have you been up to? What has Dad been feeding you?"

"Mom." Vivi rolled her eyes and wiggled out of the embrace. "It's literally only been forty-eight hours."

"Has it?" Fabiola rubbed her eyes. She'd been in her own personal time warp.

"When are you coming home?" Liam asked. He and Ben moved to perch on the edge of the bed, and Vivi sprawled at the foot.

Fabiola squeezed his hand. "As soon as I can. By the weekend, for sure."

"Aren't you even going to say hello to your beautiful baby sister?" Paulina admonished. She'd retrieved Leonora from the bassinet and held her out.

"Hi, baby sister," Ben said with a dutiful wave.

"Do you want to hold her?" Fabiola asked.

Ben's eyes widened with panic. "No way."

"I will!" Liam shrugged. Fabiola placed a pillow on his lap and nodded at Paulina, who lowered the baby onto it. "Hey there," he said, waving to Leonora with his free hand. The surprising softness in his voice made Fabiola's heart flutter. "Hey, she's smiling," he announced. "For real, look!" He pointed at Leonora's tiny face.

"Babies that age can't smile," Ben said. "I read it on WebMD."

"Dude, look. Honest to God she's—" Liam paused and wrinkled his nose. "What's that smell?"

"Pretty sure she just pooped," Vivi said.

"What? Gross!" Liam made a face and Paulina swiftly retrieved the baby. He sprang up off the bed while Ben doubled over with laughter.

"She pooped on you!" he giggled.

"It's just gas," Paulina admonished, checking Leonora's diaper.

"I'll take her," Vivi offered, sitting up. Paulina lowered the baby into her arms. "Hey, little sis," Vivi said. "Finally, another girl in the house. It's gonna be me and you against these goons." She shot a withering look in Ben and Liam's direction.

Fabiola glanced around at Vivi cradling Leonora and at Liam and Ben, now wrestling on the floor. A surge of love washed over her, only to be quickly eclipsed by a suffocating dread. She'd created this family, it was her responsibility to care for them, yet she didn't even know where they'd be living in another couple of weeks. She didn't know how she'd afford soccer uniforms for the new school year, or new shoes for Vivi, who was growing so fast. Not to mention college, which felt like a distant, unattainable dream. Her pulse quickened as anxiety gripped her. Her pulse began to race.

Noticing the cloud that had come over Fabiola, Paulina gave a soft clap of her hands. "All right, that's enough for today," she announced. "Your mama needs to rest. We'll come back tomorrow."

Fabiola hugged her three children in turn, clinging to each of them longer than they might have liked. As Paulina ushered them toward the door, she turned back to plant a kiss on Fabiola's forehead. "Remember, it will all be OK in the end. And if it's not OK, then it's not the end."

Fabiola looked up at her mother. "Dad used to say that to me."

"I know." Paulina nodded. "He used to say it to me, too."

SIXTY-TWO

Six months later

"Did my sweet girl have a good nap?" Fabiola cooed. Leonora smiled up from her crib and kicked her legs in greeting. It was hard to believe how fast six months had flown by. Leonora's cheeks, wrinkled and sunken when she'd been thrust into the world a month earlier than planned, had been replaced by twin puffs of skin so rosy and smooth Fabiola had to resist biting them.

The late afternoon March sun filtered in through the window, bathing the room Fabiola shared with her daughter in soft light. It was a beautiful room, with soft light gray walls, modern yet welcoming furniture, and expensive bed linens—everything Fabiola would have expected from Liz's guest room.

It was a far cry from Fabiola's old, cheerfully eclectic Brooklyn apartment, but she found she didn't miss her old home —at least, not the way she'd felt there. In Liz's guest room, she woke up clear-headed rather than foggy. She slept deeply, and despite Leonora's nighttime wakeups, she felt more rested than she had in years. Most importantly, she felt safe.

Liz's guest room was not where Fabiola had expected to end up. The two women were still circling each other cautiously when Liz had accepted a three-month assignment in her firm's London office. When Fabiola's Brooklyn apartment sold, Liz offered her condo to Fabiola and the kids while she was overseas. "Just until you get things sorted out," Liz had said. "I'm not saying everything's OK between us," she added. "I just think the kids should be somewhere they're comfortable."

Flooded with gratitude—and guilt—over Liz's gesture, Fabiola had done her best to find another place before Liz returned. She'd taken newborn Leonora all over the city, viewing dismal apartments she couldn't bear to consider for her kids. In desperation, she'd finally put a deposit down on a bland, overpriced high-rise in Murray Hill, mainly occupied by new college graduates. Unfortunately, the deal fell through just as Liz arrived home.

"The kids will go stay with Aron and Leonora and I will go to a hotel," Fabiola had said, already forming a mental list of everything she'd have to take with her—travel crib, bouncy seat, clothes.

Liz looked horrified. "No, stay until you find something else," she said. "I'm on a deal right now so I'll barely be home."

Guilt surged through Fabiola. "Absolutely not," she said. "We've imposed on you long enough."

"Fabi, you are not taking that baby to a New York City hotel." Liz shuddered. "Didn't you read that *Buzzfeed* piece about E. coli on hotel bedspreads?"

"Liz, we can't—"

"You're staying here," Liz said, a familiar, steely glint in her eyes that told Fabiola the matter was settled. So, they stayed, though Fabiola continued to scour apartment listings, trying to ignore the twinge of guilt she felt every time she stepped off the elevator into Liz's formerly immaculate apartment that was now cluttered with the kids' backpacks and baby gear.

Now, Fabiola lifted Leonora from the crib and kissed her fat cheek. "It's time to get dressed for the party," she said, pointing to the tiny ruffled, yellow dress laid out on the bed. "Auntie Alice gave that to you, and I think she's right—yellow is your color."

"Mom!" Ben charged into the guest room. "I scored two goals. Two!" Leonora's smile grew wider. Ben was not-so-secretly her favorite. "Two goals, Leo!" he repeated, waggling two fingers in front of her face. She rewarded him with a belly laugh.

"Sweetheart, that's great!" Fabiola wrapped her free arm around him. He was still in his full soccer kit, his hair coiled into tight, sweaty curls. "I'm so proud of you." Ben had struggled the most with switching schools after it became clear they'd be at Liz's longer than expected. At first, he hadn't even wanted to try out for the soccer team but Liam—and Liz—had talked him into it.

"Why waste your talent?" Liz had said. "And if you don't play, your muscles will atrophy. You don't want Liam to be faster, do you?" Ben had looked panicked at the idea.

"Thanks for talking Ben into trying out for the team," Fabiola said later, after the kids were in bed and she found herself in the kitchen getting a glass of water just as Liz was opening a bottle of wine.

Liz gave a wry smile. "I've been told I'm persuasive." She took out a second wine glass and held it out in invitation.

Fabiola hesitated. Typically, she would retreat to her room in the evenings, giving Liz her space. "Um, sure," she said, her palms dampening with anxiety. Despite the gradual ease in their interactions over the past few months, not a day went by without her feeling the heavy burden of the pain she had caused her best friend.

Liz poured the wine, and they sipped in silence.

"Also, thank you for everything you've been doing with the

kids, especially Ben and Liam," Fabiola said eventually. Liz had made a habit of taking the boys to shoot hoops after dinner on the nights she got home early enough, and on weekend mornings, she'd play FIFA on the PlayStation with them before coaxing them into joining her for what she called "soccer conditioning" runs.

Liz nodded. "They're good kids. All of them. You did a good job—you're doing a good job."

Fabiola flushed at the unexpected compliment. "You mean despite the whole nearly being homeless and destitute thing?" she joked.

Liz snorted. "Oh yeah, that."

Fabiola took another sip. "How was work?"

Liz shrugged. "The usual. Not enough hours in the day."

"I don't know how you manage it."

Liz set her wine glass on the counter and turned it in a circle by the stem. "Actually, I've been thinking about scaling back a bit. Maybe spending more time coaching at the YMCA, or somewhere else. I think I need more balance."

"That," Fabiola said, "is the last thing I ever thought I'd hear you say. But I think it's a great idea."

Liz shrugged. "Yeah, well, my perspective's changed a lot lately."

"Same," Fabiola said softly. Liz reached forward and touched her glass to Fabiola's. It wasn't much, but it felt like progress.

Breaking up her reverie, Liam burst into Fabiola's room behind his brother as she slipped Leonara into the yellow dress. Her happy-go-lucky child, Liam had made a seamless transition to his new school and had quickly made enough friends for both him and Ben. "Mom, I had four saves in our game!" he crowed. Then, seeing Leonora, Liam scrunched up his nose and ballooned out his cheeks in a grotesque gargoyle-like face. She gave a delighted gurgle.

"My twin superstars," Fabiola said. "Don't forget me when you're famous soccer players."

"We'll buy you a Lamborghini," Ben said.

Fabiola laughed. "A minivan might be more up my alley."

Liam wrinkled his nose. "Eww."

The doorbell rang. "That's probably the food," Fabiola said. "Go help Liz with it. And then shower, both of you!" she called after them as they dashed from the room at the mention of dinner. "No stinky kids allowed at my birthday dinner!"

Fabiola smiled as she heard them thunder into the kitchen, tripping over each other to tell Liz about their soccer triumphs.

"I like having them around," Liz had admitted one rare Saturday morning when all four kids were still asleep and she and Fabiola sat at the kitchen island with coffee mugs and laptops, catching up on work. "I mean, yeah, they could stand to work on their personal hygiene, and I don't know where they get all their energy, but it's nice to feel some life in here." She gestured at her once-immaculate kitchen counter, now cluttered with the twins' math homework, Vivi's lip glosses, and a stray baby sock.

"And by "life" you mean utter chaos?" Fabiola said with a weary sigh.

Liz laughed softly. "Basically, yeah." A shadow crossed her face. "I think it would be hard with just me here, you know? The memories, and all."

Fabiola's throat tightened with guilt. "Liz, I will never stop being sorry for what I did," she murmured. "The fact that I put Peter before our friendship—it kills me every day."

Liz sighed and shook her head. "I can tell. Sometimes I can almost feel the guilt radiating off you. You barely smile anymore, and you walk around looking like the world's about to end." She paused, then added, "If I'm being honest, it really kills the vibe—as Vivi would say."

Fabiola groaned. "God, I'm so sorry—"

Liz raised a hand to stop her. "Seriously, you have to stop apologizing. I get it. You're sorry. And while it will never be completely OK, this is where we find ourselves." She shrugged and offered a soft smile. "And it turns out, it isn't so bad."

Now it was Vivi's turn to interrupt Fabiola's thoughts as she appeared in the bedroom with Liam and Ben. "Cute," she said, pointing to Lenora's yellow dress. "Hey, can I go over to Ty's to watch a movie with them and Savannah after dinner?"

"Sure, as long as you stay here long enough to sing to me and have cake," Fabiola replied.

Vivi rolled her eyes. "Obviously."

To Fabiola's surprise, Vivi seemed to be thriving the most in her new environment. At school she'd quickly befriended Ty, a tall, nonbinary student with a flair for bowties and coding, and Savannah, a small girl with pink hair who'd told Fabiola her role model was Steve Jobs "but without the narcissism." The three had started the school's first Young Entrepreneurs club and were planning a business plan competition for the spring.

Vivi had also continued managing Fabiola's social media and was handling the occasional weekend clients. Plus, her idea to offer LEGO storage design had expanded into a full-fledged business organizing playrooms. Fabiola had made Hayley a full partner after Leonora was born, and the business had thrived even during the months she'd taken off for maternity leave. And while she treasured her time with Leonora, when she'd gone back full-time a month ago, Fabiola was surprised by how good it felt to be back in the world outside her bubble of motherhood.

"Dinner's ready," Liz called from the kitchen.

"Thank God, I'm starving." Vivi plucked Leonora off the changing table and swung her into the air. "I'm so hungry I could eat you," she said in a baby voice, pretending to nibble one of Leonora's cheeks. Leonora gave a snorty giggle.

"Coming!" Fabiola called back. For dinner, she'd ordered pizza and a chopped salad from Kesté, her favorite Italian place.

Dessert was carrot cake with extra raisins, baked by Vivi and Paulina, who'd become the family's chefs. When Paulina wasn't working her nursing shifts, she came by to help with Leonora and make dinner. Fabiola enjoyed sitting in the living room, nursing Leonora while listening to the playful banter between Vivi and Paulina over the exact measurements in their recipes. "But how much is a pinch, exactly?" Vivi asked. "Like, my pinch could be way different than your pinch, you know?"

"I don't know, a pinch is a pinch!" Paulina replied, throwing up her hands.

Paulina had bought party hats for Fabiola's birthday dinner, which she forced everyone to wear long enough to take pictures in them. The boys ate their weight in pizza and even Paulina had a second slice of cake.

Paulina presented her with a Peruvian maté pot and a tube of lipstick in her own favorite shade of red. "A little color wouldn't kill you, querida," she said. From Liz came a gift certificate for a fancy spa, and from the boys came a tube of drug store hand lotion plus a video montage of their soccer highlights from the season so far, which they eagerly screened for her—twice. Vivi gave her a black tote bag printed with MOM BOSS in large, gold block letters. Inside were a pair of gloves with touchscreen fingers to use with her phone when it got cold out.

"Dad thought you'd like the gloves," she said. "But I picked out the bag."

"I love it," Fabiola said.

Everyone laughed, ate, and laughed some more, then sang "Happy Birthday" one more time for good measure. Leonora yawned and Paulina whisked her off to bed. Vivi headed out to Ty's, and the boys drifted off to play video games. Only Liz and Fabiola lingered, savoring the sudden quiet.

Fabiola sipped the last of her wine and surveyed the wadded-up napkins and smears of frosting on the counter. She felt a swell of contentment, followed immediately by a wave of guilt. It was all so much more than she deserved.

Liz twirled her glass in her hand and cleared her throat. "So," she said. "I've been thinking."

Fabiola's heart sank. She'd always known they couldn't stay at Liz's forever, that eventually she'd have to get serious about where she and the kids would live next. Though her increasing income had opened up a few more options, the prospect of restarting her apartment search knotted her stomach with anxiety. She braced herself for what was coming next.

"I found out there's another unit open in the building, newly renovated," Liz continued.

Fabiola sighed. "We definitely can't afford your building, Liz. But I'll get serious about looking again. We'll be out of your hair soon, I promise."

Liz stared at her. "What? No. I meant for all of us."

"All of us?" Fabiola frowned, confused.

Liz nodded. "It's four bedrooms plus an office, which we could convert to a nursery. The twins could finally stop sleeping on the pullout couch in the den."

Fabiola tried to process what Liz was saying. "You want to live together? As in all of us?" She let out a bewildered laugh. "Why?"

"Why not?" Liz asked, taken aback. "I mean, this is working, don't you think?"

Fabiola ran her hand through her hair. "Me and my four children—not to mention my mom, who's around all the time—living with you is working? If I were you, I'd be counting the minutes until I got my peace and quiet back."

Liz flushed and bit the inside of her cheek. "Well, you're not me. And I had a lot of peace and quiet before. This is better. But if you don't want to..." She looked down and fiddled with the zipper on her chic, asymmetrical sweater, her eyes filling with tears.

Fabiola straightened up. "Oh my God, Liz, I'm so sorry, I wasn't implying that we wouldn't—"

"For the last time, stop apologizing!" Liz looked up and gave an exasperated laugh as she wiped away a tear. "Seriously." She took a deep breath. "This probably sounds crazy, but having you guys around makes me feel useful. Useful in a way that I'm not at work. Like I'm doing something important. Especially with the boys. I mean, yes, they are loud and annoying, but it's so easy to make them happy. I feel like finally I cracked the formula, you know? It feels good." She glanced down at her hands and picked at one of her nails. "I mean, maybe it's a terrible idea. I would totally understand if you wanted to find someplace just for you, for your family. But if not... well..."

Fabiola stared at her. A tiny crack appeared in the dam Fabiola had built against the hope of ever being forgiven for her multitude of sins, and a trickle of optimism forced its way through. "Are you saying you want to be in our family?" she asked Liz. "Our crazy, smelly, loud family?"

Liz looked up at her, her eyes shiny. "Yeah, I guess I do."

The hope inside Fabiola continued to build until the pressure became almost too much to bear. When the dam finally broke, it shattered into fragments that were swept away as she laughed through her tears at the good fortune she never thought she'd have. Then she leaned forward and pulled Liz into a hug. "Honey, it's too late," she said. "You already are."

Fabiola and Liz were still busy looking at the apartment plans online when Paulina returned from putting Leonora to sleep. She and Liz banished Fabiola from helping with the rest of the dishes and instead Fabiola sank gratefully onto the couch —her couch. Because she belonged here, she realized now. She belonged here with the kids, her mother, and most of all, with Liz.

She had eaten her fill of pizza and cake, but at that moment the fullness inside her came from the love given to her by her family—both born and chosen—and by the love she felt for them. For the first time in months, her chest didn't tighten with fear and guilt as she thought about the future. And while it might not align with the perfect picture she once envisioned—a pristine nuclear family lined up for holiday card photos—it would be beautiful in its own unique way. Beautiful, and so much more than she'd dared hope for only a few short months ago.

Sitting there, she said a silent thank you for the choices she'd made, the good and the bad, all of which had led her here.

Her phone dinged and she picked it up.

> Happy birthday.

Fabiola's heart quickened. Despite the emotional distance she'd put between them, Peter still had that effect on her. It had been a long time since she'd heard from him. The last time had been an email exchange when Leonora was two months old, telling her that he'd taken a job in Seattle, that he would help out financially but didn't want to be involved otherwise, at least not right now. That had stung, so much so that she'd considered declining his offer of financial help. Liz, fortunately, had convinced her otherwise.

Thanks, she replied.

> I hope everything's good with you.

It is, she wrote. It was true. Her kids were happy and healthy. She had just celebrated another trip around the sun with the people who loved her most. What more was there?

> How is she?

> She's good. Rolling over and trying to sit up on her own.

Fabiola hesitated, then typed:

> I can send a picture if you want.

She watched the three bubbles appear and disappear for a long moment.

> Please don't. I'm sorry.

She looked up to see Paulina and Liz in the kitchen, swaying and singing along to the music Paulina had put on. Liz paused to refill her wine glass and top up Paulina's. They clinked glasses and glided toward Fabiola in the living room, their smiles projecting all the warmth she felt inside.

She looked down at Peter's text one last time, then set her phone aside. She understood. Some people were born to be parents, and some grew into it. Some people thrived in the role and some chafed.

And others would simply never know what they were missing.

A LETTER FROM THE AUTHOR

I want to say a huge thank you for reading *The Perfect Plan*. I hope you enjoyed reading about Fabiola as much as I did writing about her. If you'd like to join other readers in hearing all about my new releases and getting access to giveaways and bonus content, you can sign up for my Storm newsletter:

www.stormpublishing.co/caitlin-weaver

You can also sign up for my personal newsletter—I promise not to bother you too often.

www.caitlinrweaver.com/contact

If you enjoyed this book and could spare a few moments to leave a review, that would be hugely appreciated. Even a short review can make all the difference in encouraging someone else to discover my books for the first time. Thank you so much!

As someone who navigated my own fertility journey to become a parent, I'm grateful to live in a world with so many ways to have (and to be!) a family. And while Fabiola's choices weren't always neat and tidy—because where's the fun in that? —I always knew she would end up surrounded by the love and support she deserved.

Parenting is *hard*, and there's no one right way to do it, despite what all the books and blogs suggest (believe me, I've read plenty). We're all doing our best, and like Fabiola, we'll inevitably make mistakes. The beauty lies in how we recover, learn, and grow into better people and parents. At least that's what I tell myself every time I screw up.

Friendship can be just as challenging. I've learned that friendships can go through dormant phases, yet the strongest ones always find a way to bloom again. Life is long, and its unpredictability is the only certainty. We're human, and we sometimes hurt each other, but grace and forgiveness can repair those bonds—and it's almost always worth it.

Thank you again for being part of this amazing journey and I hope you'll stay in touch—I have so many more stories and ideas to entertain you with!

Caitlin Weaver

www.caitlinrweaver.com/contact
www.threads.net/@caitlinrweaver

facebook.com/CaitlinRWeaver
instagram.com/caitlinrweaver

ACKNOWLEDGMENTS

I must start by thanking the whole Storm Publishing team for all their fantastic support. Special thanks go to my exceptional editor Vicky Blunden, who never fails to make me better.

Thank you also to my early readers and critique partners, who offered wise and honest feedback that strengthened this book immeasurably: Amanda Vink, Carly Wahl, Jen Craven, Kerry Chaput, Ojus Patel, and Renee Ryan.

Writing is by nature a solitary pursuit, but I've managed to make it less so by finding connections and resources in two wonderful organizations: the Women's Fiction Writers Association and the Toronto Area Women Authors.

Much gratitude goes to Laura Shachmut, who was generous enough to enlighten me about the experience of being a surrogate.

Thank you to my parents and my in-laws for swooping in with childcare when it was most needed so I could write. Also to Marcus, Elijah, and Sam for always being proud of me, and for (mostly) understanding when I needed to hide away to get words on the page. I love you all and am so lucky to call you mine.

A huge thank you to **you**, dear reader! With so many books in the world you chose mine, and for that I am very grateful.

Finally, if you've read my other books, you may have noticed a recurring theme: the power of female friendship. As a woman, there's nothing like the unwavering support of your girlfriends. Over the years, I've seen my friendships go through seasons—sometimes blooming, sometimes dormant—but those friends are always there when I need them most. Having good friends by your side is a true gift. To all my incredible friends near and far, I love you all and I couldn't do this without you.